C.C. TYLER

IN DARKNESS & DUTY

THE PROPHECY OF SORIN TRILOGY

AUTHOR'S NOTE

Please note this book contains content that might be upsetting to some readers, including violence, mature language, death of a loved one (mentioned), suicide (mentioned), anxiety, sexual content, imprisonment, and captivity. It is not intended for anyone under the age of eighteen.

DRYSTAN
LAND OF VAMPYR
THE VOID
THE SAPPHIRE SEA
MORROW
SORIN
THE NEW WORLD
NŪA
CITY OF WITCHES
DRENGR VILLAGE
THE VADON MOUNTAINS
WEREWOLF TERRITORY
CIRRILLO

Contents

For those still learning to forgive their past selves.

PART I

CHAPTER ONE

GRIEF HELD ITS IRON grip on Kade Drengr.

A restless energy swelled and pushed inside him, too, like the infinite choppy waves of the Sapphire Sea. Ahead of him, that sea stretched for miles to an indigo horizon. Seagulls squealed above, nose diving into the depths, lost to the frothy crests. Electricity perfumed the wind, the promise of a storm in the air.

"Aye there!" a sailor called as he descended the ramp of the large ship destined for Nūa.

Kade squinted against the afternoon sun's blinding light. The silhouette of a pipe became clear, jutting out of the man's toothy grin.

"You have paid passage?" he asked.

Kade nodded, rummaging in Bleu's satchel and handing him the appropriate papers.

The sailor looked them over. "Where's your companion?"

Kade searched for Evelyn amongst the townsfolk making their way home after work. No obsidian hair. No navy cloak, hem forever stained by the mud puddles of Callum. No mass of fiery red fur lost in the throngs of hurried feet.

Uncertainty wormed through Kade as he tried to gain a sense of how much time had passed. Evelyn'd gone to say goodbye to Tovi while he had remained at the docks with their things. Had it been twenty minutes? An hour? Ever since he'd read his brother Eldrick's missive—his father, Alpha Aramis Drengr, was dead—time had oozed like tree sap, while some moments zipped by.

He'd been here before, the territory painful and familiar. He reminded himself the words that had helped him through grief in the past.

One foot in front of the other.

Kade turned to the sailor. "She'll be back soon."

The wind whipped past, raising his wolf's hackles. Beside him, Bleu sidestepped, hooves clattering against the planks of the dock.

The sailor nodded. "Alright, but we're boardin' soon and raise the anchor in an hour. I wouldn't dally."

Kade nodded, the only agreement he could manage. He ran his hand down Bleu's muzzle, whispering the promise of apples once they made it onto the ship. A few packed bags surrounded them. Layered to travel—sweater snug, cloak fastened—Kade was ready to step foot on a forsaken boat and follow his brother's commands to return home at once. Blankets had been draped over Bleu for the colder nights on the ship along with parting parcels from Miss Patricia—the town's inn owner. His horse huffed, side-eyeing him. He swore he saw concern flash through his steed's gaze.

After his mother's death, he'd become lost to waves of grief with no relief on the horizon. Kade had run for miles and miles in his werewolf form, needing to release his pent-up energy, similar to the pulsing in his chest now, like an oiled lantern, growing the more it burned. Memories of that time flooded through him—wet soil wedging into his paws while he ran through the forests of home, the scent of pine awakening his senses, the crisp breeze after an afternoon shower dampening his fur coat. He'd craved it all.

And he'd found purpose. Running had led him to Carena, the first Daughter of the Goddess, and there he'd been put to work, busying himself with the last of the witch's autumn crop. He'd picked apples and tilled trees in her orchard until his muscles ached. He'd found something to do, something to busy his mind.

Movement. Action. *Purpose.*

He'd learned then that there was no sense of sitting in the past. Boarding the ship and returning home felt *right*. Though he loathed boats, it was the appropriate step forward. And Kade couldn't deny the tingle of excitement, despite circumstances, for the promise of Evelyn at his side. He searched for her and her witch familiar, Maxie, again, but neither were in sight.

None of it—the urgency, the aptness, the ease of the day—would have happened without Evelyn. She'd done more than help with packing and purchasing the tickets. She'd made sure they said farewell to their friends in Callum, and she'd accepted his silence, staying at his side as a peaceful presence, letting him process his father's death at his own pace.

Gods, he loved her.

But every time he breathed the words, they turned to dust on his lips. He hadn't been able to muster them, the timing off.

Hours ago, they'd been tangled together as the sun rose over Callum and the birds sang the morning. They'd been moments away from completing their fated-mated bond, ready to tie their souls and bodies together. And yet, lingering on the past, asking what could've been, made Kade lose focus on what lay ahead. Carena's words trickled through him.

One foot in front of the other.

Bleu reared back as a gust of wind barreled down the docks. Kade soothed the horse, clucking his tongue. Ships creaked as they bobbed in the water, and Evelyn's absence glared like the sun's reflection on the waves.

Perhaps saying goodbye to Tovi was taking longer than either of them anticipated. Yet, time ticked by, their departure growing closer. He sighed, whispering his plan to find Evelyn into Bleu's flickering ears and headed into town.

The air was thick with eeriness as he trudged along. A clatter like thunder behind him, growing louder, spun him around. A massive, black carriage barreled toward him. It didn't swerve, and the horses drawing it looked like they had the underworld in their eyes. He jumped out of the way as it sped past, wheels losing purchase on the stones as it swayed, unsteady.

Kade furrowed his brows. His wolf became alert, a growl rumbling in his throat.

He continued down the street, hoping to meet Evelyn along the way. His wolf itched for her, his heart thudding in his chest, anxious to hold her hand again. Such a simple touch that grounded him, that assured him they'd endure the voyage ahead and anything else after they stepped foot in Sorin.

Except, when he arrived at the print shop, he found no sign of her. Peering through the window, no one else moved about either. Wisps of steam rose from the fireplace, as if it had been recently doused. Where was she? Maybe he'd missed her, and she'd walked back to the harbor with Tovi?

Down the cobblestone streets, Kade ventured to the dock with haste. Yet, he found it the way he'd left it. Bleu, alone, surrounded by the packs. The sails of the ship had been let down, ballooning with the evening breeze.

Kade's stomach sank. Time was running out, and his confusion became worry. His wolf, on the other hand, bristled, pacing underneath Kade's skin.

Think.

He turned left and right, as if the southern and northern streets held answers. If he hadn't passed her on the path, where else would Evelyn have gone? Maybe she'd forgotten something in her apartment and went to fetch it. Again, Kade hoped to run into her along the way, but across the entire stretch of the town, he hadn't caught even a glimpse of her.

As he turned onto the most colorful street in Callum, he was hit with the vibrancy of shops painted blues, pinks, and yellows. His sights fell on the last building at the end of the street, the lone emerald building, Pages and Leaves's golden sign dim in the oncoming clouds. Above the bookshop, no lights shown where Evelyn's apartment had been. No Maxie waiting at the foot of the stairs. No signs of anything at all. He'd still check though—

A store door's bell chimed, and Kade collided with a lithe yet tall frame, knocking him off balance.

"Deepest apologies," the other man said.

"Riven." Kade offered a curt nod.

Tovi's brother grinned like a cat who'd already devoured his prey. Not a single white hair was out of line, brushed long and to the side. A three-piece black silk suit molded to his frame beneath a fastened jacket and leather gloves.

Riven raised a purple box, a sickly sweet aroma wafting from inside it. "Had to grab some parting treats before the journey. In my own excitement, I wasn't watching where I was going." His stare gleamed with mischief as he eyed Kade's attire up and down. "You appear to be readying for travel as well, Commander Drengr."

Kade froze at the mention of his official title. No one had called him that in some time, and yet, what was more surprising was that Riven knew it.

His surprise must've been evident because Riven chuckled. "My sister fills me in on these matters. Don't look so worried."

He stepped to the side, angling himself in the direction of the harbor. At the mention of Riven's sister, Kade regained focus, remembering why he'd ventured down this street in the first place.

"Have you come across your sister? Is she traveling with you?"

Riven tilted his head. The angle sparked Kade's wolf into a defensive posture. It teetered at the edge, barring its teeth as if a threat leered in front of them.

"No, why?"

Kade sighed. "Evelyn went to say goodbye to Tovi not too long ago."

Riven's brows shut up. "Ah, yes, Evelyn. She did come by looking for my sister at the print shop, but sadly, Tovi wasn't there. Last I saw her, Miss Carson was headed in the direction of the harbor."

Kade's brows pinched so violently, a headache pounded between his eyes. Had he missed coming across her twice? Was he so consumed by his grief he'd overlooked her? No, Kade wouldn't. It was Evelyn. His mate.

He stepped away from Riven. "Thank you, and safe travels."

"You know," Riven said, snagging Kade's attention again. "I'm surprised she chose you, after everything."

Kade paid Riven's words no mind. The *everything* he spoke of was in the past, so he didn't spare Tovi's brother a single glance as he continued to Evelyn's apartment. He climbed the wrought iron steps two at a time, his fear cementing with each clanging step. He found the door ajar, as if someone had left in a rush. Inside, everything was as they'd left it.

And empty.

Had Evelyn ran? Again? He tried recalling their last encounter. The tone of her voice. A glint in her silver eyes. Had he been so distracted by his grief he'd missed signs?

No.

Kade knew in his heart that wasn't true. Evelyn wouldn't. She'd meant those words earlier; he felt her love in his soul. But then where—

Something hissed behind the bathroom door. Someone bumped into the walls, and the door's hinges rattled against the frame. More hissing. More commotion. A stream of curses.

"You little shit," a female voice whispered.

A cat growled.

Maxie.

But it wasn't Evelyn behind the door. Kade didn't detect her warm vanilla and cedar scent. He stepped forward, caution and curiosity humming through his pent-up muscles. *Thump, thump, thump.* His restless energy mounted.

The door banged open, and a ball of red fiery fur burst out of the bathroom, scurrying under Evelyn's bed.

"Maxie!" Kade called as he collided into—

Tovi. Scratches lined her cheeks, neck and wrists, blood beading at the surface of her pale skin.

"What in the stars above are you doing here?" he asked.

Before Kade reached Maxie, she dashed past him and bolted out the adjacent door. Her descent down the metal stairs echoed unseen, hurried and determined.

Evelyn.

Kade unsheathed his sword and ran. He ascended the stairs in a blur. Behind him, Tovi called his name, begging him to stop. He ignored her.

Something wasn't right.

He sprinted down the street, Maxie, a ball of red fiery fur, yards ahead of him. An instinct, a knowing, an element of the fated-mate bond tugged him down the cobblestone street, trusting Maxie to lead him in the right direction.

Through the market square, she darted between the steps of townsfolk, heading towards the docks. Kade shoved others out of his way, never losing sight of Maxie. Frantic, she raced towards the end of the pier.

Where a black-as-soot ship sailed away.

Kade caught up to her and skidded to a halt, his boots scuffing against the wood. His breathing came out ragged, and his heart thudded in his aching, pulsing chest. Once. Twice. A third time as his vision tunneled in and out.

Dark magic sat in the air. It carried her name, as if it carried her away.

Evelyn.

The ship speared through the waters at an unnatural speed, but it was close enough from him to make out the frenzy of activity on the top deck, and amidst it all a black carriage, the same one that had almost run him over earlier. A sickening knowing rippled through him. The wind hurled in the harbor, the land rebelling against the notion.

Evelyn was in that carriage. She'd been taken. His mate had been locked away. He couldn't feel her, but he could feel *it*—an enchantment around her, locking her away from him.

It wasn't possible. He was wrong.

No. No. No.

He pushed out his mating bond but hit a wall, a strong unseen barrier, blocking his bond to Evelyn. He tried and tried to reach her, shouting in his mind. Perhaps it was so new, she didn't know how to respond on the other end.

Evelyn, please. Answer me.

Answer me, love.

Stars above, it was no use.

The carriage door swung open.

Cold horror shot through Kade. Worse than the cold, creeping discomfort the murders had caused, more frightening than the kelpie of Lake Glenn, and more haunting than the White Lady's howls on the wind. His knees weakened as a growl vibrated from his throat.

Four—*four!*—assailants held Evelyn firm as they dragged her out.

"Evelyn!" he cried, but the wind swallowed her name whole.

He had to get to her. Had to protect her. But how? He couldn't swim. His wolf bared its teeth at the water. *Frightened.* Maxie yowled and paced as frantically as Kade's racing heart.

And then a figure obscured his view of her.

At the end of the ship, Riven stood, gazing at Kade, smirking, and—

A single fang glinted over his bottom lip.

Kade stumbled back.

Riven was a vampyr.

Pain lanced through Kade's hand, sudden and burning. He dropped his sword, the metal clanging against the dock. His hand glowed a pearly blue, a magic he'd never conjured before fluttering like a star. The hilt of his sword gleamed red—he'd burned himself. His muscles froze, and a ringing in his ears muffled the sounds of the dock and sea. The light dimmed and vanished as quickly as it came, steam rising from his bloody wounds.

Stars above, where had that come from?

The harbor winds whirled. Back on the ship, a cloaked figure had joined Riven's side, hands thrust into the air. *Magic.* The air buzzed with power, the kind a witch possessed. The sails of the ship billowed, and it lurched forward, taking off across the ocean twice as fast as a ship that size should travel.

"No!" Kade growled.

He fought the urge to shift, but his rationale won out—what good would his heavy, muscular werewolf form do? Swimming was out of the question.

Longboats bobbed below. Kade sprang towards the closest one, but before he could reach it, a dagger struck the wooden post, cutting the rope that tethered the boat to the dock. It dropped ten feet into the water, and the waves took hold and carried the boat out to sea. Kade cursed, turning towards the culprit. Tovi stood there, another dagger at the ready.

"What are you doing?" he asked, heart racing like thunder in his ears.

"You have to let Evelyn go." Pain etched her features.

Kade's body stilled. She was mad if she thought he'd ever do such a thing. Another boat bobbed in the water ahead, and Kade sprinted to it, anger propelling him. Tovi moved in a blur, whizzed past him like a ghost.

Moons, that speed. Her agility. Was she a vampyr, too? Though, Kade didn't care.

He only cared about Evelyn. The winds and waves dragged Riven's ship out to sea, pulling her farther and farther away. He readied to jump into the water, his fears be damned, and brave the waves to swim to her. He had to. *Gods*, she was his mate.

"Kade, stop!"

Tovi stepped ahead of him, laying a hand on his chest and pushing him back. Tears welled in her eyes, but she gritted her teeth, resilient.

"Move aside!" he growled.

Tovi braced and pushed again. Her strength matched his, keeping him at bay.

"She is gone, and you'll kill yourself if you don't stop."

The black ship shrank more and more as it sailed into the horizon. The bell of the harbor chimed behind him, signaling the parting hour.

It rang to the tune of Kade's defeat.

Evelyn was gone.

He growled and backed away from Tovi, running his hands through his hair, a delirious haze overcoming him. *He'd lost her. He'd lost her. He'd lost her.* The truth was too heavy to bear, and Kade sank to his knees. Maxie circled him, yowling for Evelyn over and over again.

Kade raged against the gods, demanding answers. His gaze landed on Tovi. Her wounds from Maxie had already healed, not a sure sign she was a vampyr, but definitely a sign she wasn't human.

He stood to his full height, muscles quivering. "You helped him."

Tovi shook her head. "I didn't. I swear it. Evelyn is my friend—"

"Lies." Kade's wolf instincts eclipsed his rationale. "She went to say goodbye to you. You were her best friend, and your brother captured her. Took her from me!"

Tovi flinched. "I can explain."

Kade shook his head, a wolfish growl rumbling out of him. "Give me one good reason why I shouldn't kill you and be done with it, vampyr."

He charged, yet Tovi was quick. In a blink, she vanished. Kade spun, anticipating an attack from behind, but pain lanced through his skull. He collapsed onto the dock, and everything went black.

Chapter Two

Tovi

Tovi gripped the hilt of her dagger tighter. She had no desire to use it, but as the werewolf before her stirred in his sleep, she needed some sort of defense.

In case Kade shifted in the small confines of the ship's cabin.

Dried mud crumbled from her plum velvet cloak. Grass stuck out from her hair, tickling her cheeks. She did not appear entirely as intimidating as she wished. Tovi cringed, unaccustomed to appearing so drab in front of others. Well-dressed. Groomed. Put-together. Appearance was a shield—the first line of defense.

How you're seen is what you are.

Her mother's voice filtered through her mind as if the high-nose vampyr sat beside her. Tovi bristled; knowing her mother, a slew of snide comments would surely follow. *Wear this. Shoulders back. Smile. For Goddess's sake, not like that.* Tovi shook away the phantom memories. Her mother would also balk at what Tovi planned to do next, but it didn't matter—the woman was long gone and dead, and at present, Tovi had no time to care about her attire. Not when the werewolf she planned to bargain with roused from unconsciousness.

Kade's eyes snapped open, revealing pools of rage that leveled on her. As he sat up, Tovi remained still, waiting, clutching the dagger so tightly, her bones burned.

"Where are— *Moons*, we're on a boat, aren't we?" Kade grabbed hold of his bunk's frame, clamping his eyes shut and shaking his head.

"Yes." Tovi held out a steaming cup of tea, dagger still in the other hand. "Herbs to help your nausea. I heard you're not a fan of boats."

He eyed the tea, the blade, and then her. "Where is your brother taking Evelyn?"

Tovi sighed, rolled her shoulders back, rested the dagger on the table, and abandoned the cup of tea beside it. She steeled her patience by grabbing a glass of wine, readying for the arguments to come. "Drystan, no doubt," she said.

Kade inspected the room, eyes landing on the packs wedged into the corner. "And where is *this* ship headed?"

"Nūa. We're on the same one you planned to board this evening."

Her vampyr hearing detected Kade's racing heart.

"Where's Bleu?"

Tovi tilted her head—like Evelyn, the Son of the God cared so fiercely for others.

"Your horse is accounted for," she said. "I had him placed on this ship along with all your belongings. He's fine and safe."

"And Maxie?"

At the sound of her name, Evelyn's familiar scurried out from her hiding place and onto his bunk. She bumped her forehead into Kade's shaking arm. He relaxed a fraction, but his ire didn't lessen.

He studied Tovi, jaw ticking. "How is it you're a vampyr? I've seen you walk in the sunlight."

Instinctually, Tovi reached for the red stone hanging on her necklace. Its smooth surface sent shivers of reassurance through her. She pulled it free. Kade's assessing eyes narrowed. She'd expected questions. Some she planned to answer. Others she'd have to evade carefully, tactfully. But this, she could easily share.

"This is a bloodstone, a rather rare and powerful gem. It allows me to walk in sunlight as well as masks my vampyrism, scent and all."

She didn't mention the bloodstone's limitations—it worked best in obscured light, as direct sunlight still drained her—or the fact that without it, she'd combust into flames the moment the sun's rays touched her. She'd never share her weakness with anyone, regardless of her intention to convince Kade to work with her.

Tovi also didn't mention that hours ago, she'd woken in an icy panic, petrified Riven had taken her bloodstone. The bastard had buried her in a box—hence the muck—miles away from Callum. She and Riven had always danced to the tune of pranks, starting long ago as humans. Growing up on their parents' humble farm, Riven would trick her with Far Darrig sightings then sneak up behind a corner, scaring her into a paler shade. In retaliation, she'd leave worms in his boots overnight and giggle at his disgusted screams come morning.

Their sibling relationship had manifested into enemies decades ago. They'd moved past faerie scares and slimy insects. Locking each other in dungeons. Threats of sunlight. Playing the games of court. Killing their lovers. Tovi winced at a particular memory, one she liked to forget.

One where she'd been a spoiled and selfish princess.

But *something* had changed. *Riven* had changed. He'd captured Evelyn, and that unnerved Tovi. Not only because Evelyn was Tovi's dearest friend, but because of Sorin, the continent vampyrs, witches, and werewolves all called home. If Riven succeeded in his plan, they faced a threat they could not survive. She needed alliances, and Kade needed her.

Tovi sipped her wine. "Look, I know you might regard me as the enemy, but you and I want the same thing."

A growl rumbled from Kade. "Is that so? I'm not entirely convinced you didn't help your brother, whoever the hel he is—"

"Riven is a prince of Drystan, and I a princess." Her vampyr sight caught the slight tremor in Kade's clenched muscles, her own predator instinct sensing another in her midst. The dagger glinted in her peripheral, still in reach.

"What do you mean 'princess'?" he asked, eyes widening.

Tovi swallowed. Hate marred his amber stare, but she paid it no mind, used to having hate directed at her. Nothing new for a princess with a reputation. Besides, Kade also had every right to hate her—so much of what he knew about vampyrs were misinterpretations. She didn't fault him for it.

"We are merchants, though." Tovi gave him a lick of truth. "That isn't a total façade. Trade and profits feed our people." At least, that had been her goal the last hundred years. A family-run merchant business that not only imported goods her people could not access, but also allowed her people to create income, businesses, purpose, a *life*.

"You've lied for years. Lied to Evelyn," Kade said.

Guilt worked its vicious way through Tovi's unsettled gut. She'd never imagined Evelyn would find out this way, so... *horribly*. That she was not only a vampyr but also a princess. As much as her brother played a hand in Evelyn's abduction, Tovi had no one to blame but herself. Though she'd lied for years, she'd never meant to betray Evelyn. She was more than a friend—she was a sister. But Tovi doubted that sentiment still survived in Evelyn's heart.

"Believe what you want, but I had no direct part in Evelyn's capture," she said.

Kade bared his teeth and stood on shaky legs. He hissed a curse as the ship leaned left, up and over the unseen waves of the Sapphire Sea. Maxie sat squat in his bunk, those all-knowing yellow eyes jumping between Kade and Tovi.

"I don't trust you," he finally said.

Tovi seethed, inhaling through her nose. "If you want any chance of getting Evelyn back, you need to start."

Another growl rumbled through Kade. "*Stars above*, say her name one more time, and I'll throw you overboard."

She fought the urge to wince at the severity in his tone. Tovi didn't doubt his threat for a moment, but in the presence of an opponent, she knew better than to react.

She remained calm, leveling her breathing as she met his stare. "Like I said before, my brother is headed to Drystan, a land you and other werewolves, as well as witches, have no experience with." She sipped her wine, the tannins drying her tongue. The sensation of a thousand eyes crept over her skin. Though parts of her past would gain Kade's trust perhaps, admitting the truth came dangerously close to a past version of herself she didn't take pride in.

Tovi held secrets like metal armor. They protected her, protected her people.

Goddess, she cringed at the coldness in his eyes. She feared Kade's judgment, how he perceived her motives. What would he think if he learned she'd witnessed Evelyn's capture? The Daughter of the Goddess was her friend, but so much else had been at stake. Kade's life. The prophecy. Sorin, their homeland. It all hinged on that difficult decision to walk away from her brother's print shop. All for the chance her risky, outlandish plan might work. She played her own game in all this, a dangerous, tactful dance that made her heart race.

But if she had any chance of stopping Riven, she needed allies of her own.

Tovi inhaled, setting her shoulders. "He will most likely keep Evelyn in the castle—*my* home. If you want to get inside and have any chance of reuniting with her, you'll need me, just as much as I need you."

Every bit of Kade tightened—his muscles, his energy, his ire. Tovi's instinct to fight flared. Even her fangs and talons threatened to unsheathe.

"What exactly are you saying?" Kade said.

"My brother has officially become a true threat. Not only to my people, but to all of Sorin. I can't face him alone. Similarly, you can't get Evelyn back without my help." Tovi's stomach churned. She knew how it looked—using her friend's capture to her advantage. But she'd face Kade's judgment if it meant following what her heart knew was right. "If I help you, I want an alliance with the Drengr pack."

Kade shook. He fisted his hands, charging towards her. The energy in the cabin snapped. Light shined from both Kade's hands and his eyes glowed. Tovi snatched her dagger, shielded her eyes with her forearm and braced for the attack she likely deserved.

CHAPTER THREE

KADE

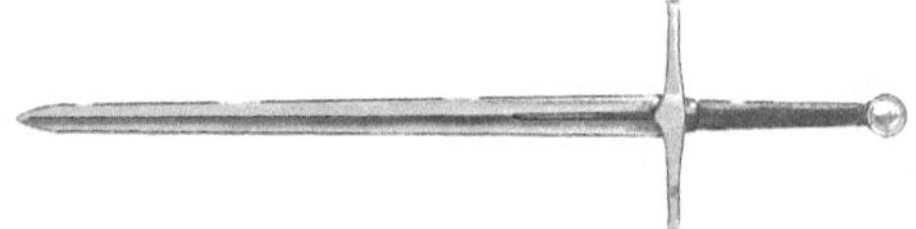

KADE'S PROTECTOR INSTINCT WARRED within him, and *power*—the same oddity he'd experienced at the docks—surged like the tidal pull of the moon.

His breathing hitched. *Stars above*, what was happening to him? He flexed and fisted his hands, trying to shake the power as if it were pesky raindrops. The light from his hands flickered a few times until it dissipated, sucking back into his core. His wolf didn't howl, wrestle, or retreat.

Interesting.

But Kade shook away his curiosities along with his unease and refocused on Tovi.

"Evelyn's safety isn't a bartering chip," he growled.

Tovi's eyes darted over him, lingering on his hands. Her lips pursed until she shook her head, silently deciding something. "I don't ask this lightly, Kade." Poised, Tovi set her shoulders back straight, but didn't lessen her grip on the dagger. "As you know, vampyrs are cursed—a thirst for blood, the inability to walk in sunlight—but not all of us perceive our innate darkness the same. There's two schools of thought. Fight it or embrace it. I, for one, see myself for what I am—cursed. My brother, on the other hand, sees the darkness as a gift. But my brother is a saint compared to some. They marvel at the darkness, crave wickedness, and are simply evil. Because my brother and I regard darkness differently, we are enemies. Siblings thrust into a political feud."

Questions tumbled one after the other through Kade's mind. His perception of the vampyrs had already been altered with Tovi's appearance and ability to walk in the sunlight. He was still trying to wrap his head around the blood-stone. She'd mentioned they were rare, but how many vampyrs walked amongst werewolves and witches, right under their noses? More unsettling, there was a royal family of sorts, which made him increasingly curious. He'd only ever been taught about one royal figure amongst the vampyrs, but that foe hadn't surfaced in decades.

Kade's brows pinched. "Your father, the king, why doesn't he deal with this divide between you and your brother?"

Tovi blinked and sipped her wine. "He doesn't interfere... which is why I try my best to keep tabs on my brother myself. I don't trust Riven. Ever since you and Evelyn were born, my brother has grown increasingly... secretive. Months ago, tensions had been escalating in Drystan court. Circumstances were getting worse. Then, out of nowhere, he left Drystan for Callum. Those close to him claimed he'd left for business-related matters, but I was suspicious."

Callum. The town they'd recently left, the town Kade and Evelyn had only arrived in a few months earlier, and where they'd fallen for one another. His blood ran cold, and any words he'd been about to say evaporated on his tongue as he waited for Tovi to continue.

"I followed him months ago to keep an eye on him. But Riven was slippery. From all I'd witnessed, he *was* here on business, building rapport with those in Torren. Our homeland relies heavily on imports. Trading relationships are vital." She sighed. "Then the first murder happened."

A creep crawled up Kade's spine, like the sensation something stalked him. Between Evelyn's capture and all of this new information about vampyrs, he'd forgotten about the murders, one of the reasons he'd remained in Callum in the first place.

"While you and Evelyn worked together, I did my own investigating, worried my brother was involved, but Riven's only connection to the murders was McKenna, a young woman who'd briefly been his lover." Tovi paused, pain flashing in her eyes for the briefest moment. "I had begun to dismiss the notion Riven was involved entirely until Evelyn mentioned a spell and her bloodline."

Stars above... Bit by bit, piece by piece, everything clicked together. The body parts. Evelyn's bloodline. Kade had feared she played a larger role in everything, but he'd let that go after killing the White Lady. He hadn't lingered on the dark witch's dying screams, ones that cried out to a dark prince. Kade ran one hand through his hair while the other palmed his breastbone to calm his rapid heart.

"Your brother's the missing piece in the murders. *Fuck.*"

Tovi didn't deny his claim, her lips set in a thin line. She was far too calm, far too *calculated,* and Kade hated it.

His wolf surged against his skin on a wave of heat. "You suspected your brother all along and said *nothing.* Why?"

Her face settled into a neutral expression. "I didn't have sufficient evidence that outweighed the dangers of revealing who I am."

Kade growled. "But you were Evelyn's best friend!"

Tovi's nostrils flared. "You're her betrothed, and yet I don't recall you rushing to tell her the truth about your identity. Weeks you let her think you were nothing but a stranger to her."

"Careful." Kade seethed, his wolf raging inside him. "Weeks are very different from years."

"Well, as someone else who cares for Evelyn, you know how difficult it is to face the fact you might lose her once you're honest. You may not believe me, but Evelyn *is* my best friend. Bloody hel, she's like a sister to me—so yes, I lied because I didn't want to ruin our friendship." Tovi sucked in a breath, eyes flashing with more pain. She gave her head a slight shake, pinching her brows and staring absently into the table as if the grooves of the wood held answers.

"Why not come forward after Aster's death at least? You knew how that destroyed Evelyn." He didn't miss Tovi's wince. *Good.* So many things could've gone differently.

Tovi hissed, a sound that reminded Kade of the sort of growl a werewolf would make when annoyed. "I'm pretty sure when a kelpie dragged Evelyn into Lake Glenn, it would've been an opportune time for you to shift into a werewolf. We can't exactly undo the past, can we?"

Kade gritted his teeth. Frustration rippled through him, but she was right. There was no sense sifting through the past. "Fine," he said. "You don't like how—"

"On the contrary," Tovi held up a hand. "I think the way you and Evelyn fell for one another is the way it was supposed to happen. I hadn't seen Evelyn happy in... a long while. Even before her parents died. She's always so worried about being good enough, failing to see how amazing and capable she is. I'm happy she met Cyrus Skender first and... you're far better than the Nūa papers described."

Kade studied Tovi's face, his muscles easing slightly. He almost—*almost*—believed her to be sincere. "You act as though you care about her."

"I do." Her tone and demeanor rang true, but Kade couldn't look past his mate's lingering absence and Tovi's part in it all.

"Do you know Riven's reasons for capturing Evelyn?"

"To finish what the White Lady started," Tovi whispered. "It's a spell to allow vampyrs to walk in the sunlight."

Kade shook his head, fighting his wolf howling in his blood. "Evelyn and I destroyed that spell."

"Not entirely. Somehow, someway, my brother was able to salvage it. He now has the last piece." Tovi paused, as if bracing herself. "It's Evelyn's blood."

Blood.

Kade's own turned to ice, freezing him in place. *Moons.* He thought losing Evelyn on those docks, watching her fade into the horizon had been the most horrifying, grim moment of his existence, and yet the possibility of her death, Riven's need for her blood rooted him in horrific numbness.

Anger and fear battled that numbness, making it difficult to speak. "W-why..." He shook his head, growled. "Why would Riven do this?" The words exploded all at once. "What does he gain?"

Tovi hesitated. "Riven cares about impressing the worst of the worst in court. What better way to win favor by giving them what they miss most? *Light.*"

Kade shook his head. "I don't understand. Wouldn't you want that for your people, too?"

Tovi reared back. "At the expense of Evelyn's well-being? No. Even if we walk in sunlight, we'd still be cursed. The more we feed our rather predatorial urges, the more wicked the darkness grows. What do you know about scáths?"

Kade almost rolled his eyes. Why was she wasting his time? "Newly-turned vampyrs, blood thirsty, reckless. Monsters."

"That may be what everyone thinks, but everyone is wrong. We call them *caillte.* The lost. Not newly turned vampyrs riddled so deeply with darkness there's no undoing it. *That* is the threat facing our homeland if my brother succeeds."

Kade tensed. Distrust coursed through him. Tovi's words challenged years of training and fighting against an enemy he now knew he never truly understood. "If your brother is so secretive, how do you know his intentions?" he asked—no, demanded—because he didn't want to accept any of this. He thought Evelyn had been captured because she was Daughter of the Goddess. The vampyrs feared her, feared her union with Kade. She'd always be at risk with her title, but he hadn't anticipated something this grave.

Tovi stared out the small window of the cabin. "I... heard Riven tell Evelyn his plans for her."

Kade's heart thumped. Once. Twice. Like a wolf stalking his prey, he didn't move, didn't twitch as he whispered, "Heard?"

"This morning, I woke in a box, buried in some field outside of Callum. When it occurred to me Evelyn may be in danger, I ran to look for her. Unfortunately, my brother already had her in his clutches."

Kade charged. "You're telling me you witnessed Evelyn get captured. Allowed it?"

Tovi flinched, jade eyes shuttering and snowy blonde hair shaking dirt onto the floor. "I had no other choice—"

"You did, and you chose to fail her!" Panic tore through Kade, the power from earlier surged forward. His vision tunneled in and out, the sensation worse than the lean of the ship. He braced his hand on the bunk beside him. Smoke rose from under his glowing palm. *Moons*, not again. He cursed, retreating from the bunk and leaving behind a scorched handprint on the mahogany wood, but his hand had returned to normal—no light in sight. Kade blinked, regaining his focus.

"What the bloody hel is that?" Tovi stared at him with brows drawn together.

"I don't know," Kade said, sweat prickling at his brow.

She pointed at his face. "Your eyes also glowed a pearly blue, like your hand."

The energy threatened to push again, but Kade fisted his clammy hands, holding it at bay with all his might. Evelyn had been captured and now this.

Later.

"We're talking about Evelyn, not me. You let her get captured, remember?"

Tovi shot him a scathing look, eyes sharp as daggers. "Riven threatened your life, and she surrendered to protect you."

Kade stumbled back. "What?"

"Riven would've done it. Your life was at risk, Kade. Evelyn didn't hesitate, not for a second. I think she, too, realized the odds were against us."

His brave mate—she'd protected him. A third-born, thick and through, Evelyn had surrendered to keep him safe. He shut his eyes. The faintest regret washed over him. If he had gone with Evelyn, she wouldn't have been alone against Riven. The past pulled him back.

No—he wouldn't waste time thinking on it, not when he needed to keep moving forward, start planning how he would get Evelyn back. Nothing else mattered. Not even his resentment toward Tovi and her lies. If Riven was taking Evelyn to Drystan, Kade did in fact need the vampyr princess. No werewolf had crossed the Void—the desolate, dark, mist-filled divide between Drystan and Sorin—successfully, at least not in the histories he'd been told.

What felt like a lifetime ago, Kade'd stood on the docks in Morrow, resentful of setting foot on a godforsaken boat. But he'd done it, he had stuck to the task at hand, swallowing his warring emotions and fear of open water. It had only been one step and then another up the ramp. His mission then had been to find Evelyn and bring her home, and his efforts had paid off—weeks later he'd found her.

Kade understood the power of moving forward and not looking back. It had gotten him through the months after his mother died. The past had no place in the present. It weighed him down. He didn't want to forget what Tovi had done, but he needed a way into Drystan, the first step in getting Evelyn back.

"You swear to get me across the Void and to Drystan Castle?"

Tovi nodded. "Yes."

Kade took on the familiar posture of a determined warrior. Resolve washed over him. "Alright. You'll be our guide. I suggest you rest up. We have three weeks before we reach Nūa, and during that time, I want you to teach me everything about your land. Now, if you'll excuse me, I need some fresh air."

He headed towards the door, eager to get out of the belly of the ship and smell the breeze. Anything to calm his wild, restless wolf. Maxie leaped off the bunk and joined him. She weaved between his legs, a faint purr vibrating through his ankles.

"You'll need to get a handle on the new power, too," Tovi said.

Kade stopped, the wood of the door groaning from his grip. He didn't enjoy being reminded he had something else to deal with. Evelyn's capture, the newness regarding vampyrs—*stars above*, his father's death, too.

"Worry about getting us to Drystan castle, vampyr." He slammed the door and the echoing bang covered up any reply Tovi might have made.

CHAPTER FOUR

EVELYN

T HE PADS OF EVELYN Carson's fingers burned.

Flesh sizzled. Steam rose. Sweat prickled at her brow.

It wasn't her own magic causing the pain—no, that was trapped, still bound thanks to Riven's bracelets.

High in a gray sky, tendrils of stray clouds reached out to the stone of Evelyn's tower, just shy of her window—her very locked, very enchanted window in Drystan Castle.

For the third time, Evelyn tried to open it. At the poor expense of her now numb fingertips, it didn't budge. Dark magic oozed from the metal latch and frame. Without access to her own magic to extend out and feel it, all she could sense was wrongness, the same kind that wrapped around every inch of Drystan she'd so far experienced.

Evelyn cursed and braced her forehead on the windowpane, a tired breath shuddering out of her. At least the glass cooled her steaming skin. Heat had flushed through her body ever since Riven had captured her, a constant stream. At this point, she was scorching, hotter than the flame coursing through her veins. Carnage, anger, resolve—they stormed inside her, thundering to be let loose.

Fucking flames, she saw it all for what it was. The lack of food. Isolation. Riven was doing this on purpose. He needed her alive to complete the spell to allow vampyrs to walk in the sunlight. He couldn't kill her, but he could weaken her. Exhaust her body, play with her mind. A weak prisoner was easier to control.

There was no *fucking flames* way she was going to let Riven break her. Exhaling through her nose, she assessed the surrounding land outside the window.

The tower stood high above the rest of the castle, alone on the east side. Not a shingle or roof to fall onto before hitting the ground below. Guards, the size of ants from so high up, scurried back and forth across a stretched battlement. Evelyn released a shaky breath. Even if the window budged, she'd have nowhere to go.

More guards flanked other walls and towers, Verena-purple uniforms dotting the inky limestone. The castle was a fortress, heavily guarded and fiercely surrounded by a murky moat and a wall decorated with iron spikes jutting upward. It was carved into a mountainside with a steep, rocky descent.

If Evelyn made it out of the castle unscathed, where was she to go next? Bouts of mist mingled through the streets of a village that sat on the edge of a snaking river. She was too high to make out anyone, and even though there was still much to learn about her enemy, she guessed the village brimmed with vampyrs.

Sure, Evelyn had managed without her flame before. In the early months after she'd run away, witches on the Guard and werewolf warriors had once searched for her, but she'd slipped past them all, undetected. She'd mastered the art of going unseen while she moved from place to place. At least then she'd had her innate magic to help her.

Evelyn massaged her sore wrists. The skin and bones trapped beneath the bracelets were bruised. Her left had been rubbed so raw, sticky blood glued the bracelet tighter. Evelyn channeled her magic, her flame swirling and flaring in her blood. It hit the walls of dark magic, and like any other creature, hitting against a cage over and over only weakened it.

She gritted her teeth and growled with frustration. She needed to keep her strength, which was slowly fading. Evelyn swallowed, shutting her eyes in hopes of some reprieve, but even in the darkness, there was pulsing pain, helplessness, exactly as there had been in the confines of the ship. Even now she bobbed up and down, not on waves, but on the ebb and flow of her despair. They'd made it across the Sapphire Sea in sixteen days, twice as fast as the usual voyage. Between the speed of the ship, a spell that needed her blood, the enchanted window, and the damn bracelets, it was clear another witch worked with Riven.

Not only was Evelyn unequipped to face a fellow witch, but it also unnerved her that one had left Sorin to side with the vampyr prince. Had the Wall failed around the city of witches? Had something horrific happened to her homeland?

Guilt for running two years ago ate away at her. Even as Riven's prisoner, she wanted nothing more than to show the people of her homeland she'd changed. Though it wasn't common knowledge she'd run, she *knew* the mistake she'd made—as did her sisters. What did they think after all this time? Did Mirella, her astute, older sister harbor years-old ire? Did Blair, her kind but reserved middle sister, resent her for the worry she'd caused?

Evelyn fisted her hands at her side. She wasn't certain what she'd face in Drystan, but no matter what, she'd make sure Riven never succeeded with his spell, one way or another. She'd earn forgiveness from those she'd left behind by defeating the darkness and protecting her homeland. When she returned, it would be as though she'd never left.

And yet, she wished she'd return to Sorin under different circumstances.

At Kade's side.

Goddess, she missed him. Her heart ached for him.

For his kindness, his kisses. His phantom touches haunted her when she drifted to sleep, his evergreen-and-rain scent lingered on her clothes. To think they'd been so close to returning home, united and determined to fulfill the prophecy together—it crushed Evelyn's spirit. She'd tried not to think of him for when she did, her questions never stopped. How long had he waited for her at the docks? Had he learned she'd been captured? Had he thought the worst?

And Maxie. Her absence was like a hole in Evelyn's chest. A fragment of her soul missing. A witch didn't part with her familiar. Ever. Had Kade found Maxie? Did she feel the separation like Evelyn did?

No.

Evelyn steeled herself, refusing to let doubt plant its weedy seed. She'd been down that path before, knew the havoc it wrecked on her heart. Never again would she let it control her like it once had. She prayed to the Goddess that Kade had found Maxie and that they were both safe. She wiped away a few tears, set her shoulders straight, and paced back and forth, rallying her resolve.

Voices resounded outside her door, and Evelyn paused. Had Riven finally decided to pay her a visit, or had the vampyr king been informed of her arrival?

Though she'd gotten a great sense of the land outside the castle thanks to her high vantage point, Evelyn had seen little inside the castle aside from her room. She'd been blindfolded before they left the ship. Deprived of her sight, she'd relied on her other senses—the smell of wet stone, the drizzle of rain, and the boots clattering on the path of whoever dragged her along. Evelyn hadn't gained any sense of who surrounded her, what their purpose was, or where they traveled. She'd half expected to be thrust at the vampyr king's feet in a throne room or handed over to Riven and his mysterious witch allies, but instead, they'd shoved her into the large suite of a tower with no indication as to when the spell would take place or how they planned to use her blood.

The door's lock rattled open, and a woman glided into her room. The agility. The swiftness. Her visitor's movements set off alarm bells in Evelyn's mind, and her bound flame rallied to defend.

A vampyr.

Her attire reminded Evelyn of a uniform, like one she'd worn on the Guard. Tight leather leggings molded to her legs, and a belt of the same leather held a black quilted jacket in place. Though, unlike Evelyn's uniform, the jacket's sleeves were high with silver embellishment. Matching wristbands held the snug tunic covering her arms in place, and the Verena crest glinted over her right breastbone. Brownish-black hair had been pulled to the side and braided in a fishtail pattern, blending in with the dark outfit.

"Who are you?" Evelyn asked, words thick and laden on her tongue after days of silence.

"Tala, a member of Riven's council," the female vampyr said. "I've been tasked with guarding you."

Her golden eyes tracked over every inch of Evelyn's frame, like some beast sizing up her prey. Yet, despite the predatorial threat steps away, Evelyn's flame danced. Even snuffed against the bracelets, it twisted with delight. A sense of familiarity tugged at her—and the stark difference compared to Riven and Tovi. The vampyr didn't possess the same ethereal beauty but an earthier kind. Regardless, in the presence of a vampyr, at Evelyn's command, her flame rallied to defend.

"Guard me? Last time I checked, I was in a cell."

Tala raised a brow. "I'd hardly call these accommodations a cell."

Evelyn scoffed—maybe delirium had gotten to her after all, and her sense of self-preservation had vanished. She was feeling rather bold. "Measly comfort doesn't negate the fact I'm a prisoner here."

Tala rolled her eyes and walked the perimeter, seemingly disinterested in Evelyn. "Call it what you want, but compared to the dungeons, it's luxury. Here you have window. A bed. A bath." She paused at the four-poster on the north wall and then the armoire. "Are the clothes not to your liking?"

Evelyn bristled. She'd found the wardrobe full of clothes tailored to her size, which meant, to her annoyance, Riven had been planning her capture for some time. She wasn't sure which irritated her more, the fact he succeeded or that he'd been plotting right under her nose. Worse, had Tovi assisted Riven? Evelyn dismissed the name, refusing to even think of the searing betrayal.

Instead, she regarded the grandiose of the room—the velvet, the silks, the amenities—for what they were.

Golden shackles.

Tala sighed with a hum. "Between us ladies, you could use a fresh set of clothes." She sniffed the air, and her nose wrinkled. "I'd also suggest a bath. You smell like shit. No offense."

Evelyn blinked, unable to stop her mouth from falling open. She clamped it shut, shaking her head. She wasn't certain if she was disoriented or if that was a true tease in the vampyr's tone. Embarrassment washed through her. Grime and stench clung to her. Grease matted her hair roots. She wore the same clothes since the day she'd been captured, and she'd been locked in a cell during her time on the ship, her accommodations a humble chamber pot and her cloak as a bed.

She crossed her arms. "Offense taken, considering it isn't exactly my fault I've been locked away for weeks."

Tala waved her hands in the air. "Don't overheat yourself, fire witch. What's in the past is in the past. Would you rather stew in what can't be undone or wash?"

The female vampyr sauntered over to the table situated between the sofa and pair of reading chairs where a decanter of wine sat, two goblets glinting from the light of the fire.

"Here." Tala poured a generous glass of wine and handed it to Evelyn. "It'll calm the nerves."

She eyed the alcohol. While wine sounded lovely—*Goddess*, the chance to calm her nerves even with a sip or two—she didn't trust the effects it would have on her already tired, weary mind. "I'm good, thanks."

Tala exhaled. "You're afraid. Hiding it well, but I can still hear your racing heart." She tapped her one ear. "Vampyrs have keen senses, don't forget it."

Fucking flames. Evelyn clenched her jaw and breathed through her nose. Not only did she hate knowing Tala could sense her nerves, but she also hated not understanding her enemy. For so many years, she'd fought scáths who attacked for one thing—blood. They didn't play games or observe their opponent close-ly.

Evelyn took the glass, pausing as she glanced at the liquid. Distrust, icy cold, flushed through her.

"It's not poisoned. I swear," Tala said. As if to prove her point, she poured herself a glass and sipped it. The burgundy stained her white teeth, no fangs in sight though.

Evelyn raised a brow. "How can I be so sure?"

She shrugged. "Poison isn't my usual method of killing."

Evelyn scoffed. Perhaps it had been a tease in Tala's tone earlier. Curious, she asked, "And what is your usual method?"

"Axes."

Evelyn raised a brow, intrigued, but no weapons of the sort hung from the adviser's belt. Her agile frame suggested the female vampyr was accustomed to fighting and being active. But clearly she also enjoyed wine. She downed her pour in a single gulp, abandoning the empty goblet on the table with a *cling*. A red-stoned pendant dangling from a delicate necklace reflected off the gold cup and caught Evelyn's attention.

She froze mid-sip, the tannins turning sour on her tongue. Evelyn'd seen the likes of it before.

Tovi.

She'd worn one, a pearl-sized crimson stone set in black metal. *A rare stone of my homeland*, she'd said.

"What is that?"

Tala followed her line of sight. "It's called a bloodstone. It allows me to walk in the sunlight. And it keeps others from knowing, entirely, that I'm a vampyr."

Tears threatened to spill. The sight of the bloodstone answered questions brimming in the back of Evelyn's mind for weeks. Tovi had walked alongside Eveyln during the daylight. Shopping, to and from classes at university, strolls in the park. How had she never suspected her best friend was a vampyr?

Her best friend.

Could she even call Tovi that? No. She'd tried her hardest not to think of Tovi, but now, locked beyond dark stones, it had become increasingly difficult. *This* was Tovi's home. *This* had been her castle. Or was it still? Did she roam these halls as Evelyn stood prisoner in a tower? The betrayal was blinding. It seared through Evelyn, so hot, she saw red. Tovi had lied about not only who she was, but what. The more she thought of her, the more often she asked the most painful question of all.

Had any of it been real? Their laughs. Their friendship. The times they'd held each other through heartbreak. Tovi had been there for Evelyn more than her own sisters in the wake of her parents' deaths, and yet she'd known who'd killed them. It didn't make any sense. Why hadn't Tovi said anything? Perhaps Tovi had lured her close, assisting Riven in his plot.

Evelyn downed her wine, setting the drained goblet on the table with a loud *clang*. She crossed her arms and dug her fingernails into her biceps, using the pain for something else to think of. Stewing over Tovi was as helpful as opening the enchanted lock on the window without her magic.

Her efforts only hurt in the end.

Escape wasn't in the cards—*yet*. But that didn't mean she'd sit around idle. Wine, a bath, some rest. Time to gather her wits. Recharge her resolve. Figure out what to do next. If she wanted any chance of victory, of escape, Evelyn needed to learn more about her enemy.

"Dinner will arrive in an hour," Tala said, striding for the door.

"Splendid." Evelyn didn't hold back the sarcasm.

"I take it you haven't been enjoying the chef's soup, then?" Tala asked, a playful glint in her eye.

"I'd hardly call it soup."

Tala laughed. "Maybe I'll put a word in with the cook and get you something nicer tonight. Wash up. If you've already forgotten, you stink."

Evelyn grasped her arms a little fiercer. "Will I get the chance to bathe alone, or do you plan to guard me every minute of every day?"

Tala raised her hands in surrender. "I'd rather not stay for your bath. I'll grant you some privacy. But I'll be right outside the door, and remember"—she tapped her ears—"vampyrs have excellent hearing, better than that mate of yours, even. Try to leave this room without me and you'll end up in the dungeons, but this time with chains connected to those bracelets."

Evelyn sucked a breath, the mention of Kade gluing in her place. She didn't bat an eye for Tala's threats, not when she craved Kade's touch and kind gaze. She'd give it all up—the room, the comfort, the promise of fresh air—to know for certain he was safe.

Tala paused at the door. "Also, a fair warning: Riven is close to getting what he wants. I wouldn't push him. Follow my orders, stick to me, and you'll survive the coming weeks."

The vampyr shut the door behind her.

Evelyn's head ached. She wasn't sure what confused her more. The fact Tala had warned her about Riven's progress or that the guard had said, "what *he* wants"?

Chapter Five

Eldrick

Eldrick Drengr stood with arms crossed, leaning against his desk, a migraine forming from his tight, grinding jaw.

Large, smooth bricks of gray stone made up the walls of his office, and the color closed in around him, sterile and cold. Few windows lined the fortress, but Eldrick's office possessed two opposing views. One was situated on the west wall, facing the Vadon Mountains. The tips of pine trees stretched for miles, like an evergreen army standing at attention. White-capped mountains lined the horizon, the first signs of winter evident in his homeland.

Behind him, the south window he'd situated his desk in front of, gave a bird's-eye view of the Drengr Village. From eight stories high, Eldrick could watch the market, smoke stacks, corner bonfires, and even the outside perimeter where warriors patrolled.

His heart tugged towards the west window. The scant rays of evening sun peeking through the hovering clouds glinted off his axes resting beside him, lost in the sea of letters, parchment, and maps. What Eldrick would give to venture outside in the crisp air, grasping his axes and sparring until the moon hung above.

But the latest missive he'd received, taunting him a few feet away, had him glued to his duty, the contents of the letter too grave to dismiss for an evening sparring session.

More missing werewolves.

Seated at the oak council table, his uncle, Claus, studied the news from the Johannes pack.

"That is a total of forty missing werewolves," he said.

"I know." Eldrick gritted out. He didn't need reminding of the tallying number, keeping count just well as Claus was. But he said nothing more. There was no sense in feeding the tension between him and his uncle as of late.

Months ago, Eldrick had screwed up, earning Claus's unsolicited help. It hadn't taken long for his uncle, also a commander and warrior, to discover Kade was no longer at the Void with the Gray Fenris, his brother's team of werewolf warriors. Eldrick's attempt at a ruse had, as Claus put it, allowed Kade to "abandon his duty" becoming no better than "that selfish witch who'd ran like a scared bride who'd gotten cold feet."

Thank the stars Kade hadn't been around to hear those words from their uncle. The two had never gotten along like Eldrick and Claus had, and even though Evelyn had run, Kade always demanded respect for his betrothed. He honored her no matter what.

If only Eldrick's brother were here. He could use Kade's grounding patience and apt focus. He himself couldn't focus on the various missives spread out behind him without the latest one blaring like a village warning horn.

Gone. Missing. Vanished into thin air.

"You said the efforts at the Void had doubled," Claus said.

"The efforts are doubled. I saw it myself during the summer visit. Double the warriors, double the posts. There isn't a mile of the Void not being monitored. The efforts have also helped. Less scáths and demons are getting through to Sorin."

Eldrick felt lousy, directing the conversation to a separate issue. They were discussing the missing werewolves—not the threat of darkness creeping over the Void. But what else was he supposed to say? He had put extra measures in place, but they weren't working. Like other accounts, the Johannes's missive detailed no evidence of foul play. No blood. No signs of a struggle. No clues at all.

Not even the scent of an assailant.

When the disappearances had first started, Eldrick had assumed it had been vampyrs, the vile creatures. Who else would take werewolves other than the bloodsuckers from the north? But there hadn't been the sharp, citrus scent of vampyr in any of the areas where werewolves had gone missing. Besides, how or why would a scáth take werewolves in the first place?

"It might be time we consider one of our own," Eldrick whispered with a shake of his head.

Claus growled. "That is what vampyrs wants us to believe."

Eldrick gritted his teeth, digging his nails into the muscles of his arms.

Some rumors had circulated regarding a demon of sorts, but scholars hadn't found anything. Even his middle brother, Lorkan, the best scholar he knew, was stumped. They'd debated on demons, ones that stalked and dragged away their prey like lions, but those resided closer to the far west side of the mountains and sand wastelands. Ialtógs plucked their prey from the sky but were relatively unforgiving in the devouring part of their attacks. There had been little blood at the sites of the recent attacks and few signs of a struggle. Nothing added up.

For a month's time, fingers had pointed at the mages beyond the wastelands. Their magic connected them to the earth, a projection of the Earth Goddess's power, and it made sense they could clear their tracks, make it appear as if werewolves had vanished into thin air. The mage king's impromptu visit to their village over the summer had put that theory to rest. His visit had also cleared half the whiskey stores of the Drengr pack—a devastating loss Eldrick still lost sleep over.

He sighed, the tightness of his jaw joined by the pinch between his brow. Sore teeth and an onsetting headache—neither pain outmatched the frustration eating away at him. With no suspects, no new clues, it left Eldrick without answers and nothing to reassure the other packs it wouldn't happen again.

Claus rubbed the scruff on his jaw. His deep-brown eyes landed on Eldrick with a severe stare. "We need to write to Alpha Johannes about how we plan to proceed. Aside from our own, his pack was the one left untouched by this mystery. Now, all the packs have been affected, and we need to present a cohesive image before they grow restless."

But what would they tell Alpha Johannes? Eldrick was supposed to be a leader. But how could he lead when he had no facts to offer? Could he promise another search party? Ensure more reinforcements were placed at the Void? Call to aid from the witches?

Except the werewolves hadn't uttered a word of this to witches. Pride over precedent. The alphas wouldn't dare look weak to the Elders, as if they couldn't control their territory. Ever since Evelyn Carson had run, tensions between witches and werewolves were high. But perhaps they didn't have any other choice.

One, two. Eldrick breathed in, breathed out. The practice grounded his racing mind, brought his heartbeat back to a relatively slow speed, and in this instance, calmed his worry regarding the missing werewolves.

"I should write to Blair Carson," he said. "We could at least trust her to keep it a secret while she helped."

Claus scoffed, rising from his chair. Tall and stocky, his uncle exuded wolf and warrior head to toe. "Because she's good at keeping secrets doesn't mean we can trust her. If I recall correctly, she's also the one who convinced Kade to leave in the first place."

Eldrick's jaw ticked. "He didn't *leave*. He went *searching* for the Daughter of the Goddess."

Claus's eyes narrowed. Doubt. Disappointment. He'd glowered the same look down at Eldrick the day his mother had died. Then he'd deserved his uncle's ire. His mistake had cost his mother her life. But letting Kade go? No. Eldrick wouldn't budge on that decision. The prophecy. The sake of their homeland. Defeating the vampyrs once and for all.

He moved from his desk to stand closer to the window, away from his uncle's stare. Claus had always been hard on him, seeing as he'd one day be the alpha of the Drengr pack. Eldrick peered down at the village. A different view, a different perspective to help reign in his wild thoughts.

"You've always taught me to lead with my head," Eldrick said, turning back to his uncle. "Facts, logic, not emotions. Letting Kade go made sense. Still does. We need Evelyn, and he was the best chance of getting her back."

Claus relaxed a fraction, sighing as he folded his arms over his broad chest. "Yet, we have no idea where he is."

Eldrick nodded. "True, and I'd be lying if I said I didn't wish Kade was here, offering his cutting insight."

Kade gave others hope, not only because he was Son of the God but because he understood how to bring people together. Often at the expense of what he needed. Pride swelled within Eldrick, not jealousy. He'd always admired Kade. He'd not only kept their family together—he, Eldrick, Lorkan, and their father—after their mother died, but had also helped hold their pack together. Eldrick had stepped up, too, leading alongside his ailing father, but Kade had shown up in the small areas Eldrick couldn't reach—the training grounds, the village streets, the Shield-maiden. Moons, if only Kade would return home with Evelyn. That would be the hope the werewolves needed, the Son of the God leading the investigation against this mystery, the Daughter of the Goddess, hopefully, at his side.

"What do you suggest we do then?" Claus asked. "I think writing to Blair is hasty."

"Fine. We let the news settle about the Johannes pack. Let me think of a response. Until then, we hold off on reaching back out."

His uncle nodded. His eyes held more, but he said nothing as he left Eldrick's office, leaving him alone.

He shut his eyes as the door's lock clicked shut. "Fuck." Eldrick exhaled, a sourness coating his tongue. He peered down at the Drengr's prosperous village, a sight worth calming him. Yet, his heart ached, too, knowing other packs grieved.

The Shield-maiden, the village's tavern, swarmed with activity. Fond memories flooded Eldrick. Kade at his side, enjoying a blueberry ale while the band played. Lorkan would refuse to dance but would tap his foot perfectly to the tune. With winter on the horizon, the songs would be heavy and sad while the stew would be meaty and hardy.

Loneliness settled over him. Both brothers were gone. Kade had left over a year ago, and Lorkan was on sabbatical. At least he'd gotten letters from his middle brother, detailing the wonders of Vísdómr, the werewolves' most renowned library, but he'd not heard from his youngest brother in months. Eldrick hadn't sent word to Kade either—he hadn't the slightest idea where his brother was or what progress he'd made finding Evelyn.

Eldrick was about to turn away from the window when hair white as a dove's caught his gaze.

Below, a woman walked through the current of werewolves, so light on her feet, she appeared to float like a snowflake.

The village faded. Eldrick's emotions evaporated. Time stilled.

Her ethereal beauty cast a spell over him—snowy hair, a slender frame, nose and cheekbones to match. She reminded Eldrick of the snow that fell in the winter months, silent and delicate. Not once had he ever seen her in the village. Was she a werewolf? A witch? A human? It wasn't uncommon for either to pass through the village to trade or shop.

One, two.

Fresh air, even a walk. Perhaps that was exactly what he needed.

Chapter Six

Evelyn

A week passed.

The days moved as slowly as the clouds over Drystan. Evelyn's prospects at learning anything about her enemy felt as bleak. Her maddening, mundane routine left her disheartened. She woke with the sun, readied for a day of being attended to by human servants, paced around her tower, and shared meals with a silent Tala. Evelyn bristled from the comforts—silk sheets, three-course meals, an endless wardrobe.

Her guard surveyed her every move, making it difficult to do anything but sit and remain a well-behaved prisoner. At first, Evelyn had attempted to get answers out of Tala, but she'd remained tight-lipped. She answered in smirks, sighs, scoffs, and the occasional rolling of the eyes when Evelyn threw an insult.

If Evelyn wanted answers, she wouldn't get them from Tala.

Her door swung open, and servants wheeled in a cart brimming with silver platters. *Human* servants. Another question, another unknown Evelyn hadn't managed to understand. Why did humans live in Drystan? Were they here willingly?

Tala sauntered in next, her walk possessing equal parts ease and grace. The movement reminded Evelyn so much of Tovi, she had to look elsewhere blinking away the memories of her poised, proud, once best friend.

Tala sat on the large velvet sofa in the center seating area. She patted the empty seat beside her. "Join me for lunch. I could hear your stomach growling down the hall."

Evelyn grinded her molars together, fighting the urge to roll her eyes. The female vampyr never failed to remind her—or warn her, Evelyn wasn't sure—how impeccable her hearing was. She couldn't gauge the vampyr, couldn't figure out what game she played. One moment, she was teasing, the next, she threw threats, only to offer her a salve for her wrists after that. But Tala had never hurt Evelyn, which begged the question, who exactly was Tala, and why had Riven appointed her as Evelyn's guard?

Evelyn didn't enjoy taking orders like some child being babysat. Stubbornness led her to one of the reading chairs across from Tala. The vampyr smirked, one of her fangs making an appearance. It wasn't as long or sharp as a scáth's. Why? Yet another question to add to her growing list.

"Drystan fashion suits you," Tala said, sarcasm dripping like syrup from her words.

Evelyn's nostrils flared. Dresses. Skirts. Slips. And, *fucking flames*, more damn dresses. She hated each of them. The layers. The fabrics. The inability to move freely and securely. The skin of her legs prickled, the expensive material reminded her too much of Tovi's fine taste in clothes.

After the servants laid out lunch and left, Evelyn and Tala ate their meal in utter silence, as usual. Evelyn ate as much as she could. The food had improved since the bland broth on the ship. Roast chicken. Crispy potatoes. Herbed gravy. Evelyn had tried to regain her strength by eating, but nausea ailed her in waves.

After the third bite, she abandoned her plate on the side table, inhaling through her nose. Her head pounded, and she grew flush again, sweat slicking down her neck. If she forced another forkful, she'd be sick.

Tala's golden eyes hesitated on her abandoned plate, brows pinching slightly. "How about a walk, witch?"

"A walk?" Hope sparked in Evelyn's gut.

Tala nodded, setting down her own plate. "Fresh air. A moment out of this tower. What do you say?"

The vampyr rose from her seat. That had been something else Evelyn had gathered. Tala proposed questions but didn't leave room for objection. They were going for a walk. Evelyn was getting out of this tower.

Fucking flames, what an opportunity.

She practically shot out of her chair, far too quickly. Her sight narrowed, the circular room tunneling in and out of focus. She blinked away the dizziness, refusing to let her nausea ruin this chance of getting a better lay of the castle.

Drystan's cold bit like a frozen viper. Evelyn's cheeks burned rosy, and her fingers stiffened to a horrid numbness. But the cold helped. The clean scent of snow sat in the air, filling Evelyn's lungs with freshness. It beat the thick brine of the ship and the suffocating tower. Goddess, she could breathe again, and the temperature dulled the pain of the bracelets.

Tala didn't seem in any rush to escort her back. They'd walked a steady pace through a large, well-manicured garden. Wintergreen hedges lined rows and rows like a squat maze. Snow dusted the vacant flower beds. Some ferns remained, frost as clear and thick as glass magnified their lime-green hue. There was a lack of life in the garden, though. Oh, birds flew above, and surely worms tunneled down below, but the still garden possessed nothing... lively, no bright energy. Without her magic, she couldn't detect anything for sure, but something in the air, something rooted the in land was odd, as if her instinct sensed an otherness.

A *wrongness*—like the dark magic on her window. What exactly clung to the land of Drystan? Was it the darkness of the Void seeping into it? Yet, Evelyn had no idea how near or far the Void was in relation to the castle. She shook her head, ignoring the onset of a headache.

Over the white-capped mountains to the north, the sun hung like a silver dollar in the sky. Thick, slate-gray clouds stole most of its light, casting the castle in haunting shadows, but it was still day.

Evelyn had taken note of the guards stationed around the castle grounds. *Humans.* They hadn't come across a single vampyr. Perhaps not all vampyrs possessed a bloodstone. She'd never encountered a scáth with one either.

Tala veered left, leading them under a rusty archway and out of the garden. They entered a courtyard where fountains sat in every corner. Large, black carved vases rested in the center of water pools. Mounds of ice fell over the rounded fountain tops, the slow but mighty trickle of a few water currents cascading into a delicate chime as they hit the icy basin.

"Why is it you have a bloodstone and others do not?" Evelyn asked.

Tala sighed, dipping her cold fingers into the fountain's basin and combing through the icy water. "Only a select few have them. Those usually within Drystan court who possess a high status, a lord or lady."

Which explained why Tovi had one. She was their princess after all. Yet, worry wormed through Evelyn, unrelated to her old friend's secrets. How many other lords and ladies used their bloodstone necklaces and walked amongst witches and werewolves in Sorin, unbeknownst to everyone around them?

"Who gave you yours?" Evelyn asked, the question tumbling from her lips before she even considered she might not like what she heard.

"Tovi."

The name was like a bucket of ice water. She'd forgotten others knew Tovi—knew her like Evelyn didn't. Her betrayal riled Evelyn's flame deep inside her. She didn't want to linger too much on Tovi's lies, but Riven had said Tovi was a thorn in his side, and Tala claimed she was part of *his* council.

"Simply because she is your princess or because you're acquainted?"

The vampyr studied Evelyn, golden eyes fleeting over her face. She'd seen that look before, an intense apprehension as the other refrained from saying something, as if Tala held back. Evelyn's brows pinched together, chalking up the flicker of familiarity in the back of her tired mind as unreliable. What about Tovi would Tala hold back? Why tell her anything at all?

Tala smiled, both fangs flashing. "I'm not entirely certain that's any of your concern, witch. Come. Sundown approaches, and I'm sure you'd like to walk—"

"Lady Tala."

A young guard stood in an entryway leading into the castle. Adolescence still clung to his rosy cheeks, and he'd yet to grow into his gangly limbs and height. His innocent human eyes landed on Evelyn, fear flashing through them. He held a folded lettering gripped tightly in his hand.

Tala shook her hand dry and gave Evelyn a pointed glare. "Don't wander from the courtyard."

She left Evelyn alone to discuss with the young guard in a hushed voice. The sight of the descending sun sent Evelyn's heart rate up. Back in the tower. Locked away. Alone. She moved onto the next fountain, frustration gripping every fiber in her being. Time ticked like a phantom omen approached.

Riven intended to use her blood to allow vampyrs to walk in the sunlight. That knowledge alone unnerved her. How? When? Why hadn't the prince made himself known or the king? Snow flurries began to fall, their icy exoskeletons landing on the black limestone and dissipating into the foundation of the castle. Evelyn followed their trail, her resolve melting as quickly as the new snow. What good did the fresh air do if she didn't get answers?

An exasperated *humph* snagged Evelyn's attention. Beyond the courtyard, one of the prettiest young women she'd ever seen sat at the edge of a pool. A statue stood at the center. Her dainty hand hovered over the water, shaking, as her brow furrowed. A few droplets rose into the air like beads of suspended rain.

They reflected the women's sage suede dress. Wait—*fucking flames*—the young woman was a witch who possessed a water bronntanas. Was she working with Riven?

Evelyn's heart skipped as she headed in the witch's direction. The joint courtyard was rather simple, the center statue the single ornament along with evergreen trees, neatly pruned, lining the perimeter. A tall, lanky man had been carved from the same dark stone of the castle, but Evelyn paid the figure no mind, her sights set on the witch.

As she approached, the witch's brows pinched more, exasperation turning her beautiful face red. She gasped, and the water droplets fell. The witch muttered a curse and slapped the water's surface. Evelyn paused behind an evergreen, hiding as she continued to take in the young witch.

She hovered her hand over the water again. Again and again, she flexed her fingers, and Evelyn's racing heart dropped. She'd been there before. Frustrated. Angry. Her magic lost to her. The feelings were as familiar as yesterday. What she would've given to not be alone in that struggle. Cautious, Evelyn stepped out from her hiding place, approaching the younger witch on silent feet.

She cleared her throat. "Try again."

The witch whirled. Barely twenty years old, her eyes held a young innocence. They shined a shade between blue and green. Her golden blonde curls, weaved with silver tinsel, spilled over her shoulder as the witch scrambled back.

Evelyn held up her hands—black bracelets taunting her. Perhaps this had been a foolish idea. "I'm sorry. I didn't mean to startle you. I... I noticed you were a witch and—"

The witch retreated another step. "Stay back. I'm not supposed to talk to you. My sister told me you aren't to be trusted."

"I'm not here to hurt you. Your magic—I thought I could help."

The young witch blinked. "You want to help me?"

Evelyn nodded. She gestured towards the water surrounding the statue. "Why don't you try again, and I can..." Words had been etched into the rock where the statue stood, clearer at this distance, and the first word rooted Evelyn in place.

King.

Tall, lanky, like another vampyr she knew. Long hair pulled to the side with delicate braids weaved by his temples. A humble crown, what appeared to be a metal ring, sat atop his head. The man's cheekbones were carved from stone, figuratively and literally. The astute nose and square shoulders, Evelyn realized who Tovi and Riven resembled the most—their father.

It was a statue of the King of Vampyr.

This had been the enemy her people had whispered stories about late at night, the villain both adults and children feared, but Evelyn's blood ran colder than the Drystan air as she read the rest of the plaque.

King Harold Verena, May the Goddess Let His Soul Rest in Peace.

Evelyn's heart raced. Her vision tunneled in and out as she read over the words. Rest in peace. Rest in peace. As if he were...

"The king... is he..." Goddess, Evelyn couldn't manage words. "Dead?"

The witch's eyes narrowed, her head titling. "Yes, he's been dead for some time."

Evelyn's mind whirled. Dates had been carved into the stone as well. Years, centuries ago. Centuries before the first Daughter of Goddess and Son of the God. *Fucking flames.* For so long, Evelyn had feared this vampyr the statue represented. She'd feared he'd storm across the Void with his armies and destroy her homeland. She'd trained day in and day out, losing herself to nightmares over his wrath and darkness. She'd *ran away* from home, desperate to ensure he'd never learn she lost her flame.

And he wasn't even alive.

Bloodstones. Vampyrs walking in the sunlight. The differences between scáths. None of it outmatched the newest truth.

For almost twenty-six years, Evelyn had feared a ghost.

Her flame raged within her, heating her from the inside out. *Out! Out! Out!* it screamed. Where had the winter chill gone? Was that steam rising from her arms? A sharp pain pierced through Evelyn's head, and she collapsed to her knees with a cry.

Hands gripped her shoulders. Gentle hands. The stone's cold was a comfort against her limbs as she crumbled. Someone cried out her name. Black dots bubbled through her vision until they morphed together, and darkness took Evelyn under.

CHAPTER SEVEN

KADE

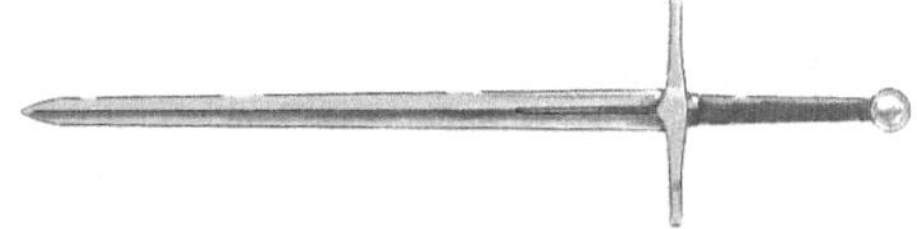

KADE INHALED THE AIR of home, and cold filled his lungs.

The white of winter had begun its eclipse on the mountains, snow-capped peaks disappearing into gray clouds. Summer trees had lost their leaves while evergreens and pines stood stiff with frost. Snow dusted patches where the sun didn't reach, the promise of more in the air.

His eager wolf wrestled to be unleashed. It craved the plush ground of the Vadon forests, to be surrounded by proud, tall trees. The untouched terrain and mountain chill whipped through his fur coat. Nothing compared to the mountain chill.

Crisp, clean.

It awakened Kade's werewolf spirit and the new power forming at his core—the one he ignored as he made his way through the Drengr Village. The current of his pack moved like nothing was amiss. Pups wrestled and played. Weavers gossiped over their looms. Metal clanged from the smithy. Not a tuberose hung from doors. No pack member wore black.

To Kade's surprise, the time of mourning for his father had come and gone. He and Tovi's voyage had been three weeks, but he'd at least expected frankincense and myrrh in the air—an incense symbolizing his father's spirit rising and leaving this world—and sandalwood, representing his mother as the two mates were reunited again. Kade passed a huddle of warriors, laughing and joking, not a line of solemness etched into their faces.

One foot in front of the other.

Kade didn't have time to ponder. He weaved down the streets of home, headed to meet his brother. Cabins, cottages, and shops lined the perimeter of the village, leaving the center open, leading to the main fortress. Lār loomed like some beast, rising taller than any of the other buildings and the palisade wall surrounding them. Sharp, shaved tips of the wooden polls pointed to the gray sky, strapped together with clay and rope. Still, the mighty wall was no match for the stoned fortress ahead, werewolf runes etched into the framed entrance.

Kade had sent Tovi to meet his team, the Gray Fenris—alone. Unease swam in his gut. Perhaps he was a fool to trust her, but Kade cringed at the thought of Eldrick meeting the vampyr princess. It was best he found Eldrick by himself, and hopefully Lorkan, too, so they could mourn their father as brothers.

Kade's feet turned heavy as he ascended the stairs of Lār. Its lack of windows and warmth had frightened Kade as a child. His mother had held both him and his brothers during summer storms, when the wrath of the winds and rain were unseen past the stone. Kade swallowed, a sadness overcoming him. He'd not resided in Lār since his mother's death. After meeting Carena, he'd learned purpose, to stay busy. Outside his training, he'd built himself a home of his own, a cottage tucked into the forest, a safe haven for him and his team.

A place he'd readied once for Evelyn, a place he so desperately wanted to show her.

Kade shut his eyes and held his breath, grimacing against the mounting pressure on his chest. Missing his mate hurt like fuck. They hadn't even completed the mating bond, sharing flesh and bodies to tie their souls as one, and yet his magic, his soul, yearned for her insatiably. How maddening would this need to protect her be once they lay together?

Shaking his head, he tuned into the echo of his boots as he passed under the open doorway, the main hall lined with tables. Ahead, the alpha's chair—now his brother's—sat empty. Kade paused, brows pinching, at the sight of his father's furs still layered atop it as they had been before he'd left. He glanced between the seemingly settled village and rather neat hall. No stains of mead. No evidence of a feast. Kade steadied himself, a contrast to his fidgety body, as he sent out his tracking magic for a moment.

To snuff the spark of hope in his heart.

Colors sprang in the space while emotions washed over him like sheets of rain. Cheer. Joy. Amusement. Purple, blue, and peachy pink. The hall was painted in anything but the colors of grief or sadness. Kade blinked, shifting foot to foot.

Time had passed since he'd received the news, enough time for the Drengr pack to have worked through grief. Kade shut his eyes and shook his head, the pressure in his chest mounting in tune with his racing heart.

Down the hall and up the stairs, he arrived at Eldrick's office only to find it empty. With the dip of the sun, Kade headed east through Lār to the training grounds, a place his brother de-stressed. As he hurried on, the large iron doors to the drawing room were cracked, flashes of red, yellow, and orange reflected on the right side. His father's favorite chair sat beyond those doors, one where he used to sit with Kade's mother, sharing a glass of whiskey and enjoying the fireplace.

The pop and crackle of logs beckoned.

He inhaled, puffed his chest, and slipped inside the room. Someone sat near the fire, but the armchair's back was tall and wide, obscuring their identity. He sniffed the air, a Drengr scent close by, but the firewood's woody, sweet aroma thickened the air, making it difficult to distinguish which Drengr male sat ahead of him.

Kade fought the heaviness in his foot and knees, negated the fear coursing through his blood, and the racing of his anxious heart. He rounded the chair, the heat of the fire singeing the cold of the outside off of him instantly, and shedding light on—

His father, his very much alive father.

Aramis Drengr blinked past Kade's looming shadow and peered over the rim of his gold-framed glasses. His spring-green eyes grew wide.

"Son! Stars above, please tell me I'm not imagining things now!"

His father sprang out of his chair and grabbed him in a fierce hug. *Touched* him so he knew it was real. Kade could not move. His boots, it seemed, had melted into the furred rug. His father pulled away, never letting go of his shoulders as his crow's-feet-rimmed eyes drank him in.

"Father..." Kade swallowed, his throat thick and tight. "It's so good to see you."

He whispered, as if his energy had completely drained after so many days of oscillating between hope and loss and grief. To witness his father's face and wide, joyous smile with his own eyes was overwhelming.

All the relief Kade had found dissipated at the sight of his father's frail frame. He swallowed bile and blinked back tears. They'd been the same height once—eye to eye—but his father's shoulders had hunched, and with the strength in his knees gone, he stood inches shorter.

"Kade, I know I look like death, but there's no need to stare at me like I'm a ghost." His father chuckled, always one to joke, and palmed his cheek and stared with wonder at Kade's face. "I see you've changed, too."

His father retreated to his chair, sighing as he fell into it.

"I thought you were dead."

Aramis's brows furrowed. "What?"

Kade nodded. He opened and closed his mouth, unsure where to begin. He had so many questions—about his father, about the letter that had brought him home, proclaiming his father's death, but those could wait. He wanted to revel for an hour in father's living. And he needed to answer his alpha's questions first. Steely eyes and obsidian hair, a determined witch and a big heart that cared deeply—his mate, Evelyn.

Kade started from the beginning.

He told his father everything. The murders. Working together. Pretending to be a huntsman. That'd he'd lied. How everything had changed. Why Evelyn had left in the first place. And the last day on the docks, headed home because they believed his father had been killed.

His father listened, silent and observant.

"I've rushed home ever since Riven took her," Kade said. He stared longingly into the fire, the dancing flames a beacon of remembrance for Evelyn. He grit his teeth. "My sole mission is getting her back. It's what brought me home."

His father smiled, small and thoughtful. "A mission didn't bring you home, Kade. Love did."

Kade's brows furrowed. It's not that he didn't cherish the love he had for Evelyn, it pulsed deep in his heart and sang to his soul, but he wasn't certain it drove him forward. A mission. Action. It was why he prided himself on being a commander, why he'd fallen into his role as Son of the God with ease. It had given him a tangible purpose.

As if conjured by fate, a fiery touch, warm and inviting, reached through the crevices of his mind. Something pulled at Kade, tugged at his mind so strongly, he fell to his knees. Sights, sounds, smells—she invaded his senses.

Cedar and vanilla. Eyes like night. Strands of spilled ink.

"Evelyn," he rasped, taking hold of their bond.

His father grasped his shoulders, squeezing firm as he held him upright. "Moons, Kade, what is wrong?"

Kade clung to his father's hands, voice cracking as he said, "It's my mate—I can feel my mate."

CHAPTER EIGHT

LIGHT BRUSHED AGAINST EVELYN like the gleam of a full moon.
Pearly, powerful, and tender. Her heart reached for the light—farther, farther, farther—until it grasped its source... another heart, so like her own.

Kade.

She whispered his name into the nothingness where she floated, her mind, her subconscious elsewhere, somewhere—she didn't care. Her fated was near. She could feel him.

Kade.

Her magic and their bond no longer hit against a mental brick wall. No steely cage. The bracelets were gone. How or when, Evelyn didn't know. Exhaustion still gripped her body, and the unknown plane of existence where she floated held her firm, the tug, tug, tug of her werewolf growing stronger.

Evelyn!

Panic laced Kade's beautiful, gruff voice. Hope swelled through her—he'd heard her at this distance.

Evelyn! Are you alright? Where are you? Love, talk to me.

She couldn't recall where she was last. Drystan, yes, but where? Black stone flashed through her mind. A villain, a tall, stoic villain standing over her. One made of stone. One she no longer had to fear. It was the unknown that frightened her. The truth of her enemy she had yet to discover.

Evelyn!

Her subconscious snapped to attention. She missed his voice. His touch. His amber eyes. Her heart, her flame brushed against his mind. The moon and sun danced together. Slowly, closely. Her mind cried tears of joy. Evelyn couldn't fracture this peace.

Kade, I'm alright.

Silence stretched, but their connection didn't falter. There was a tug, a sense of desperation pulsing down their bond. Did he hear the lie in her words?

I'm in Drystan. Are you safe?

Fear spiked, and flashes of red bloomed in the darkness. Where was he?

Kade!

Yes, yes, I'm safe.

Evelyn relaxed, her heart pulsing with relief. She sighed and held onto Kade, the strength of their bond grounding her.

Evelyn, I need you to hold on a little longer. I can feel our connection fading. It's probably the distance. Where in Drystan are you? What has Riven done?

Her other senses fought against the bond, against her subconscious floating. The elsewhere she'd found began to fade.

Kade...

She didn't want to lose him—not the peace she'd found amidst the darkness.

Evelyn!

Kade's cry filled with anguish, and Evelyn's heart ached with it.

I miss you. I love you. The castle. A tower.

She rushed the words over the bond. Light—not Kade's—brightened against Evelyn's mind. The light had sound, like the sudden whistle of an oncoming hard and violent storm, sucking away Kade's presence. As their connection drifted, waves and tides pulled them farther and farther apart, her fated's last words shouting into oblivion.

Hold on, Evelyn. I'm coming for you. I'm coming.

CHAPTER NINE

TOVI GLIDED ON LIGHT feet through the Drengr Village, heading for a tavern with a warrior's shield outside the front.

"It'll be in the ground," Kade had said. "Weathered, but there's no missing the Drengr navy."

A retired shield-maiden, Lucy, owned the tavern. Tovi shook her head, disbelief coursing through her. Werewolves treated females differently, but it was always a shock to see it firsthand. The respect. The equality. She marveled at it. She'd fought fangs-out to have female vampyrs own establishments back home, and yet they still faced prejudice, especially if they were unmated and independent. The sight of a squat, round establishment ahead, werewolves, witches, and a few humans coming and going, strengthened her strides.

Kade's letter to Gray Fenris had detailed meeting at dusk, and by the way the sun hung over the mountains, rays reaching out to the jagged white peaks, she had less than an hour. She kept glancing at the sun, though, tallying its descent inch by inch. Her insides churned as her snowy hair whipped behind her. The haunt of *when* Riven planned to use Evelyn's blood hung in the air, too, chillier than the winter evening.

Tovi battled a sense of urgency along with her nerves. Fingers numb. Mouth dry. She'd meet Kade's infamous team alone. Over the years, she'd faced plenty of foes independently, yet this felt different. Her allies then had been vampyrs; she'd been unable to risk meeting with witches and werewolves, the price of failure too great. Riven had allies, too, ones who leaned into darkness. *Who* those allies were, she had never discovered. Tovi had had to be tactful, fearing her brother's retaliation if he caught her red-handed, digging into his secrets. Instead, she'd waited and protected the promise of the prophecy. Her own secrecy and patience were two of the strongest weapons she'd wielded these last few decades.

She swallowed, attempting to set her shoulders back. Tovi had purchased new clothes in Nūa, a detour Kade had argued against. He didn't understand the needs of a princess—pristine attire, not a hair out of line, schooled expression. Tovi hadn't been a princess her entire life, but she'd been one a majority of it. How she presented herself mattered. Her appearance, her allure, her evident status.

Tovi never forgot she was a vampyr, one of the cursed things wreaking havoc on Sorin. An outfit that created an impression of a strong diplomatic presence would prove she was more than—as werewolves called it—a scáth. She'd chosen dark-green trousers, an unassuming color unlike yellow and one that complimented her pale skin and hair without drawing too much attention like red. *That* had been her mother's favorite color as it attracted every eligible suitor in all of Drystan. More shivers ran up Tovi's arms.

From the memory of hungry male gazes.

Her parents had changed when they became king and queen, the decades to come overshadowing their origins. Their political goals and ambitions had changed, but so too had their perception of Tovi. Her father no longer saw the hunter who'd fed their people in the beginning, but a bargaining chip in trade and alliance. *Marriage.* Her worth had whittled down to that of cattle, all because she was female. She'd retaliated, using her sex whenever she wanted, showing them it belonged to no one but her. Their ashamed gazes still haunted her, leaving a creep on the back of her neck like she was always being watched.

Judged.

Tovi bristled as flurries collected on the furs of her cloak and the tufts of Maxie's ears. Evelyn's familiar gave her a yellow-slitted stare. Neither enjoyed the makeshift sling Tovi had created, securing Maxie against her chest while they'd traveled across Sorin.

"Don't give me that look, or I will eat you," Tovi muttered.

She wouldn't, of course, and Maxie looked away, unbothered as if she too knew Tovi's threat to be empty. Out of all the things she and Kade had argued about the most, *who* took Maxie had secured top place. The phrase "worse than a demon" had been used by the werewolf commander, and keeping Maxie hidden like a tightly snug babe versus bringing her into the werewolf fortress had been the best plan of action.

Tovi rolled her eyes at Kade's ridiculous assessment and the cat's own aloofness, pulling her plum cloak closer, thankful the storekeeper in Nūa had been kind enough to enchant it clean of any dirt. She'd send Riven, the bastard, the cleaning bill. Tovi seethed. If her mother were alive, she wouldn't bat an eye at what Riven had done. She'd twist the story so it was somehow Tovi's fault.

If you were married, like your father and I desire, you wouldn't be in these childish quarrels with your brother.

She exhaled, her breath coming out in a puff. Goddess, how she wished this was a silly, sibling quarrel, but Riven's plan threatened to destroy their people and with it, Sorin. Hurt wrapped around her tired, ancient heart. How could someone she loved also be her enemy?

As muddy streets turned into stone ones, Tovi dismissed thoughts of her brother. Ahead, a shield made of brass bolts and rust-colored wood had been wedged into the dirt outside the tavern door. The battered shield had clearly seen many years, but the image burned into it remained visible from far away—three werewolves howling at the center of a moon.

Columns of redwood tree trunks framed the tavern's doorway, and various watering pails had been used as planters. They sat under hazy tavern windows, filled to the brim with ferns.

Maxie squirmed against her chest as they entered, the rambunctious crowd jarring Tovi, too. Laughter and conversation boomed in the space. The clattering of clay cups and cheers resounded in the one-story tavern. The sight of axes, swords, and shields piled atop tables reminded her she'd entered an establishment packed to the seams with her enemy.

Not for long, Tovi assured herself. She had a plan—help rescue Evelyn and secure an alliance with the werewolves. Simple. Maybe. Probably not. She'd do her best to secure it, at least, starting with this meeting with the Gray Fenris first.

Sighing, Tovi headed towards the bar, keeping an eye out for colorful hair, a detail Kade had supplied to help her recognize his team. His healer, apparently, fashioned bright, dyed hair. *A mage thing*, he'd said. What color she'd chosen this season, he hadn't the wildest guess. It changed so often, he couldn't keep up, but his details were rather simple.

It'll be bright, whatever color Linx decided on.

A woman, a foot taller than Tovi, pushed past with a tray of drinks.

Wine.

Bloody hel, a glass of wine. Tovi groaned. The promise of the notes of sharp tannins and black pepper and, *oh*, perhaps jammy blackcurrants added a pep to her step.

At the bar, Tovi searched the bottles on display. The numerous glasses glinted against the copper bar top. Hammered smooth and flat, blotches of green stains decorated it with a well-used charm. It reminded her of the Runaway Radish. Shutting her eyes, Tovi imagined Evelyn. Her laugh. Her smile. The wiggle of her brows when she teased. Even in Callum they'd managed to find time to share a drink, as if their friendship had picked up right where it left off.

Would sharing one while her friend was her brother's captive be wrong?

"I suggest the blueberry ale. Lucy's summer supply is dwindling fast, and you won't get another chance soon."

An unwarranted shiver traveled down Tovi's spine and tingled in her toes. The man—no, the werewolf by the scent of him—discussed ale, but the timbre of his voice was like a whisper of seduction.

Absolutely ridiculous.

She turned to face him, which was a catastrophic, foolish mistake, because he was sinfully handsome. With a clean-shaven square jawline and cropped brown hair with rivets of gold from the sun, tousled strands fell over his forehead as if he constantly ran his hands through it. Lean and tall, with agile muscle etched into his shoulders, arms, and torso, he stood with arms crossed. His severe stare gave her wicked thoughts.

She'd been staring, too, and had been far too silent for far too long, and her words came out rushed and wrong. "I... I don't drink ale." Tovi cursed. She'd sounded so pompous, so *ugh*, and she hadn't meant to. "I'm sorry, what I meant to say is I prefer wine."

The werewolf's lips tugged into a playful smirk, and damn the Goddess, a dimple formed, molding his handsome, masculine face into a softer, brighter sight. Tovi blinked. Perhaps he wasn't a werewolf, but a demon in disguise. There was no one in the living world who could be so beautiful and sharp at once.

"Sadly wine's hard to come by in the Vadon Mountains, and Lucy prides herself on her personal brews." The werewolf's eyes roamed over her, green like the forest of the Vadon Mountains, as if the gods had mined the color and gifted him emerald gems for sight. "I take it you're not from around here?"

His question brought Tovi back to the present. Right. She'd arrived at the Shield-maiden to find the Gray Fenris, not to converse with strangers, certainly not ones that made her stomach warm and fluttery.

"No, I'm not," she said, flat and to the point.

She evaded his attention and searched for bright-colored hair again, but no one matched the description.

"Magu!" the tall woman from earlier beamed, rounding the bar.

Tovi swiveled towards him, Maxie's claws clinging because she moved so quickly. Oh, no, no, no. *Magu*. The term broke the spell Tovi had fallen under, and she went rigid. She'd heard it before. A term of endearment her friend had used. It meant *son* to the werewolves, but not any son, the alpha's son, the next in line.

Eldrick Drengr stood next to her.

Frigid fear rose through her already cold vampyr body. Kade had warned her no werewolf hated vampyrs more than his brother. They'd discussed it at length, to Tovi's annoyance, and decided to keep her out of his sight. It felt contradictory to evade the next-in-line alpha of the Drengr pack if they were to be allies, but Kade had been adamant they didn't have time to convince his "stubborn-headed brother." They'd deal with him after they saved Evelyn.

Tovi's instinct to flee quickened her pulse. But what would running do? Make her appear suspicious? Tovi had been in the midst of enemies before and needed to remain calm. She inhaled, stilling her nerves. She'd wait until the Gray Fenris arrived.

"It's good to see you, Lucy," he said, greeting the woman who'd called out to him.

"Aye, likewise. Did you rush in for the last bit of blueberry ale? Just in time. I'm going through my last keg."

"Can I get two?" He gestured towards Tovi. "She's never had it."

Lucy scoffed. "Now, you look like one of those city women who sips wine. Sure you can handle an ale?"

Tovi raised a brow. "I can handle anything."

The tavern owner threw up her hands. "That's a woman after my own heart right there, stars above! If you don't flirt with her, Magu, I will."

Lucy walked off to pull from a wooden barrel with a spout. Tovi glanced slightly to her left. Eldrick ran a hand through his cropped hair and sent an annoyed glance towards Lucy. The female werewolf didn't seem affected in the slightest as she slid the two pints of pinkish ale towards them.

Tovi maneuvered Maxie to reach for her pouch of coin. Her fingers skirted across the edges of cut gems, far too hefty a price for an ale, but before she grabbed a coin, Eldrick slid enough for both across the brass bar top.

"That wasn't necessary," she said. "But thank you."

Eldrick turned to her, eyes so alight, they may as well have been the gems in her pouch. "You could thank me by enjoying it with me."

Tovi debated. She searched one last time, but nobody possessed bright hair like Kade described. Beyond the hazy windows, the sun hadn't fully fallen past the mountain peaks. The Gray Fenris had time to arrive, and until then, she'd manage the Drengr alpha.

"Alright." She clanked her clay mug against his, swigged, and— Tovi's entire face pinched, her eyelids fluttered, and a jolt traveled down her spine. "Bloody hel that's sour," she spat after swallowing.

Eldrick broke out in a wide-brimmed grin. "Still certain you can handle it?"

Taken aback, Tovi straightened. He didn't underestimate her. Playfulness rang in his tone, but she wasn't one to not prove a point. Her eyes bore deep into the mug's contents. The pinkish froth mocked her. Inside her sling, Maxie fidgeted, as if eager for her to get on with it.

Tovi chugged.

Lucy's voice chanted in the background and the beat of fists on the tables egged her efforts on. One, two, three, four... Tovi slammed the empty mug on the bar top and wiped her lips with the back of her hand. She turned to grin at Eldrick and stopped. Their gazes connected, two shades of green, and her entire being sighed. The chaos of the last three weeks ceased, and a lightness settled over her like the gentle fall of a snow flurry.

Eldrick shook his head. "That was—"

A ball of fiery fur burst into the air, leaping off Tovi's chest and landing with a catlike grace. Maxie peered back at Tovi, narrowed her gaze, and then took off.

"Maxie!" Tovi cried.

Annoyance thrummed through her. She hated that cat, had hated her since she first locked gazes with those yellow all-too-knowing eyes, but Maxie belonged to Evelyn, and Tovi had to keep her safe. She couldn't stomach letting Evelyn down again, like she had in Callum.

Tovi moved past Eldrick, sights set outside the Shield-maiden.

"Wait," he said.

She stopped, sending him a soft smile. "It was great meeting you, but I have to go."

She threw the words over her shoulder and quickened her pace. She caught the tip of Maxie's tail scurrying around the redwood tree doorway.

As her cloak billowed behind her, Tovi struggled to rein in her vampyr speed. She weaved between those in the village, keeping her sights on Maxie's ball of red. The cat veered left, and Tovi followed. Toes numb. Fingers tingling. Hot and cold, her muscles quivered with a frantic, disoriented pace.

Maxie ran faster, darting under carts, disappearing into the loose foundations of buildings, and appearing in the throngs of the many muddy boots in the evening activity. She leaped off stone steps and down the next street. Tovi skidded to a stop at the cusp of the two buildings. At the end of the deserted path, Maxie sat, waiting. Her tail swooshed back and forth, as if taunting Tovi.

She lost all sense. She fisted her hands, running after Maxie, when an iron grip grabbed her arm and pulled her into an alleyway. Her back slammed into hard stone, and before she could counterattack, silver flashed in the dark, and the feel of a blade pushed up against her throat.

"What are you?" Eldrick whispered in a calm yet lethal tone.

What. Not *who.* His suspicions caught her off guard.

"I have no idea—"

"Don't you dare. I can smell it on you!" he hissed.

Tovi's heart pounded. That wasn't possible. Her bloodstone hid her vampyr scent.

Theories whirled in her mind, but she couldn't think straight. A scent, fresh and spicy, like basil and spearmint, reached to her baser instinct, eliciting a desire she'd left dormant for years. Her body shivered with Eldrick's hard form flush against her, firmly pressing her into the stone wall.

Whatever spell she'd come under snapped her back to reality.

"Let me go," she hissed, holding back fangs that instinctively pushed to be released.

Eldrick held her harder, the stone of the wall grating against the bones of her shoulder blades.

"I'll ask one last time, what the fuck are you?" he whispered again, cold and cruel.

"It's who I am," she spat. "Not what. I'm not some sort of animal or beast—"

"I beg to differ."

She snickered. "Says a werewolf."

Eldrick snarled. Metal kissed her pale skin like a feathery touch as he shook with rage. She didn't flinch, didn't let the fear thrumming in her veins show as strands of hate twisted into the green of his eyes. *Shit.* If she didn't do something, say *something*, he was going to kill her. His intent clouded the air, contorting his handsome face. But she couldn't fight at the risk of hurting him—*that* jeopardized her chances with the werewolves.

Her secrets whispered on the wind, taunting her like the pesky flurries twirling around them. Every fiber of her being fought against the notion, growing taut and steely. And yet Eldrick's blade pressed deeper into her skin, the sharpness of the axe sending shudders through her. The wooden shaft groaned under his grip, whining as his shoulders tightened and—

"Kill me, and you'll start a war you cannot win!" Tovi said.

Eldrick blinked. "Why is that, bloodsucker?"

"Because I'm Tovi Verena, Princess of Drystan and vampyrs."

Eldrick backed away a fraction. "Princess? Vampyrs have a king—"

"The king is dead," Tovi said, each word rushed into the other. "And I'm the rightful heir to the Drystan throne."

Bare, exposed, she stood there as the truth hung between them, colder than the Vadon Mountain's air.

Chapter Ten

Eldrick

Wind gusted by with the vampyr's words.

War. The term was like a bucket of ice over Eldrick, chilling him stone-cold to the bone.

"You're a liar," he hissed.

Everything Eldrick had known about vampyrs suddenly replayed in his mind. Every scáth he'd fought. Every detail he'd read in missives. Every defense he'd planned against them. And even the day he'd watched them overtake his mother and kill her.

"I *know* you're kind," he said.

Indignation flashed in her jade eyes. With considerable strength, she pushed against him, but Eldrick held his ground, not daring to let her out of his hold.

"Perhaps there are things you don't know about us," she said.

Us. She admitted it proudly, as if it weren't a death sentence. As if it weren't wrong. His blood heated, and Eldrick snapped.

His axe met her throat again, ready to slice up and to the side, a clean cut to the vein pulsing in her neck. It wouldn't kill her, but it would be enough to disarm her and deliver a death blow to her head or heart.

Yet, she didn't beg, didn't falter.

Eldrick egged himself on, but those jade eyes enchanted him with a sensation he couldn't shake. His body was taut against hers, adrenaline rushing with each rise and fall of their chests in unison. It was a feeling—it meant nothing.

She'd entered his village and put his pack in danger. Who knew why she was here, what her intentions were. Yet, sense and reason sparred in Eldrick's mind. What if she told the truth and he caused a war?

He'd followed her out of the Shield-maiden because he'd smelled the enemy—that awful, familiar scent he associated with death, with the vampyr. Sharp, acidic. Her fluttering hair left a trail of it. At first, confusion had frozen Eldrick in place. Had no one else detected it?

But now, up against the alleyway wall, there was no denying it. Past plum and lilac, there was something cutting, like the white of a lemon. No black spidery veins rimmed her jade eyes, and no talons jutted from her delicate fingers. Yet, two needlelike fangs flashed in a snarl, challenging him—challenging everything he knew of vampyrs.

They raged and ravaged, slaughtered, and sucked their victims dry. They didn't walk the streets in a hurry. They didn't walk in the *sunlight*. They weren't so... beautiful.

Her eyes, the lightest shade of green, were like the first signs of spring. Saplings, flower buds, blades of grass sprouting from dirt. Winter, spring. Ice, warmth. Everything all at once. She held him under a spell.

Like a queen.

A vicious, bloodsucking queen.

Hate had wormed its way into Eldrick's heart long ago for the creatures that destroyed their continent—yet why was it so difficult to kill her and have one less vampyr roaming his homeland?

He growled, pulling away from her. Facts, data, logic. Though he didn't trust it, this princess hadn't demonstrated a wish to harm anyone in his village. She hadn't even fought him. Eldrick's anger and hatred drove him to end her, not reason.

Perhaps there are things you don't know about us.

He grabbed her wrists. "You will say nothing between here and the fortress, do you understand? Or I swear, I will kill you."

She gritted her teeth but nodded.

Eldrick dragged her down the back alleys to Lār, sticking to the shadows and corners so none of the Drengr pack saw them. She'd made it past the gates and into the village undetected, and he wanted to keep it that way. If anyone else discovered her, there'd be chaos and uncertainty. Her presence would strike fear into his pack, and he couldn't afford to fracture the little peace they had compared to the other packs in the Vadon Mountains.

To his surprise, she complied the entire way, not saying a word or putting up a fight. He led her to a side entrance into Lār and pushed her through, making sure not a single guard or warrior spotted them.

Eldrick urged her forward, down a hall, and up and up until they stood outside the main foyer. Voices murmured inside, and Eldrick hoped his father and uncle waited. Together, they could learn more about this Tovi Verena and figure out how to proceed. He thrust open the doors, axe still at the ready, and threw her to the ground—

Eldrick stilled.

Across the foyer, standing by the fire with Aramis was his brother.

"Kade."

Eldrick's brother rushed towards the drawing room's entrance, but not to him. Kade's hair had grown, half pulled into a bun. Time at sea had tanned his skin while worry plagued his amber eyes, an expression he'd never seen so deeply etched into his brother's expression. He collided into Tovi, grasping her shoulders.

"Be careful!" Eldrick gripped his axe, moments away from attacking. Screw reason and logic, Eldrick needed to protect his brother.

Kade paid him no mind, and a tinge of hurt grated through Eldrick.

"I heard her through the mating bond," Kade said, his chest heaving. "She's in the castle. In a tower."

Mating bond? Tower? *Stars above*, Eldrick spun with questions.

Tovi nodded, her attention fleeting between Kade and Eldrick. "Kade…"

His brother blinked, finally focusing on Eldrick and pulling Tovi behind him, shielding her—

"What is going on?" Eldrick let his alpha baritone bleed into his voice. "Kade, are you aware she's a vampyr?"

His brother shut his eyes and grimaced. He whispered a curse. "It isn't as it seems."

Silence fell, aside from the crackling fire. As if the Vadon Mountains sensed the unease brewing between brothers, too, a gust of wind passed the window. The forest to the west swayed back and forth, waving in warning as the threat of the unknown neared.

Eldrick didn't care how it seemed. He had the facts. Tovi Verena was a vampyr. The type of monster that killed their mother. He'd never imagined this sort of reunion with Kade, one where he stood between Eldrick and one of their enemies.

Feelings, ghastly and strong, rippled through Eldrick and seized his heart. A year, a damn full year since he'd seen his brother. They'd never spent longer than a month apart. Brothers and best friends. *Moons*, the gods and goddesses knew how much he'd missed Kade, and standing in the foyer with a threat to his pack present, it clouded his judgment.

One, two.

Eldrick steadied his breath, and one blaring question shot through him. Stepping farther into the room, he said, "If you are here, where is Evelyn?"

His brother's entire body turned rigid, his shoulders taut as his jaw ticked. He swore guilt, perhaps sadness, flashed through his eyes.

"She's been captured by the vampyrs."

"What?" their father growled. His cane banged against the stones as he approached closer. "I don't recall that being in your grand tale of finding your mate."

More silver lined their father's hairline than a week ago, and he'd lost additional weight. His tunic swallowed his thinning torso, and his knuckles were like knots on tree branches, bulging and swollen as he grasped his cane with both hands, hunched over as he peered up at them all. With each day, with each sign of decline, Eldrick was reminded of his past mistake.

He shook his aching head. *Focus.* A vampyr who walked in sunlight. His brother home. Now, Evelyn was a captive of the vampyrs. He'd also never heard of a witch and werewolf sharing a mating bond. Eldrick couldn't keep up. He gripped his weapon to steady himself.

"If the vampyrs have Evelyn, why is *she* here?" He cast a glance like a dagger at the vampyr princess.

His father held onto the armchair for balance, his stern stare boring into Eldrick. "Why are you convinced she is a vampyr?"

Eldrick tried to dismiss the doubt in his father's question. Why couldn't he trust his judgment? He smelled it on her, sharp and lemony against the plum, stone fruit of her scent. How could they not? It clotted the air and fought the burning wood at the fireplace.

"I am a vampyr, Alpha Drengr," Tovi said. "The Princess of Drystan. I've agreed to guide Kade and his team across the Void and through Drystan in exchange for an alliance with the werewolves."

Cold fury froze every fiber of Eldrick's being. "Werewolves don't ally with bloodsuckers."

"Eldrick." Kade held out his hand, attention flicking between his axe and stance. "Tovi's brother, Riven, plans to use Evelyn's blood in a spell that allows vampyrs to walk in sunlight. We need Tovi."

The vampyr nodded. "If Riven succeeds, the darkness you all know will spread farther than it ever has before."

Eldrick lowered his axe stomaching clenching. "Are you suggesting vampyrs like you would walk amongst us?"

Tovi nodded. "Yes."

"That would be a grave turn of events. We've relied on our advantage of day and night for centuries." Aramis shook his head, his weathered frame trembling.

An hour ago, Eldrick hadn't known there was a vampyr princess and prince, now he had to comprehend an unfathomable, devastating future as well.

He studied the enemy standing in his foyer. Tovi wasn't like the vampyrs that slaughtered his mother, but he still saw her as a killer, and perhaps what made her different made her more dangerous than a scáth.

"Kade, how are you certain she isn't a part of the plan?" Eldrick asked. "For all we know, she's luring you to Drystan so Prince Riven has both the Daughter of the Goddess and Son of the God as his prisoners."

His brother shook his head. "No, Riven had his chance to capture me. I've been in Callum, on the continent of Torren, and weeks ago, I received a missive in *your* hand, stating father was dead and I was to return home at once."

"It was forged," Tovi whispered.

The hair on the back of Eldrick's neck rose.

"I believe Riven did it to separate me from Evelyn." Relief flashed over Kade's face as he glanced back at their father. "He knew how to send me home without a second thought."

"How would this Riven accomplish such a thing?" Eldrick shook his head.

"He has allies," Tovi said. "Perhaps ones amongst the werewolves."

For a moment, the missing werewolves crossed through Eldrick's mind. That morning, he'd thought it time to consider one of their own as the culprit. He shook away the notion, refusing to believe it. Not a single fact pointed to a werewolf. Nothing pointed to the vampyrs either, but they were the enemy. His own people weren't.

"I know it may be difficult to see past that Tovi is a vampyr," Kade said. "But she is on our side."

Eldrick scoffed. He'd never dismiss the facts. How could his brother? Her kind had killed their mother. They were monsters, blood-hungry parasites that invaded their homeland. He didn't care how alluring she seemed, the way his pulse quickened when their eyes connected, or the fact she challenged everything he knew about his enemy.

"Are you sure?" Eldrick asked. "The vampyr king is dead, and she is the rightful heir. I believe her motives are selfish."

Kade stilled, shooting a glare at Tovi. "Is this true?"

Tovi shut her eyes and grimaced. When they sprang open again, they never left his brother as she said, "It didn't seem relevant to mention."

Kade growled. "Relevant? If you are the rightful heir, then march into Drystan and stop your brother! Why all this secrecy, all this plotting?"

"I can't!" She stared at each of them. "Werewolves have female alphas, do they not?"

Eldrick's brows pinched. "Of course."

"It isn't the same for vampyrs. Females are regarded differently. By right, I am the firstborn. The time separating our births is mere hours. Many believe I should step down or abdicate the throne because he is the male."

"Simply because you're a female vampyr they question your ability to rule?" Kade asked, shock ringing in his tone.

The vampyr's nostrils flared as she sighed. "Yes. It is one of the reasons my brother and I are at odds. It's why I need allies. To secure my throne. Trust me, I am a far better choice than my brother as king. You don't want him ruling Drystan."

Eldrick shook away the lick of sympathy he had for her—to simply not respect her because of sex angered his inner wolf—but she had already withheld information. What more was she not telling them?

"Kade, you can't trust her," he said.

A low noise rumbled in his brother's throat. "I don't, but Evelyn is my mate, and I will do whatever it takes to get her back."

The severity in Kade's words made Eldrick pause. Never had his brother held so much resolve, so much emotion. Yet, that was the issue, wasn't it? Eldrick understood the way of mates. Werewolves celebrated the bond. He'd witnessed the beauty and power of it between his parents, but he'd also witnessed its downfalls, how the bond consumed and overrode reason, ruining body, soul, and mind.

Eldrick understood it more than anyone else.

The sight of his father—once a proud, strong man with a boisterous laugh that filled a room with joy—reminded Eldrick of the day he'd convinced his brother to skip training and trail their mother's unit across Sorin to Morrow. They'd led the vampyrs straight to their mother's stronghold.

Straight to her.

All to help his brother *feel* better.

Eldrick blinked back the memory of that wretched mistake, the knots in his belly tightening into a sharp, severe pain. He'd once let his feelings get in the way of the facts; that had led to his mother's death, had caused his father's current state.

He'd sworn to never do it again.

And, *moons*, Eldrick hated he had to do this. He and Kade had finally reunited, but his brother wasn't thinking straight. He wasn't seeing the facts, the logic. But as future alpha, that was Eldrick's job, and he'd take Kade's anger in order to lead his pack through this.

"I can't allow her to accompany you. Nor can I promise an alliance," Eldrick said. "As of this moment forward, Tovi Verena is a prisoner of the Drengr pack until we decide how to proceed with her offense of trespassing on our lands."

A growl rumbled from Kade's chest. "Evelyn is my mate. She might die because of this spell, and Tovi is the best guide we have through a land werewolves have never crossed."

Eldrick shook his head. "I'm sorry, brother."

Kade charged, eyes glowing.

Aramis stepped between the brothers, moving quicker than Eldrick had seen him move in years. He rested a hand on Kade's shoulder. "Your brother is only trying to protect the pack, Kade. We can't trust her. Not yet."

Assurance shot through Eldrick, but he couldn't meet his brother's eyes—their mother's eyes—marred with such betrayal.

"What about protecting the Daughter of the Goddess?" Kade shouted. "The prophecy, even!"

His eyes shifted from amber to a blue glow, and both Eldrick and his father froze. What in the *stars above* was that?

"Kade..." Tovi's tone was soft, gentle even.

"The decision has been made." Their uncle's deep, gravelly voice came from the corner of the foyer as he emerged from the shadows. How long had he been standing there? Sometimes, his uncle's beastly ability to sneak up on his prey unnerved Eldrick.

Tovi leaned closer to Kade and swallowed, but kept her gaze glued to Eldrick. Unable to handle the sapling green of her stare, he returned his attention to his uncle who strode farther into the foyer. His beefy, calloused hand rested on his axe, the blood of his enemies still staining the blade.

"Claus," Kade muttered. "This is a matter between my brother and me."

"Yes, you're correct, though your brother is the future alpha of the Drengr pack. You may be Son of the God, but you had no right to grant this bloodsucker alliance in the first place. Not to mention your father *is* the alpha of this pack and has agreed with your brother's sound judgment."

Eldrick shut his eyes and grimaced, hating that his uncle had weaved in birth order. Traditionally, Eldrick as alpha outranked Kade as a protector, but as Son of the God, his brother's title created a gray area. They'd long followed an unwritten rule—Kade stayed out of politics. But more importantly, they'd always acknowledged they were brothers first and foremost. Eldrick swallowed, attempting to squash the guilt souring on his tongue. Today was the first day those lines had been crossed, but he refused to let his own feelings or his brother's hurt get in the way of his decision. He had to lead his pack. With everything still to learn about his enemy, he wouldn't let anything cloud his judgment.

"I'm sorry," he said and meant it. "You must go after Evelyn and get her back in any way you see fit, but I can't trust the intentions of the vampyr princess."

Kade charged towards Eldrick, the blue glow returning to his eyes, hackles raised, and wolf shaking under his skin.

"Unhand me!" Tovi hissed, capturing everyone's attention.

Claus had reached her, drawing her into a tight hold, her back to his chest as she struggled against his strength.

His brother growled. "Eldrick, see reason!"

"I am. She is a vampyr—"

"You send your brother to his death without me!" Tovi cried. True fear shined in her jade eyes, and for a moment, Eldrick paused.

Was he willing to risk his brother's life?

He gritted his teeth. Her words were merely that. *Words.* His brother was the best third-born protector to ever climb the ranks. If anyone could cross the Void, it was Kade. No matter what, Eldrick could never trust Tovi Verena, Princess of Drystan.

"Lock her in the dungeons, Claus."

Chapter Eleven

EVELYN'S EYES SNAPPED OPEN. The bracelets, in fact, were gone, her wrists bare and lighter. She didn't have the slightest idea how or who took them off. Her head ached while Kade's declaration echoed in her mind. It brought comfort, a radiating brush of warmth. Her body shivered. His strength. His resilience. *Fucking flames,* she'd match it, and they'd be together again. Her soul sang with a declaration of her own. She'd get through this. She—

"The bracelets almost killed her!" a voice, one Evelyn didn't recognize, hissed. "You're lucky she didn't combust from her own magic."

The present pulsed into focus. Evelyn lay on her side, facing the stone wall in her room located in the tower. Her head rested on a plush pillow, feathery blankets pulled over her, shielding the fact she'd awakened.

"Whose fault is that? I didn't make them—you did, witch," Tala said, her voice strained. Her voice was louder, closer to Evelyn.

Evelyn dared not move, staring at the dark wall ahead of her. By the way Tala and the witch bickered, neither had noticed she'd woken yet. Evelyn evened her breath. Perhaps they'd reveal something, anything useful if she pretended to remain asleep.

"I warned you and Riven, binding a witch's magic—especially one like hers—could be deadly. Neither of you listened."

"Don't get your cloak in a twist." Evelyn practically heard Tala's golden eyes rolling. "Riven gave strict instruction. Bind her magic. Keep her away from others. I didn't have much choice in the matter."

"Perhaps you can remind Riven that without her *alive*, there's no chance of the White Lady's spell working. We need her."

Evelyn knew as much, but her interest piqued anyway. Who was this other voice, and how did she know the White Lady's spell?

"Will she be alright, Ingrid?" another voice asked. This one—sweet, hesitant, and farther away—jogged Evelyn's memory.

"Yes." That voice belonged to Ingrid, then. "Why were you in the courtyard? It's dangerous to be alone, Belle. We've been over this."

"It was daytime."

"That doesn't matter. Some of the worst have a bloodstone. You know better."

The chastising tone reminded Evelyn of Mirella, her eldest sister. A pang of longing shot through her. She'd hated her sister's haughty, arrogant verbal lashings, but after so many years, Evelyn missed them. A chase through the house because she'd stolen her sister's favorite blouse, an aghast reaction at dinner after hearing stories of Evelyn and Blair's *entanglements*. What she'd give for one sisterly argument again, but the one happening behind her sent shivers of worry down her spine. What had happened to Nūa, if anything, that two sibling witches resided in Drystan?

Wait, sisterly? Evelyn paused, her memory hanging onto the third voice. The young witch in the courtyard—Belle—had said her sister—Ingrid—told her not to trust Evelyn.

"None of them venture outside. It's dreadfully depressing out there." The younger witch's voice dripped with sadness, her voice sullen, small, and full of longing.

Ingrid clicked her tongue. "Then why would you go outside?"

"Because I'm bored. If…" The younger witch hesitated. "If you would let me join you, teach me—"

"No."

The word was so final, absolute, Evelyn flinched from the coldness.

Ingrid sighed. "We've discussed this too many times." Patience warred against annoyance in her tone. "If the wrong person learned of your magic, it might be held against you. Taken advantage of even. It's safer this way. *You're* safer, Belle."

Evelyn furrowed her brows. During the Great Burnings, witches who had possessed a water brotannas had fled far south. They'd fared better against rougher seas and now called the southernmost continent home, trade business their only connection to Sorin. Others had traveled east, past the Vadon Mountains, and found their place amongst the mages. Their water brotannas was so similar to the mage's *magik* that overtime it intertwined with their bloodlines. Not lost, but no longer a brotannas as witches knew it. It was extremely rare to come across a witch in Nūa with a water brotannas—Evelyn had only met one, and she'd been a merchant visiting Sorin from the south—but its rarity wasn't a risk. What did Ingrid fear? Or *who*? Vampyrs? Other witches?

Evelyn tried to piece together everything she'd learned—so much with so little. Riven had at least two witches as allies, and one of them knew the spell the White Lady had crafted. She fought her excitement, continuing to lay still as they continued.

Tala sighed. "You will need to figure out another way to contain her flame. We can't have the Daughter of the Goddess walking the halls with access to her magic."

"Why not throw her in the dungeons until we need her?"

Evelyn bristled at the suggestion, unamused at Ingrid's aloof tone. More upsetting, though, were the witch's latter words. *Until they needed her.* They had a timeline. Her heart raced a little. Kade had said he was coming, but how long would it take to cross the Void? She feared the risk Kade was about to take.

But Evelyn knew they'd risk it all for the other, a shuddering, reassuring truth she couldn't shake.

"You know we can't do that. It'll make Riven appear weak, as if he can't handle her."

Someone rose from a chair—wooden legs scraping across stone. "If the spell works, we break the curse. Is it worth the risk of weakening her when we need her? All for the sake of his precious, pompous reputation, when in a couple of weeks' time, he'll have the court in the palm of his hand."

Evelyn's heart skipped. *The* curse—as if the darkness surrounding the vampyrs was a tangible thing.

Before she had time to think more on it, Tala was beside her, sighing rather loudly. "I'd suggest you keep a tight lip, Ingrid. We have a rather avid listener amongst us."

Fucking flames. Evelyn clamped her eyes shut, but the ruse was up. Three sets of eyes burrowed into her back. Cringing, she sat up in bed. Tiredness clung to every bone, fiber, and muscle in her body. The three women sat around her—one vampyr, two witches. Outnumbered, but not outmatched. Her flame danced at her fingertips, ready to ignite.

"I'd think twice before you strike, Evelyn." Aside from their petite noses and delicate chins, Ingrid was the opposite of her bright, airy sister. The eldest of the two had straight raven hair, cut right below her chin where it bobbed as she approached. Her dark eyes, a brownish-black, pierced Evelyn like an iron dagger, sharp and vicious.

She held in her outstretched hand a folded piece of parchment with a broken wax seal. It taunted Evelyn, and she snatched it, a creep crawling up her spine. She didn't recognize the teal seal, the symbol a tansy flower. They waited as she opened the letter in silence, not even the Drystan wind whined. It seemed to pause with the calm of anticipation.

Evelyn read the words carefully, the script thin and achingly neat, relaying an address in Nūa. She read it again, letting the familiarity of the street name sink in. It had been years—two to be exact since she'd hurried down the sidewalks, surrounded by brick townhomes. Past marigold flower beds, copper lampposts, coven flags. It was the afternoon of her wedding dress fitting, hours before she ran away. The plan had been laid out then, ready to enact, a dirty little secret she'd withheld from...

Blair.

Fucking flames, the address was her sister's townhome in the art district.

"Where did you get this? *Why do you have it?*" Had Tovi, also her sister's friend, given it to them? Evelyn didn't ask the last question as her voice cracked and her hands turned clammy.

Ingrid crossed her arms, seemingly unbothered by her outburst. She jutted her chin towards her wrists, still red but free. "You almost died, burning from the inside out, which means we can't place the bracelets back on you."

"What does that have to do with my sister?" The bite in Evelyn's tone snapped the air. The room grew hot, her magic rising to a dangerous degree.

"Riven has allies everywhere, close to the ones you love. Step out of line, and your sister pays the price."

"How dare you," Evelyn hissed, rising from the bed and charging towards Ingrid. A *whoosh* and breeze flew past her, and Tala appeared, blocking her path.

"Stand down," Tala said.

Evelyn ignored the vampyr, sights set on the witch who'd threatened her sister. "How can you possibly be helping him? You're witches."

Belle winced, only slightly. Ingrid, on the other hand, smiled, smug and proud.

"There's a lot you don't know, Daughter of the Goddess. I wonder how witches in Nūa will react when they learn you ran from your duty and aren't little miss perfect." Ingrid scoffed. "It's too bad you can't spread your legs and beg for forgiveness like you did with your werewolf."

Evelyn cursed a storm, and her right hand ignited, flame stretching up her elbow.

A sound, like a hiss and growl combined, vibrated from Tala. It echoed off the walls—the cry of a predatorial warrior. She held out one inky-taloned hand towards Evelyn, the other towards Ingrid, holding them apart.

"Out in the hall. *Now.*" Her command barreled out of her. Ingrid's upper lip rose in a snarl, but she obeyed, spinning towards the door. Her black dress billowed around her, sheer layers like Drystan mist.

"Come, Belle," Ingrid said.

"Belle stays," Tala said.

There was no room to argue in her tone, not a fraction, but Ingrid, a fierce and protective sister, halted.

With dark eyes wide, she said, "I'm not leaving Belle alone with *her.*" The word a snarl aimed at Evelyn.

"She's to attend to Evelyn's wounds. Like you said, Ingrid, we need her. Besides, you threatened Evelyn's sister. I doubt she'd do anything."

Ingrid's jaw worked, and her eyes blazed, but she left the room at Tala's side, hands fisted in her skirts and head held high. She slammed the door behind them. The locked clicked, then raised, but muffled voices permeated the wooden door and bounced off the walls of Evelyn's room.

She regained her breath, drawing back her flame. Tiredness hit her like a tidal wave, and she staggered from foot to foot. The effects of the bracelets lingered, and her strength had paid the cost.

"I brought a salve with me," Belle whispered. "If you'd like me to take a look at your wrists." The younger witch wrung her hands together, rising and falling on the balls of her feet.

Evelyn sighed, assessing her. Though related to her nasty sister, she didn't seem as much of a threat. She sauntered over to the seating area, sinking into the sofa. Belle joined her, the poor witch's nerves bubbling the air.

"How is it you're a healer if your sister is the eldest?" Evelyn asked. Usually, firstborns, like Mirella, were trained to be healers. Unless a witch's brotannas was better suited to be a healer within their birth order, say a scholar turned teacher for other healers, or a medic amongst the guards, perhaps, but Belle's brotannas had been water in the courtyard. Something didn't add up.

"Tala overpromised. I'm not a healer exactly. I know a few remedies, ones I learned to heal my sister when we were younger."

Pain flashed through Belle's eyes as she dabbed salve onto her wrists. Evelyn's mouth went dry. What sort of wounds had Ingrid faced to need healing? And why had she not been taken to an actual healer as a child? More questions, but Evelyn wouldn't push for these answers. The subject felt horribly off-limits.

"Did something happen?" Evelyn asked. "In Nūa, I mean."

The witch shifted in her seat. "As far as I know, Nūa is much the same. Why do you ask?"

"Are you sure?" Evelyn asked with a frown. "Were you brought to Drystan?"

Belle's brows shot up. "You say it as if we are here against our will. I assure you, that is the farthest from the truth."

It was Evelyn's turn to shift in her seat. "I assumed something happened. I've been away from home, and I thought the worst."

The younger witch giggled. "Drystan is dreary, I know. But it isn't all bad. It's much safer than where we once were in Nūa in fact, but not for the reasons you may think. The city, last I read, which was the past week's pamphlet, is well and riding out their autumn before winter hits them, too."

The vibrant fresh scents of spearmint and eucalyptus relaxed Evelyn despite the mounting uncertainty. Belle claimed her home fared well, so she found it hard to believe Drystan was safer, especially when Ingrid had indicated it wasn't wise for Belle to be out alone in the gardens. Was it the mere worries of an older sister, or a knowledge of the vampyr horrors Evelyn was well acquainted with? Evelyn sat with her thoughts as Belle continued to apply the salve. It cooled her burns.

I'm coming for you.

Kade's words granted Evelyn a sense of relief. She trusted Kade with all her heart. But they also fueled her resolve even more. She'd promised to return home with him and had sworn to finally fulfill the prophecy. She intended to keep that promise, to demonstrate that she'd changed, to undo the mistake of ever running in the first place.

At Ingrid's early words, guilt lay heavy on her shoulders. She *had* run, and the weight of it caved her in. What would witches think if they learned the truth? Evelyn hated to consider the possibility, and a heaviness settled over her shoulders. No. She'd return home with insight regarding their enemy.

But where to begin? A curse. A spell. Those details were a start, and her flame danced in her blood, eager to learn more. Her determination became as fierce and wild as her flame, and an idea formed, gentle and subtle, like the death of a snowflake on her skin.

Belle.

The young witch had said little, nervousness still clinging to the beautiful witch's demeanor. She moved away from the sofa, gathering a satchel full of bottles and canisters of salve.

"Thank you," Evelyn said.

Belle smiled, but it was tight and didn't reach her eyes. "The bracelets were made with dark magic, and you wore them for a dangerous amount of time. You might feel the effects for a few days. I recommend some rest."

She turned to leave, and Evelyn swallowed. It was now or never. "I don't suppose you'll tell me about the spell your sister mentioned." She waited four even breaths, heart racing while Belle stood, back turned, body unmoving. Slowly, the witch faced her again, blue-green eyes fleeting over Evelyn.

"Even if I wanted to, I can't. Ingrid tells me nothing. Look, I really shouldn't be talking to you. Rest like I said, and I'll try and come back to check on you in a few days."

"I can help, you know," Evelyn said, inclining her head to Belle's wringing hands. "With your water brotannas."

Evelyn wanted answers, but a deep-rooted part of her also saw an older version of herself in Belle, and the need to help sparked, wild and untamed inside her.

Those stunning, blue-green eyes widened. "My sister doesn't want me learning it. She says it's dangerous. If the wrong person discovered my power, they'd take advantage of it."

"Your sister is wrong." Evelyn tried to rein in the bite of her words, but her earlier anger rose. "Your magic is yours and no one else's." Even if Belle refused, she *had* to know that. She deserved to know that.

Belle stared at the floor, shaking her head. "You ran away and left us witches behind. I'm not sure I trust you."

Evelyn winced, shutting her eyes tight. "You're right, I did. Perhaps if I share why I ran away, you'll trust me a little. I lost my flame."

"*What?*" Belle hissed. "You're lying."

Evelyn scoffed. "I wish I was. The day my parents died, it left. I struggled for two years to get it back. I know, Belle, what it feels like. I saw the look in your eyes today. The frustration of not being able to grasp onto your power. I know I sound like the enemy, but I can help you. I swear it."

Her truth lay out in the open, her body suddenly heavy with the weight of it. Admitting it out loud didn't take away the urge to shed it like a skin, as if losing her flame had never happened.

Belle frowned. "Everything comes at a price. Why help me?"

"I need... to know what's really going on here."

"You want me to spy on my sister? I can't give you secrets. You're the enemy."

"Do you actually believe that?" Evelyn shook her head.

Apprehension brewed in Belle's eyes. A rosy tint flushed her cheeks, and she opened and closed her mouth, unable to form words. Evelyn fought the urge to say something more, to convince her, but she didn't want to push the nervous witch and lose the opportunity all together.

Finally, Belle stepped back, shaking her head, blonde curls swaying as she did so.

"I'm sorry, but I have to go."

She rushed to the door and knocked. The guards opened it and let her through. Green suede passed through the wooden door, and Belle left Evelyn alone with the resounding click of the lock.

The dark stone of the tower closed in around Evelyn, the twisting shadows on the walls her only company.

CHAPTER TWELVE

ELDRICK BLOCKED WITH HIS right axe and attacked with the left, the weapons like extensions of his body. The wooden shafts were his bones, their leather wrappings indented by his grip and swing. Their familiar weight and shape felt good. He felt good, as he always did sparring, training his mind and muscles. Adrenaline ran through him hot and cold, fueling his spirit despite the day's events.

Eldrick readied his weapons with a smirk. Across from him, Claus grinned, his square jaw twitching with tension. Metal clanged, iron against steel, as the werewolves sparred. Eldrick's smirk fell into a blank expression of pure concentration while Claus continued to smile with each swing after swing of his long sword.

Everyone had retired for the evening, leaving the training grounds of Lār empty aside from Eldrick and his uncle. Despite the cold evening breeze, they'd stripped their shirts and sweat dripped down their rippling muscles. All day, Eldrick had replayed his decision in the drawing room. Tovi's fury. Kade's disappointment. His own worry. With axes in hand, he breathed in the fresh air, relished its openness compared to Lār's stony, windowless, thick walls. He faked his axe left, then spun right and swung.

One, two.

A beautiful vampyr sat in the dungeons, a princess, and her brother had captured Evelyn. What an absolute, migraine-inducing mess. He turned to movement and tuned out his endless worry.

One, two.

He advanced on the offensive twice that time, Claus matching each blow with as much muster.

"You're getting old," Claus said.

Eldrick laughed. "You'd know, wouldn't you, uncle?"

Claus's head tipped back, and he roared with laughter. Claus was four years younger than Aramis, and at 110, he was far from old. He appeared only a few years older than Eldrick aside from finer lines around his eyes and the various scars over his body from decades of fighting as a warrior. As one of the best commanders in the Vadon Mountains, he'd spent much of his time at the Void. When he wasn't there, he'd trained Eldrick to be a leader, to be the future alpha of the Drengr pack.

Claus's beefy arms grasped his sword, and he gritted his teeth at Eldrick, a menacing werewolf growl rumbling from his chest. His wolf always sat on the surface, the beastly magic only hairs away from unleashing.

Leaner and shorter than Claus, Eldrick possessed speed. Swift and efficient, he jabbed Claus with the blunt end of one axe in the gut and the other in his lower back as he toppled over.

His smirk returned, and triumph thrummed through his werewolf blood.

Claus whirled around, eyes dancing with delight. He sidestepped, spinning into an attack Eldrick almost missed, the curved edges of his axes colliding with the edge of his sword at the last second.

"Also getting slow." His uncle winked.

The desire to disprove his opponent's playful taunts steeled Eldrick's resolve. Anticipation quickened his heart. He steadied his breath, gripped his axes tighter, and calculated his next move. To demonstrate how slow he wasn't,

Eldrick advanced towards Claus, attacking to the left, to the right, and head-on, repeating the assault with each step.

One, two. One, two.

Lār was the center fortress of the Drengr Village. It spanned over the north side, made up of an eight-story eyesore of a tower looming over everything with twin three-story annexes jutting east and west. On the backside, a wall extended from the annexes, outlining the perimeter of the training grounds for the Drengr warriors.

Eldrick hated Lār's stark contrast against the lush Vadon Mountains, but at present, took advantage of its layout. He inched closer and closer to the surrounding wall. Claus's focus began to waver between escape and defense. He flicked his gaze to the left, the moment of hesitation costing him and giving Eldrick the second he needed.

He overextended his reach with both axes, instead of clashing with Claus's sword, he went over the blade and pulled. The hooked underbellies of the iron yanked the blade from his uncle's grip, and Eldrick swung against his opponent's dominant wrist. The blade glinted as it flew through the air and landed in the sandy training ground.

Weaponless and stunned, Claus's eyes grew wide when Eldrick kicked him square in the chest. The brawny werewolf fell onto his back with a resounding thud.

Claus cursed to the stars and moon, a laugh latent in his breathless retorts.

Eldrick returned an axe to the holster on his trousers, extending his free hand to assist his uncle. "It is you, uncle, who is getting old and slow."

Claus eyed him, his gaze so different from their father's green one. Something lay in them. *Mirth.*

Eldrick reacted too late. Something hit his legs and he fell back. The night sky flashed above him as he crashed to the ground. He rolled as his uncle's bludgeoning fist boomed into the sand. A laugh rumbled from his uncle, dark eyes elated.

Engaging his core, Eldrick righted himself and lunged. Muscles stretched. Bones broke. Fur sprouted from his sun-kissed skin. The bones of his face ached as they elongated into his werewolf form's snout, and he bared his sharp canines. He charged, landing over his uncle in a single jump. With claws grasping Claus's shoulders, a growl emitted from him deep, long, and with his alpha baritone.

The muscles in Claus's rather taut body had no other choice but to stand down—the animalistic power in Eldrick's blood commanded him to. As he released Claus and backed away, his uncle's face split in a wide grin, a deep laugh shaking the werewolf's chest.

"You needed the fight, didn't you," he said.

Eldrick shifted out of his werewolf form and sighed. His uncle never missed anything. He raked his hand through his hair, the wisps over his forehead soaked with sweat. Adrenaline coursed through his spent muscles, his heart pounded in his chest, and yet Eldrick's mind still reeled with his decision to lock Tovi Verena in the dungeon. He tried to tell himself his father had agreed; it had been a sound alpha decision. But his brother's anger and hurt-filled eyes flashed through his memory.

Never let your emotions cloud your judgment.

Claus had taught him that lesson the day his mother died. A stern lesson. A harsh lesson. A lesson Eldrick never wanted to learn again. He couldn't afford to when he became alpha, not when good leaders led with their heads. He'd sought the training grounds to release his emotions, to rid his guilt of denying his brother and the attraction for Tovi. Both still wormed in the pit of his stomach.

"Out with it already," Claus said. "I can hear the gears turning in your head."

Eldrick shook his head. "Did I make the right decision?"

Claus raised an inquisitive brow and scratched his clean-shaven jaw. He headed for the watering jug near the training grounds veranda. Warrior ruins—swirls, phases of the moons, and variations of the wolf—had been carved into the pillars. The specks of silver embedded in the etched stone twinkled like the stars awakening in the sky above.

"Why do you think you didn't?" Claus asked.

Eldrick followed in step beside him. "I let Kade down, and I'm also risking his life without a guide."

"True," Claus said with a tip of his head. He handed Eldrick a mug of water. "Why didn't you agree with the terms your brother set and form an alliance with the princess, then?"

Eldrick took a swig of refreshing water. "It's too much of a risk. Hours ago we learned she even existed."

"Is that why you haven't killed her?" Claus asked.

Eldrick's grip tightened on his mug. "Yes, I figured we could learn from her. We've never seen a vampyr like her. Her existence shows us how little we know about the enemy. It would be stupid to kill a source of more knowledge. Besides, seeing she's a princess and the heir, killing her might be an act of war. I'd rather not start one, especially with a foe we don't fully understand."

Claus sighed. "Ah, that is true and smart. Yet, you haven't rushed to tell other alphas."

Eldrick scoffed. "And cause an uproar for no reason? If I told the rest of the packs, I'd have to reveal Evelyn Carson is also a captive of the vampyrs. That would cause more fear on both fronts, the witches and werewolves. If that news was released, it would be disastrous. With the missing werewolves, sanity is barely holding on by a thread. If our people also learned we'd been lying for the last two years about Kade and Evelyn's union..." Eldrick shook his head. "We'd rob them of the false hope we've created."

Claus sighed. "That is true. So, why are you doubting your decision? Your reasons are sound."

His brother's anger flashed in his mind. "I've been unfair to Kade—"

"No," his uncle said, "you're looking at the situation with a rational perspective. It's wise."

Eldrick straightened, his uncle's approval catching him off guard. Ever since the day his mother had died, ever since he'd led to her death, Eldrick had chased making the right decision and snuffing his emotions. To hear his uncle acknowledging his efforts brought on a wave of grounding reassurance.

"You think so?"

"Evelyn is a part of the prophecy. Your brother should go after her, regardless if she is his mate or not." His uncle sighed. "As for our prisoner, it's best if you have a sound judgment on how you handle that situation before it's too late."

"You think I should kill her and be done with it?" The words came out like sticks and stones, scraping his throat. He didn't understand why. He'd killed vampyrs before. To keep his pack safe, to protect them, to do what was right. Perhaps it was because she was so different from the vampyrs he'd faced in the past. What he didn't know about her made her a worse threat. Moons, she'd made it into the village right under everyone's noses. How many other vampyrs were doing the same? Eldrick exhaled. He'd underestimated vampyrs once before. He wouldn't do it again.

His uncle crossed his arms, dark eyes narrowing as he thought. "You could kill her and be done with it. It's an act of strength amongst the packs, and it would send a message to our enemies: don't step foot on our lands. But..."

"But?" Eldrick's heart thudded in his chest.

"What if you considered the alliance?"

Eldrick's heart skipped a beat, and he blinked, unsure if he heard his uncle correctly. "You said—"

"Your instincts are right, Eldrick. There is nothing wrong with your choice, but perhaps there is more than one right choice in this scenario."

Eldrick swigged his water. "Enlighten me."

"Accompany your brother and the Gray Fenris *with* the princess. Enter Drystan and you get a firsthand experience of what our enemies truly are like. You said it yourself, you hadn't killed the princess because you wanted to learn from her. Think of the things you could learn in her homeland."

Anticipation quickened through Eldrick. "Are you suggesting I actually make a deal, or are you saying I should manipulate her?"

Claus shrugged. "*Manipulate* is such a harsh word, but there are times as a leader you must twist a situation to get out of it what is best for you and other werewolves. Make the deal. Assess her and Drystan along the way. Good riddance if she doesn't prove herself. She's the one that claims to need the alliance, not us. We have nothing to lose. Though, I doubt she'll prove trustworthy, even if she helps get Evelyn back."

"She's a vampyr," Eldrick said, curling his lip as he downed the rest of his water. Its chill ran down his gullet, freezing his rib bones.

"Precisely." Claus gave a curt nod. "It might also give you a chance to show Aramis you're ready."

"Ready?" Eldrick asked.

Claus's dark eyes studied him. "Between the missing werewolves and what we now know about the vampyrs, the Drengrs need an alpha fit to lead. Look, you know I respect your father, as my alpha and my older brother, but he is declining, Magu."

Magu.

A nickname used only for those next in-line to become the alpha—a reminder for Eldrick's future, his duty. He'd been preparing for years to become alpha of the Drengr pack, and his blood ran with alpha strength. The firstborns were leaders, but not all were alphas. That was magic, a fate bestowed to their wolf. Eldrick's grandfather had possessed it, as had the many generations before him. But being leader of the Drengr entailed more than any other alpha. Ever since the first whispers of the prophecy and the first Son of the God, Finton, had been born, a ruling pack and alpha had been declared. Back then, the honor had been bestowed on the Johannes pack, Finton's pack, but ever since Kade had been born, it had transitioned to the Drengrs.

Eldrick inherited that responsibility.

"You're suggesting my father would let me ascend," he whispered.

Alphas traditionally ascended when their predecessor died, and the werewolf magic zapped the title into place. With his father still alive, Aramis had to grant

Eldrick the honor directly. There'd been whisperings of it over the last year, especially since Eldrick had stepped into many of the alpha-expectant duties, helping his father lead. Meetings with neighboring packs, visiting the Void for routine updates, receiving guests in their own village and welcoming them. Yet, his father had never once mentioned ascending.

Had his efforts not been enough already? He tried not to care or worry, tried not to be angered and saddened all at once.

One, two.

Eldrick breathed away his disappointment. There was no sense harboring it when it didn't help.

Claus sighed. "You and I both know the rarity of an ascension. I think it might be less of your father believing you're ready and more of a battle of pride, but if you showed him something worth considering, something he could not dismiss, you might have a chance at persuading him in the right direction."

"You think learning more from the princess will do that? I am needed here."

Claus held up his hand. "You're also needed in the fight against the vampyr. Keep a close eye on the princess. Learn her motives. Her true intentions. Perhaps you can learn information about the missing wolves, too, and if the vampyrs are to blame. Learn your enemy, Eldrick, and when you return home with the Daughter of the Goddess and the secrets of the princess, perhaps your father will see you in a new light. Lead with your head, come back with the facts. Return home an alpha."

An alpha.

Eldrick's nervous heart slowed. That's what he'd always wanted, wasn't it? He'd been destined to be the Drengr Alpha, the leader of his pack and people. He'd dreamed of it, had trained for it. Eldrick had to allow the data and facts to outweigh his emotions.

The fact was, his uncle was right. By joining Kade's mission, he'd get insight about Drystan as well as the opportunity to learn more about the princess who desired an alliance. He'd have a front seat to facts, and when he came home, he'd present them to his father and demonstrate he was ready to ascend and finally assume the duty he'd been born for.

Determination swelled in his chest.

Eldrick took a deep breath, meeting his uncle's gaze. "Alright. I'll do it."

CHAPTER THIRTEEN

STARLIGHT AND A SLIVER of the moon shone from the lone window in Tovi's cell. Night darkened the Drengr dungeons. Kade hadn't come and neither had his arrogant, scowl-faced brother. Tovi seethed and crossed her arms. The shackles around her wrists tugged against the wall they were secured on.

Not only had she been thrown into a cell, but she'd also been chained like some wild animal with little room to move about. Tovi inhaled through her nose, shutting her eyes, and tried with all her might to remain calm, but the creeping sensation she'd failed to secure an alliance with the werewolves started to settle in.

She'd lied to Kade. It hadn't been intentional. Withholding who and what she was had come as natural as breathing. The more others knew, the more they judged. The moment lords and ladies of Drystan court had learned she'd not renounced her title as heir, the snickering and cutting stares began. Perhaps old wounds had aided her in keeping that tidbit to herself. Besides, it wasn't the truth about her father that led to this cell but the uncontrollable fact she was a vampyr.

The incessant drip of water against stone was like the ticking of a clock, wasted minutes as her brother worked towards completing the spell. She prayed to the Goddess that Kade was trying to persuade his brother to reconsider or was starting his journey without her. She'd rot happily away in this cell if the efforts to get Evelyn back were in motion. As much as she wanted an alliance with the werewolves, Sorin had worse problems on the horizon if her brother succeeded.

The echo of boots descending the stairwell broke Tovi from her thoughts. Her heart quickened. Had Kade come to release her? Or had Eldrick decided to use that axe and execute her?

She mastered her posture, keeping her arms crossed and shoulders back—proud despite the grime clinging to her clothes.

The figure, tall and sure, approached down the hall. As he walked past the nearby sconces, Eldrick's golden-brown hair, shining wet, glinted in the flickering light. No axe glinted at his belt though, not a weapon to speak of strapped to his lean physique. Unless he had one tucked into his tight trousers. Though, there wasn't much room with the way his leathers molded so close to his muscles.

Tovi blinked and averted her gaze to his watchful, stern eyes, trying to convince herself she'd been searching for a possible threat and not ogling the werewolf's body.

"You know, I can't tell if these accommodations suit you, bloodsucker."

Eldrick's nickname iced over any attraction she had. How could she forget? He only saw her as a monster.

He leaned against the adjacent wall, oblivious to her internal annoyance as she leveled him with a fierce stare.

"Since you are a vampyr, after all," he continued, "I imagine you're used to dark and damp places. Though, you are a princess so maybe..."

Tovi didn't answer, grinding her teeth to fight back a retort. Despite his insults, she had no idea why he'd come down here, and she couldn't risk the opportunity to convince him to let her accompany Kade by lashing out.

Eldrick's emerald eyes tracked her, but his features gave nothing away. The man was as stony and rigid as the wall he leaned against.

Heat stretched between them, a beckoning lust, and Eldrick's scent—thickened by recent sweat—perfumed the air, fogging Tovi's rational mind. Hours ago, the alpha had held an axe to her throat, but her body didn't seem to care. She tried to grasp the cold of the dungeon and sniff out the mildew, anything to rid her senses of him.

If he was as affected by her as she was him, he didn't show it. Though, desire had flared in his eyes when he'd approached her at the tavern, and there'd definitely been intent. Was any of that still there?

"When was the last time you fed?"

Tovi stilled. His question elicited an array of images she'd worked hard to tamp down. Blood. Red. Warm. She swallowed, fighting the push of her fangs, refusing yet again to let him get under her skin.

His lips upturned. The bastard enjoyed this.

"I've studied your kind, learned a vampyr's tells. Three days, that's about as long as a vampyr can go before feeding. But you're different, aren't you? Can you go longer?" He shrugged. "Though, the bags under your eyes suggest no matter the days that have passed, you're hungry, bloodsucker. You need to feed soon, don't you?"

She transformed her growl into a scoff. "You'd be surprised to learn I can go quite a while without feeding compared to the 'scáths,' as you call them, but I do appreciate your concern."

A half lie. Tovi, compared to a *caillte*, maintained more control over the urge to feed, but she shared the same dreaded timeline: she needed to feed every three days. An affliction of the curse and not her true nature.

Eldrick's eyes darkened. "I'm not concerned."

She raised a brow. Perhaps she affected him after all. She threw the plan to play nice out the window, eager to have a little fun.

"Why bother asking, then? Are you taking requests, perhaps? Elk's my preference, but after seeing the splendors of your village, I'm keen to try the local venison."

Now, it was her turn to get under his skin, and a lick of satisfaction snaked through Tovi. It was slight, but Eldrick's jaw ticked, and she caught the way his hands gripped his arms tighter. Then, his brows pinched. He didn't ask, but she saw the question brewing in those eyes of his.

"Ah, yes. It may surprise you, but I drink animal blood. So, before you go off on some speech about 'not touching your people,' I have no plans to, wolf."

Eldrick's nostrils flared. "I don't believe—"

"Are you here to discuss my eating habits or far more pressing matters? We need to figure out a way to get Evelyn out of my brother's clutches. Should I also spell out the risks if we don't succeed?"

"No. I'd rather you explain why you keep mentioning 'we,' as if you're a part of the plan."

His spoke with hard authority, as if he talked down to her, and Tovi saw red, hating it.

"I *should* be a part of the plan," she hissed. "The mission to get Evelyn back is dangerous enough, but I guarantee you're making it far more dangerous by not letting me join your brother and his team—"

"You actually expect me to believe you care for my brother's safety? All you want is the alliance."

Tovi inhaled through her nose, trying to calm the heat rising in her usually cold body.

Perhaps she was still that wretched princess who only cared about herself. The thought caused sharp pain to lance through her chest. *No.* She cared for Kade and Evelyn and the prophecy.

Eldrick peeled off the wall, starting to pace. "I care for my brother and his team, and I haven't failed to recognize the benefit of having the vampyr princess join our efforts to get the Daughter of the Goddess back, but I don't trust you."

"You don't have to trust me."

He stopped and whirled. "What? You want to have an alliance and not trust one another."

The notion to share her feelings about the prophecy snaked through her mind, like a dragon slinking by with a precious jewel. Tovi's stomach flipped. She could barter it, present it to Eldrick like an offering. Like so many of her secrets, it was intertwined into who she used to be, as well as weaved with secrets that weren't her own, ones that weighed heavier in Eldrick's presence.

How you're seen is what you are.

She set her shoulders straight, mastering her breath. "I'm over 700 years old and well aware trust takes time, and yet we don't have that on our side. I'm asking you to recognize one key element. We share a common enemy. My brother. His plan threatens to destroy all of Sorin. You may not trust my motives, but it is to save my people. You're an alpha, are you not? You know what it means to take care of your people. To lead them, protect them. To go any lengths to make sure they prosper."

Eldrick studied her, eyes searching her face. His hands flexed by his sides.

Had she said too much? Too little? His rigid exterior gave nothing away aside from a flash of something in his emerald eyes. The charismatic werewolf she shared a blueberry ale with no longer existed, and a pang of remorse went through Tovi. All because she was a vampyr, she'd lost something.

Eldrick cursed under his breath, raked his hand through his hair, and shook his head. "Fine. Alright." He reached inside his pocket and retrieved a key.

By the time Tovi blinked, he'd unlocked the cell door and grasped her wrist. One opened shackle clattered to the ground. The second followed soon after, echoing in the silent truce between them.

"Mark my words, bloodsucker." Eldrick leveled his gaze with hers. "I'll set you free and allow you to lead us through Drystan, but I'm not agreeing to anything"—Tovi sucked in a breath—"until you prove to be a worthy ally."

"I swear I will get Evelyn back," she said, trying to rally thoughts to form another argument. Was the Drengr that stubborn? How could she convince him?

"Getting her out won't be enough."

Tovi's head ached. "What else do you want from me?"

"Show me I can trust you, that you'll be a worthy ally." Eldrick shrugged. "That's my deal."

"Show you?" Tovi's mind reeled. Her secrets whispered like cackling ghouls.

Eldrick lips tilted in a smirk. "Yes, show me. I'm coming with you, Tovi Verena, and you better hope to the gods you aren't hiding anything, because next time, I won't hesitate to use my axe."

With that, Eldrick stalked out of the dungeon. Tovi followed, numb, as if a new pair of shackles wrapped around her wrists. Between convincing Eldrick she was a good ally and getting Evelyn out of the castle, she believed the latter would be the easier.

Goddess, help her.

Chapter Fourteen

Kade

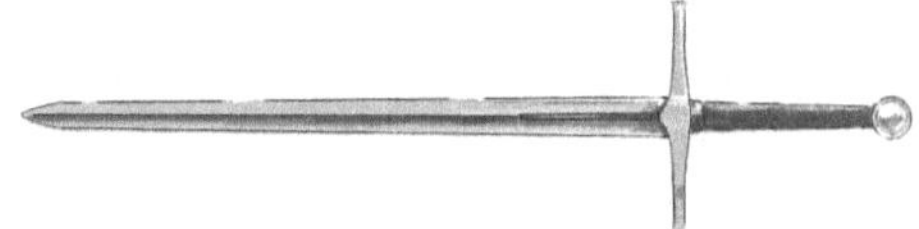

Maxie sat atop a center table in the Shield-maiden. She cleaned one of her paws, calm and unbothered by onlooking werewolves who shook in their boots. Despite their tattooed muscles and beaded warrior braids, they gave her a wide berth, avoiding her table—the *best* table in all the tavern with eight seats. Some had even sacrificed a chair, standing with backs to the walls, one eye on their companions, the other on Maxie. Her red fur shined a deeper orange under the firelights of Shield-maiden's, and the tufts of her ears appeared like golden tinsel. The crowd was quiet, watchful of her, one hand holding a cup of ale and the other hovering shy of their axes or swords.

The sight of Maxie warmed Kade's heart, but it did nothing to subside the mounting pressure in his chest. Frustration, anger, worry, all of it wrestled within him like a raging mountain storm during the hottest months. Like the winds and rain and electricity, it all stalled against the mountain range and sat, staying put until it ran its course and emptied its fury upon the lands. But unlike those storms, the energy manifesting in Kade had no end in sight.

It didn't lessen, it grew.

A sigh shuddered out of him, and at the shaky sound, Maxie peered up. She greeted him with a loud meow. Commotion echoed in the tavern. Chairs scraped against the floor. Metal screeched as it was unsheathed. Mugs slammed against tables. Maxie puffed out her chest, eyes half-slits. Kade managed a smile and sauntered past her, assured she'd be fine.

Tucked behind the bar, unseen unless one rounded the column of carved redwood tree the size of four huddled men, was an area Kade and the Gray Fenris had dubbed *their* spot in the tavern. Drengr-navy drapes, velvet and thick, added another layer of privacy. Tucked away from other pack members, the cozy dimly lit spot gave them room to enjoy an ale or two in peace, without the watchful eye of curious werewolves.

Kade's hand hovered over the curtains, and he sucked in a breath. The color and material reminded him of Evelyn's cloak. He swallowed, craving her in his arms, wishing he could weave his fingers through her obsidian hair. Kiss the pink blush on her cheeks. Or gaze deeply into the silver of her eyes.

He *would*. No matter what he faced and despite his brother's frustrating decision.

Kade snuffed the energy in his chest, yet again, to no avail. Hours. He had hours to plan with his team before they headed north, *without* their guide. They had no minute to spare. Voices murmured beyond the curtains. Someone clucked their tongue, another giggled. One moved, boots skidding across the floor followed by a sudden "*oof.*"

"What was that for?" a male voice hissed.

Before anyone could answer, Kade parted the curtains.

The music and murmurs of the Shield-maiden faded as his team saw him. Two beats passed, and they erupted out of their seats. All of them barreled into him, forming one massive hug. A sense of calm and lightness settled over Kade as he held his friends for the first time in over a year, and for a moment, the pressing energy in his chest subsided, and he allowed himself a calming exhale.

"I can't breathe!" someone yelped and wiggled against Kade's torso. A pink bun popped through the pile of them, then another. "Let me out!"

Everyone laughed as they parted, and Linx, the mage healer of the team gasped for air. Far shorter than the rest, Linx stood below their chests at a proud five foot—no taller, no shorter. Well, aside from the two buns of pink hair twisted on either side of her head, offering a few inches of extra height. Her yellow, catlike eyes sized him up.

"I see you're sporting a bun, too?" She gestured towards his head, raising a brow at Todd, the team's weapon master. "See, I'm trendy!"

Todd groaned, as did his leathers as he fell into a worn, quilt-patched armchair. "I'd hardly call buns a trend, Linx. Besides, I don't see an inch of pink on Kade."

The mage healer rolled her eyes. "You're jealous of my fashion sense. You don't have a lick of it, dagger boy." She waved to blades of all sorts that had been strapped to his physique like accessories.

He scoffed, flicking his dark hair out of his eyes. "I have style. It's less subtle."

"I hardly call 'stabby' a style."

Everyone chuckled. Bétar, Kade's second-in-command, sat on the curved leather booth on the west wall. He wiggled his red-as-dawn brows at the team's archer, Yennifer, who bumped her shoulder into his. She flashed him a wide, radiant smile, and the mountain of a man melted in his seat. The two had mated two summers ago, and their love for one another was warmer than the lit fireplace nestled into the corner.

Kade had missed this—the teasing amongst friends and the natural camaraderie. He grappled with a pang of loss. Evelyn would fit well with the team and even better at his side, his equal to lead. Yet, he'd been gone over a year, and it felt good to be home, surrounded by his friends.

"I'm happy to see you all," he said.

Bétar smiled, wide and toothy. "Likewise, Commander. You've been missed."

Todd stretched, crossing his arms behind his head. "Well, I for one haven't missed the ungodly hour you liked us waking up at. It's been nice to sleep in once in a while."

Kade leaned across the table, unable to fight the smirk twitching on his lips. "When did you ever adhere to my start times in the first place?"

"Seventy percent is passing." Todd winked.

All of them groaned, but Kade laughed, allowing it to bubble out despite the anxious energy tingling through him. The reunion was a much-needed distraction.

"I chose my pink for the occasion, Kade. Happy your home, but I also chose it for your vampyr friend. Easy for her to spot."

"Aye." Bétar nodded. "Easy indeed, but this Tovi Verena you mentioned never showed."

Kade sighed, removing his cloak and sword. He crossed his arms and leaned against a wooden beam. His body, tired and worn, needed purpose, but his insides were too frenzied to sit. "Eldrick came across her before she had the chance to connect with you all."

His team went rigid. Yennifer paused her work sharpening an arrowhead. Her lake-blue eyes flashed with concern as she peered up at him.

"Is she alive?"

Kade nodded. "For now. He threw her into the dungeons, intent on learning more about his enemy."

Bétar shook his head. "Does he understand we need her?"

Todd rested his elbows on his knees, tanned skin paling. "No one has ever made it across the Void successfully. She was our best chance."

"I know." Kade gritted his teeth. Why did his brother refuse to see reason?

The issue was his brother thought he was seeing reason. Facts, data, logic. Kade understood the importance of a level head, but sometimes his brother became stubborn. He'd never imagined Eldrick risking Kade's life or his team's in the process.

"We could break her out." Linx nibbled her lip, wheels turning underneath her colorful hair. "Lorkan created some new wicked weapons for me. I've been dying to try them."

Kade shut his eyes and dropped his head back in a grimace. What Linx lacked in shifting and size, she made up for in cleverer ways.

"*Moons*, don't tell me it's more explosives," Kade said.

His brother, scholarly and scientifically inclined, enjoyed making weapons for all his teammates, but especially for Linx, who had a knack for blowing things up—a talent that got the Gray Fenris in trouble over the years.

"It is!" Her eyes danced with mischief.

"We can't blow up Lār." Todd rolled his black-as-night eyes.

"He's right," Kade said. "We can't fight against our own, and we also don't have time to figure out a plan to break her out."

Bétar tapped the table. "We read your letter front to back. Are you sure there's no indication of when Riven will perform the spell?"

Kade shook his head, words like glass in his throat. He'd debriefed his team in an extensive letter he'd sent days ago. He kept assuring himself, as did Tovi, if Riven had succeeded, they'd know. Fear was as cold as ice in his throat. The spell needed Evelyn's blood, but they didn't know *how* much, either. A drop from her sliced palm or... Kade clenched his jaw, staring into the grooves of the floorboard. He refused to think of the worst or any of the unknowns.

One foot in front of the other.

Kade, at least, empathized with his brother when it came to making difficult choices. He'd recognized Eldrick's pained stare—the safety of the pack versus Evelyn. He hoped his father or brother had the sense not to execute vampyr royalty, enemy or not.

"Since we have no indication of when Riven plans to use the spell, we have to act quickly."

The team nodded, deliberate and curt.

Bétar clapped. "It's good to have our commander—"

Something nudged the back of Kade's legs, a familiar plush softness, while the rest of his team stared on in horror.

"What in the stars above!" Todd said.

One of his small knives flew through the air, embedding into the wooden floor between Kade's boots—inches from Maxie.

"Todd!" Kade roared.

Maxie hissed, weaving through Kade's legs and settling between them. She cast a slitted stare towards his weapon master, who had proceeded to stand atop his chair, a second knife at the ready.

Fear coursed through Kade, and his mounting worry shattered his control. His power unleashed. Light burst out of him, pearly and bluish, like a pulsing disc. Everyone ducked. Bétar shielded Yennifer, and Todd dragged Linx out of her chair to hunker with him. Even Maxie dashed underneath the table, Kade's power reflecting off her yellow eyes.

He threw out his arms, stumbling from the post he'd been leaning on. Burnt flesh and wool clotted the air—he'd scorched his biceps with his own hands. They wavered bright to dim to nothing, but the light, his power, didn't go out. It was sucked back inward. Kade's heart raced. This newness, this other, he didn't *want* it. It left him off balance, unsure of himself. Something he couldn't afford as he tried to get Evelyn back.

"Well... that's new," Todd whispered.

Kade blinked. He'd forgotten his team had even been there, his power taking away all his focus. Stars above, this *really* wasn't the reunion he'd envisioned. Kade ran his hands through his hair, taking a deliberate step back from everyone.

His mouth went dry, but he said, "Is everyone alright?"

Yen shook her head, blue eyes narrowed. "Are *you* alright?"

He nodded, but it felt like a lie and everyone's hesitant stares said they knew it, too.

"Does that demon belong to you, then?"

Rattled and wide-eyed, the lot of them whirled their attention to Lucy as she rounded the corner, a piled-high tray in hand.

"You mean Maxie?" Kade asked.

"Wait, it has a name?" Todd said. He and Linx stood, gathered around the table.

"*It* happens to be Evelyn's familiar," Kade said.

Linx gasped. "But how are they apart? Mages have familiars, too, and they don't ever leave each other's side."

Kade swallowed, bending over and picking Maxie up. She curled into his arms and rested against his chest. The Gray Fenris and Lucy cringed. A small sigh escaped Maxie, though, and she shut her eyes in contempt, tail swinging behind her.

"That's because it's a matter of the heart, right?" Lucy asked. She placed platters of pulled pork, lemon-steamed trout, and roasted greens onto the table. Fresh, meaty, and filling. The scents of his homeland's cooking eased Kade's tautness. "I reckon she's faring fine with her witch's other half, the mirror to her soul, so to speak."

Intrigued, Kade tilted his head away from the food and back to Lucy.

Yennifer nodded. "That makes sense, seeing as you're mates."

"Ah, mate or not, that"—Lucy pointed at Maxie—"is a demon. Scared half my patrons away tonight. Worse than if a vampyr had walked into my tavern."

They all stilled, not meeting one another's eyes. The irony that a vampyr *had* entered her establishment wasn't lost on them.

"Sorry, auntie," Todd said, helping her with the rest of the food. Two baskets of buttered biscuits with blueberry preserve followed. "If we'd known what she was, we'd have lured her away."

"I mentioned Maxie in my letter," Kade said, exasperated.

"Did you?" Bétar *humphed*.

"Missed that detail," Todd said.

Kade leveled an annoyed stare at his teammates and held Maxie tighter.

Lucy laid her hand on Todd's shoulder, her gaze softening as his did in return. Todd's mother had died at the Void, and her sister, Lucy, had taken Todd in and raised him like a son. Her tavern was more than a tavern for the Gray Fenris. It was a second home.

She gently squeezed his shoulder. "No ales for you all tonight. You'll need your rest and energy. Come by in the morn, and I'll send you off with some provisions."

The team thanked her as she left, and an awkward quiet fell amongst them.

Linx, usually the brightest of the group, had paled. "Kade, that is a power unlike any other werewolf, or mage or witch even."

"But Kade is the Son of the God," Yen said.

Bétar cleared his throat. "Could it have surfaced because you found your mate, the Daughter of the Goddess?"

"I..." Kade paused. With everything in the last few weeks, he hadn't considered *why* the energy had formed. He had, though, considered Linx's concern. Werewolves didn't cast magic or wield power. Their magic was rooted in abilities. Shifting, tracking, healing. Sometimes heightened senses or strength. He himself had a tracking ability connected to time and emotions, common in protectors and third-borns. Yennifer had keener and crisper sight—she never missed a target with her arrows. Bétar could lift ten times his strength, and Todd moved so fast, it was as if he could gracefully bend and twist like water. Yet no one, not even in the histories written about Finton, the first Son of the God, did a werewolf possess such power. It unnerved Kade.

"Kade's bond with Evelyn might actually be the cause," a new voice said from the doorway, "seeing as it happened the first time at the docks when Evelyn was captured."

For the second time that night, the Gray Fenris team whirled towards a newcomer.

Tovi Verena, washed and dressed in traveling leathers stood at the wavering curtains. Her white snowy hair fell softly, as if she'd run here and stopped abruptly.

A moment later, a flustered, angered Eldrick burst through the curtains. "You maddening woman. I told you to wait!"

Tovi rolled her eyes, not sparing Eldrick a glance.

"*You're* the vampyr princess?" Linx asked.

Biscuit tumbled out of Todd's mouth as he said, "You're far too pretty to be a vampyr."

Tovi raised a brow and smirked, flashing a fang.

Bétar crossed his arms. "You've seen Kade's light power, too?"

Kade bristled and Maxie squirmed against his chest.

"Yes—"

"What light power?" Eldrick asked, his voice stern and unbending. His green gaze collided with Kade's. "Is that why your eyes glowed earlier?"

"It's nothing," Kade said.

"Nothing?" Bétar repeated.

Kade ignored his stare. They didn't have time for this. Navigating, learning more about his new... magic? Kade blinked rapidly to clear his head. He'd deal with it later—it seemed the least of his worries when Evelyn wasn't at his side, a prisoner in the north, enduring gods knew what.

"We have more pressing matters. For starters, why are you both here?" Kade spoke without breaking eye contact with his brother. They'd never been so at odds, not even when he'd decided to leave and find Evelyn.

"Your brother finally decided to come to his senses," Tovi said and sauntered farther into the room.

Someone choked on their food, perhaps Bétar, and another spit out their drink, spluttering as they caught their breath. Todd by the sounds of the dramatics. Even Linx, the brashest of them all, stood with her mouth in a definitive O.

"Oh, I think I might like you," Yennifer said. She tossed her long wheat-colored braid across her shoulder, a playful smile brightening her face.

Gods save him.

"You agreed to be allies, then?" Kade asked.

"Not quite," Eldrick said. "The princess and I have come to a different agreement." He looked at Tovi. Again, she paid him no mind, making herself a plate of biscuits and preserves. "She and I will join you to get Evelyn back. I'm sorry for being an ass earlier."

"Thank you, Eldrick," Kade said. An understanding passed between the two brothers as they clasped hands. The reunion they'd both wanted, the brotherly bond restored. "Think nothing of being an ass," Kade said, "but know I will tease you relentlessly now that you're joining us."

Eldrick exhaled. "I deserve it. Now, what exactly is the plan?"

Kade turned to his archer. "Do you have a map, Yen?"

The Gray Fenris, Eldrick, and Tovi gathered closer as Yennifer rummaged in her satchel. She retrieved a parchment, the fold lines paper-thin and brittle as she opened and splayed it over the table. On the map, the Void was depicted with clouds of fog and mist. North of it, Drystan's topography was a mystery.

Kade pointed to a center section of the Void, not too far from the great river running down the center of Sorin. "Like we predicted before, Tovi confirmed there is indeed a canyon pass located here."

"You don't say," Bétar said.

Before Kade'd left, they'd been searching for a way through the Void. No witch or werewolf had successfully tracked across it, but they'd sought to be the first. Through it, they'd enter enemy territory and attack at the source.

Tovi nodded, analyzing the map. "It can be dangerous, but for a group our size it's a good option."

"What are our other options?" Eldrick asked, eyeing her across the table.

Tovi waved a hand in the air. "Pirates, but that's rather expensive."

"And risky," Kade said. "Riven will suspect one of us—Tovi or me—to break Evelyn out of the castle."

"Yes," Tovi said, "but I doubt he'll suspect a bunch of werewolves working with a vampyr. We need to make sure he doesn't learn that we're working together or that we've made it into Drystan."

Kade nodded. "Surprise will be our advantage."

He and Tovi had discussed at length the best way to get across the Void, into Drystan, and head north towards the castle. They hadn't yet figured out how to infiltrate it, but getting there was the first step.

"What about demons?" Eldrick asked. "They're more concentrated at the Void, right?"

Tovi hesitated and swallowed. "Yes—but as a vampyr, darkness is already in me. Darkness is attracted to light, hence why demons cross into Sorin, I'll throw them off within your company. Not foolproof, but a pack of madras won't hunt us."

Kade shuddered. He'd fought plenty of madras, the demon equivalent of a wolf, with his team, but as they ran usually in packs, he'd rather not encounter them during their journey.

"Is that why witches and werewolves haven't been able to cross the Void before?" Yennifer asked. "The light in us?"

"It does play a factor for sure," Tovi said. "But the Void is simply a dangerous place. Even vampyrs stay clear of it, terrified they'll become *caillte* that close to the darkness."

"*Caillte*? Lost?" Eldrick said, translating the word.

"Yes," Kade said. "It's what we call scáths."

"But you crossed the Void and so did your brother," Yen said with her brow raised.

Tovi nodded. "We both have bloodstones. The magic within the stone is a sort of cloak, hiding us from the darkness in a way. Its why my people in

Drystan can't leave. They'd perish through the Void like you all, but for different reasons."

"Our light is like a beacon whereas they'll fall to darkness, become it, then?" Linx asked.

"Yes," Kade said. "But we have fought our share of demons before. We can handle the Void."

"Aye." Bétar nodded. As the team listened intently, tension released from Kade's muscles, and he fell back into his commander role. *This.* Standing in their secluded room at Shield-maiden's, peering at Yen's worn map, static prickling with the promise of their next mission—Kade not only missed this, he *needed* it, welcomed the ease of purpose flowing from his next steps forward.

"Is there an option without demons, though?" Todd asked. He spun a dagger, the sharp point embedded on the table.

Tovi exhaled. "Well, that would be the pirate option, smuggling us through the underground, but again, expensive." She ran her finger up the mountain range and to the spot on the map. "The canyon pass is also quicker. We could get there in a day or two, right? Getting access to the underground might take some time, possibly a week."

The team glanced at each other, committal nods jumping from one to the other. It appeared, they had a plan.

Evelyn.

Kade sent her name down the bond, even if she couldn't hear him, he hoped her soul *felt* it, knew his commitment to her.

I'm coming for you.

PART II

Chapter Fifteen

Evelyn

RAIN POURED OUTSIDE IN unrelenting sheets, wave after wave like beads of glass clattering against Evelyn's window. Her afternoon walks had become her only reprieve out of the tower. Every trip outside her circular stone prison cell soothed her restlessness, but by the looks of the raging rainstorm outside, today she wouldn't get that opportunity.

Evelyn tapped her foot against the cold stone floor. Despite the lively large fire at the hearth and access to her magic, Evelyn couldn't escape the chill of Drystan. It clung like some hungry, angry invisible pest, an *otherness* settling over her like dew she couldn't brush away. It reminded her of the presence of the White Lady, the darkness in the air oozy and wicked.

She slumped into the sofa, Tala paid her no mind across the way, reading a series of parchments and letters. Her golden eyes skittered across the words, fully immersed. Evelyn peered down at her own reading, an abandoned encyclopedia by Matilda Moore. She'd succumbed to such boredom, reverting to rereading the works of a witch she'd studied during her tutelage. Matilda was an infamous scholar. The Nūa Library had an entire wing dedicated to her work. Infamous or not, why were her works in the vampyr castle?

It wasn't one text, either—the bookshelf near her bedpost had an entire anthology, the leather and gold font in pristine condition, one Evelyn recognized as originals her sister had coveted and paid a hefty price to find and keep as collectables. The mystery was much like the scholar herself, who'd up and disappeared without a trace hundreds of years ago.

Before Evelyn could ask Tala about the books, a tentative knock resounded. The vampyr peered up from her papers, amusement shining in her eyes. She rose and sauntered towards the door, a bemused smile playing at the corner of her lips. Evelyn reached out with her magic, and a serene, calm, graceful magic, like that of a bending riverbed, tickled against hers.

Belle.

Her heart raced, and she ground her teeth together to fight a smile. On the other side of the door, Belle's freckles dotted across flushed cheeks. Her blonde curls had been left free and wild, spilling over her shoulder like golden-spun threads of sunlight.

"I..." Belle swallowed, eyes darting to Evelyn. She raised a basket full of ointments and supplies. "I came to check on Evelyn's wrists."

Tala's brows shot up, and she narrowed her gaze. "A day or two late, aren't we?"

Belle cleared her throat, smiling with no teeth. "You know how my sister can be."

Tala hummed. "Fair. Come in."

Belle entered, slow and hesitant. Her mahogany heeled boots clapped against the cold stone of the tower floor. She stopped at the seating area, hovering at the edge of the intricately weaved carpet, eyes darting between which seat to choose. Tala's papers messed up the left reading chair, and Evelyn's pile of Matilda Moore's books occupied the sofa.

Tala smoothed her hands down her quilted jacket. "I have some evening errands to attend to. Perhaps you can join Evelyn for dinner tonight instead of me?"

Belle nodded. "I'd be delighted."

"I trust neither of you will get any fine ideas that include Evelyn leaving this room?"

She raised a brow at Evelyn who bristled underneath her golden stare. She chewed the inside of her cheek. Tala's tone suggested she was some young, naive schoolgirl in need of a rehashing of the rules. She didn't appreciate the reminder she was a prisoner, but unwilling to jeopardize alone time with Belle, she nodded.

"Good. I'll see you in the morning for our usual scheduled time." She winked at Evelyn as she left.

Her nerves grated, Evelyn's flame rose to the surface. But again, Evelyn did nothing—it was too great a risk to upset or aggravate Tala and earn back her bracelets, an unsaid threat that lay in the air.

Alone, awkwardness beat between Evelyn and Belle, vibrating in the circular room.

"I'm glad you came back," Evelyn said.

Belle swallowed. She didn't meet Evelyn's gaze as she set her basket of supplies on Tala's now empty chair. "How are your wrists?"

Evelyn overturned her hands in her lap. Green bruises outlined where the bracelets had once been but were no longer sore to the touch. Evelyn hadn't bruised for this long since she was a child. After maturity, a witch's magic expedited the natural healing for simple wounds like bruises and cuts, which meant the bracelets' magic had been darker than she'd thought. Bouts of drowsiness still hit her from time to time, and she blamed her drained energy for being unable to reach Kade again through their bond.

Sighing, she dismissed any thoughts of him. He was coming, risking his life, and she had her own task at hand.

"They're getting better."

Belle approached, lifting Evelyn's wrists with a tentative touch. "The scabs are closed over. That's good."

"Yes."

It occurred to Evelyn that this witch's sister had created the bracelets, and their stark difference was as blinding as the sun after days of rain. Even if Belle hadn't mastered her brotannas, her fluid, dancing magic was there, alive and vibrant. Not a lick of darkness bubbling in the current of it.

The fire popped as Belle returned to her basket, rummaging for something. She walked back to Evelyn, handing her a pamphlet.

"I brought you this. Something to reassure you I hadn't lied about Nūa. I know both your sisters live there, and I didn't want you to worry."

Last week's date had been printed in the right-hand corner above the newspaper's title, *The Magic*. Evelyn steeled her hand from shaking as she read over it. Things were much the same since she'd read the one Tovi had given her weeks ago—fashion experts writing about transitional pieces needed in one's closet, the trendy dinner spot serving Old-World-meets-New-World flavors, and the latest efforts at the Void. There was no mention of any unrest, and it reassured Evelyn nothing had gone awry since leaving Callum.

She swallowed, words thick. "Thank you for showing me this."

Belle nodded. "Of course."

Evelyn tilted her head, studying the witch. "If Nūa is much the same, why are you and Ingrid here?"

"My sister met Visha, her fated. Seeing as she resided in court, we moved to Drystan."

"Your sister's fated is a vampyr?" Evelyn asked slowly. It wasn't necessarily disbelief—Kade was her fated and a werewolf, so she understood the possibility one's fated might not be a witch, but the fact it was a vampyr still surprised her.

"Yes, a vampyr." Belle twisted her hands as she swallowed. "Does your offer still stand? To teach me magic?"

"Are you agreeing to help?" Evelyn asked.

Belle's blue-green eyes widened, and she set her shoulders an inch straighter. "Let's see how helpful you are first."

Evelyn scoffed, but she enjoyed the young witch's sass. A spark, a hint of that powerful water brotannas hovered at the surface like a wave ready to crash down. A heaviness clung to Evelyn's limbs. Her magic had been like that once, a whoosh of flame roaring to life before reverting in on itself, a dying ember she could not feed. Evelyn sank deeper into the cushions. Purpose settled over her, like a gentle Callum mist. She wanted to help Belle as much as she wanted to learn more about the vampyr.

Evelyn sighed. "Well, here's to hoping I prove to be a good teacher."

She rose out of her chair and walked to the bathing chamber. She returned with a small bowl, burgundy clay whitening her pale fingers further. Evelyn placed it on the woven carpet, her determined stare reflecting in the fresh, stone-cold water.

"Sit with me." She beckoned Belle to join her, outstretching her hand.

Belle, nervously, twisted a finger around one of her honey curls. After a beat, she released a heavy breath and took Evelyn's hand. Together, they sat on the carpet. Belle's flowy, powder-blue dress ballooned and settled around her like delicate petals. It looked wrong against the maroon, woven carpet and onyx stone walls.

Evelyn fidgeted in her own skirts, detesting every layer. Goddess, she hated dresses. Her bare legs felt exposed, prone to the terrible Drystan chill. Outside, the rain continued, the constant patter against her window calming, while the fire crackled and popped with no rhythm or reason. Its wild and unpredictable power reached Evelyn's in a familiar greeting, giving her the courage to try and help this witch.

"Where does our magic live?" Evelyn asked.

Belle nibbled her lip then tapped over her heart. "Here. It's a kernel of power in our soul."

"Yes, exactly. Our brotannases are there, too, woven into our magic, but we have to train them differently. Like a muscle, we have to work them and make them stronger. Use it too much, we tire it out. Use it too little, it grows weak."

Evelyn reached out and grabbed Belle's hands. She gave them an encouraging squeeze and brought it against the witch's chest, placing it over her heart.

"Alright, I want you to close your eyes."

Belle's cerulean eyes studied Evelyn, dripping with apprehension. Finally, she closed them, her lids twitching.

"Take a deep breath for me, Belle."

The witch listened, her chest rising and falling as her nostrils flared. Her shoulders eased, and the flush on her cheeks faded, her bridge of freckles more prominent.

"Can you feel your water?"

"Yes," she said.

Evelyn nodded. "The first step is to recognize your brotannas, your magic is *you*. It's not separate, it's not its own. You are one and the same."

Belle's eyes snapped open. "What?"

Evelyn's heart skipped. For a brief moment, the youngness and innocence in Belle's expression brought back the memories of her dear, bubbly friend.

Aster.

Such wonder, hope. All of it swam in Belle's clash of green and blue, too familiar and recent. Aster's death was still an open wound on Evelyn's heart. It didn't matter she'd succeeded in killing the White Lady. Grief had planted its thorny root and from time to time slithered like an invasive vine closer to the surface.

Yet, that was what fueled her, right? She'd made mistakes. She'd failed. She'd run, risked the safety of her homeland, and brought a darkness to Callum they'd never deserved. She wouldn't let that darkness continue. Not Riven or the spell. Evelyn didn't let doubt—or grief, even—hold her back. She faced her fears, no matter how ugly or risky.

"Yes," Evelyn said with a shaky breath. Out of sight, a loud pop in the fire echoed in the room. "Your water and you are the same. Our magic is tethered to our souls, but our brotannas are unique to us, weaved into who we are. It is us, as we are it. One and the same. When you reach for it, what's it like? How does it greet you?"

Belle closed her eyes again, inhaling as she fell into herself. "It's calming, serene, and... gentle." Her mouth opened and closed. "Am I allowed to say it's beautiful?"

Evelyn laughed. "Of course."

Belle laughed with her, a gentle kind of sound, like her brotannas. "It's blue."

"Like the sea?"

"No. A glacier blue."

Belle's brotannas rose to the surface, her magic twisting and turning in the air around them. Evelyn's flame wavered in greeting, excited and warm, but Evelyn pulled it back, letting Belle feel her magic only.

"It's like the lakes at the bottom of a mountain. I don't smell or taste salt, but the forest and life. Rain, dew, and creek beds." Her eyes popped open, and Evelyn swore the blue against the green bent and turned like the surge of a river. "Now what?"

Evelyn pushed the bowl of water in between them. "I want you to start with ripples. No droplets or trying to grasp the water. Make movement in it, connect your power to it. That's all."

Side to side, Belle leaned as if warming herself up. One hand remained over her heart, and she placed the other on top of it, exhaling as she closed her eyes. Her chest rose and fell with no rhythm, frantic against the sound of rain outside. Evelyn's attention jumped between the bowl and Belle. *Goddess,* the young witch's magic was present, certainly not lost like hers had been, but the young witch's breath hitched and wheezed.

Her brows pinched together, and she sighed. Her stare met Evelyn's. "I can feel it. It does feel a part of me, but grasping it is... difficult."

Evelyn nodded. "That's alright. It might take practice. Have you wielded it before?"

"When I was younger." Belle placed her hands on her knees. "We had a well outside our manor. We hardly used it, more for decorative purposes, but one day I was playing with Ingrid. We used to shout into the never-ending tunnel in the earth, giggling as our words echoed to meaningless sounds of nothing. And then it erupted, water shooting to the sky. It felt like I'd found something of my own, something that was mine. Ingrid had her wind brotannas, and now I had mine." She shrugged. "Our parents and older brother died three weeks later. Scáths—well, I mean—never mind. Vampyrs attacked, yet we lived. Our uncle in Nūa took us in after that."

"And he never had you tutored for your brotannas?"

Belle shook her head. "Our uncle wasn't a kind man. He was rich and single and didn't care for his snot-nosed nieces. He paid for private tutors, but my sister made me keep my water brotannas a secret. She didn't want him to notice me more than he already did."

Something flashed in Belle's eyes, secrets or memories of the past, and Evelyn didn't pry. She respected what Belle had told her. A trust was brewing between them she didn't want to shatter.

"Can I try again?" Belle asked.

Evelyn smiled. "Go for it."

Belle readied herself, same as before. Her breath steadied, her lids stilled, and a calmness washed through her. A beat passed and a surge of fluid power filled the air. The water in the bowl rippled—once, twice, a third time like the trembles after a quake.

"Did I do it?" Belle hunched closer to the bowl, and it rippled again, this time mightily enough to splash a wave over the clay bowl and seep into the rug. Belle erupted into gleeful giggles. She covered her wide, toothy smile with her hands, the water reflecting her overjoyed expression. "Goddess, I did it!"

Evelyn laughed, too, a feathery, warm lightness settling over her for the first time since Callum. For a moment, the stone walls of her tower prison crumbled to make way for a bright magic, eclipsing the rain and impending spell. She sat back, her own magic dancing with delight. The power of Belle's successful attempt peppered the air with promise.

Belle relaxed, glancing at the bowl of water in wonder. The edge of her lips downturned. "I'm sorry for what I said the other day."

"What do you mean?" Evelyn moved towards the sofa, leaning upright against it, tucking her knees to her chest.

"I said you ran away and left us witches behind."

Evelyn shrugged, picking at a loose strand on her skirts. "Nothing wrong with the truth."

"But it wasn't fair to throw it in your face. Being unable to master my brotannas has been frustrating, and I took that out on you, but I never considered what it must've been like. You're Daughter of the Goddess, and witches and werewolves looked to you to defeat the darkness. I know how lousy and lonely it can be, but especially for you, it can't have been easy."

Evelyn forced a small smile. Her mouth felt thick, words too heavy. Belle was right. It had been lonely moving place to place, her secret growing heavier with each passing month. The more she'd tried to get her magic back, the farther out of reach it had become. She'd felt vacant. Hollow. Evelyn didn't want to return to that place, not even in memory, and yet the what-ifs nagged at her. What if she'd never run? What if she'd never placed herself in Riven's path? Would there even be a spell threatening her homeland?

Never mind all that. She had an opportunity to undo her mistake, and she would grasp it with both hands.

"Do you know how the king died?" Evelyn asked.

Belle shook her head. "I don't know, but as I'm sure you've noticed, vampyrs aren't exactly what us witches believed."

"That's an understatement," Evelyn scoffed.

Belle smiled, but it didn't reach her eyes. "I'm afraid I can't give you answers. Ingrid cares for me in her own way, sheltering me, keeping me ignorant of

Riven's plans or her part in them, but I can tell you what I've observed during my time here."

The witch's account of her time in Drystan shattered more of Evelyn's beliefs regarding the vampyrs. The king had been dead for five hundred years, and Drystan hadn't had a ruler since. Scáths weren't newly turned vampyrs, but *caillte*, vampyrs overtaken by bloodlust. The Void was as dangerous for vampyrs as it was for those in Sorin, and worse, they couldn't cross it without a blood-stone.

The timing of the king's death jarred Evelyn, her palms growing sweaty. Witches and werewolves had always believed vampyrs had emerged five centuries ago, and yet that was when the king had died, so they'd existed far longer than that. Was the timing a coincidence? Worse, the king was Tovi's father, which meant, Evelyn's friend was... ancient. The fact sent shivers down Evelyn's spine. So many years to perfect her cunning, lying ways. But more importantly—

"Attacks, ones we believed were because of the king, ceased years ago," Evelyn said.

Belle shrugged. "The prophecy might've played a part. Perhaps Prince Riven and Princess Tovi got better at maintaining the *caillte*. The princess has taken significant strides to help vampyrs in the surrounding towns and villages."

"Tovi?" Evelyn didn't hide the surprise in her tone.

Belle hummed. "She is the rightful heir, after all."

The rain worsened outside. Wind rattled the metal frame of her window and thunder boomed against the stone walls. Evelyn's heart raced in unison, the fire at the hearth flickering higher as the sense of betrayal stormed inside her. During their friendship, Tovi had alluded to "the family business" and her part in it. Never would Evelyn have ever imagined that business was running a country and Tovi was rightfully queen. It at least explained the divide between her and Riven. Did that mean Tovi had no part in Evelyn's capture? Evelyn swallowed, ignoring the stinging in the corner of her eyes. Even if Tovi wasn't involved, she was still a liar.

If Belle noticed her withdrawing, she didn't say and continued on. "But most at court, lords and ladies, don't honor her claim."

Evelyn stilled, a thought sparking in the back of her mind. "Is that why Riven wants vampyrs to walk in the sunlight? Will it make him king?"

"Maybe, but I think he's more concerned with breaking the curse."

"Your sister said the same thing. *The* curse as if it were—"

"Its own thing, yes." Belle nodded. "Vampyrs haven't always been this way."

Belle rummaged through the basket of supplies she'd brought and retrieved a journal. She handed it to Evelyn. The weathered leather was soft under her touch, numerous water stains blooming into the tan material. She opened it, the entry page similar to journals her scholarly sister, Blair, kept when conducting research—she never left the house without one tucked under arm.

Evelyn scanned the long, delicate writing and gasped—the owner's name as well as the book's title rooted her in place.

Vampyrs by Matilda Moore.

"But... she never wrote a book on vampyrs. No witch has." Her voice shook while the thunder boomed outside.

"Yes, and she's quite knowledgeable about them. You'll also find her account of vampyrs is starkly different to what we know, and the dates all preceded the king's death."

Evelyn shook her head. All the questions she had answered were replaced with new ones. "But I don't understand. Where did you find this? Why is her research even in Drystan? Why was it never translated to text?"

Before Belle could answer, the door opened, and servants began wheeling dinner into the room. Belle snatched the journal from Evelyn's hands and wedged it between the sofa's velvet cushions. The two remained silent as the servants laid out dinner. Evelyn's heart raced. It quickened to a pace her core hollowed out. The scent of cream, tarragon, and mustard chicken roiled her stomach, and she fought the urge to throw up.

The water witch sent the servants away, requesting privacy. To Evelyn's amazement, they listened. Whoever Belle and Ingrid were, they had position within the court. Once gone, the fire and rain crackled and pattered together as Belle made herself a plate of food and rejoined Evelyn on the rug.

"I found it in the library, thinking I'd stumbled upon someone's diary. I can't even begin to guess why Matilda's journal is here or why we've never known these facts," she said. "Maybe she wanted to protect witches, thinking that keeping us ignorant would keep us away. Maybe it wasn't even intentional. I've read it front to back multiple times, though, and I've come to the conclusion vampyrs aren't darkness itself. They are cursed by it."

Evelyn's brows pinched. "*By* it? You're suggesting darkness and the curse are two separate things. Vampyrism is a curse."

Belle considered, nibbling her lip. "Earlier, we discussed a brotannas is a kernel of power in our souls. Our powers are us. Not a separate thing. From what I've seen, it is different for vampyrs. Whereas a demon is all darkness, vampyrs possess only a kernel of darkness inside them. They fight against it every day."

"I have studied vampyrs for two decades. This threatens everything I believe," Evelyn whispered.

Belle pointed her fork at the journal. "Read some of Matilda's passages."

Evelyn, despite the chill running down her spine, obeyed. She skimmed, far too frantic to care for every word. Culture. Sleeping habits. Mating bonds. Matilda's passages and notes were observations made of a people that didn't align with vampyrs. Scáths—or *caillte*—weren't mentioned once, in fact Evelyn didn't find a single passage detailing the insatiable hunger for blood. The words *honor* and *sacred* had been underlined with ink.

"They were a peaceful and prosperous kingdom," Evelyn whispered.

Witches and werewolves regarded vampyrs as cursed, like all creatures of darkness. That's what she'd been taught. Two decades of tutelage warred against the notion there was more to it, but she couldn't discredit Belle's suggestion or Matilda's notes supporting it.

Evelyn rose on shaky legs. She poured herself a glass of wine, leaving a scant distance between the burgundy liquid and the glass's rim, needing the heavy pour. The first sip sent a chill through her gullet. The hairs on her arms prickled, and she grasped onto the warmth bleeding through her belly.

Third-borns will defeat the darkness.

She'd learned in Callum the prophecy was up for interpretation. *The truest of unions.* Scholars had inferred that to mean a binding of souls between third-borns. But after discovering Kade was her fated, Evelyn believed that the prophecy meant something deeper, something that spells or rituals couldn't create. It was more about matters of the heart, about destiny. If those who had interpreted the prophecy could be wrong about her bond with Kade, could they also be wrong about the vampyrs? Perhaps she wasn't meant to destroy them but to free them.

No. The prophecy stated she and Kade would *defeat* the darkness together. Her soul, her magic sang with that promise. That future. Yet, Riven didn't need Kade for the spell. He'd had a chance to capture Kade in Callum, but instead he'd threatened his life, not a sliver of hesitancy in his words. To the prince, Kade was expendable, which assured Evelyn he only had plans to use her, but it didn't answer a blaring question.

"Why is Riven convinced walking in sunlight will break this curse?"

Belle shook her. "I haven't the slightest idea, and between you and me, my sister isn't convinced it will. Others around her seem wary, too."

"Then why go through with it?"

Belle sighed as she rose. "Because Riven wants something, deeply. No one would dare get in his way."

Evelyn gritted her teeth, jaw aching from the force. She'd get in his way, Goddess damn him. If the spell didn't break the curse, which Evelyn was inclined to believe, *caillte* would have the ability to roam day and night, wreaking never-ending destruction across Sorin.

Belle teetered from foot to foot. "Will you still help me with my magic?"

Evelyn nodded, jarred by the switch in subject. "Of course."

Belle released a pent-up sigh. "Good. My sister isn't aware I came to see you today, so I must hurry before she discovers me gone. Read more of the journal, and I'll try to learn more."

"When will you come back?"

"Tomorrow if I can, but if not, the day after. I swear it."

With that, Belle dashed out of Evelyn's room and the lock to her tower door resounded against Evelyn's endless questions and sense of unease. The rain continued, and Matilda's text beckoned her.

Read me. Read me. Read me.

Chapter Sixteen

Evelyn

E VELYN DIDN'T SLEEP.

After Belle left, she poured over Matilda's words, entrapped by the scholar's findings. The journal splayed open in her bent knees pulled close to her chest, she sank deeper into the feathery pillows of the bed as she fell further into the history of vampyr. A candle on the nightstand flickered light across the old pages. Sleep clung to her aching eyes by the time a skirt of wax had bunched against the brass candelabra.

Matilda's notes ended three-fourths of the way through the book, the remaining empty pages taunting Evelyn. She shut the book with a long exhale, the sound slamming like the truth.

Vampyrs had not always been cursed.

Matilda's notes had been weaved with facts, accounts, and observations. Vampyrs ate food for vitamins and sustenance. Blood was treated as a delicacy, and usually only between a vampyr and someone they respected. A lover or a friend. Vampyr or not. When sex got involved, how they craved and needed blood got murky.

Vampyrs were, similar to faeries, immortal. They could have children, but like witches, it took years, sometimes decades to conceive. Usually, a mated pair had the best chances. They, too, called it mates, like werewolves, but from what Evelyn gathered, it was similar to fateds.

Those turned remained their age at the time the vampyr venom touched their veins while those who were born vampyrs stopped aging around thirty years. The Verenas were filthy rich, which explained Tovi's high-end fashion and ability to pose as a wealthy merchant, but vampyrs in general possessed money and extravagance. With a hidden underground for trade, a land with patches of vibrant, nutrient-dense soil, and a coastline with a current leading to the southern continents, Drystan possessed many riches.

The most interesting of all, vampyrs once walked in the sunlight.

Fascination gripped Evelyn, and she hadn't found anything related to darkness, demons, or the Void once throughout Matilda's journal, confirming the curse had happened after her time here.

And after the king's passing.

An eagerness flushed through her, as if she'd chipped away at something bigger. It could shed light on how to defeat the vampyr, or the curse for that matter. With so many scholars studying the prophecy, information like this would be vital.

Evelyn sighed, resting the journal on her nightstand. She needed sleep, a moment to rest. Wear and tear gripped her muscles, and her mind spun. So much information, and yet so little on how to stop Riven. Why did he think allowing vampyrs to walk in sunlight was the solution?

Her heart ached and yearned for Kade. *Fucking flames,* tears stung at the edge of her eyes. Those amber eyes of his, always believing in her. His kind touch, a gentle kiss to her temple. Kade was always calm, collected. He'd remind her to believe, and she did.

The rain had stopped, the night eerie still compared to the wild day. Outside, the moon shone high beyond a veil of gray. Unlike the sun, which glowed silver, the moon gleamed a pearly hue. Her heart swelled with her love for Kade, and she pushed under the covers. She inhaled and exhaled, thought of his promise to come for her, and let his words and phantom touch calm her to rest.

As sleep eclipsed Evelyn, voices murmured outside her door, and the distinct clatter of boots against stone echoed down the hall. Her eyes popped open. Her magic surfaced. Something lay in the air, thick and cold.

The lock clicked, and her door eased open. She sprang from her bed, bare feet hitting the cold floor as she jolted awake. But no one stood on the other side, only the shadows from the flickering sconces framing her door.

Was it her guard or Tala?

Unsure and uneasy, she stepped forward as her magic rose to the surface. Her fire obeyed, so in sync with her now, so a part of her, it weaved strongly and tightly to her soul and will, hot and fiery and ready for a fight.

"Evelyn."

Her name was like breath on the wind, so slight she barely heard it.

"Evelyn."

A female voice whispered her name. Movement flashed in the hall—a blur of white snowy hair. Evelyn's heart skipped. *Fucking flames*, she recognized that hair.

"Tovi!" she hissed.

Riven's sister, her best friend, had found her. Evelyn reached the door frame, her unease warring with relief. Her mind raced. Riven made it crystal clear he and Tovi were enemies, but why would Tovi help her? Could she be trusted?

Another blur passed through the hall, and Tovi stilled, lurking in the center of the hallway. Jade eyes glinted in the dim lighting, and her hair shined like the moon, the only features Evelyn could make out at this distance.

Her guards were gone.

"Tovi, what are you doing?" Evelyn asked.

"We don't have time. Trust me."

Trust her?

Was she out of her mind? Had she forgotten she'd lied all this time? Because Evelyn hadn't, the wound of betrayal was still fresh and raw on her heart. But before she could argue and call out her friend's lies, Tovi zipped past again.

"We must hurry. Follow me!"

Tovi dashed down the hall, her frame thinner than Evelyn remembered. Shadows danced on the dark stones of the castle walls, swallowing Tovi.

Evelyn teetered foot to foot. Her scalp prickled, the hairs on her arms rising. Tovi's betrayal rooted her in place as did Kade's promise. Though she didn't enjoy sitting around, locked away in her tower, her instinct screamed something wasn't right.

"What are you waiting for?" Tovi hissed.

Evelyn spun, her once friend's words tickling the shell of her ear, as if she'd snuck up behind her in the shadows.

"I don't trust you." Admitting the truth aloud was like swallowing shards of glass. It hurt worse than Evelyn had imagined it would, the pain ripping her heart out of its steady rhythm. She hadn't fully processed Tovi's lies, their fake friendship, and being forced to do so now ached.

"Why?" The question echoed in the hallway, its speaker out of sight in the shadows.

"Show yourself!" Evelyn whispered. "Are you that much of a coward you won't face me?"

Silence echoed.

"Come on now." Ahead, Tovi emerged from the darkness of the hall. The hood of her cloak—black, a color her friend never wore—cast her face in shadow. "Don't you want to see your wolf?"

An edge, a slight reediness rang in her tone, unlike Tovi's usually chiming one. Evelyn stepped back. The tone alone made her magic flighty, but her friend's word choice set off alarm bells in the back of her mind. Never had Tovi referred to Kade as a wolf. Huntsman. Betrothed. Valiant commander.

But never wolf.

Tovi tilted her head in that same way Riven did, like a cat ready to pounce. A slippery creep crawled up Evelyn's spine, slinking up one vertebra at a time. Her instinct snapped into the defense.

In a blink, Tovi appeared a breath away from her, toe to toe, jade eyes burrowing into Evelyn's silver ones. Except, this wasn't Tovi. Her face was gaunter with hollow cheeks, her thinner lips curved into a sneer. This vampyr shared a likeness with Tovi as if they were sisters.

Evelyn didn't have time to think about it further as the vampyr pushed against her chest. She lost her footing from the force, but her muscles quivered for a fight, and heat flushed over her, righting her posture. She flared out her hands and ignited her fingertips. The extra light cast the female vampyr in an orange hue, illuminating her frail frame, razor talons, and unruly hair. She wore a fitted dress in gray and a black velvet cape, an onyx broach clasped at the center.

Most definitely, undoubtedly not Tovi. She'd never be caught with her hair so untamed and wearing such dark, drab colors. Not in a hundred years. That much, Evelyn knew.

"Who the fuck are you?" she spat.

The vampyr flashed her thin needle-like fangs in a wicked smile and pounced. She swiped her razor hands at Evelyn as if she wielded a blade. Evelyn lifted an arm to block the vampyr's claws.

The bruising clash of forearm against forearm ricocheted her backward. She ignored the pain and threw her flame. The vampyr dodged it, and the ball of fire blasted into the wall behind her, dissipating and leaving a scorched mark in the stone.

The vampyr attempted to move around her and catch Evelyn from behind, but Evelyn was faster, twisting and grasping the vampyr's wrist mid-swing. Her flaming hand seared pale flesh, and the vampyr filled the air with a shrill screech. With her other hand, she hit Evelyn across the face.

Pain assaulted the bones of Evelyn's nose. Her eyes watered, and her bottom lip stung. Warm liquid traveled over her upper lip while another trailed down her chin. She prayed to the Goddess her nose wasn't broken while a single finger to her lip told her that was split.

"Your blood smells like sunshine." The vampyr clutched her wrist, the smell of burnt flesh permeating the hall as her skin fused itself back together. "Do you taste as sweet?"

The fierce likeness to Tovi frightened Eveyln—clearly they were related, confirming her best friend had withheld so much from her. But that voice. The malice. They were also so different.

The female vampyr charged, but something flashed in front of Evelyn and stood between her and the attacker. Tall, lean, and with long blonde hair swaying behind him, Riven shielded her from the approaching vampyr.

"Stand down, Visha."

Visha.

His command rumbled down the hall like some beast at the end of a cave.

The female vampyr stopped and rolled her eyes as if she were a child told playtime was over. She gave Riven a forced smile with narrowed eyes. "I only planned to bite a little."

Plenty of retorts sat heavy on Evelyn's tongue, but the tension radiating off Riven's taut shoulders made her clamp her mouth shut.

"I gave you an order that Miss Carson was off-limits." His words and anger echoed off the stone.

"You're no fun anymore, brother." Visha peered over his shoulder, her hate and lust-filled eyes drilling into Evelyn. She wanted to pounce, but her shoulders relaxed inch by slow inch. She'd not disobeyed her brother's orders.

Brother.

Evelyn sucked in a breath, looking between Visha and Riven. The vampyrs declaration only solidified what she'd guessed. The likeness to Tovi—the same snowy hair, the otherworldly green eyes, lithe frames. Tovi had a sister. Another secret. Evelyn bristled, hurt and betrayal turning her rigid.

"She never mentioned me, did she?" Visha crossed one arm over her chest and propped her other arm on its elbow, flicking her wrist back as if she couldn't be bothered by her furious brother or Evelyn's flame, still dancing at her fingertips.

This was the enemy Evelyn envisioned. The vicious stare, as if a demon of pure evil lingered in Visha's blood. She was not a scáth or *caillte*. Evelyn's magic sensed the curse, the wrongness prickling the air while that kernel of darkness Belle had mentioned was present in every twitch, movement, and crease of her lips, reminding Evelyn of the White Lady.

"Always so embarrassed of her *other* siblings." Her voice came out shrill, scraping across the surrounding stone. "She barely acknowledges Sven exists."

"Sven does that to himself," Riven muttered.

"Wait." Evelyn shook her head, taking a step forward. "There's another brother?"

The question burst out of her. Resentment clouded her judgment. On the one hand, Tovi's never-ending betrayal made her want to shrink away into the hall, for the castle's darkness to overtake her and swallow her away from Visha's wide, triumphant smile. While the other part of her raged for answers.

"Extinguish your flame," Riven said, not moving an inch.

Evelyn gritted her teeth, ignoring him. She kept her sights on Visha. Why had she attacked Evelyn when Riven needed her blood? Why risk it?

"Miss Carson, Ingrid shared your lovely sister Blair's address a few days ago. Am I wrong?"

Evelyn seethed, exhaling through her nose.

"Extinguish your flame *now* or your sister pays the price," Riven said.

Evelyn drew back her magic, the flames weaving and wavering out of sight and back into her being. The loss of extra light blanketed the hall in more darkness.

"Isn't that a good little pet you—"

"I'm no one's pet!" Evelyn charged, but Riven held out his arm. Vampyr strength held her back.

"She's our prisoner, Visha, one we need alive!" the prince shouted.

"For a spell that might not even work." Visha rolled her eyes. "She's a waste of a good time. Throw her into the rings and let our court have a good laugh. *That's* how you treat a prisoner. Not by pampering them."

A spell that might not even work. *Fucking flames.* Another person who doubted Riven's plans. Evelyn assessed Riven from the corner of her eye. He'd gone tauter than before, his fangs jutting over his bottom lip in a snarl.

"Visha, leave," he commanded.

She harrumphed, jutting her lip into a dramatic pout. "At least punish her for hurting me. Little bitch."

"You attacked me!" Evelyn pushed, but Riven's arm didn't budge.

"And you fell for my little trick, thinking I was Tovi. That was your first mistake. Your second was thinking she'd ever come for you. She won't. All my sister cares about is herself. Don't ever forget it." Visha spun and disappeared, her clattering boots in sync with Evelyn's hammering heart as the darkness swallowed her whole.

Visha's words felt like salt in her already festering wound. She hadn't trusted Tovi's intention earlier, but she had for a moment believed she'd come.

In the stretching silence, Riven headed down the hall. Evelyn followed, her sister's well-being fresh on her mind. The moments ticked by with the clattering steps of Riven's boots and the slapping of Evelyn's bare feet. The static between them extended in the hall until it felt as if the walls were closing in on Evelyn. She could feel the phantom scrape of the stone prickling her skin.

"You tried to escape." Riven's words came down like a gauntlet as he entered her room and stopped at the seating area.

"Your sister tricked me."

Riven shook his head, his jade eyes meeting hers. "Tricked or not, you still tried to leave!" He outstretched his hands and gestured around the room. "After extending some grace, providing you with comfort—"

"Grace?" Evelyn hissed. "I am your prisoner. Do you truly think a grand room and meals negates my reality?"

Riven prowled towards her. Evelyn's spine stayed straight and strong. She drove every ounce of hatred she had for him into her stare.

"You should be more grateful. You deserve a dungeon like Visha implied. But I am trying to keep you alive."

Evelyn hadn't seen Riven in weeks, and time had worn the prince. He still possessed his slinking, arrogant walk, but dark circles rimmed his eyes. Not hunger. Wariness. Fatigue. Something had rattled him, and Evelyn, far too curious, couldn't help but try and get answers out of him.

"A spell only you and the White Lady thought might work. You're risking the entire continent."

In a blink, Riven vanished and then he stood in front of her. His strong, lithe hand grasped her throat and squeezed, forcing Evelyn to look him straight in the eye. Malice spoiled the jade color.

"Tell me, Miss Carson, what would you risk for the ones you love?" he hissed.

Evelyn couldn't answer, struggling to breath. Riven's grip didn't lighten, his vampyr strength crushing her airway. White dots bubbled and popped in her vision while her heart slowed. *Thump. Thump... Thump.* She clawed at Riven's hand. Images of Kade flashed through her mind. His kind, golden eyes were such a beautiful sight amid so much pain.

"Because there are no limits, no extent I wouldn't go. I would do *anything*. Even if it destroyed this world."

With one final squeeze, Riven released her, thrusting her away from him. Evelyn grasped her throat, smoothing her hands over her skin like it might rush air back into her. She glanced at Riven. She trusted his words, felt them because she too understood them. Knew them like her own. Because she'd do the same. She'd burn the world for Kade. For the one she loved the most, she'd burn it all.

The air in Evelyn's room began to move, twisting and collecting into a circle by the door. Through it, the hall shimmered, morphing into a new place, a *different* place. Ingrid stood at the center of a room, one hand outstretched as she drew the circle with her magic.

A *danu*.

Evelyn had seen her sister Blair create them from time to time, a rather powerful ability one with a wind brotannas possessed—to travel from place to place by drawing fractures in the wind. They took considerable energy. The more miles between places, the more draining, and a witch couldn't create a portal to a place she'd never been. The witch's creed was a good rule to follow. Their eyes must've drank it in, their head full of memories, heart beating with familiarity, while their hands must've touched the ground.

Ingrid seemed unfazed, the *danu* within the castle a simple feat. She stepped into Evelyn's room and the circle snapped shut, the view of the hall returning. A black silk nightgown draped around her, as her narrowed stare landed on Prince Riven.

"We're trying to keep her alive, remember?"

"That's Tala's task." He hurried towards the door like a cat prowling its territory. "See that it's done."

Riven vanished into the hall, not even his boots sounding his exit.

Ingrid's bob had a slight curl, and a velvet headband bushed the dark strands out of her face. Sleep clung to her dark eyes. She too had bare feet and a flush blossomed on her cheeks, as if she'd rushed here from bed.

"You're a fool," she whispered through clenched teeth.

"Are insults your only way of communicating?" Evelyn crossed her arms and raised a brow.

"For someone who's a prisoner, you're far too bold."

"Then throw me in the dungeons and be done with it."

Ingrid's eyes flashed with surprise. "Do you have any idea what vampyr court is like? Placing you in the dungeons is a death sentence. Here, you're safe and you'll make it until the end of the spell."

"And when will that be?" Evelyn dared to hope Ingrid would slip the truth.

But the witch shook her head. "That's none of your concern."

She held out her hand. The red pendant of a necklace dropped like a noose as it extended to its full length. It swung side to side, ticking to the inevitable.

Evelyn tried to dampen her fear, but her words came out thick as she whispered, "What is that?"

She recognized the red jewel—a bloodstone like Tala's and the Verena twins'. Yet, the dark metal encasing the stone was different. Strong. Powerful. *Wrong.* The dark magic twined into the jewelry screeched and grated against Evelyn's flame.

"The bracelets were going to kill you, so I made something else. It'll bind your magic but won't have the same fatal effects."

"*No.* I'm not wearing that!" Evelyn stepped back, retreating from the darkness. Panic washed over her. Having her flame back the last few days had been her only reprieve since getting captured. She tried to grasp the mating bond with Kade, tried to warn him they'd lose connection again.

Kade. Can you hear me?

Nothing. Silence and miles rang between them. Evelyn stretched the makings of her heart, sent her love, not her words down the bond.

"You are a prisoner." Ingrid shook the necklace. "This is your shackle."

Kade didn't answer down the bond. The emptiness between their souls was worse than the promise of losing her magic. She had to warn him, make sure he understood.

Evelyn shook her head. "I'm a fellow witch. How could you do this to me? Binding is an atrocity."

Ingrid chuckled. "You demand witch camaraderie, but where was that two years ago when you ran from your betrothal?"

Evelyn gritted her teeth. Ingrid didn't deserve the truth of why she ran like Belle did. Her energy was spent better elsewhere.

Kade!

Moonlight caressed her, a cold and warm touch all at once.

Evelyn. What is it? Are you alright?

Ingrid stepped closer, the dark magic of the necklace whispering and pricking against Evelyn's skin and breaking her contact with Kade. She recoiled at the witch's ability to hold the dark magic, confirming how far the witch herself had played with the wicked.

Evelyn!

Ingrid charged, inching so close her breath mingled with Evelyn's. Dark eyes drilled into her.

"I threatened your sister, but trust that Riven meant what he said. He will stop at nothing. Nothing, Evelyn. If he must scour the entire continent to find your wolf, he will. When he does, he'll make you watch as he kills him. It won't be slow. It won't be merciful. Before he is done, you may as well be dead, too. *Put the necklace on.*"

Ingrid's tone grated against Evelyn's bones while the threat to Kade's life dug its irony talon's into her heart and twisted. What would she do for the ones she loved? The earlier question steeled her resolve.

Anything. No matter the risk. No matter the pain. No matter if she lost a piece of herself in the process.

Kade, I'm alright, she lied down the bond.

What's wrong, love? Tell me. Talk to me. Kade's voice was frantic. Pained.

Evelyn shut her eyes, her breathing shuddering out of her.

But you won't be able to reach me. My magic will be bound again.

A growl echoed in her mind.

It's alright. I'm alright. And I'm going to learn all I can, Kade. I love you.

What? No. Evelyn, listen to me. Stay put. I'm coming—

Evelyn grabbed the necklace. The dark magic against her skin instantly severed the connection with Kade, like a knife sliced through her mind. Her knees weakened, the pain winding down to her heart and cutting the tendons like tiny scissors shearing away. Sweat built at her temples, but Evelyn refused to fall and let the effects of the necklace weaken her resolve.

They may have made her a prisoner, locked her in a tower. They may have threatened the ones she loved and robbed her of her magic. But they could not snuff the fiery rage to defeat them. It coursed and fueled Evelyn's every breath, thought, and action even as she placed the necklace on, even as the sickly, oozy dark magic entrapped hers. More than ever, she understood the lengths Riven would go. She'd do anything for Kade, anything to keep him safe.

Even if it meant risking her own life in the process.

Chapter Seventeen

Kade

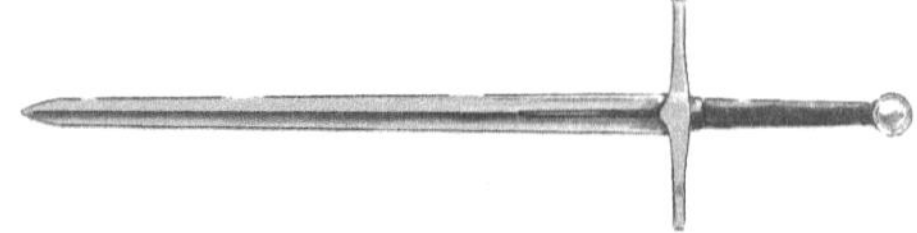

Kade burst from his tent, the wails of distant demons no match against his own.

Evelyn was in danger. No matter what she said, he didn't believe it.

Bound magic.

Kade clutched his stomach, rushing to the misty wall of the Void. Darkness and decay seeped between the divide of Drystan and Sorin. Yet, the air was cold, refreshing against Kade's panicked state. His heart hammered, and he tried and tried again to reach her down the bond.

Evelyn. Evelyn. Evelyn.

His wolf hit a mental wall, different from the one he'd encountered weeks prior. Evelyn's soul, her magic down the bond was close, but he couldn't touch it. Some sort of shield surrounded it, and it bounced and trembled against Kade's efforts. No amount of force cracked its dark walls.

He could no longer reach her.

Ahead, the Void stood as an unmoving wall of thick, gray mist. It ran from the coast to the mountains, miles and miles of mists and fog. It dissipated a foot above Kade's height. Above, endless clouds created a sky of stone. The moon, half visible in Sorin, half lost beyond the clouds, cast a white light onto the Void's wisps.

It felt different, gazing into the gray with plans to journey through it. Kade's wolf had always bristled near it, an underlying *other* in the dew settling in his fur during patrols. The ooziness clotting the air shared a likeness to the White Lady.

Evelyn's presence was gone. Gone. A hole in his heart. In his body and soul. And he could do nothing about it. Trying to grasp it was entirely futile. Attempts fell through his fingers like sand, leaving him far emptier than before.

I'm alright, she'd said.

Moons, Evelyn's voice hadn't shook, hadn't wavered, and yet, through their bond he *felt* the lie.

I'm going to learn all I can.

Kade gritted his teeth while his heart swelled so heavily he had to palm his chest. Fear and pride warred within him. It was so like Evelyn, endeavoring what she could, taking risks. He'd admired it in Callum. The way she entered the castle ruins and the Gray Wood without a glance back. Her bravery had been one of the many reasons he'd fallen for her.

And yet now it left him spent, maddened with worry. If he wasn't there with her, how could he protect her? Kade mustered all his strength, all his might to not rush into the Void and run to her. No matter the many miles. No matter the unknown demons. He'd reach her.

Boots crunched against the frostbitten grass. Behind Kade, Bétar approached, wrapped in a wool blanket. The others rested, their campsite still in the cold, eerie night. Tomorrow, they ventured into the Void.

"When's the last time you slept?" Bétar asked as he joined his side. His breath floated like a lone cloud and bled into the mists, lost.

"I slept earlier." Kade didn't meet his second's stare, focused ahead.

Bétar sighed. "A true sleep. One that wasn't a mere three hours."

Kade furrowed his brows. "Some missions that's all we get. You know that."

"This isn't any mission. You need your rest."

Kade's wolf rose to the surface, a growl sitting at the edge of his throat. He turned to Bétar. "You think I don't know that?"

His second shut his eyes, the moon casting his face in a nightly gray glow. The beads weaved into his red beard glinted and shook as he exhaled.

"I know you're worried," he said. "About Evelyn."

Kade nodded. He didn't have the energy to agree out loud or bother denying it.

"I heard her through the bond again. She called my name." He paused, trying to see through the Void as if Evelyn might emerge. He swallowed the foolish wish. "They bound her magic again. She was warning me, assuring me she was alright."

"Do you trust her?"

"Of course," Kade said. "Evelyn's brave and resourceful. She can handle herself."

"How would I know? You haven't told us about her. You're my best friend, and you found your mate, and it's been dismissed like nothing ever happened."

Kade whirled. His wolf howled, his temperament threatened. "My homecoming wasn't exactly a celebratory moment, Bétar."

"I know!" his second growled. "But ever since we left our village, you've barely slept, ate, or talked to any of us. I've never seen you like this."

Three days had passed, the journey north harsher than usual as the first winter storms froze the mountain terrain. They'd rushed here and had decided to rest for a night before continuing. Kade hadn't wanted to at first, but he'd seen reason. They needed their wits in a land they'd never explored, and a night's rest might make a difference in his team's awareness in a fight. They were on a mission to get Evelyn back. Kade was putting one foot in front of the other. What didn't Bétar understand?

"I'm remaining focused."

The edges of Bétar's lips turned down in a frown. "You're too focused, so much so you're not letting yourself have a moment of peace."

Peace.

Kade wouldn't feel that until he had Evelyn back in his arms, until his lungs inhaled her cedar-and-vanilla scent.

"If it was Yennifer out there, a prisoner of your enemy, what would you do?"

It was dangerous to even challenge a mated male about his mate's well-being. Werewolves were beasts, their powers weaved with shifting and the nature of wolves. Territorial, protective. Bétar, though wide with muscle and the scars of a protector, had practiced patience and kindness when it came to Yennifer. Over the years, Kade had witnessed the love in his second's eyes for the archer, long before he'd ever muttered a word of it—highly motivated by the influence of blueberry ale.

Bétar searched Kade's face. "I'd be maddened with worry, but I'd feel assured she could manage."

"I feel the same way about Evelyn."

Bétar scoffed. "Then why are you strung tighter than Yennifer's bow string?"

"Because I'm on a mission." Again, Kade turned, refusing to meet his second's stare, focusing instead on the mass of mists and shadow.

Bétar sighed. "I'm worried about you."

Bare without his sword and armor, Kade's third-born instinct to protect against more than danger, surfaced. He was supposed to lead by example, put one foot in front of the other, account for every detail, every possibility for his team, and inspire hope and purpose in those around him. His actions, his focus, were not intended to make Bétar concerned.

Did others on the team see his worry for Evelyn? Did his brother? The pressure on his chest, one that pulsed every minute of every day, surged. His skin ran cold, his heart drummed in his ears. Thoughts and reason vanished.

Kade didn't need to see to know his eyes glowed again. They reflected in Bétar's stare and the beads of his beard, blue brightening the moon's light on his second's face. Again, his new power returned on its own accord. Kade tried to grasp it, but unlike his wolf, it didn't feel a part of him.

He blinked a few times, shook his head, and the light eventually dissipated. The pressure in his chest remained, though.

"You need to get that under control."

"It is under control," Kade said.

"You almost blew up the Shield-maiden," Bétar said. A tease sat in his second's tone, the usual banter he'd expect from him. It didn't settle the mood into a lightheartedness, not when Kade didn't have time to hone a new ability, one that frightened him more than fueled him.

One that risked the well-being of others.

"Bétar is right," Linx appeared to his left.

Beside him, Bétar jumped. "Haven't we been over announcing yourself? You about stopped my heart!"

Linx giggled, biting her lip. "Where would the fun be in that?"

Bétar muttered a curse about mages.

Next to Linx, Maxie sat, tail curled around her feet like some bushy blanket. The two had actually bonded during the team's journey north, and side by side, their shared stealthy, mysterious likeness was more apparent than ever. The sight eased a bit of tension in Kade—the fact Evelyn's familiar was faring well enough amongst his team brought him some comfort.

"Kade, no werewolf has possessed a power like that," Bétar said. "Not even Finton."

He exhaled, breath pluming into the Void's mists. "I know."

"Then why aren't you more worried?" Linx asked with a shake of her head.

Worried? Kade didn't have any more worry to give. Not when every ounce was spent thinking of Evelyn.

"My attention is set on getting my mate back." Kade studied the Void, not looking to his friends. The gray taunted him. "It is also not the time or place.

Like you said, no other werewolf has possessed a power or ability like this. Its best to wait until we're home with the help of scholars, witches even."

Linx sighed, eyes softening. "I know you want to get Evelyn back as soon as possible, but I don't think learning this power will stall our progress, not when we need to rest from time to time. Though I am a mage, and your ability might be different from my magik, I can try and help."

"Aye, can't believe I'm saying this, but that's a fine idea," Bétar said.

Kade wrestled with reason. Learning this new power had its benefits. But something deep inside him fought the notion. His worth, his purpose were defined by his abilities to be a protector. He'd experienced it in the wake of his mother's death. He responded and protected his family and pack, honing his potential and setting the example others needed. This new power left him off-balance. As if he weren't good enough to complete this mission. And the more he worried, the worse the pressure on his chest grew.

One foot in front of the other.

Kade repeated his mantra, his teachings from Carena, despite the mounting pressure. Containing it was for the best. He'd deal with this power after he rescued Evelyn.

"The mission is priority," Kade said, allowing his commander baritone to crack the still night air.

Kade left the Void, not leaving room for Bétar or Linx to challenge his decision. Their disapproving gazes scraped across his back with each step to his tent.

CHAPTER EIGHTEEN

ELDRICK

ELDRICK, TOVI, AND THE Gray Fenris trekked through the Void, a barren wasteland of fog, mist, and death. Husks of scorched trees appeared from the mists like skeletal remains, crooked and ominous. Demons howled and mewled unseen, the growls of ones Eldrick had never heard before, grating against his spine and awakening his inner wolf. Desolate, inhabitable. The lack of sunlight for centuries had left its mark on the land swallowed by fog.

Eldrick avoided actual skeletal remains littering his path. Deer, birds, and—

He averted his eyes from a skull that didn't belong to an animal. It jutted halfway from the gray sand, empty eye sockets and molars distinct compared to the animal remains. Perhaps his own kind, a witch, or human. He shuddered. His inner wolf grew restless, agitated, desperate to shift and prowl through the wasteland as a stealthy beast.

But Tovi had warned them not to shift unless absolutely necessary.

A werewolf's magic had been gifted by the Moon God, a deity who possessed light. Darkness lived in unison with the Moon God, the moon shone brightest in the night, but there was no balance in the Void. Darkness craved light, to overshadow it completely. Shifting, using their magic, only called to the darkness more, luring the surrounding demons closer.

More aggravating, Tovi led them. Light on her feet, the enchantress glided through the fog, agile and alert. She squatted to inspect tracks, stopped to listen to surrounding sounds, and sniffed the air at certain junctions.

They'd barely spoken since they'd left Lār. As if Eldrick's angry thoughts reached her, Tovi looked back at him, jade eyes snaring his. For a breath, their two green tones connected. Eldrick's heart skipped. And then, she whirled back around, the connection severing like a snapped rope.

She continued to guide them onward. As a firstborn, *he* was a leader, and the sight of her, beautiful yet a vampyr, leading them forward, made his insides twist. He didn't enjoy following her or how the way she moved made him feel.

Eldrick tempered his pride and attraction.

Though Tovi appeared concentrated on her task guiding them through the Void, not a flicker of alternative agenda, he still didn't trust her—a detail he'd shared with his Uncle Claus in a recent missive.

He'd hurried and sent an update with the last werewolf they'd come across before entering the Void. They were on course, but he was still wary.

There was no place for the warmth in his belly or dangerous thoughts whirling in his mind, not when one fact above all else overrode everything. Tovi was a vampyr, and Eldrick's hate for the monsters marred his perception of the princess. The facts spoke loudly, ones he refused to forget.

The fog began to thin and part, like a curtain unveiling the canyon, and Tovi paused. The others joined her, peering down a sloping descent of boulders and brush, the first signs of vegetation since they left Sorin.

Eldrick's werewolf sight caught the plush canopy of a forest. His brother and Bétar joined him while the others paused to rest.

"There are trees," he said, unable to keep the shock from his tone.

By the set of his brother's taunt jaw and Bétar's furrowed red brows, they were surprised, too.

Tovi nodded. "We're at the edge of the Void, about six miles south of Drystan. The canyon pass bleeds into the southern forest."

"A forest? What else is after the Void?" Todd asked.

"Villages, but I'll make sure we stay clear of them as we head towards the castle."

Yennifer paused her water canteen mid-sip. "Vampyrs have villages?"

Tovi rolled her eyes, inspecting the canyon below like a bird of prey would high up in a tree. "Yes, yes. I know we're all surprised by vampyr civilization, but we don't have time for a rehashing of it all or a full geography lesson."

"Speaking of geography," Bétar said. "The canyon pass looks like rather tight terrain."

Vines and ferns intertwined into a dense brush. Snow and ice clung to branches, and fog filtered through the empty spaces. Eldrick assessed everyone's gear and packs. Bleu snorted into Kade's ear while Maxie sat at the edge, yellow eyes expectant.

"We will have to reconsider our supplies and pack everything else onto Bleu," Kade said.

Again, the horse snorted into his brother's ear, shaking his head as if to say, *How dare you.*

"We should split up," Tovi said. "Some can assess the canyon pass, making sure it's clear while the rest sort out the supplies sooner rather than later. The sun might not shine here, but there is still night. Demons and scáths roam in the later hours."

Silence stretched amongst the group, and Eldrick clenched his jaw. Years of learning strategy warred within him. A narrow, one-way path with no additional exits. She could be setting them up for an ambush. She was wrong. They shouldn't split up. The team's silence indicated they agreed.

Kade's amber eyes flashed with a hint of distrust. They shared a slight glance, a silent conversation. His brother's left brow twitched a fraction, questioning.

Demons wailed again in the distance, far away from the canyon which was eerily still. Only the fog moved, like a ghost skittering between bushels of green and frost.

Eldrick laid his hand over his axe strapped to his hip. The hilt brushing against his palm gave him comfort. Facts and reason ran through his mind while his dislike for Tovi swam in his gut. Emotions aside, Tovi had a point. The canyon pass *was* tight. Eldrick couldn't deny that. In the event they came across scáths or demons, they needed to remain agile. Full packs strapped to their backs wouldn't do. Eldrick's instinct as alpha pushed him to keep his pack, his team, safe, and if he had time alone with Tovi, he could assess her further.

"I'll go," he said. "The rest can work out the supplies."

His gaze snagged with Tovi's. He expected frustration or annoyance, contempt even, but she looked relaxed, thoughtful.

Kade nodded. "That works."

Eldrick discussed with his brother and second-in-command how far they'd travel, no more no less.

"Ready?" Tovi asked him once he met her at the canyon's edge.

No, he wasn't. In the last few days, though they hadn't spoken, they'd been together. They'd hiked through the Vadon Mountains, slept on bedrolls under the stars, and traveled across the plains. Nothing separated them, yet a distance existed between them like the canyon they were about to enter, and through that distance thrummed a palpable tension. It pulled and buzzed, despite Eldrick's better sense. At least he'd had the Gray Fenris as a buffer, the eyes and ears of five others watching.

Now, he'd agree to be alone with her, and it spiked his heart rate higher than the thought of whatever darkness lurked in the canyon.

Eldrick inhaled—*one, two*—grasping for something, anything to give him resolve.

Don't let your emotions cloud your judgment. His uncle's voice filtered through his mind.

That's what he was doing, wasn't he? He was letting his emotions blur his rational judgment. Those emotions had taken root the moment Tovi had begun leading them, and Eldrick had grasped them tightly instead of letting them go and finding solid ground with the facts.

Tovi was their guide, and as much as he hated it, they needed her. This was part of the mission. Get through the Void. Make it to Drystan. Get Evelyn out of the castle. With those facts, Eldrick dismissed both his prejudice against her and his unwanted attraction.

"Let's get moving." He set his shoulders straight and tamped down all that worming emotion deeper and deeper, until he couldn't feel its wiggling madness any longer.

CHAPTER NINETEEN

ELDRICK WAS FUCKED.

He walked alongside Tovi, ensnared by her allure. With the grayish-white sky above, her porcelain skin and hair as white as a dove's, she blended into the wintry landscape as if she were the ruling creature of it. Eldrick supposed she was, as the rightful heir, a fact that showed in her proud, poised walk, in her firm, thoughtful brow, and in her determined jade eyes. Her thoughts swirled there as she assessed their surroundings.

She paid him no mind, and Eldrick wasn't sure why it bothered him. Now that it was the two of them, the silence didn't feel right. Should they have casual conversation? Discuss the weather, perhaps? They barely tolerated one another. Yet, why did that thought leave a sickening feeling in his gut?

His uncle's proposition came to the forefront of his mind. A blaring torchlight of a reminder. Assess Tovi. Learn her motives. Create a sound judgment of her character. Learn what he could about the missing werewolves. At the thought of the latter, he grimaced and looked away from her. He still believed vampyrs were behind the attacks on his people.

A few snowflakes fell, lazy and tranquil, from the never-ending sky of gray. Aside from their crunching footsteps, nothing else moved or rustled until the calming trickle of water sounded from up ahead. Snow blanketed every surface aside from the stubborn needles of the fir trees poking up from the icy layer.

The sound of water grew louder before they reached a creek bleeding into an icy marsh. Trees with bulbous roots rocketed into the sky, trunks enveloped in ice. A sage vine-like plant sprawled across the frozen patches of water. Eldrick struggled to see through the dark water and detect its depth.

"Is this where you kill me?" Eldrick said. "Leave me behind before the others join us?"

Tovi exhaled, schooling her features. She crouched. "Killing you is not on my agenda. At least not today." She flashed him a radiant smile, a hint of fang peeking over her bottom lip.

Eldrick scoffed. She continued her assessment, and he trailed behind her. She stopped, listened, and inspected the forest floor, then repeated the pattern three times.

"What *is* on your agenda?" he asked.

"I'm looking for signs of anything that might kill you instead of me," she muttered.

"I thought you said madras stayed out of the canyon pass during the winter months."

"I said *usually* they stay out of the canyon pass, but if the season gets tough enough, they wander for food. It's why some of them cross the Void. By the looks of the frost, summer was short and bleak this year." She sighed as she brushed her delicate fingers over the fronds of a fern glassed in ice. Her brows scrunched as she shifted her touch to a patch of disturbed snow. The indent was deep, the width of her slender forearm. Tovi rose from her haunches, moving past him and looking out into the marsh. "And so we're clear, there are more than madras demons in Drystan."

Eldrick fought his curiosity of the land no werewolf had entered in centuries. "I suppose you're an expert on all things demon, bloodsucker."

Her nostrils flared, and her knuckles popped as she fisted her hands. She breathed deep through her nose. His words riled her, but she ignored him. Eldrick felt like a child, a young boy teasing a girl he had a crush on. *Moons.* He shook his head. It was this place. It was Tovi's allure. Her enchantress energy.

Whatever it was, Eldrick needed to get a grip.

"We'll wait here until the others join us. The water is moving, so it'll be safe to drink and wash in," Tovi said.

"And when the others join us, what do you suggest we do next? Make camp or move out?"

Tovi crossed her arms, looking towards the sky. "Well, my guess is they'll make it back right before evening and resting during the night would be safest. We need the rest, but I'm not convinced Kade will want to delay."

Eldrick paused. He'd forgotten they were on this mission for Kade and Evelyn. After so many months away, Kade had assumed his role as commander so effortlessly, like he'd never left. He always fell into his duty far easier than Eldrick. His focus was unparalleled. Eldrick didn't envy his brother; instead, he was proud of him, admired his discipline.

"Kade knows his team best," he said. "We trust his instincts."

Tovi scoffed, rolling her eyes as she searched the trees.

"What?" Eldrick asked.

She sighed. "Look, I should preface I think Kade and Evelyn are great together, but I'm not sure Kade's instincts were as sound as you think in Callum. He acted as a huntsman, Cyrus Skender, hiding his werewolf and identity from her. That's how he got close to her."

Eldrick's brother was honest to a fault. Loyal, dutiful. Pretending to be someone else didn't sound like him, so distrust didn't worm its way into Eldrick's belly, but curiosity did.

"Didn't you do the same? Act as Evelyn's friend to get close to her?"

Tovi paused, a flash of something crossing over her features.

Eldrick cursed. "I'm sorry. I wasn't trying to be hurtful, that came out wrong."

"No." Tovi shook her head. "You're right in a way."

Eldrick waited. Snow continued to fall between them. With his arms crossed, Eldrick's inner wolf sat rigid, almost feral to learn more about her.

"I pretended to be someone else, but I never pretended to be her friend. I *was* her friend. About ten years ago, vampyr court was getting worse and worse. Many were falling to darkness, farther than ever before. As my brother became more secretive and gaining favor in the court, I thought it best to keep an eye on her, but..."

"But?"

"I never intended for us to be friends. I was only keeping tabs on her from afar, and then our paths crossed, and it sort of happened. It became real. So real. I've been alive for centuries, and not once did I have a friendship like I did with Evelyn or even her sisters for that matter. It was like she was my sister, too."

Anguish dripped from her tone, and the urge to reach out to her flexed in Eldrick's fingers. He kept his arms crossed, snuffing the urge.

"Why didn't you tell her?" he asked.

Tovi shook her head, blinking wide. "I wanted to, and every time a moment came where I could, I'd talk myself out of it. Maybe she'd hate me? Maybe she'd not accept me as a vampyr? I worried, too, that telling her I could walk in sunlight would put my people at risk. Would she and others on the Guard think we were worse of a threat and march to war? In the end, I remembered the prophecy, and I couldn't jeopardize the promise it held. Not when she hadn't met Kade yet."

Eldrick sucked in a breath. The prophecy. The one that claimed the darkness could be defeated, the one his people had always believed meant defeating the vampyrs. This belief of Tovi's was what he needed to learn more of.

He took a step closer to her. "You really believe in it, don't you?"

"Yes." Her jade eyes tracked his movement.

Conviction. Poise. Adamancy.

All of that enveloped Tovi, and a need— no, a want—etched into Eldrick's tightly woven body. A snowflake fell onto her eyelash. An itch to brush that snowflake away flushed through him. To touch her. Feel her. Stand in her orbit.

Don't let your emotions cloud your judgment.

He lurched away from her, putting her out of arm's reach. Then he cleared his throat and said, "Earlier, you were looking for signs of demons. Show me what you know, what you're looking for. I can help."

Tovi assessed him, head to toe, her eyes narrowing. "Alright." She fell back to the original print in the snow. "I'm looking for signs of what's about." She pointed to the disturbed patch of snow. "Something's been here, but it's not fresh. The snow has frozen and there's a layer on the top."

"Do you know what type of demon?"

Her shoulders slumped. "I'm not entirely sure. It's definitely not a madras. There's only one print, something of the insect variety."

A crawling sensation tickled Eldrick's skin. *That* sounded dreadful.

Tovi hurried away, scouring the snow. Eldrick inspected in the opposite direction, trying to find similar prints as well. In the Vadon Mountains, demons always made themselves known—madras, italogs, béars. They attacked anything in their wake past the Void.

He caught movement in his peripheral vision, but when he turned, the marsh rippled as snow fell on the glass-like water. His hackles rose.

"It's probably best if we meet the rest of the group closer to the canyon base," Tovi said. "Whatever it was—"

The iced marsh cracked like glass as a blue-hued beast burst from the depths. It cried out a piercing roar as water and vegetation dripped from its exoskeleton. Large oval black eyes peered down at them while pincerlike teeth chattered together.

All six of them.

The demon dove for Tovi first. Eldrick ran, his instinct snapping into place as his blood ran cold. He shifted—earlier warnings be damned. Tatters of his shirt burst around him while his leathered armor and axes fell away, and his enchanted trousers molded to his newly enlarged, furred muscle. Across the frozen ground, Eldrick's elongated feet thundered. His face and torso stretched, the muscles screaming. As he grew a foot taller, his vantage widened, and his agility strengthened.

He collided with Tovi before the demon landed a blow, encircling an arm around her waist and pulling her with him as he dove to the side. Jointed arms stabbed into the ground right where Tovi had been standing, leaving an indent similar to the one they'd found in the snow moments ago.

The demon roared again, the sound ricocheting off the trees and surrounding canyon walls. Eldrick and Tovi pulled apart, rolling to opposite sides as the demon pierced the ground again. Eldrick jumped to his feet, squatting into a fighting stance with claws at the ready. He roared, luring the demon's attention away from Tovi.

It's insect-like head tilted and swayed as it came closer and closer to Eldrick. Its body never seemed to end, emerging foot by foot from the depths of the marsh. Eldrick had never crossed paths with such a demon, but he'd seen the likeness in the small centipedes that crawled throughout the forest floor of the Vadon Mountains. Farmers hated them in the Drengr Village. Pests that munched on crops. Yet, this one was clearly not on the hunt for carrots or cabbage. It was a demon of Drystan, hungry for him and Tovi.

The thought of Tovi in danger sent a shiver up Eldrick's spine. *Stars above,* he didn't understand it, but he manifested it into anger, into fight, meeting the demon's attack as it dove for him. He grabbed each of its elongated skeletal arms. Back and forth, the demon and Eldrick shoved and pushed in a game of tug-of-war and wills. Eldrick's paws skidded through the snow while his clawed grip tightened on the demon's pincers.

Beneath his claws, the exoskeleton began to crack and splinter. The demon screeched, flicking its head to the side. The momentum threw Eldrick into the air. After a few moments of flight, he landed with a thud and body-jarring *oomph*.

Dazed, Eldrick struggled onto his back. The demon loomed over him, lowering inch by inch. It had him cornered in a cluster of trees. Eldrick bared his werewolf teeth, sliding backwards.

A chill flushed through. Where was Tovi? Had she run at the first chance she could?

He was a fool. An utterly distracted—

The cry of a female warrior captured both Eldrick and the demon's attention.

Tovi flew through the air, her snowy hair flowing behind her. Eldrick stared, mouth agape. Tovi had transformed. Her fangs had lengthened. They glinted like razors as she landed on the demon's back. She held Eldrick's axes, one in each hand. Both crunched into the demon as she saddled its massive head, one embedded into the back of its skull while the other protruded from one of its oval eyes, black gunk oozing onto the curved blade.

The demon screeched in pain. Yet, Tovi held firm, baring her fangs. She knew how to fight. Her hold on the demon, her grip on the axes. Tovi had held a weapon and fought a foe before.

Eldrick couldn't look away. His stomach fluttered. *Stars above*, he suddenly saw her in a new light.

This beauty, this enigma who threatened to shatter all he knew of this world...

The dark and the light, what was wrong versus right...

Everything turned upside down.

The demon began to shake and writhe above the marsh, and Tovi's snowy, bright silhouette shook with it.

Eldrick growled in his werewolf form, came to his feet, and ran to the marsh's bank. Snow and sheets of ice pushed onto the shore as the water sloshed. He prepared to jump, to latch onto the demon too when it suddenly plunged back into the marsh's depths, bringing Tovi with it.

Eldrick skidded to a halt. The water of the marsh rippled back and forth, sucking Tovi and the demon down into its frozen darkness, then it calmed again. He shifted back into his human form, the cold tightening his sweaty skin.

"Tovi!" he shouted.

Panic chilled Eldrick through skin to bone. He clenched his fists. What should he do? How could he help? He had no weapons, and his werewolf form in water did him little good thanks to sheer size and mass.

But why did he care? Because she'd saved him. *A vampyr*. As a leader, he couldn't look past the honor of what she'd done.

Fuck.

Eldrick paced the marsh's edge, searching for any signs of Tovi. His breath came out ragged.

Nothing.

Not a ripple or a bubble.

"Tovi!" Desperation laced his tone.

Diving in seemed to be his only option. Weapon or not, he couldn't stand idle. Waiting. Worrying. *Stars above*, this was maddening. Muscles bunched, poised, Eldrick was ready to dive into the marsh, but the demon rose to the surface with a ferocious cry, an ethereal princess hanging onto its back.

Tovi had blinded every one of the demon's eyes, where now there was nothing, but ghastly indents left from the axes. One pincer hung limp while the other was gone entirely. Eldrick swore it bobbed on the marsh's surface behind them.

With one last battle cry, Tovi swung around the beast's neck, bringing her to the front. Blind, injured, and spent, the demon had no energy to react as she planted the axe where its neck met its belly. The blade sank so deep that her weight dragged her body and the blade downward, opening the demon at its center.

Its slain form wavered then plummeted to the marsh's shore with a resounding boom. In the chaos, Tovi's slender figure disappeared. Without thought, instinct kicked in, and Eldrick ran. He simply ran. Hoping. Wishing.

What for, he didn't know, not until Tovi's breathless, panting face came into view. Relief washed over him. Eldrick rounded the demon's corpse, crouching down to inspect her. Her fangs had retreated and, though she was drenched to the bone with frigid water, there wasn't a scratch or mark on her.

A million words, a million things, *stars above*, a million emotions expanded and ballooned inside Eldrick's calculating and factual mind. She was safe. Relief. They were alright. Gratitude. She was breathtaking. Awe. Eldrick pocketed all of them. He didn't push them aside, but he didn't let them lead his next words.

"You're full of hidden talents aren't you, Tovi Verena."

Tovi's eyes went wide, her mouth falling open ever so slightly. Then she smiled and laughed. Sweet and songlike. Something embedded deep into Eldrick's core awakened at the sound, and his mouth split into a wide grin and his own laughter bubbled to the surface.

Aside from a dead demon's body and the Void's chilly mist settling on their shoulders, he and a vampyr laughed together until their bellies ached.

CHAPTER TWENTY

E VELYN'S FINGERS HOVERED OVER the crimson pendant resting on her chest.

Once on, the necklace's dark magic burned her skin like a branding iron. The hope of taking it off when alone had died the moment she'd dropped it over her head—the thought of taking it off glued her arms to her sides, the compulsion to not touch it freezing her hands.

The night prior, Ingrid had only watched as the altered bloodstone seared her skin on contact. She claimed to not have known the full extent of its power, but she also didn't seem to care that Evelyn's flesh sizzled two strides away.

Red, blistered burns ringed Evelyn's neck under the necklaces chain. Under her oversized sweater, she'd hidden her wounds, but she wasn't safe from movement, even the simplest twitch. Wool caught on the scabs dotting her chest, and the friction made Evelyn grit her teeth. Tala hadn't returned since the afternoon before, leaving Evelyn alone with her pain, thoughts, and loss of magic yet again.

Her new form of a shackle shared the same, wicked enchantment encasing the window ahead of her. Made of onyx, it shared a likeness to the castle's stone, too. Unlike with the bracelets though, the cage around her magic was not as tight with the necklace. It was like a metal setting, a cage wrapped around Evelyn, encasing her magic behind an invisible wall. It moved freely and lively in her blood, but she couldn't conjure it to the surface or wield it. The contrast was cruel, to grasp hold of it only to be snuffed the last inch before it ignited at her fingertips and raged.

But Evelyn inhaled and exhaled, found her breath, and fought against the temptation to *feel* the rage so close to the surface. It felt dangerous, as icky and heavy as doubt. She could hold onto her rage, her anger and borderline hatred for what Ingrid had done, but how did that help her?

She'd dealt with challenges before, and despite the unfortunate addition to her situation, last night had granted her insight.

Tala, Ingrid, and Belle weren't alone in believing the White Lady's spell wouldn't work. Riven's own sister doubted it, enough she'd risked Evelyn's life for a bit of fun. If so many doubted the spell's efficacy, why did Riven trust it? The question nagged Evelyn like a terrible itch she couldn't reach.

One thing was certain as she laid her hand over the black-as-ink brick beside the window. A winter chill seeped into the burnt pads of her fingers. An ooziness, wicked and thorny, wrapped around her sore digits.

It was all the same.

The dark magic in her necklace, the one she'd faced in Callum against the White Lady, as well as the darkness befalling the castle around her. The darkness and the curse were one in the same. *That* was certain. Evelyn fought her rage and grasped her resolve instead.

Behind her, an audible release of air broke her thoughts. She whirled. Dust fell in the outline of rectangle, like that of a door. Stone gears rattled and grinded unseen as a chunk of the wall fell backward, farther and farther.

Evelyn's first instinct was to defend herself. Perhaps Visha had returned, Riven's order thrown to the wind. She didn't have her magic, didn't have her staff, and the nearest thing was the unlit candelabra. She grabbed it, taking a step back towards the window.

Behind the door, a curse echoed. A *nervous* voice. Evelyn's flighty heart skipped a beat. She recognized that voice as did her magic. Brightness burst from the sliver of darkness and tumbled into Evelyn's room.

Not brightness itself, but a heaping mass of yellow skirts.

"Oh dear," Belle said as she rose on shaky legs. She tossed back her golden curls, revealing her flushed face.

Evelyn lowered the candelabra, her grip not lessening with her fear. "What in the Goddess are you doing?"

The witch scrunched her petite nose. "I'm here to learn more about my brotannas."

"You"—Evelyn shook her head—"revealed a hidden doorway, and you want me to tutor you?" She abandoned her makeshift weapon on the love seat as she hurried over to the new door in her room.

Belle grasped her wrist, halting her investigation. "No, I didn't risk using the secret passages for you to ruin them!"

The young witch glared at the main door to Evelyn's room. *Ah*— the guards. But seeing it was daytime, humans stood beyond the stone walls. Their hearing wasn't as keen as a vampyrs, but still, Evelyn didn't chance them listening in.

She whispered, "*Secret passageways?* Why didn't you tell me about them sooner?"

"First of all, I still don't fully trust you."

"I feel the same way about you," Evelyn said. "You failed to mention Visha was a princess. Your sister's fated is the royal family."

Belle blinked, rearing back. "I assume you knew Visha by name because she is Tovi's sister. She's your friend—"

"Was," Evelyn corrected. "Though I don't even know if I believe that. She withheld a lot from me, including the fact she had other siblings besides Riven."

The blue and green of Belle's eyes softened, and her shoulders slacked. "I'm sorry. I didn't mean to keep that from you, I swear. But I did keep the tunnels from you, because of this." She gestured her dainty free hand at Evelyn. "You'd want to use them."

"I *am* using them." She tugged out of Belle's grasp, eager to learn what lay beyond her room—and equally eager to distract herself from Tovi's bruising betrayal. "How did you even discover the passageways?"

The young witch shrugged. "One gets bored with no friends or anything to do. I found one in my own room, and I've been using them ever since."

"Why?"

Belle furrowed her brows. "Well, it's easier to get around the castle using them. The vampyrs have no idea they exist, so I stay out of their sights."

"I promised you I would help with your magic, and I will, but have you considered the fact that the vampyrs you try to stay clear of, and the one's your sister fears, might be able to walk in the sunlight if I don't get some answers?"

Belle wrung her hands together. Her gaze landed on Evelyn's bloodstone. "I hate that Ingrid made that but... she's my sister."

Evelyn swallowed, bile rising in her throat. She'd betrayed her own sisters by running away and worried about their forgiveness the most. She'd changed. She knew she had, and Goddess, she wanted Blair and Mirella to witness it, too. It's why she needed answers, information. But Evelyn understood a sisterly bond, knew the cost of hurting them and didn't want to place Belle in that position unless she truly believed it.

"I'll teach you your magic now and navigate the passageways alone if that's what you want."

Belle nibbled her lip and gave Evelyn's hands a firm squeeze. "No. I'll come with you."

A draft of colder, mustier air escaped from the hidden passage, and Evelyn glanced through the opening. Glassless windows gave a glimpse of the outside world. A stairwell spiraled down the side of the tower. The darkness below, the fresh air. It buzzed with the secrets of the ancient castle.

And the promise of answers.

CHAPTER TWENTY-ONE

A LUSH DEEP-GREEN FOREST sprawled around Tovi. Ferns covered the path and ivy wrapped around fir trees. Patches of snow and ice dotted the canyon's forest. Flurries fell from a forever gray sky above. The gentle landing of the snow greeted Tovi, and she inhaled the air of home.

Despite the mist, chill, and overcast sky, it *was* home. Down here in the canyon, the remnants of a Drystan winter brought back memories. The splintered, sap-scented wood as her twin brother chopped it for fires. The fresh scent of snow on Tovi's hands as she readied a ball to throw at Riven's head. Their younger sister's laughter when she hit her target, and he cursed. And Sven, the youngest, hunkered unseen and most likely to throw the next.

The weight of memories puffed as a sad and lone cloud as she exhaled. That sibling fun was long gone now. She hadn't broken the bond between them all, but she'd started the first crack. From then, it had split like aging wood. Shame shawled her ancient bones.

It had been miles since the rest of the team had joined her and Eldrick by the swamp. Like she'd predicted, Kade had urged everyone onward. For hours, they dredged the dense thicket of the brush, intent on journeying as much distance as they could before nightfall cast them in wicked darkness.

Or another demon struck.

The feel of its tough exoskeleton against her hands and the burn of its blood as she'd driven Eldrick's axes into its head was a phantom memory sending shivers up Tovi's spine. Its presence in the swamp and its size swirled nerves in her belly. Darkness, heavy and hungry, overtook her home like a parasite she could not destroy. No matter how many demons she killed, another would surface.

Eldrick marched ahead of her, pushing aside an icy branch she'd been too distracted to notice. She smiled softly in thanks and ducked under it. Ridiculous, unwarranted feelings rushed through her, so hot they might defrost the vegetation around them. Worse, Eldrick's words from earlier replayed in her mind.

Tovi Verena.

He'd said her name. Not "bloodsucker." Her actual name, and the sound of it in his voice had sent a jolt to her stomach, sparking a heat she didn't even know she could conjure anymore. Two emotions had flickered in those gemstone eyes of his, but Tovi had been too frightened to see something she wanted to see.

But more importantly, something she didn't need.

Eldrick had told everyone, in dramatic detail, about their account with the demon. Tovi recalled his eyes alight with awe, but the team's reaction had stopped her short. Todd had gripped the dagger at his belt tighter. Bétar's eyes had narrowed, and Yen's blue eyes had widened. Eldrick's tale had made them see her in a new light.

Gaining their trust would be harder now. She wasn't some princess on a diplomatic errand. Tovi could fight. She'd trained with daggers, swords, sometimes axes for two decades. *Goddess,* she'd mastered a bow and arrow at seventeen. She wasn't simply a vampyr in their eyes, but a trained one who'd withheld her skills. Kade, too, held an edge of new distrust. She'd not shared her fighting abilities during their time on the ship. And she'd give him no new information now. Revealing how she was trained and by who entered dangerous territory.

With their deepening apprehension, questions would follow. Tovi tensed, straightened her shoulders and continued walking. Those were questions she'd rather avoid, especially with Eldrick.

"Is Drystan always like this?" Todd asked.

Tovi paused, turning to look back at everyone on the team.

"Like what?" Her tone came off harsher than she'd intended, but days of judgmental stares, comments, and energy had begun to wear her down. They might as well have been throwing Eldrick's axes at her, and every so often a few would graze her skin and cut her open. Her need to feed soon didn't help either. Hunger nipped in her empty belly.

"Well," Todd shrugged. "Wet and dark." His eyes peered above the tree canopy. The gray from earlier shifted to a darker gray. Soon night would wash over them.

"Sadly, yes," Tovi said. "The darkness causes the clouds, which blocks the sunlight."

"All year?" Yennifer's eyes went wide.

Tovi nodded, her lips thin and eyes downcast.

"What about food and farming?" Bétar asked. "How do you feed your people with no sun?"

The mood of the team shifted. Bétar cursed as someone hit him in the stomach. A glance back, and Tovi found Yennifer with the end of bow jabbed into her mate's gut, sending him a withering look.

"We've adapted our crops to fit the climate better, ones that like the rain and the overcast. Everything else we import."

Again, silence stretched except for Tovi's boots crunching on the frosted path. She dreamed of potato or pumpkin soup, the promise warming her tired bones. Her mouth watered at the thought of blueberry biscuits slathered with butter.

"It's actually persimmon season if I recall—"

"Persimmon?" Bétar annunciated the word slowly.

"I still can't believe vampyrs eat food," Todd said.

Tovi stopped and whirled. "What?"

Todd shrugged. "Well, I thought—we thought—you only ate, you know…"

She didn't wait to see the judgment, confusion, or horror regarding the fact she drank blood. She turned her back on them, continuing up the path, trying to tell herself she didn't care. Besides, it was hard to get angry at the weapons master. Todd was far softer than his blades, a naturally kind soul.

"Also, what is it with this bloodstone of yours? Why do you have a bloodstone and others don't?" Todd asked another question. "Wouldn't that make the days and nights easier?"

Tovi shut her eyes and sent a prayer to the Sun Goddess to save her. "They're extremely rare. Only a handful in court have them."

"Like?"

Tovi didn't think, she answered Todd's question to get it over with. "Some of my siblings and I, of course, and some of those on the royal council."

"Siblings?" Kade's voice barked from behind.

Shit.

He walked up the path. "How many siblings do you have?"

"Three," Tovi muttered.

The two Drengr brothers shared a glance, but Tovi didn't balk. She remained still, shoulders back.

"Three? Two more than I knew of." Eldrick asked, "And are they enemies, too? Riven's allies? Does he have the entire vampyr court on his side?"

"No, he doesn't have the entire court. He has Visha, the youngest of us, because he doesn't leash her violent tendencies." Tovi sighed. "Sven, on the other hand, is a different story. He stays out of vampyr court and royal affairs entirely. I last saw him fifty years ago, and it was only in passing amongst traders."

"Those are rather important details you failed to mention," Eldrick muttered, walking ahead.

"How so?" Tovi narrowed her eyes.

Eldrick threw up his hands. "You don't have sound relationships with a single sibling. Tell me, how many allies do you actually have amongst your own people?"

"If it was an equal fight of vampyrs against vampyrs, I wouldn't be seeking out alliances with werewolves, now would I?" Tovi said.

"Arguing is a waste of time." Kade pushed through them and continued farther up the path. "We have a few hours before nightfall. Let's keep moving."

"We can't ignore the fact she lied—"

"Lied?" Tovi scoffed. "I didn't tell you something you never asked about. That's hardly lying."

"Fine. You withheld information, but what else are you withholding?"

Tovi steeled her spine and charged towards Eldrick. Singing her praises one moment, accusing her of being a liar the next. *Goddess*, his mood swings, his perception of her, was giving her whiplash.

"Let's get this straight, wolf," Tovi jabbed her finger into his chest. Someone gasped behind them, and another breathed a curse. "I am withholding plenty, because similar to how you feel about me, *I. Don't. Trust. You.* Trust goes both ways. When you learn to trust me, I'll grant you the same courtesy."

Eldrick gritted his teeth, a growl rumbling low in his chest. "I'm glad to hear we're on mutual ground then."

"Splendid." Tovi strutted past him. "Kade's right. Let's keep—"

A scent settled into the fog and ferns. Sharp lemon. Tovi inhaled again, willing her senses to be wrong. Her nostrils stung from the cutting smell while another more distant scent mingled with it.

Tovi whirled, searching the mists. *Please be wrong.* Sounds in the distance, voices, disturbed the silent canyon.

"Does anyone—"

Tovi sprinted and laid her hand over Eldrick's mouth. His gem-colored eyes widened as their skin made contact.

"Everyone off the path! Now!" she hissed.

The team darted out of sight, some going left, others going right. Kade hurried Bleu and Maxie farthest away, falling under the drape of mossy vines.

Heavy booted steps grew closer. Tovi cursed, pushing Eldrick off the path. They landed, tangled together in overgrown ferns, with Tovi lying atop Eldrick's chest. She tried to fidget off, but he wrapped one arm around her waist and held her firm while the other laid a finger over her lips, silencing her. Covered by a canopy of large, wide fronds, they were hidden from sight, but face-to-face with Eldrick, Tovi couldn't see those who now strolled their path.

With scent alone, Tovi guessed. "Vampyrs," she mouthed to Eldrick.

He nodded, eyes trailing every inch of her face. The footsteps stopped, but so did time. Eldrick's stare ensnared her, and for a moment, she forgot they were hiding. Her heart slowed, her breathing stopped. The rivets of green wavered like the polar lights in the far north, the dim light glinting at different angles.

Alive. Breathing. Warm.

Wonderment washed over Eldrick's face, and unlike on the path or after the demon attack, Tovi couldn't look away, not with other vampyrs so close. His eyes dropped to her lips, which she'd bitten to remain still. Eldrick's nostrils flared, and a warmth spread from her belly to her toes, time and tension pushing and pulling between them.

"I swear I smell wolf," a male voice muttered.

Tovi and Eldrick snapped to attention. Tovi released a breath while Eldrick blinked rapidly. Leaning away from him and whatever moment they'd shared, Tovi tuned into the conversation on the path.

"Of course you smell wolf," a female voice said. "There's five them up ahead in chains."

Eldrick's entire body trembled then his hand on her waist tightened with a clawed grip. Tovi chanced a quick glance behind her and internally cursed. His hand was shifting, fur sprouting from his sun-kissed skin.

"Stop," she mouthed. "Wait."

Eldrick bared his teeth but listened. He breathed through his nose, in a simple one, two tempo. Tovi rose and fell on his chest as he calmed.

"I know we're escorting werewolves," the male vampyr hissed. "But I swear I smell more, like it's coming from over there."

Eldrick pulled Tovi closer to his chest, and she buried her head into the crook of his neck, molding against him. Eldrick's heart hammered beneath her, and his scent consumed her, the pumping of blood at his neck over and over again, the way he held her fiercely yet gently, his arm around her waist. Her fangs pierced her gums, screaming to be set free and sedate her growing hunger with the delicious, warm blood coursing inches from her.

A boot stepped closer and into the brush, fern leaves crunching as one of the vampyrs approached. Tovi readied for a fight, her fangs jutting from her mouth.

"Come on, Laz," the female vampyr said. "It's the fog making you wary. I'm ready to get out of this cursed Void. Let's go, we also have fighters to deliver."

Boots retreated from the ferns and back onto the flattened path, their steps became faint, distant, and then nothing at all.

For three whole breaths, Tovi and Eldrick remained as they were, molded to each other. His heart raced like a caged bird. She nuzzled closer to him. Neither were inclined to move.

Until someone on the team whistled light like a songbird.

"Eldrick? Tovi?" Kade whispered.

Like their bodies suddenly burned the other, Tovi and Eldrick separated in an instant, rolling and standing in the ferns. Eldrick avoided making eye contact with her, and Tovi stepped farther away, creating a wide berth between them.

Kade ducked under the vines and back onto the path with Bleu and Maxie. Linx emerged from foliage, and then three other silhouettes in the fog sharpened to Yennifer, Bétar, and Todd.

"Did everyone else hear them mention werewolves?" Todd asked.

"I have the same question," Kade said.

Before Tovi could comment, a clang of metal accompanied by the creaking of wood sounded in the distance.

"Move!" a voice hollered deep into the fog.

Metal chimed like chains being rattled together. Tovi's gut churned, and she hurried up the path.

"Stay quiet," she whispered to the others.

Eldrick scowled so hard Tovi feared his jaw might crack his molars, but he moved without a word, staying quiet as Tovi instructed.

The canyon walls shrank to scattered boulders, the fog and mists lowering and lowering until an army of fir trees stretched for miles.

Flattening herself against a boulder, Tovi peered out into the forest, finding the snaking path through the patches of snow and layered pine needles. Ahead, the worst of her fears manifested, and a stone, as heavy as the boulder she pressed herself against, plummeted in her belly.

"Stars above," Kade whispered at her side.

Five werewolves walked in unison, one behind the other, chained together. Ten vampyrs surrounded the formation. Tovi swore their taloned hands glared black in the dim light.

"*Moons*, did we stumble upon the missing werewolves?" Bétar asked, his ruddy cheeks as red as his beard.

Yennifer gripped his shoulder, tears brimming in her eyes. "They're in chains."

"You knew this was happening, didn't you?" Eldrick's voice trembled behind her.

"What?" Tovi seethed.

His golden-brown hair was matted to a forehead sheened with sweat, and he shook with rage. Hatred laced the rivets of his green eyes.

"Don't pretend like you didn't know." He stepped towards her, a hand on his axe.

Tovi shook her head. "I didn't know, I swear." Her voice came out shriller than she expected, desperate. "I've been away from Drystan for months."

"You're a liar."

Eldrick's constant doubt of her was worse than any blade carving her skin. Each attack left a mark, scarring her battered heart and dampening her resolve.

Yet, Tovi *hadn't* known. Amongst so many secrets, this was the truth. Never, not even when Tovi was at her worst, would she have placed werewolves or anyone for that matter in chains.

"I am not a liar," she said, back straight and poised.

"You never mentioned your siblings or your ability to fight. Both would've been nice to know on our end. What if this is another detail you've chosen to *withhold*?" Eldrick asked.

"If you recall, my ability to fight saved your life hours ago!" Tovi yelled. "What difference does it make if I told you or not?"

She and Eldrick had met step for step and now stood toe to toe. Jade clashed with emerald. Winter eclipsed spring. Their wills warred. Fog dissipated around them, their heated argument raising the temperature of the air.

Tovi's chest rose and fell. Only moments ago, it had risen against Eldrick's under a canopy of fronds as their bodies molded together. Now, there couldn't be enough distance between them, miles apart from seeing eye to eye.

Hot with rage, Tovi's fangs pricked her bottom lip, and the tip of her talons pierced her fleshy palms. She may not shift into a wolf, but a monster lay in Tovi just the same. *Goddess*, this werewolf unraveled her and threatened to unleash that monster at every turn.

Tovi tightened her fists despite the cuts. The pain kept her balanced and in check. This journey was supposed to be difficult. Traveling across the Void, through Drystan, encountering demons. Not to mention everything they faced when they arrived at the castle.

Yet, Eldrick made everything worse. How could Tovi solidify this alliance if she was up against this stubborn, suspicious werewolf at every turn?

Stepping closer, he whispered, "How can we possibly trust you when there are so many secrets?" Eldrick gestured towards the werewolves. "Or that you knew this was happening—"

"I didn't—"

"Stop!" Kade roared and stepped between them.

Tovi shut her mouth, shame washing over her.

"We don't have time for this bickering." Kade eyed each of them. He tied his hair into a small bun with a leather cord, slicking his damp hair away from his face. "We're freeing those werewolves, understood?"

All of them nodded, and Tovi shifted from foot to foot. *Her* people had chained theirs. She swallowed bile, digging her nails into her palms once more, and refused to meet Eldrick's hateful stare.

She wanted to claw at his face and wipe that hate right away. But she had a worse enemy to fight at the moment—her own people.

CHAPTER TWENTY-TWO

KADE

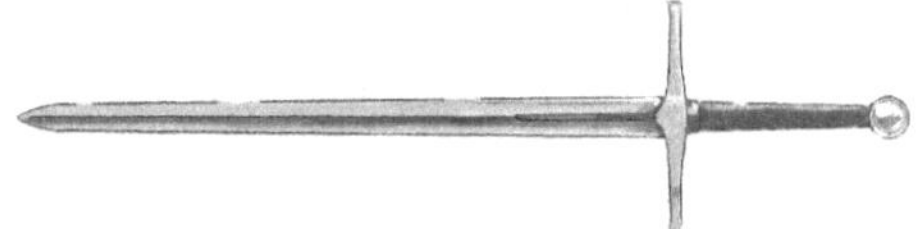

MINUTES TICKED BY. PINE needles crunched. Their hushed breaths became lost to the forest breeze.

Linx's magik snuffed the sound of their approaching steps. They stalked the chained like a pack of wolves, uniformed and on course.

Upon closer inspection, there were eleven total vampyrs. Two rode war horses, one stationed at the front and the other at the rear. Two vampyrs walked alongside each horse and the rest flanked the chained werewolves.

The crack of a whip broke the ominous air, and a growl rumbled through Kade's chest. He and his brother locked eyes twenty yards apart. They'd been here before, stalking prey as a team. Bétar spotted Eldrick and Todd behind Kade. The four of them approached, tree to tree, inching closer and closer to the chained werewolves.

Farther behind, a swirl and dance of leaves fluttered on the path as if wind kicked up the debris. When Kade narrowed his eyes, his werewolf sight detected a petite silhouette.

Linx.

Another crack of a whip demanded his attention. Todd cursed behind him.

"I'm going to fucking gut them," Todd whispered. "Slowly."

A similar sentiment flushed through Kade, and his heart hammered in anticipation.

Tovi and Yennifer were nowhere to be found amongst the trees, as planned. Tovi had proven to possess a considerable amount of strength that negated her size, allowing her to carry Yennifer, bow and all. If it had been any other instance and not moments before a fight, Kade would've roared with laughter at Yennifer's scowl as Tovi carried her farther up the forest, out of sight and undetected. He'd give money to see that disgruntled look on his archer's face again.

Bétar had managed a chuckle, but his second's downturned brows and narrowed eyes were full of concentration now. Flush against a pine tree, the brawny werewolf stalked with the grace and poise of a real beast.

In formation with his team, sword in hand, a rightness settled over Kade. A purpose. A target. Perhaps journeying day after day had felt like little progress, Evelyn out of reach no matter the miles or days that passed. But did freeing his people veer him too off course?

He and his wolf both itched for a fight. The restless energy pushing in his chest festered under his skin, threatening to unleash. Kade tried to rally it in, tugging and pulling his last shred of calm dangling at the end of a rope. The rope groaned, ready to snap. This energy, this feeling, built within him at an alarming rate

One foot in front of the other.

He peered around the trunk of the tree and through the crossing branches. Twenty-five yards ahead, chained werewolves continued on. He flicked his fingers forward twice, Eldrick nodded, and they began their approach. They ran, crouched, from tree to tree, weapons at the ready.

Unlike the Vadon Mountains, no songbirds chirped, no squirrels rustled in leaves, and no deer scraped against bark. The trickle of a stream didn't even sound in the distance. Silent and still, the forest raised an eerie chill on Kade's arms.

Above, the low blanketing clouds stuck tendrils of mist into the canopy of trees like the outreach of a ghost's hands, waiting to grab them from above. Fog that fell in dollops moved like slithering shadows, seemingly sniffing out the team and inspecting their presence.

A whistling sound broke the silence, and the pop of a shattering breastbone followed. The vampyr leading the convoy slumped on his saddle, an arrow protruding from his dead heart. The other vampyr reared his horse, shouting to the others. The werewolves' chains rattled as they drew closer together.

Chaos ensued.

Kade and his team rushed from the tree line. Eldrick ran with his axe at the ready, his war cry bellowing with Bétar's. Todd threw his daggers, silver dashing through the air. One embedded in the center of a vampyr's forehead with a deafening thud. With wide eyes, the vampyr sank to his knees as his flesh festered black. The other dagger grazed the arm of a vampyr flanking the back of the line of captive werewolves. He screeched in pain, flaring out his taloned hands.

He charged, but Kade swiped up and across his chest. His blade made contact, slicing through the vampyr's armor and pale skin. The vampyr turned black as stone before he hit the ground.

Three down. Eight to go.

The vampyrs weren't scáths—no black veins rimmed their eyes, and their movements were calculated, trained. Not hungry beasts out for blood but warriors, ready for a fight.

That pulse deep within Kade traveled upward. Energy compressed and expanded within him. His breathing quickened, but Kade swung his sword left then right, slaying the next vampyr that charged.

Moons.

Exertion, fighting, release. Kade relished the ability to fight away his worry.

To his left, Todd shifted into his black werewolf form, towering over two screeching vampyrs. To Kade's right, Linx appeared out of the flurry of upturned pine needles.

"The werewolves, Linx!" Kade cried. He clashed with a vampyr, offering Linx a clear path.

"On it!" she said.

Sparks sprayed from Kade's sword as it clanged against vampyr's sharp talons. They were black like a scáth's, the talons dipped in ink, but the black didn't travel up his arm. For a breath, the shift reminded Kade of a werewolf. But a different magic, that familiar ooziness, fizzed in the air. His opponent wasn't a *caillte*. It had not yet given in entirely to darkness, as Tovi had warned him of. But it had leaned into darkness, and the black of its nails, that oozy magic, hinted at the horrible monster that would leap into life when the vampyr finally lost himself.

Had Evelyn faced the horrors of these talons or fangs?

Kade lost focus and sidestepped too late. The vampyr sliced one shoulder with his blade and the other his talons. Kade roared. Pain blinded him, and his inner wolf howled. Kade unleashed weeks of buried wrath.

Left, right. Defend, counter, attack. With each step and slice of his blade, Kade advanced.

A simple overstep, and the vampyr stepped into Kade's attack. His blade sliced his taloned hand clean off. The appendage dropped with a thud and bounded over Kade's boots. As the vampyr screeched to the misty sky, he left his middle exposed. Kade swiped thigh to neck. Split open, the rest of the vampyr's flesh blossomed black, and his dead body dropped.

Kade flicked blood off his blade and took in the rest of the fight. A second arrow fell from the sky, killing the one vampyr left atop a war horse. Eldrick struck one axe into the shoulder of a vampyr, and then struck again to the throat. Bone and blood crunched under the blade.

Ahead, Todd fought in his werewolf form, dark fur matted with sweat and blood. His claws dug into his opponent's shoulder, and he thrust them into a pine tree. Bones snapped, the tree shuddered, and the vampyr didn't rise to attack again.

Seven down. Four to go.

Beastly pride flushed through Kade.

Out of the fray of fighting, Linx had gathered the werewolves farther back. Chains and shackles littered the forest floor. Those freed had joined the fight, assisting Bétar with a vampyr wielding two swords.

They were winning—

"Ah!" Kade growled. He dropped to the ground, pain lancing through his ankle.

A female vampyr, disembodied from the waist down, crawled across the forest floor with her talons. A trail of crimson streaked behind her severed torso, and she swiped at the back of his knees despite her grave injuries. She wailed, fangs glinting like daggers.

"Son of the God," the female vampyr hissed.

Kade flipped onto his back and pushed away from the vampyr. His wolf wrestled to be released, his skin rippling with the urge to shift. He scurried away on his elbows, kicking his boot's heel into the female vampyr's chin. She laughed and crawled faster.

"Are you as fun as your witch? Will you scream like she did?"

Kade went cold.

Silence rang in the forest. His icy fear sucked the noise of the chaos around him, and—

Kade shifted.

His wrath, worry, fear, and strength took over and forced him into the beastly warrior he was. He roared in his werewolf form, claws elongated, muscles rippling.

Stronger. Faster. *Angrier.*

Kade's inner beast and power met, collided into a newness he gladly embraced.

No one threatened his mate. *No one* harmed her. *No one* said an ill word about her.

And lived.

The vampyr's earlier glee faded. Her eyes widened in terror.

Kade grabbed something—he wasn't sure, maybe an arm or her neck. He didn't care. It didn't matter. He pulled, enough the vampyr met her end in more pieces than she'd been in, this time, dead.

Kade roared. *Moons,* he wished Evelyn heard his battle cry. Felt it down the bond.

A crunch snapped him back to the present. His brother's axe stuck from a vampyr's skull, blood seeping over the wedged blade.

"Two to go," his brother said.

Kade shifted from his werewolf form. His hands flexed at his sides, sticky with the stain and crust of blood. He joined Eldrick, scouring the fight for the last two vampyrs.

"You're our Princess!" one cried.

In a cluster of trees farther up, Tovi held a dagger to her kin's throat, fangs bared. Her hands had transformed to talons, fangs elongated into an animalistic snarl.

"We are your people," the vampyr said. *Pleaded.* His eyes begged for mercy.

Tovi hesitated for a fraction of a moment. A flicker in her scrunched brows, but then she lowered herself eye to eye with the vampyr.

"No subject of mine chains innocents."

A single, deliberate swipe against the vampyr's throat and red droplets scattered across the princess's face, along with pain. She shut her eyes, hurt evident in her usually poised posture. Princess Tovi Verena had killed the vampyr, but she hadn't wanted to.

Eldrick stiffened, and he lowered his axe. Dirt and grime covered every inch of his brother, even in his knitted brows.

"She meant those words." Eldrick blinked and shook his head, as if he hadn't intended to speak out loud.

Kade, too, heard the truth in her voice. He'd heard it for weeks now, and his anger for Tovi's betrayal had simmered to frustration. But would his brother ever look past her being a vampyr? The glimmering of his eldest brother's eyes held a twinkle of promise, but Kade didn't linger on it. Later. When they had a moment alone, he'd finally talk to his brother.

Ten down. One more to go.

Kade scanned for the last vampyr, accounting for his team. Bétar and Yennifer reunited, forehead to forehead as they leaned against each other. Linx attended to the wounds left on the once chained werewolves. Kade half expected to see Todd wrestling with the remaining vampyr, but Todd had shifted back, bare torso and feet dirtier than Eldrick. Confusion speared through Kade. Where—

A horse galloped past, a pale rider atop of it.

No. No. No.

Kade cursed and whistled. Bleu galloped by at full speed, and he swung atop his gray steed and urged him forward.

"Faster!"

Bleu obeyed, hooves thunderous under his ferocious gallop. Voices cried behind him, but Kade ignored them, his target the vampyr ahead. Twenty-five yards away.

To the music of the horses' pounding hooves, Kade's energy twisted and turned with a drumming fear. He thought of Evelyn, the vampyr's earlier words ricocheting in his worried mind.

"Will you scream like she did?"

Stars above. He wasn't with Evelyn, protecting her. Kade knew there was chance the vampyr had lied, but it didn't matter. Kade didn't know what Evelyn endured. The unknowns ate away at him, as did his inability to be there at her side through whatever she faced.

Her silvery-gray eyes. Her soft smile. The way her brow furrowed while she thought. Kade tried to ground himself with thoughts of her, thoughts of who he was fighting for.

Bleu caught up the other horse. He bumped into it, shoving the vampyr off his saddle. Kade dismounted Bleu in one fluid motion and blocked the vampyr's oncoming attack. Talons hit steel. Black battled silver. Hit after hit, step after step, push and pull as Kade and the vampyr fought, the energy in his core rising to the surface.

"Kade!"

Whoever called his name, his brother, a team member, whoever it was, they were too late.

Kade exploded.

A wave of energy, *his* energy, of uncontrolled power sucked the sounds of reality to a deafening silence and then released into an invisible wave.

Magic. Power. Strength.

All of it emitted from him. It collided into the vampyr, sending it through the air as pale flesh flayed away until it was nothing but naked bone.

Kade fell to his knees, spent. He dug his hand into the earth, trying to ground himself and regain his breath. The vampyr wouldn't make it to Riven. The werewolves had been freed. He'd continue to Evelyn—

"Kade!"

Eldrick appeared in front of Kade. His eldest brother's eyes were wide, roaming over him. He placed his hands over Kade's shaking shoulders, steadying them as the other members of the Gray Fenris surrounded him. Linx pushed Eldrick aside, grabbing Kade's face and peeling his eyes wider as she inspected his pupils.

"Moons, Kade, what in the stars above was that?" she asked.

Kade tried to stand, but his legs buckled. His new power had exhausted him. Eldrick grabbed his shoulder before he fell completely to the ground.

"I think you need to be still for a moment. That... power or magic or whatever it was, Kade..." His brother shook his head. "It was immense."

Ahead, only the husk of the vampyr was left, steam rising from its scorched body. Kade blinked. He had done that. His *power* had done that.

Kade tried to move again, blinking past the heaviness and jarring sensation behind his eyelids. His fractured reflection, tired and worn amber eyes, stared back at him in the crumbled pieces of his sword. His torment was as sharp as the shards.

"Fuck," he cursed. He peered up at his team. "I don't really remember what happened or how I did it. Something... exploded."

"*You* exploded," Bétar said with a shake of his head.

Kade blinked, looking to the others for more of an explanation.

"It was like a bluish moonlight," Yennifer said. "As if you were wielding it like some sort of magic."

Kade swallowed, a stone of worry dropping to the pit of his stomach. "Like a witch's magic? A brotannas."

Linx shook her head. "Not like one I've ever seen. It wasn't wind, earth, fire, or water. It didn't even look like flame."

Kade's body wavered, unbalanced and pulsing.

"That was worse than in Callum," Tovi said.

Worse. As if he were some liability.

Questions gripped Kade, but he had to keep pushing forward, to remember his mission. He was the protector, the leader. He set the example, was the glue that kept everyone together. He didn't have the time to face this, not when it begged the question of whether he was capable of getting Evelyn back in the first place.

"I'm fine." He rose on shaky legs, fighting his exhaustion.

"You're not fine," Eldrick said. "Whatever this new power is, you can't control it."

Kade gritted his teeth. "We aren't going to find answers in this forest. We rest for the evening and tend to the werewolves. At daybreak, we continue our journey north."

No one objected, no one questioned, but Kade didn't miss the hesitancy in everyone's movements or the quick glances the rest of the evening.

As if he might explode again.

Chapter Twenty-Three

T HE SCENT OF WET stone and the howl of the high winds wrapped Evelyn and Belle as tightly as the stairwell's spiral. Snow snuck through the windows they passed under, melting into the dark stone of the tower and melding with the bleeding mildew stains.

They had about an hour before the servants arrived with lunch. Not a moment longer to spare. Evelyn had been keeping track of their comings and goings, along with Tala's. She risked a surprise visit from the war adviser, but the chance to explore was too valuable to ignore. Eagerness thrummed through Evelyn, and her snuffed magic danced with excitement.

Prior to descending, Belle had drawn what she knew of the castle. The layout provided more context to the buildings and halls Evelyn had studied from her tower. This part of the castle wasn't used, according to Belle. The grand hall, the throne room, residential quarters, a library, even the dungeons were located levels and stairs away from her prison.

"I think it was abandoned after the king's death," she had said.

Silent and steady, Evelyn and Belle explored where the stairwell led first. Evelyn counted three doors as they passed, two turns between each. Before the lowest level, there was an iron gate with rusted hinges; its spiked finials squeaked from the tunnel breeze.

"That's where I came out of," Belle confirmed.

"And where's it lead?"

"Abandoned servant halls." The young witch shivered.

Eveyln nodded, pocketing the information for later.

When they reached the bottom, the stairs sank into an icy sludge puddle, the water murky and rotten. Evelyn plugged her nose, and Belle rushed back up three flights of stairs, putting distance between herself and the smell.

"That's horrid," Belle said.

"I couldn't agree more." She peered up, the underbellies of the stairs dripped with icy dew. "I suggest we try the first door. If we run into trouble, it's the closest to the tower."

With a swallow, Belle nodded and followed Evelyn.

Once there, Evelyn placed her ear flush against the stone. Nothing else but stuck air sang on the other side.

"Can you send out your magic?" she asked. "See if anyone or anything is on the other side?"

"I can try."

Belle flattened her hands against the door and closed her eyes with an exhale. With the bloodstone, Evelyn couldn't feel Belle's magic or power enter the air, but she recognized the witch's focus—the furrow of her brow, the ease of her shoulders as she connected with her magic. Longing spread through Evelyn, and she swallowed the unpleasant taste of it.

Her eyes fluttered open, and her shoulders relaxed. "Nothing, not even a human servant."

Evelyn brushed her fingers over the outline of the door and pressed against it, expecting to find resistance, but it budged. The door groaned open, and both of them held their breath.

"I'll go first," Evelyn whispered.

She took a deep breath and crept through the passageway, poking her head out first.

Books awaited her.

Endless stacks of them. Goddess, Blair would've been envious. Evelyn tripped over a few as she stepped into a small area, books lining shelves, piled high in the corner, and arranged on the ground so they acted as a bench for others. Large ones, leather-bound ones, one's tiny enough to fit into a back pocket. Evelyn ran her finger over some of the spines, titles of Old World and New World classics textured against her finger.

Belle emerged from the stairwell, cerulean eyes bright. "Rather delightful surprise, don't you think?" she whispered.

Evelyn smiled in agreement but remained cautious as she slunk against the right side of the library. Without her magic, Evelyn felt at a disadvantage. It hadn't been the first time she'd walked into the unknowns without it, but Drystan castle was different, its secrets felt like static in the air compared to Callum's ancient magic.

She inched farther into the space. The nook curved around a bend, as if this space were a back closet, filled with texts its owner had abandoned.

"Can you send out your magic again?" Evelyn whispered.

Belle nodded. After a beat she said, "There's nothing near."

As they entered the larger space, more mess greeted them. Books, maps, scrolls. A large floor-to-ceiling window drenched the room in a grayish light. Bookshelves lined the left wall while a map of their world, Sorin and Torren, stretched across the right wall, giant pins scattered across it. A desk manned the front, a sitting area overrun with books to the left, and a large table covered in maps to the right.

Evelyn weaved her way through columns of books to reach the desk, eager to learn more about its contents and possible owner. Belle followed behind her, both silent on the balls of their feet.

On the desk, piled shipping logs sat in the left-hand corner, and the purple Verena crest, angry and deep, glared at them.

"Oh dear, is this Riven's office?" Belle whispered.

Evelyn grabbed the first letter, heart pounding in her chest. Signed at the end of each was the prince's name. She triple-checked a few more, and *Goddess.*

"You're right. It's his office." She stilled, as if he lurked in the shadows, but nothing moved about. Not a servant. Not magic. Not the sense of darkness.

Beside her, Belle had grown stiff, as well, hands fisted at her sides.

"Best hurry," Evelyn said. "I'll check the desk while you take a look around."

"Alright."

To the witch's credit, she was light on her feet as she weaved through the books. Evelyn swallowed a pang of sadness, realizing Belle might been used to tiptoeing her way through the castle.

With care, Evelyn searched Riven's desk. Maps, trading catalogs, letters from merchants. She came across nothing related to the spell. Before she became disgruntled, her fingers brushed against worn leather near the lampshade. She found a journal buried under the desk's clutter. Uneven parchment pages stuck out of its edges, while a tied leather string secured the bursting contents. Evelyn pulled, and the knot unraveled with ease due to the years of wear and tear smoothing down the leather. The pages flew free once released, littering around Evelyn's feet.

She squatted and grabbed a few that floated before hitting the ground. Dates sprawled in the corners ranged hundreds of years, depicting the same two people—a gorgeous woman and a young boy around the age of five.

The woman's hair, curly and long, fell to her hips. It had been shaded darker than the boy's. Vampyr fangs jutted over their lips when they smiled or laughed. The two always seemed to be looking elsewhere, never at the artist, as if the images had been sketched without their knowledge. Moments of them laughing, smiling, reading. Even sleeping. Though charcoal lined the sketches with not a single hint of color, Evelyn recognized the little boy's eyes.

They belonged to Riven.

Was this his child?

Tovi had never mentioned a sister-in-law or nephew, but she'd never mentioned a younger brother or sister either. Perhaps these were more secrets, more family members she'd not uttered a word about.

As Evelyn flipped through the sketches, she caught a chilling detail. The young boy never grew older. His age ranged from infant to a young child, but never past that, which begged the question, what had happened to him or the woman?

More recent sketches revealed what Evelyn had guessed back in Callum.

The first young woman to die at the White Lady's hand, McKenna McCarthy, draped in blankets and appearing sultry, stared at Evelyn like she'd stared into the eyes of the artist. That look alone... Evelyn shifted in place. There was passion. Want. *Desire*. She sifted through more and noticed Riven had taken time to sketch McKenna's smile, capturing the details of her face close up. He shaded the twinkle of her eye, the dimple on the right cheek, her curls messy and splaying in the wind.

These were the lines of one who noticed the details, *cared* for them.

Evelyn struggled to accept the notion. Riven was callous and cold. The memory of his grip on her throat remained, and the absence of her magic another blaring truth of how cruel he was.

She gathered the sketches and placed them back how she'd found them. She set her sights on one of the desk's drawers. She fiddled with an aged bronze handle, and the old wood groaned as she eased the drawer open. Letters cradled inside ripped envelopes took up most of the compartment.

Evelyn thrummed her fingers through them. Two symbols kept appearing—an upside-down paw print and a tansy flower. No addresses, no names. She grabbed the first letter. The wax seal had broken through the upside-down paw, smudging black onto the envelope.

> *Prince,*
> *Phase two of my plan is in place.*

*Phase one continues. The missing
werewolves are causing unease. Loss of
faith will come next.
The Lone Wolf*

Evelyn hadn't read anything in the paper Belle had given her indicating there was trouble in the Vadon Mountains. But witches and werewolves lived separately. Aside from the prophecy and the trade, little else brought them together. Still, such news made Evelyn uneasy.

Sweat pricked on her scalp, her breath shallow. She opened a second letter, this time one with the flower symbol. She hoped the contents would give her more clues, but as she read, her heart thumped as loud as drums.

*Prince of Light—
Your news brings great joy to our cause
and efforts. May your recent win en-
courage others to act. As promised,
here is the sister's address you may
find useful in the coming weeks while
taming the Daughter of the Goddess:
38 Penny Drive
Nūa, Sorin*

Evelyn's hand shook as she ran her finger under her sister's address. She flipped the letter over, but nothing indicated who had supplied it. Only the flowered symbol. Her vision tunneled, the study fell away, and a coldness crept over her skin.

One of their own had supplied Blair's address to Riven. Who? An important question, but not as important as the grief welling in Evelyn—Blair was a target because she'd left.

"Evelyn."

She snapped back to the present. Her thoughts slowed down, and she settled into the stillness of the study again, her fear calming as she turned her attention to Belle.

Answers. She'd risked leaving her room and exploring the secrets of the castle to find answers regarding her enemy. She refused to return home empty-handed with nothing to show her sisters, something that proved she'd changed.

Belle stood by a giant map that took up most of the western wall. Its edge wavering from a draft, the continent of Sorin rolling with the movement. Evelyn joined Belle, the letter still in hand.

"Look at the pins." Belle pointed to two distinct symbols.

A wolf and a flower.

Evelyn's one brow pinched, a headache forming from all her rampant questions. She passed Belle the letters.

"They're code names."

The wolf pin, the same black as the wax seal, punctured various villages in the Vadon Mountains. Evelyn rattled off the village names, each correlating with a different pack. Her heart squeezed at the sight of one tucked at the center. She reached up on her tiptoes and ran her thumb over the name Drengr, her mate's home. A hollowness stole her breath.

"I recognize this one." Belle traced her finger over the flower.

"I've seen my sister read letters with it." Belle's cerulean eyes scanned the words, the edges of her lips down turning. "But, I have no idea who it is."

Evelyn had never seen the symbol before her time in the Drystan Castle, but nestled in the city of Nūa, it sat, pushed flush against the fabric of the map. Riven had admitted he had allies, yet her gut twisted at the evidence of his reach.

The White Lady. Witches living in Drystan. One in Nūa.

Like the strings connecting the pins and places, his contacts weaved deeper threads. Her sister's address. Missing werewolves. A cause. A plan. Did it all relate to the spell, or was it a bigger plot?

"Uh, Evelyn..." Belle whispered, tugging the sleeve of her oversized sweater. She followed the witch's line of sight.

Dangling from a metal perch protruding from the stone wall, high above and adjacent to the floor-to-ceiling window, was a large, furry bat.

And its rust-colored eyes were zeroed in on them.

"What is that?" Evelyn whispered.

"That's Riven's pet," Belle said. "Their bond sort of reminds me of a familiar."

At the mention of a familiar, a lump formed in Evelyn's throat. She missed Maxie, and every time she thought of her, tears stung the edge of her eyes. Nights had been lonely without her familiar curled at the end of her bed or her paws kneading her feet when it was time for breakfast.

Yet, the creature eyeing them above wasn't like any familiar she'd seen before. The massive bat dropped and zipped towards them, chaotic and sudden. Its high-pitched screech echoed off the walls, disturbing the study's quiet. It dove towards them, and its leathery wings brushed against Evelyn's temple, ruffling her hair.

"What do we do?" Belle asked, creating a shield with her arms, the letters she still held flapping under the circling bat. It seemed to have zeroed in on them, seemed to want them. Impossible, but...

Evelyn snatched the letters away, and the bat changed course, flying around her instead of Belle. Like Maxie, it guarded Riven's things.

Goddess—the ruckus might alert the prince. Evelyn sprinted towards the desk, intent on placing the letters exactly where she'd found them.

"Cover me!"

"What?" Belle hissed.

The bat darted in front of her, cutting her off the path towards the desk. She took a step, but again the bat intercepted her.

"Belle, help me!"

Evelyn jumped between stacks of books, sidestepping left and taking the longer route. As she reached the desk, the bat leveled high and shot towards her. Evelyn braced for impact, but instead, the bat screeched as a sphere of water splashed its torso. The bat spun. In the time it took to collect itself and regain balance, Evelyn was able to place the letters back in the drawer. Neatly and right where she'd found them.

Recovered from Belle's attack, the bat assessed Evelyn, apparently found her harmless without the letters, and returned to the barred perch. It swung like a furred pendulum, wrapping its leathered wings around it's body. Glossy rust eyes glared upside down at them.

Evelyn hurried to Belle and grabbed the young witch's hand, making for exit. "Nicely done," she whispered.

Belle beamed, and they rushed from the study, through the hidden door, and back up the tower's stairwell in minutes. Sweat and the scent of snow wrapped around them as they burst into her room.

They'd beaten the lunchtime servants, and when they arrived, none batted an eye at Belle's presence. While the young witch practiced her brotannas over a cup of water, Evelyn considered all she'd learned. Not much in the sense of the spell or the curse, but her mind continued to linger on sketches she'd come across first, and Riven's question from the night before.

What would you risk for the ones you love?

"Belle," she said, "did Riven have a wife and child?"

The droplets she controlled fell and splashed back into the cup. "Yes, a long time ago."

Evelyn nibbled her lip. The dates had indicated as much, but Riven's earlier words, the desperation in his tone, the craze in his eyes still nagged Evelyn.

Allies. Efforts. A spell...

A sickening realization washed over Evelyn. What if Riven's plan had nothing do with breaking the curse? What if it had everything to do with his wife and child?

There are no limits, no extent I wouldn't go. I would do anything. *Even if it destroyed this world.*

"What happened to them?" she said in a breath, as if answers would explain Riven's plans.

Belle began, once more, to raise the water up, but there was sadness in her eyes, a heaviness in her hands. "Rumors claim his twin sister killed them."

CHAPTER TWENTY-FOUR

Bˡᵒᵒᵈ.

Soaked into clothes. Splattered across the pine needles of the forest floor. Dry and crusted in Tovi's nail beds.

Red. Red. Red.

The haze of hunger washed through her, waves of monstrous instinct pulling her from the shores of rational thought.

Tovi needed to feed.

She'd gone too long without feeding, so long Tovi didn't recall the last time blood crossed her lips. Three damning days. That's all she ever had before hunger gnawed at her. And she'd gone over. How many days? Two? Three? When she tried to think back, her hunger shattered her concentration, and her tongue lashed out, licking the blood dribbling down her chin.

Bloody hel, she was so far gone.

Like the predator she was, she assessed the company around her with a keen eye. Eldrick and Kade, huddled together, discussed in hushed voices. Concern hadn't left the alpha's brow since the commander had exploded with moonlight. Linx attended to the freed werewolves—fresh blood seeping into the air as she stitched above a werewolf's brow. Both Bétar and Todd worked to set up camp, popping squat tents to fight the chill of frosty mornings.

Their efforts to free the werewolves had surfaced her hunger. Talons unsheathed, fighting, spilling blood. It awakened the darkness in her, inciting her hunger, and drawing her further into the shadows of her making.

Tovi swallowed. To leave unseen, without uttering a word was a risk, but sharing the fact she needed to feed was out of the question. The team already distrusted her and slapping them in the face with the damning truth she drank blood, craved it, *loved* it... Tovi swallowed. Any more judgment and her ancient heart might crumble.

No one noticed as Tovi slunk back into the trees, the proud trunks and spiny arms pulling her farther away and out of sight. She planted her feet, soft and delicate, so not an inch of snow crunched under her boots. She took less steps to hide the sounds of her movement the farther she slipped from the team, and what few sounds she'd made were replaced by a nearby trickling stream and the rustle of tiny creatures she planned to hunt.

Tovi's head snapped east. The hesitant, slow pattering of paws forced her fangs free. Shutting her eyes, she sniffed the air. The sound and scent indeed traveled from the east.

Gamey. Plump. Small.

Rabbit.

Not Tovi's first choice in the line of animals ranging across the forests of Drystan, but it was far easier and quicker to kill than an elk. She'd be back without anyone noticing she'd left, fed and sedated until they reached Drystan Village.

She stilled her breath, sights set on the direction of the scent. A hundred yards away, the bristling of brown fur against the forest floor caught her eye.

The rabbit rose on hind legs, frozen as if it felt her gaze locked on it. Hidden by faraway trees, Tovi tracked the rise and fall of its chest. Slinking forward, she stalked closer, intent on not spooking it. The yards dwindled until she was so close, the rise and fall of its furred chest matched the *thump, thump, thump,* singing to Tovi's insatiable hunger.

A branch snapped, and Tovi whirled.

With arrow knocked, groaning from tension, Yen stood behind her. The archer lowered her bow.

"Moons, Tovi, I thought you were something else."

Words died on Tovi's tongue. She wrestled hunger and self-preservation.

Yennifer's brows scrunched over her blue eyes that looked past Tovi. The crunch of leaves and sticks signaled the rabbit's retreat. Yennifer tracked the movement, then sized Tovi up and down.

"I see both of us are hunting then?" She replaced the arrow in its carrier and shouldered her bow.

Bloody hel. The very incident Tovi had attempted to avoid found her. But she was her own fool. Her hunger had been so rampant, she'd overlooked Yennifer's absence amongst the team.

"I was only getting a bit of space after the fight." Tovi's words rushed out, pitched and wrong. "A moment to be alone."

Yennifer smiled. "And I was merely practicing how to fly."

Tovi blinked as the archer walked past her. No tension. No wariness. No *judgment.*

She paused, pushing her long, blonde braid over her shoulder as she squatted and assessed the forest ahead.

"How long has it been since you fed?" She threw the question over her shoulder.

A flush crept across Tovi's cheeks, and she froze, her body colder than the Drystan air.

"I..." She'd never discussed feeding with anyone but other vampyrs. It was social, sacred for some, and no one hid their hunger. They drank blood almost every day. A drop there. A glass here. It was so ingrained in who they were, Tovi had only grown accustomed to remembering her feedings when she'd lived in

Nūa. Discussing them with a werewolf felt like peeling back her skin for Yennifer to peer at her muscles and bones.

Earlier, Tovi had evaded the truth. But the archer had seen her in the act, so there was no sense in lying. Without her usual tactics at her arsenal, Tovi resorted to saying nothing.

Yennifer sighed as she rose, thoughtfully eyeing Tovi. A genuineness wafted from the archer.

"You know, werewolves get the urge to shift from time to time. It's the beastly magic in us. We can't always fight off our baser instinct."

Tovi stilled, the comparison throwing her off. She'd never considered the similarities between werewolves and vampyrs. Shifting. Beasts. Except, they were touched by the light of the Moon God, not... cursed like she was.

Yennifer walked off, headed in the direction the rabbit had scurried off to. Mists collected by her ankles as a darker shade of gray merged into the clouds above. Night dipped its toe into the forest, inch by inch, minute by minute.

"So, when is the last time you fed?" Yennifer asked, turning back with a knowing brow raised.

Tovi sighed. She might have to peel a bit of herself back this time. Just a bit. "I don't remember."

Yen hummed. "How about you and I hunt together?"

Such surprise shot through Tovi, she didn't have the energy to compose herself. "Are you sure?"

The archer shrugged. "Wouldn't offer if I wasn't."

Tovi's stomach backflipped. The offer rocked through her, and Yennifer meant it. A truce. An offering. An understanding. Tovi wasn't sure what to call it, but she set her shoulders back, appreciating the archer's kindness.

"Alright," she said. "But, if you'd allow, I'd love to use the bow and arrow. It has been some time since I've had the chance."

Yennifer laughed. "Only if you swear to tell me when and how you learned the skill."

Tovi smiled and told a truth.

CHAPTER TWENTY-FIVE

ELDRICK

EVEN IN THE LATE hours of night, gray gripped the Drystan forest. High above the canopy, the moon's rays shifted the blanketing clouds to a slate hue, the coverage casting the forest into a dusty darkness. Fog slithered between pines, and the cold descended as the hours of night ticked by.

No fires, Tovi had said.

Despite the team's added numbers, Tovi feared her cursed blood wouldn't be enough to hold off prowling demons with such a large group. Fire—power and light—though a fierce weapon against them, called to them to ravish and dampen.

Luckily, they'd packed Bleu to the brim, sparing sleeping furs and blankets to cover the shivering bones of the captured werewolves. Linx had tended to their wounds, minimal bruises and cuts, the worst around their wrists. Bracelets enchanted with dark magic restricted their abilities to shift as well as their considerable strength. Now free, a restless bristle shook their pent-up muscles and magic as they sat, huddled together, chewing dried meats and the last of Lucy's bread.

Eldrick had given them time to decompress as well as time for the Gray Fenris team to recoup after the fight. Sleep beckoned behind his heavy eyelids, but it proved no match for his eagerness to learn what had happened to the werewolves. The sight of them in chains still riled his wolf, enough to outweigh his sore muscles. He approached cautiously, keeping his alpha strength at bay.

Eldrick grabbed a pine stump and used it as a makeshift seat while Kade and Bétar stood off to the side, arms crossed and focused. Closer, Eldrick took in the freed werewolves' attire and recognized a few of their faces, the latest missive from the Johannes pack coming to the forefront of his mind.

"You're Alpha Bjorn's son, aren't you?"

His tunic's color was familiar, the signature shade of the Johannes green. Square jaw and an unruly dark head of curls, the werewolf resembled his father, the alpha of the Johannes pack. But his missing son, *eldest* son, had been left out of his missive. Eldrick understood the severity of such a loss to an alpha and to the Johannes pack, but had Bjorn left the information out because he was ashamed or because he didn't trust Eldrick?

Eldrick flexed and unflexed his hands, hating to imagine a fellow alpha didn't trust him or didn't think him worthy of such information.

The young werewolf, twenty-two perhaps, nodded. "Sam Johannes."

"Can you tell us what happened? Do you remember anything?"

Sam sighed, sharing fleeting glances with the rest of the werewolves.

He cleared his throat. "I, along with the others, woke up in Drystan—well past the Void—already in chains, guarded by the vampyr guards you all killed. Before that, the last thing I remember was being on patrol with Erik. We were scouting the outskirts of our territory, the wind picked up, and then everything went black."

"It's true," a blond werewolf with piercing blue eyes beside Sam said. "One moment we were home. The next, I blinked and awoke in this land, no memory of how I got here."

The account aligned with meek clues from the last eight months—the missing werewolves had vanished without a trace. But regardless how the story fit, it didn't shed any new light, and worry wormed through Eldrick. He'd been relieved they'd freed them, but they didn't have enough to prevent others from suffering the same fate.

"None of you saw who or how the abduction happened?" he asked.

All five werewolves shook their heads, wearing grave expressions.

"What about scents?" Bétar asked. "You mentioned wind picked up before everything went black. Do you remember anything in the air?"

"Yes."

Eldrick recognized yet another werewolf in the group—Siv Drabek, an alpha's daughter. She'd visited the Drengr Village the summer before with her alpha mother, who, unlike Alpha Johannes, had been forthcoming about her daughter's disappearance. Another beside her wore the same color, lavender uniforms of the Drabek pack.

Two alpha children, two next-in-line alphas.

"You went missing roughly three weeks ago," Eldrick said.

Siv nodded. "Gyda and I were headed north to the Void for assignment when the same thing that happened to Sam and Erik happened to us. But I remember the scent. It was the last thing I remember before the wind. It was gone when I woke, but I'll never forget it. An unpleasant sweetness with spiced herb."

"Like licorice?" Kade asked, stepping forward.

Both Eldrick and Bétar straightened. Siv and Gyda's eyes went wide.

"That's it," Siv said. "Licorice candy."

"What does that indicate?" Eldrick asked.

His brother's brows furrowed. "It's the same scent that surrounded the White Lady."

They exchanged warry glances.

"I think it was her dark magic," Kade said.

"That means dark magic was used to capture the werewolves," Eldrick said, his words slow and thoughtful.

"But dark magic would mean a witch is helping the vampyrs," Bétar said.

Kade nodded. "The White Lady was a witch helping Riven. I wouldn't be surprised if others are helping him, too."

"None of you saw a witch though, did you?" Eldrick asked.

All five shook their heads, but the fifth, the one who'd been silent amongst the group, locked gazes with Eldrick.

"I don't think it's only witches." He crossed his arms, the tattered sleeves of his tunic stretching. A nasty bruise surrounded his eye, purple clashing with green.

"What do you mean?" Eldrick swallowed, like a piece of glass was lodged in his throat.

Siv shook her head. "Gyda and I were thrown into holding pits with Tam for weeks, and the vampyrs did a lot of talking."

"More than talking. They bragged," Tam said.

Kade growled, and Eldrick's inner wolf shared a similar sentiment.

"They talked about how much coin they'd get, saying this was the best delivery of werewolves the..." Siv paused, glancing to the forest floor.

Gyda swallowed. "That the Lone Wolf has ever delivered."

Cold washed over Eldrick. *Moons*, Eldrick couldn't fathom another werewolf turning on his own kind. Loyalty. Pride. Pack. Those were values a werewolf lived by. There was also the facts to consider—werewolves had lived peacefully for centuries. He leaned his elbows against his knees, driving them sharply to avoid the sensation of being sick.

"It has to be a code name," he whispered. "Perhaps related to the fact that whoever this bastard is, they capture werewolves, not because they are a werewolf."

Kade's jaw ticked. "I hate it as much as you do, Eldrick, but we can't dismiss the possibility."

Before Eldrick could argue the facts, Tam spoke up.

"Commander Drengr's right, and the reasons the vampyrs claimed we were the best delivery is because the Lone Wolf had finally brought alpha blood." His gaze passed over Siv and Sam.

"Yes, one of the things they bragged about, how the rings could use stronger fighters." Siv shivered.

"The what?" both Kade and Eldrick growled.

"Fighting rings," Gyda said, spitting to the floor. "Our destination was Drystan Castle, to fight in some arena. But whoever captured us knew who Sam and Siv were, like they were targeted."

Eldrick shook his head. "A witch could have discovered that information. It's not privy to solely werewolves."

"We should consider the fact that if a witch did capture them, how did they get the location for ones on patrol? Or that Siv headed on assignment to the Void," Bétar said.

Kade tipped his head, brows shooting up. "That information would be werewolf knowledge. We can't dismiss the possibility it's one of our own."

Eldrick refused to accept it, *believe* it.

Every fiber of his being raged against the notion a werewolf would betray their own kind, especially when his kind had been captured and brought to Drystan, destined for some fighting rings in the castle. *Moons,* he had to write to Claus about this.

The thought of werewolves being used for some sport reminded him of the vicious blood-hungry monsters that overtook his mother and slaughtered her, fang-filled smiles flashing glee and triumph. His festering hatred didn't blind his reason. It reminded him of what he knew—vampyrs were the enemy. Dark magic and the Lone Wolf aside, the missing werewolves centered around vampyrs and Drystan, affirming his belief all along.

Eldrick's ire itched to lash out. He needed something to blame. Or someone. He searched their makeshift camp, sights going red when he couldn't find her.

Tovi.

"Where is she?" His words were half man, half wolf.

Anger wrestled in his chest. Heat pricked his skin. He searched the tree line and sniffed the air. Plum and lilac—the scent no one else seemed to detect past that necklace of hers—were fresh, close, but Tovi was nowhere to be seen. When was the last time he'd kept tabs on her? Had she abandoned them, left when they'd all been distracted with the werewolves?

Moons.

He'd been stupid, reckless. He thought her valiant efforts to save the werewolves had been true. Had it been an act? Had he let hope steer him?

He stopped, his breath hitching. What exactly did he hope for when it came to Tovi?

A branch snapped across the way.

Tovi emerged from behind two pine trees, blonde hair free and pulled to one side. Like snowy silk, it shined and shimmered in the dusky night. She appeared rested, fresh, a faint color illuminating her cheeks. Beside her, Yen shared a soft smile, bow and arrows tossed over her shoulder.

Eldrick charged towards them. "Where have you been?"

Yennifer's eyes widened at the alpha demand in his tone, grip tightening on her bow.

Tovi, on the other hand, blinked with indifference. "Excuse me?"

"Where have you been?" he roared.

"That is not your concern!" Tovi shouted, charging towards him.

"You're mistaken, *princess*. You're a—"

"Oh, for Goddess's sake!" Tovi threw up her hands. "What? I'm a vampyr? A liar? A bloodsucker? Which one do you fancy tonight?"

Their argument had gained everyone's attention. Linx and Todd had emerged from their tents. Kade and Bétar lingered closer behind him, hovering at a distance. Yennifer remained where she'd been, lips in a thin line.

"You're a liar." Eldrick pointed towards the freed werewolves. "They were destined for the fighting rings in Drystan Castle. Try to deny that you didn't know."

Tovi's expression fell. Her mouth opened, and she stumbled back. "What did you just say?"

Eldrick scoffed and rolled his eyes. "Don't play coy with me. You knew and lied."

Tovi shook her head. "I didn't. I've never heard of the fighting rings. I haven't been home in months. I swear it." Her jade eyes fleeted past him as they connected with Kade. She turned to Yennifer. "I swear I didn't know."

Eldrick's heart skipped a beat. The desperation, the slight crack in Tovi's usually calm, poised voice made him pause. Her eyes bounced to everyone, fear flashing through them.

"I didn't know," she whispered. "Believe me."

And Eldrick's earlier anger morphed into hate. Not for Tovi. But for how he *felt*. He fucking hated that the vampyr before him compelled him to reach out and hold her. To comfort. To soothe. To whisper he was sorry, wrong, and wretched. Because he hated that he'd made her feel that way. Small and afraid. That he'd broken through her usually proud stature.

She conjured such desire, such an insatiable lack of reason inside him.

And he hated it.

Stars above, why her?

Eldrick's hate bubbled over, ready to spout worse words and accusations—

"I believe her," Yennifer said. "If she says she didn't know, she didn't know."

Tovi whirled, and Eldrick wasn't sure who was more surprised, him or the princess.

"Alright," he said. "Then where were the two of you?"

Yennifer straightened. He'd used his alpha tone again, demanding answers.

"No," she said.

Eldrick's wolf bared his teeth while a growl vibrated behind him. *Bétar.*

"Stand down, Eldrick." *Kade.*

"I won't let you be cruel, Magu," Yennifer said.

The slight plea in the archer's tone only intrigued Eldrick more. He shifted his attention to Tovi. "Tell me. If you are so trustworthy, where did you run off to?"

"Is that what you think, that I ran off? Did you hit your head in today's fight?" She jabbed her finger into her chest. "I fought alongside all of you. I killed my own kind to set werewolves free. Why is it so hard for you to accept that I am trying to help?"

Eldrick asked himself the same question. Why had he assumed the worst? His eyes roamed over her lithe frame. Her jade eyes assessed him back like a lioness, a predatory killer, shoulders shuddering with rage.

That was it. A predator. A monster. Tovi *was* a vampyr. No matter the days, no matter the minutes they spent together or the things she did, he couldn't look past that fact. How could Eldrick ever make a sound judgment about her if he couldn't look past what she was? Perhaps, he never would and that was the point.

Perhaps he'd already made his judgment.

"Tell me what you were doing," he said with a deadly calm.

"That is none of your business." She bit out the words, snarling as she did.

Eldrick laughed, crossing his arms. "If you can't admit it, then it has to be something traitorous."

"Eldrick." Yennifer approached in several sharp strides. "Stop."

"I won't ask again—"

"I went to feed." Tovi's face was stone.

Eldrick balked, his mouth turning dry.

Tovi laughed, jade eyes snaring his. "Exactly. Despite how often you remind us all I'm a bloodsucker, perhaps you forgot I need to feed. Happy? Oh, and since you're so fucking curious, tonight was rabbit, and it tasted divine."

The color to her cheeks. Her rested aura. The life in her eyes. She'd recently fed, and Eldrick had missed it.

He teetered on his feet and ran a hand through his hair. "Why didn't you say something?"

"And endure this awkwardness? I'd rather rot."

"Well…" Eldrick struggled to find words. With the audience, he couldn't afford to appear like he didn't have control over the situation or his relationship with Tovi. "With regards to our deal, it's important I know where you are and what you're doing."

Tovi sauntered past him. "Alright then, I'll be sure to inform you of every move I make, even when I'm off to take a shit. Happy?"

Eldrick stumbled back. "I…"

Everyone laughed.

Tovi rolled her eyes and shook her head. "Don't tell me you're one of those males who thinks females don't shit. I hate to break it to you—"

"I am well aware, thank you." Eldrick held up his hand to stop her. "I thought…"

Tovi's furious jade eyes searched his face, then widened in understanding. "I'm cursed, not dead."

Stars above.

Eldrick couldn't keep his head straight, his decisions so muddled, thinking like trudging through mud. Frustration soured on his tongue. He tried to bury his emotions, the explosiveness of the last few moments.

One two, one two.

Eldrick exhaled and inhaled, attempting to bring himself back into the night. He let Tovi walk off, unsure what direction she even went. A thousand words fluttered through Yennifer's eyes as she passed, but she didn't say a single one.

A presence, strong and familiar, joined his side.

"You need to back off," Kade said.

"What?" Eldrick asked. "You can't be serious. She *is* a vampyr."

"Doesn't mean you need to be an ass. She's trying to help us."

Eldrick narrowed his eyes. "Most likely for her own gain. How can you defend her when she's one of the reasons Evelyn's captured in the first place?"

Kade stared out into the dark forest, the moon's reflection getting lost in his amber eyes. "I pretended to be someone else, you know."

"I heard," Eldrick whispered. "Cyrus Skender was it?"

Kade chuckled. "Did Tovi tell you?"

Eldrick nodded, uncertain where this conversation was going.

"Well, I lied to Evelyn for weeks, and with each day that passed, it got harder to admit the truth because of the fear of losing something. I still had no clue why Evelyn ran from our union in the first place. What if it was because of me?" Kade shook his head. "I let fear get in the way, fear I'd fail at my duty. Duty wasn't what I wanted in the end, though, Evelyn was."

"What's this have to do with Tovi?" Eldrick asked.

"She is trying, and more than anyone on this team, I didn't want to see it, but she cares for Evelyn. She may have lied. She may be the princess of our greatest enemy. Yet, she wants to get Evelyn back as bad as everyone else."

Eldrick scoffed. "Her wants aren't the same as yours, Kade. You can't trust it."

"*You* can't trust it." Kade stepped away from him, shaking his head. "I've made my peace with Tovi's decisions and her hand in all this. For the sake of the team and this mission, you need to as well."

"What—"

"*Stars above*, admit you're attracted to her," Bétar grumbled, knocking the back of Eldrick's shoulder. "No one will fault you for it. She's a beautiful woman."

Red flashed across Eldrick's vision, but he said the only thing that made sense.

"She's a vampyr."

Why was Eldrick the only one who could remember that *very* important fact?

"That doesn't mean she's not a beautiful woman. Look past it for moon's sakes."

It's not that Eldrick couldn't. It was that he didn't want to. Holding onto what Tovi was seemed easier than facing the feelings heating his body.

Bétar sauntered off towards his and Yennifer's tent. She waited from him, a new level of ire blatant in the archer's expression when her stare fleeted in Eldrick's direction.

"I mean it, Eldrick." Kade's words snapped him to the present. "I don't know what's going on between you and Tovi, but we don't have time for this constant bickering. Drystan will be different, full of vampyrs. We must work as a team, whether you like it or not."

With that, his brother left him alone in the middle of the camp.

A chill descended over Eldrick, and he couldn't decide if it was the snaking fog or his shame.

CHAPTER TWENTY-SIX

EVELYN

S NOW SHOWERED OUTSIDE EVELYN'S window, for once replacing the gray land with bright white. Dense flurries obscured the view of the rest of the castle, too, locking Evelyn from the outside world further.

Isolation made her reckless, and she chanced one more glance towards her door as she eased open the hidden passageway, careful to grate the stone gears slowly.

The week since discovering Riven's study had inched by, the frustrating sameness of her captivity lightened only by one surprising change. Tala had agreed to let Evelyn teach Belle magic, and she watched their daily efforts with an often-suppressed smile.

Tala's lenience a mystery, like so many other things she'd discovered—Riven's study and the symbols there, his dead family, the confirmation he possessed allies. Not that the discovery of these things offered any answers to her many questions. There existed no connection that she could see between it all.

And time was running out. Maybe? She had no idea when Riven planned to use her blood for the spell. She had no way to communicate with Kade, no way of knowing when he would arrive to break her out of this damned prison either.

The unknowns left her unsettled.

The only solution was to explore at night. A risk, especially without Belle helping, but Evelyn was willing to take it. She crept down the hidden stairwell, determined to explore the second door this time. Snow flurries twirled, trapped in the tower as she descended on tiptoes down the steps.

She passed the door to Riven's study and went down another flight to next door below. Her toes and fingers tingled, her breaths shallow. Without hesitating, she faced the stones and pushed against the loose ones, readying to handle whatever waited beyond the door.

Dust plumed from the creases where the door pushed inward. It moved slower than the last one, as if older and stuck in place. The debris filled Evelyn's lungs and tickled the back of her throat. She coughed, covering her mouth with the oversize maroon sweater she'd dug up in the wardrobe.

Unlike the other doors, it didn't open wide. Wool knitting caught on the rugged stone as she squeezed through. More dust lay on the other side, like a gray snowfall had blanketed the space.

A destroyed, wrecked room.

A curtain rod hung halfway down the window, curtains ripped and tattered. The bed on the left-hand side had been turned over, pillows and quilts in a pile and dusted in place. The pieces of a shattered armoire littered most of the room, and Evelyn had to tiptoe over jagged piece and loose nails.

An energy, not dark and not light, marinated in the air. Lost, weary, timid. It clung to the walls like the dust clung to the surfaces. Without her magic, Evelyn couldn't fully sense what it meant, and nothing she came across—no books, papers, or items—suggested anything other than an abandoned room.

Except the destruction lay in a circle, the center of the room untouched. Curious, Evelyn wandered inward and peered up at the cobwebbed chandelier. She shivered, a creep traveling up her spine as spiders scurried across the crystals, magnifying their bodies. Backing up a step, the soles her feet scuffed against the wooden floor, and underneath her toes, black paint shined through.

Evelyn furrowed her brows, sliding her foot across the floorboards again, revealing more black paint. She ran over and tugged the curtain, ripping a piece off and using it to brush away the rest of the dust. A black, painted mass sat in the center. No shape. No symbol, just a blob of nothing. Evelyn frowned, her mind racing.

What did it mean? Who had the room belonged to?

Snow flurries from a broken window escaped through the cracks, tumbling across the floorboards before they melted into grooves. No—Evelyn studied the lost snow again, the tiniest of puddles left behind, resting atop scrapes in the wood. *Carvings* peeked through the paint.

Evelyn backstepped, trying to decipher whatever lay underneath at a new angle, but whoever had covered the area with paint had also scratched through the carvings.

A letter lay untouched at the top, an *a* or *e*, Evelyn couldn't be sure with how it'd been etched into the wood. Aggressively. Quickly. The penmanship a mere scribble. She moved down the scratches and counted lines, one after the other. Her breath hitched on a certain stanza, the lines left untouched. She ran her hands across, splinters catching on her fingertips, but Evelyn didn't feel it, her heart thudding in her chest and stomach twisting into knots.

She had to learn the words. With no regard to consequence, Evelyn dashed back to her room, grabbing pencils and paper from the writing desk she'd mostly ignored. Back in the wrecked room, she used the charcoal and etched it across the paper over the words. The letters were so big, she went through ten pages of parchment. But the words became clear on the cream material as Evelyn laid them out.

Words she'd known all her life.

The truest of unions between the third-borns of the Sun and Moon will defeat the darkness.

On her hands and knees, Evelyn crawled back up and down the destroyed floor as if another word she found would make it clear why her prophecy, the one referring to her and Kade, had been written into the floorboards of Drystan Castle. She tried to make sense of it, tried to soak in more of the room and where this was in the castle, but nothing clicked.

Nothing made sense.

She crawled back up the carved floorboards and backtracked down again, this time noting the number of etched lines. Deliberate breaks after certain ones, like stanzas. Her and Kade's prophecy was the last. She wrote the numbers down and drew the lines out, spacing where the etchings and carvings stopped.

Evelyn sank to her knees, staring at the length of the poem, song, prophecy—she didn't know what to call it. Her mind ran wild, leaving her floaty, like she'd woken from the oddest dream. So much of what she knew about vampyrs had been altered, and she wasn't sure she could handle the prophecy being more than what she believed.

The other lines had been etched so viciously, so violently, as if whoever had done it had wanted to erase them from existence. Running her hands over them, it was difficult to make out the lost words. Her thumb ran across the bulbous script of a letter *d*. The letter *o* followed, and an idea struck. Using the spare paper she had left, she ran the tip of her pencil over the letters. One word after the other, she gathered in total five words—*dove, unite, seeds,* and *Light,* the *l* deliberately capitalized—and a single, incomplete line.

Land... in red.

Evelyn scribbled the words and phrase over the mock lines she'd drawn, placing them where they fell in hopes to make out what they could possibly mean. Evelyn's heart hammered in her chest, her confusion and unease rooting her in place. The visual provided no clues, and out of context, the words didn't make any sense. Yet, the third-born prophecy had been carved into the vampyr castle.

It felt like something and nothing at all.

The increasing sense she'd escape the castle with nothing of value trickled like the snow outside the window—something she couldn't stop or control—and yet, a small part of her warred against that doubt. For the first time in a long while, Evelyn's instinct screamed with hope. She had no threads to connect these scribblings to her and Kade's prophecy or the curse, but it was more than she'd ever had. It was a start, right?

The wind tossed the curtain into the air. The rippling of paper drummed against the winter's howl, snagging Evelyn's attention. She abandoned the black paint and words, discovering a loose brick under the windowsill. Shoved into a crevice, a series of letters flapped from the draft. Evelyn grabbed hold of them, dirt and rock falling away as she pulled them free. Mildew and water stained the envelope, bleeding the ink of the *To* and *From* script, but the contents appeared neatly folded and intact.

Intrigued, Evelyn gathered her notes along with the letters and decided to take them back to her room. An eerie draft circled her bare feet as she climbed the stairs, but a constant beat made her pause. She stopped on the step, listening over the snow storm. The beating stopped. Perhaps it had been a trick of the wind stuck in the open tower. Evelyn continued on, but the beating began again, like a drumming in the distance.

Boom. Boom. Boom.

It built faster, faster, then stopped—

The distant cries of a crowd echoed off the stone. Curiosity nipped at Evelyn again. She peered down the stairs, as if the phantom voices crept close by. The secrets and shadows of the castle called to her.

Seeking the noise out, searching for it would be utterly foolish. It was night. Vampyrs were out, and she didn't have her magic.

But maybe this was an opportunity to learn more about the vampyrs in the castle.

Again foolish, but the scribbles of the prophecy and random words had hollowed her out, made her desperate to learn more. Eager, too. Like she'd tasted sweet promise and craved more. She *could* read the letters tucked against her notes, but Evelyn couldn't bare another night in her tower. Alone. Locked away. Waiting while Kade journeyed to save her.

And Evelyn wouldn't let fear—*risk*—get in the way of opportunity.

Decision made, Evelyn ran to her room and hid her notes and unread letters. Tomorrow. She'd revisit them tomorrow. She rummaged the closet for boots and a thicker sweater and traveled down the stairs two at a time, letting the distant rumbles of the castle lead her. They resounded the loudest near the door leading to the old servant's hallway Belle had used.

Darkness and debris met Evelyn on the other side. Skylights had been covered in snowfall, the lighting dim and ominous as she padded downward, continuing to let the beating guide her direction.

Belle's assessment had been fitting. Abandoned. Eerie. *Haunted*. The passageway was similar to the room she'd previously explored, destroyed and dusty. Paintings hung at off angles. Mirrors had been cracked, multiplying her focused reflection. Unlit torches lined the walls, scorch marks bleeding into the mauve wallpaper.

What had happened to this corner of the castle? Why had it been abandoned?

As Evelyn rattled questions to herself, answers seem to smear across the walls and floor. Patches of crimson, so old and dark they looked like rust, grew more frequent the farther down the passageway she crept.

And then there was the *remains*.

Skeletal remains.

Slumped against the walls with empty eye sockets. Others laid at odd angles. Some had been scattered like they'd been torn apart. They all wore purple uniforms, tattered from time. Moths fluttered around them, dust collecting on the whites of their bones.

A shudder went through Evelyn as she eased between two ancient, crumbling bodies. She recognized the uniforms—servants who attended her room wore the same kind. And the blood. So much blood. Even after all this time, it was stark against the mauve and molded carpet. Evelyn grimaced. From the imprint of time on the hallway and those dead around her, Evelyn's instinct screamed to keep moving, the darkness and ghosts of the castle too still.

Ahead, yellow light flickered across fallen boulders. At the end of the hallway, the ceiling had crashed down.

But a sliver of space, big enough for Evelyn to squeeze through, led to the light. She didn't hesitate, her breath and heart rate even as her resolve hardened like steel. Answers felt in reach, insight to the enemy she'd fought all her life. Her chest and arms scraped against the fallen stone until she popped free. Evelyn blinked in the new light. The echoes she'd followed sharpened and overtook her senses.

Drums. Screeches. Howling and horns.

The cheers of a well-entertained, wild crowd vibrated around her.

A crowd of *vampyrs*.

Fucking flames.

The path had deposited her into a tucked-away hall. Above Evelyn, rafters of an arena circled a cavern, filled with a hundred vampyrs. Her enemy dressed in silks and velvet laughed above, oblivious to her hiding place as she lurked. Not scáths, not caillte. They were vampyrs like Tovi, Riven, Tala, and Visha. Aside from their fangs and complexions, they appeared normal, like the vampyrs Matilda had described in her texts.

Wine and blood dripped from the rafters. She followed the droplets, down, down, they went, and—

Evelyn's breath hitched. The entertainment driving the crowd sickened her. She tilted, grabbing onto the wall beside her.

Below, a werewolf fought for its life against to two madras demons. The wolf of the moon and the wolves of darkness sparred. Blood soaked the sands of a pit. Servants hammered at goatskin drums on the first level, beating a rapid tempo to slashing, swiping, and chaos of the blood bath.

Rings.

Evelyn's memory snagged on Visha's words. She'd been too focused on the revelation Tovi had a sister and hadn't considered what that meant.

Throw her in—

Evelyn's blood heated. Visha had suggested Riven throw her into this arena for them to watch, laugh, and howl over. She searched for the princess and prince. Across the way, the first few rows had been sectioned off, purple banners lining the seats where Riven, Visha, and Ingrid sat. They were tangled together in their seats. The princess laced her fingers through the witch's blunt bob. Evelyn had yet to witness them together, to see this fated bond they had.

Rage rolled through Evelyn that they could revel in their mate bond while separating her from Kade. Suddenly, Evelyn's heated exterior froze. *Fucking flames,* what if... She stared down at the rings. The werewolf had been wounded to the shoulder while one madras demon bit onto its hind leg with unrelenting grip. The werewolf's grayish fur transformed to a golden-brown like that of her fated. She blinked, her mind playing tricks, *fear* tricking her.

Had that been why she hadn't reached Kade? Had he been caught in his efforts to break her out of the castle? Had he been thrown into this ring?

No. No. No. That couldn't have happened. It wasn't possible. But an unrelenting cold showered over her, and the wall wasn't solid enough to hold her upright. It felt like her heart was being ripped from her chest. *No.* Wouldn't Riven dangle her fated like a prize? Wouldn't the prince celebrate such a win and make sure she knew it?

It was the distance. It was the time. It was her snuffed magic.

Yet, her fated's kind fought below. One was now dead, limp in the sands as the madras fought over their kill. Evelyn's heart sank. Kade's people. Being *used.*

Evelyn's head spun, her insides twisting. She couldn't stand by while innocents were *murdered.* Anger and fear weaved together, and her blood danced though unable to be used. Evelyn took a single step forward—

She stopped, falling back into the shadows. A breath whooshed out of her. *There.* Seated two rows above Riven, Tala sat with another vampyr female. She glared in Evelyn's direction, her amber eyes sharp. Had she noticed her?

Evelyn stayed still, heart pounding in her chest as she waited. Tala blinked and turned her attention back to the female vampyr, continuing their discussion. Evelyn slumped against the stone wall, laying her hand on her frantic heart. She shut her eyes, shuddering against the flashes of possibilities. If Tala had caught her...

Foolish.

Kade, Blair, everyone she loved was at risk if she stepped out of line. Riven needed *her.* Not them. He'd not harm her, not enough to jeopardize the spell. Her loved ones wouldn't be granted the same courtesy.

Evelyn slunk farther back into the shadows and darkness. She'd give anything to scorch the arena and defeat the wicked vampyrs, but she steadied her breath and found reason. Attacking now would prove rash. She'd learned so much tonight—the rings, the gut-wrenching enjoyment vampyrs found from the death and violence below. She didn't dare ruin an opportunity to keep learning more about them. Not when she needed to defeat the darkness now more than ever.

Her feet were heavy as lead as she left. She'd wait for Kade, buy time. With reinforcements, she'd come back, she'd save them.

Evelyn returned to her room, her resolve no longer steel.

It was fire.

CHAPTER TWENTY-SEVEN

WIND WHIPPED UP FROM the rapids of Drystan's main river, scant droplets kissing Tovi's cheeks.

Everyone had agreed the freed werewolves couldn't track south through the canyon pass alone. Without Tovi and her cursed blood to deter the darkness, they'd draw the attention of demons or nearby scáths, and the Gray Fenris didn't have the weapons to spare. But with five extra werewolves, they moved slower than before, and food reserves were running low. Tovi hated to delay, but they needed to stick together, and once in Drystan, she could ensure safe passage home for the younger werewolves. But it meant they'd need to sail upriver, and that meant they'd need a ship.

So, they took a risk and headed east instead of north. Aside from a pack of madras they'd dealt with swiftly, and no injuries for Linx to attend to, they'd met no other troubles and delays. By some Goddess-gifted miracle, they'd discovered a slaver ship guarded by only two vampyrs. They'd handled them like they had the madras and were on their way upriver to Drystan. The route dropped them straight into the village—risky, but between Linx's magik and Tovi's vampyr blood, they'd at least have time to dock and find a trusted contact before discovery.

Tovi swallowed her hope. It was an untrustworthy emotion. She'd hoped before. For her mother to live. For the survival of her settlement. For those in court to see she wasn't the party princess anymore. For strength and purpose. Hope had never served her, and she didn't trust what it granted.

Yet, as the winds of home continued to whip by her, the land seemed to sing at her arrival.

Welcome.

Despite the curse, she loved this land. In all its gray glory, she knew its potential, had witnessed the greenest summers, the crop-filled autumns, and the gentlest winters. Maybe this once she'd allow the hope to kiss her rosy cheeks, let their last few wins fuel her resolve and push onto the next part of getting Evelyn out of Riven's clutches. Maybe, just maybe, she'd allow herself the belief she was one step closer to ridding her homeland of darkness.

With eyes closed, Tovi inhaled the scent of snow and wet rock, willing herself to hope when she sensed a certain presence, an alpha's energy close by.

Behind her, Eldrick descended the steps of the ship's bridge. Shadowed by the single sail, Linx and Todd manned the steering. The others had retired below deck. Poor Kade had been green before they left the river's edge, muttering how he fucking hated boats.

The eldest Drengr brother fared better. He headed in her direction with a determined stride. Shoulders back, jaw tight. The ship's rocking didn't affect the alpha's approach.

Tovi's defenses immediately snapped straighter, her grip on the ship's railing tightening. They hadn't spoken since he'd accused her of running off, forcing her to admit she'd gone to feed. The others hadn't seem to care, talking, joking, sharing their reserves with her, but Eldrick's avoidance and fleeting glances had been worse than the hundreds at court.

He was her biggest opponent, the largest obstacle in gaining an alliance with the werewolves. At every turn, he challenged her intentions, her *secrets*. Goddess knew she had them, harbored them like a dragon coveted gems, but they didn't mean her efforts weren't genuine. Effort and will thrummed through her veins.

And yet, she had to convince Eldrick of that.

The werewolf riled her, and she hated her lack of composure, hated that she'd had to reveal her thirst for blood so openly when she hadn't been ready. It felt like there was no avoiding, no hiding what she was anymore. Blood and vampyrs went hand in hand. She doubted he'd see past it now.

Tension formed in Tovi's shoulders, but she stood her ground. "Bored enough you'd talk with a bloodsucker and liar?"

Eldrick, to her surprise, winced. He gripped the back of his neck, eyes darting to the ship's wooden boards.

"Actually, I wanted to talk to you about that."

Tovi stilled. "Discuss what exactly?"

Eldrick released his neck and ran his hand through his hair instead, those stubborn tousled strands falling over his forehead. He dropped his arms to his side, both hanging lowly as he sighed.

"The things I said the other day, I wasn't being fair."

"Oh." Tovi's one-word response mimicked the shape of her open mouth.

"I'm sorry." Eldrick rushed the words, but he meant them. "I know you're trying to get Evelyn back."

"Thank you..." Tovi blinked, trying to process what he'd said. "Where is this coming from?"

Eldrick scratched his chin. "Aside from the fact I have been unfair, Kade reminded me we need to be a team."

"That's true."

He shook his head. "But it isn't that. You saved me from the demon, and you've gotten us this far. What would you say about starting over? A fresh start?"

For a beat, the two stared at each other, shades of green clashing as the river roared under them and the gray sprawled above them. Eldrick's proposition hung in the air. Tovi wasn't sure which she trusted least—the makeshift truce or her eagerness to grab hold of it. In the end, it didn't matter. His truce was one step closer to securing an alliance, one step closer to defeating Riven. She needed the werewolves, so she needed Eldrick.

"Alright, as long as you swear to stop calling me *bloodsucker*."

"I swear it," Eldrick said. "You've stood with us every part of the journey, and I know killing your own kind wasn't easy. I saw it in your eyes."

"It wasn't," Tovi whispered, days-old pain resurfacing. Cruelty, hate, anger... None of those things were her people. It was the darkness. A parasite changing her people, corroding them from the inside out. When she'd killed that soldier, she'd seen the briefest flash of who they used to be, until the black spread through their eyes. Yet, she didn't tell that to Eldrick, her people's secrets whispering for her not to.

Instead, she said, "I saw the blood lost in their eyes, the shift to a *caillte*. It was only a matter of time before they fell completely into darkness."

Eldrick stepped closer to her. He morphed into her orbit, his spearmint scent overtaking the salt and dew of the river. "Perhaps death was mercy."

Mercy? Tovi only felt she'd been too late. Too late to save her people.

"Perhaps. But I wish for my people... wish more were on my side. Goddess knows I pray my brother will have a change of heart before it's too late."

She missed Riven. The *old* Riven. They'd been friends and siblings years ago, sharing chats over the fire as Riven showed her his latest sketches. She'd told him her latest endeavors out in the wild, awe in his eyes. Despite his rigid exterior, Riven possessed a gentleness like no other. Years of torment and heartache, one she certainly caused, had hardened him into an impenetrable stone.

"What happened between you and your brother?" Eldrick asked.

Tovi blinked away her fond memories while a terrible one remained. Could she tell Eldrick? Her heart pulled and tugged, egging her on. When years blurred as quickly as months, memories flashed in fleeting visions. Some remained like wine stains in cloth. No matter the number of times one scrubbed, the faintest red remained. This particular memory was one of the stains, except it marked her heart. She swallowed, fighting the urge to tell him. They'd finally reached a truce, common ground. Did she dare break it by revealing the worst part of herself?

Their gazes connected, and Tovi let out a shuttering breath. Secrets whispered and cooed in her mind, reminding her this was a wicked idea, but for once, Eldrick's face was void of judgment, almost welcoming. She managed to take a deep breath, breaking their eye contact and facing the forest lining the river. She'd tell him, she decided, but couldn't bear to watch the emotions in his eyes while she did.

"Years ago, I was…"—Tovi searched for the right word—"different. As king and queen, my parents' power came hand in hand with greed. They were status-obsessed monarchs. It influenced how they viewed me, *what* I was to them, no longer *who*. A bargaining chip, an alliance, a breeding mare to be used in some transactional deal with the highest bidder."

Eldrick stiffened, but he said nothing.

Tovi inhaled. "And I grew angrier with each passing year, frustrated they'd forgotten what I was capable of, what I'd done for our family and our kingdom. I—" Tovi paused, unable to convey what she'd done with words. She'd hunted. Fed them. Protected them. Released the arrows that killed their worst enemies. Her hands still ached from jagged stone jutting into her muddy hands as she built the Drystan castle. All of her efforts forgotten in what felt like a blink of time to her parents.

She chanced a peek at Eldrick's reaction. He remained thoughtful, jaw tight but eyes softer than usual, like grass covered in dew.

"In my anger, I rebelled. I drank. I partied. I fucked anyone I fancied. If my parents presented a suitor, I made sure they ran in the opposite direction by the end of the night. Eventually, I became the partying princess Drystan court detested. The only one who saw me for what I'd used to be was Riven. He supported me when I turned down suitors and tried to keep my parents' efforts to marry me off at bay. Goddess, he often paid interested males to fuck off with a handsome sum, but..."

Tovi sighed, her next part of the story raging to be let out.

"Riven listened to my parents. He was the 'obedient son,' the one that led by example. When my parents made a match, he embraced it. Iona was a sweet, tender-hearted human from a distant land. She didn't belong in Drystan, but she and Riven fell deeply in love. After two years of marriage, he turned her into a vampyr, their marriage intertwined with eternity. Not soon after, Oliver, their son, was born. He too was a sweet, tender boy. So much of his mother and father were in him.

"One night, Riven asked me to escort Iona and Oliver to dinner. Again, Iona was sweet, timid. She truly didn't belong in vampyr court, she simply belonged with Riven. She didn't trust others, only Riven and I, but I was angry that day, so bloody angry. Everyone else had been invited to a royal hunt while I was left behind. 'Hunting is no place for a princess,' my mother had said. So, I ignored Riven's request. Partied all hours of the day, and when the time came to retrieve his wife and child, I didn't. I left them."

Tovi blinked away sorrow, ancient sadness that wrapped around her bones like chains. She'd lost count of the wine bottles she drank, how many men she'd dragged to her bed. Tannins, flesh, laughter, blood. It was all a blur of red and softness. Of lust and euphoria. An endless chase to fill a hole her parents and others had carved into her heart.

Tovi swallowed, tears stinging at the edge of her eyes. "It was the same day Drystan was cast into darkness. None of us understood what was happening. Court was in utter chaos. The sun still hung in the sky and the endless gray hadn't yet blanketed the land. Iona had been passing time in the gardens with Oli, their favorite place, waiting for me. But I never went to get them and..." Tovi blinked back tears and damning words she wasn't ready to utter. "When the rays touched them, they... died instantly. Because I'd been selfish, cruel, and horrible."

Eldrick, unlike she predicted, didn't step away. In fact, he stepped closer and laid a hand over hers that held the railing of the ship. Such a warm touch, like the spring sun on a late afternoon, ridding the lingering winter chill.

Tovi took a shuddering breath. "Riven's never forgiven me. He lost who he loved most that day, his wife and child."

"He blames you for their deaths..." Eldrick trailed off.

"Rightfully. We didn't even know, initially, that the sun could kill us. It all happened so fast, not to mention so many vampyrs turned to *caillte* immediately. It was madness that day, and by the time I even started looking for them, it was too late. If I had gone and retrieved them, brought them inside. If I hadn't been so selfish, they'd be alive. They died because of me. Oliver would be well over five hundred years old. I'd give anything to see the man he would've become. The world needs kindness like he and Iona had, and yet I'd robbed the world of it, because of one single mistake."

The wind twisted Tovi's hair, and a tear skidded across her cheek. A strong yet gentle touch caught it before it fell, and Tovi and Eldrick's green gazes locked as he brushed her sadness away.

He neither agreed nor objected to her ridiculing assessment of herself. Yet, neither his silence nor his stare possessed putrid judgment. He appraised her, eyes soaking her in, and those eyes held a sense of simply *seeing* her. That was all. A constant in the chaos, Eldrick kept her steady. Tovi's past didn't feel any less wrong or wretched, but to have spoken it out loud, to be *seen*, felt liberating.

And yet, she didn't trust the moment in the slightest. Too many letdowns and years of judgmental eyes still crept up her spine. Not long ago, Eldrick had judged her as well. Her instinct screamed this moment of seeing, of understanding, was a fluke. He was a werewolf, after all, and she'd revealed she'd been selfish, only thinking of herself, perhaps like he believed her kind to be.

"So," she whispered, "are we back to square one of you not trusting me?"

Eldrick scoffed, the left side of his lip hitching into a smirk. "No. Perhaps I misjudged your secrets to be dangerous, and yet they are parts of your past. We all have them."

"Have what?" she asked.

"Pasts." He sighed. "Even though I am *much* younger than you, I also have a past with mistakes I regret."

Tovi stilled, her heart skipping. *Mistakes.* She didn't indicate she understood what he referred to even though she knew—

"What do you mean much younger?" A laugh bubbled through her words, half forced, half genuine. "Are you implying I am old, wolf?"

Eldrick laughed, too, oblivious she'd changed the subject, evaded the awkwardness of one secret she wasn't ready to tell—*couldn't* tell, because it wasn't hers to share.

She'd promised.

"You are centuries old, am I right?" Eldrick asked.

"I am." She leaned in closer. "And with age comes wisdom."

Eldrick hummed. "True, fine wine also gets better with age."

Tovi smiled so wide her cheeks hurt. "You're quite right."

He searched the deck. "Linx and Todd found stores of wine barrels at the bottom of the ship. Should we give them a go?"

Tovi's heart raced, skipped, and almost burst from her chest. Why were her insides fluttering? Her past and secrets kept surging to the forefront of her mind, and yet, moments ago, Eldrick had listened. She'd admitted the worst part of her, the decision she regretted the most, and yet he'd stayed with her at the front of the ship, beside her.

He hadn't run, hadn't judged, and though fear still lingered, she wanted, *needed* to dive into the newness, this constant with him, despite everything screaming at her to not. Something she couldn't explain—or perhaps didn't want to face yet—pulled her towards him. It had been there since they met at the Shield-maiden, present even when he held a blade to her throat, and now, she gave into it.

Like the ship piercing into the river's rapids, she dove.

"Alright," she said, "but for one glass only."

CHAPTER TWENTY-EIGHT

A STRONG CURRENT HIT the bow of the boat, lurching it forward. Murky water sprayed Kade in the face, and he gripped the front banister to steady his weary legs. Splinters scraped against the calluses of his hands. The sting offered him a moment of reprieve from his roiling stomach.

Laughter filtered from below deck, the others enjoying a round of cards and wine. He remained above—the fresh air far nicer than the confines of the maddening boat, and he didn't dare allow anyone to witness his motion sickness. Not when the power inside his chest worried everyone else.

Linx had provided him some herbs, which left the soapy taste of dandelion muddled with dirt in his mouth and no reprieve. The younger werewolves they'd freed steered on the quarter deck, the five intent on soaking in fresh air, too, after being released from chains.

Kade didn't blame them.

"Thought we'd find you up here," Todd's cheery voice said from behind.

Kade muttered a curse, bile working his way up his throat. As he turned, he inhaled the scent of river and rock and found both Linx and Todd approaching, Maxie at the weapon master's heels.

His team's healer snapped her fingers, and the pink in her hair faded and bled to a yellow-green, like a sour fruit from the southern continents.

"That's the shade you are," Linx said.

Kade scoffed, finding the energy to smile. "I prefer the pink."

Linx giggled and snapped her fingers, pink returning as quickly as it had left.

The boat lurched over choppy rapids, and his wolf howled from the jostling sensation. Kade needed a distraction. Something. Anything other than the tilt of the world locking into his knees. Kade focused on his friends.

"Why are you both up here?" he asked, peering over their shoulders. Below, Bétar's booming laugh cracked against the wind, and two audible groans of defeat followed after. Yennifer's distinct snort when she drank too much rounded out the chorus of fun.

Linx wrinkled her nose. "It was a little bit too much of a love fest down there."

Love fest? Kade blinked, and for the first time since setting foot on the boat, his body and mind stilled. Moons, did they refer to his brother and the princess?

Todd shuddered. "Indeed. Thought we'd pay you a visit and possibly find you some relief."

He thrust a leather money pouch into Kade's hand, but he found it empty of any coins or jewels. Small, folded pieces of parchment had been stuffed inside.

"What's this?"

"A little game of chose-thy-weapon." Todd flashed a devilish grin.

Kade blinked, bracing his free hand on the ship again. "You want to spar? I can barely stand."

He hated to admit his inability, but it was obvious. He hadn't left this little corner of the ship in hours. Kade was a fool to think his team *hadn't* noticed. Discussing it, shedding light on it made his insides roil even more.

"I think some fighting and movement can do you some good, Commander," Todd said.

Kade exhaled, the folded parchment taunting him. His knees didn't connect to his mind, but anything was better than holding to the boat like his life depended on it. According to Tovi, the journey might take a half day. They had hours left and passing time was better fun than suffering through it.

His restless energy pulsed. Did he chance hurting someone he cared for or derailing their journey on the boat? Sparing, fighting—a risk. And yet, admitting *that* out loud showered more shame over Kade than his motion sickness.

"Alright," he said. "But I can't make any guarantees I won't hurl on your boots."

Linx crossed her arms. "I knew I picked the more exciting activity."

Kade rolled his eyes and drew a folded parchment from the pouch, handing it to Todd next.

"Stars above," Kade cursed as he opened his choice.

"What did you get?" Linx asked. She came up to his elbow in height, standing at her tiptoes to read the scribbled, three-letter word.

"Oh dear," she said. "Axe."

That was his *brother's* weapon, not Kade's. Too bulky at one end, off balance. He'd never adapted to the heavier end of an axe's blade—one that needed precise delivery and harsher force. He much preferred a sword, something parallel to his tall frame and moved as one with him. A glide, a slice, a pivot. A dance.

"Appears the Moon God favors me today!" Todd said.

His folded parchment read *dagger*, the weapons master's usual choice in weapon.

Kade groaned.

Linx got to work sectioning off a fighting ring in the largest area of the upper deck. Todd thrust a sack onto the wooden boards. Like clattered against like, and Kade found the contents to be *practice* weapons carved from wood. Regardless of the lighter, more forgiving material, the axe weighed more at one end, throwing Kade off as he spun it in his hand.

After Linx applied a white lacquer to the edges of their weapons, Todd and Kade faced the other off at the center of the makeshift ring, two strides apart, no more, no less. Maxie sat beside Linx, chest puffed out and tail whooshing side to side.

"The first to make contact and leave a mark wins," Linx said. She threw her hand down, signaling the sparring match's start, then retreated.

Todd lunged first, reaching for Kade's lower belly. But Kade sidestepped, bringing the axe down to scrape across his opponent's back. Todd squatted, dodging downward out of reach and swiping his leg across Kade's. The blow threw Kade off balance, and he dropped to the ground. The bones of the ship ricocheted through his rib cage. He cursed to the gray sky above.

He rolled and righted himself as Todd retreated a few steps, regaining his own posture and form.

"How's that axe treating you?" he taunted.

Kade growled, gripping his weapon tighter. He attacked this time, swiping left and down and spinning forward to deliver a blow to Todd's leading arm, but the axe sent him too far right—the lack of balance rearing him off course, hair's away from his opponent. He gritted his teeth, but Todd advanced, he and the dagger like one.

The white lacquer flashed across Kade's line of sight. He reared back as Todd attempted to punch him in the gut. The weapons master stayed close, so close, Kade only had the space to deflect and block. Over and over, wooden weapons popped and clunked together. Moons, Kade was losing. The energy in his chest rose and fell, the pull and release of gravity like hanging off a cliff. Weight pulled him downward, his grip on the stony ledge weakening.

The dagger remained in Todd's dominant hand, his right. His left arm protected his torso, like a shield. Kade charged, matching Todd's attack of proximity and brought his weapon down towards his shoulder. Kade's plan worked—Todd lifted his left arm to block the blow. Wood connected with his forearm. Victory flushed through Kade, sedating his festering energy. He'd landed a hit.

His lips twitched into a smile, but Todd was eyeing his belly. So did Linx, her lips etched into a thin line. Kade peered down. A line of white ran across his oblique, staining his fighting leathers. Stunned, he averted his gaze back upward, Kade's weapon hadn't made a mark. He'd delivered the blow with the axe's shaft, not the blade.

No winning lacquer in sight.

The two werewolves stared at each other. Both of their long hair whirled in the wind, the tension between wolves vibrating in the air, sweat soaking their clothes and brows. Kade broke away from their locked hold, shaking out his frustrated muscles. He rolled his shoulders, letting the wound to his pride simmer.

"Well done," he managed.

Todd backed away slowly, step for step, dark eyes still alert, as if the fight weren't over. "Do you remember one of the first lessons of fighting?" he asked.

The question jarred Kade's racing heart. "What?"

"Never fight with a weapon you don't know how to use," Todd said.

Confusion rippled through Kade, rocking him like the surge of current hitting the bow of the ship. "I didn't exactly choose this weapon."

"You didn't choose your new power either, Kade," Linx said.

He flickered his attention between Todd and Linx. The boat grew smaller, like walls closing in around him.

"That is different. I am not wielding it; I'm not meaning to anyway."

"You're not doing anything with it except ignoring it," Todd said. "And like using a weapon you haven't mastered," he pointed towards his marked torso, "you will get hurt or worse—harm someone else."

Bile, not from the motion sickness, rose in him. His memory flashed to the burnt husk of a vampyr. That had been the enemy, but what if he did it to someone he loved? But thinking about it, worrying about it took energy, energy he didn't have when his focus was elsewhere. On Evelyn. But perhaps ignoring his new power was just as depleting. At least he could admit that to his team.

He sighed. "You're both right."

Todd's demeanor lightened, and Linx's face brightened.

"But I *need* to rescue Evelyn first." He shook his head. "I swear, after, I will figure out this new power, but until then, I need to focus on the mission—getting my mate back."

Neither of his friends said a word for a bit. Silence and gray stretched around them. Mists and opinions. Shadows and shame.

Todd exhaled. "Fine. As long as you know we're here for you, Kade."

"Always," Linx added.

Warmth bloomed in Kade's chest. "Of course."

After, he told himself.

"Another round?" Todd asked.

Kade smiled, forced and tired. "Fine, but I'm using a sword."

The weapons master scoffed, throwing one his way. Kade didn't miss the weariness in his friend's stare—as if he'd heard the hesitation in Kade's tone, too.

More sparring had helped Kade's nausea and calmed his restless wolf. He felt lighter, more himself than he had in days. The pressure in his chest had lessoned, too, and he found he could breathe more easily. His steps up the ship held more strength, more hope. Linx and Todd stood off to the side, and he gave them a nod of thanks. He appreciated his friends who'd allowed him to be vulnerable and respected his decision to focus on rescuing Evelyn.

Suddenly, the new power growing in him was less unnerving. He had a plan to deal with it. Later, of course, but he was no longer willingly ignoring it—he'd rescue Evelyn and return home, and *then* deal with it.

Decision made, it was if the land of Drystan had shifted in their favor. The wind had changed an hour ago. Fiercer, sharp, whipping across the deck with a mighty chill. Tovi had said any minute they'd reach Drystan Village. The river, too, had changed. Darker, choppier. Yet, Kade's legs held strong, unbending against the faster current.

Their ship sped down the river towards their final destination.

Kade narrowed his eyes, honing his werewolf's sense of sight to make it out. Delicate curls of mists hovered over the rushing river. As the ship speared through the clouds of fog, more rolled in their wake, making it impossible to see ahead. And yet Kade felt how near they were, how close Evelyn was in reach. He inhaled the crisp winter air—the same air Evelyn breathed.

His wolf howled—not a whine, but a call of strength, of purpose.

Kade shut his eyes and imagined her vanilla-and-cedar scent, the feel of pine needles under his paws and the tune of songbirds back home. It grounded him, fueled him.

And that sparked a wild idea.

Kade's team had suggested his new power might be related to his mate bond with Evelyn. With consideration to when it surfaced, Kade was inclined to agree. He hadn't been naive to notice, too, that when he worried for Evelyn, the power surged forward, furthering his assumption that the magic was tied to them meeting in some way.

But with his new sense of calm, how could he tap into it?

Kade shut his eyes, loose hair from his bun whipping in his face. He inhaled, the frigid wind chilling his lungs dry. He inhaled again, reaching for the manifesting power in his chest as well as grasping onto another.

His tracking ability.

Kade hadn't used it since being in the halls of Lār. Nothing during their journey through the Void and Drystan had called for it. Usually, his tracking ability needed to be grounded within a space, but seeing he and Evelyn were connected through the mind—a thread between their souls—he wanted to assess how far his tracking ability could now reach. Since his new magic might be connected to their mate bond, too, and Evelyn was so close, he wondered if it might aid his tracking ability.

He extended down the bond, desperate to feel what he could of Evelyn. Anything, even the pulse of her fiery spirit.

Clouds of darkness, much like the mists and fog surrounding the ship, blurred his vision. His wolf hit the same shield he had for days. Lightning flashed—the power surrounding Evelyn was a storm of anger and hate. It nibbled like gnats on Kade's skin, and he growled through it. He reached out further, following the emotion his tracking ability sensed, a pearly blue twinkling behind his eyelids. Kade didn't pause time, he paused his senses.

Anger, frustration, *restlessness.*

Through the haze of gray, bursts of rust and swamp green pushed through.

Evelyn.

Stars above, he'd reached her. Past the dark magic. Past the shield blocking her.

Fire flattened against the shield. Kade's own magic ran parallel to it. Red, orange, and blue danced side by side. Despite the storm, the dark magic separating them, their love pulsed through and ebbed against each other.

A gust of wind blew past Kade, and when his eyes sprang open, he held onto his connection with Evelyn, held her tight as his sights set on where she resided.

The fog thinned and parted, revealing an onyx castle. Slim yet tall, the castle stood as mighty as the mountain it'd been carved into. Kade counted over twelve turrets, clusters of them sprouting out of the windowless base. Spires shot into the sky, some lost to the overbearing clouds of gray. A wall surrounded it, much like the one that surrounded Nūa. An inclined bridge curved and winded down to the mists of the river, docks waiting up ahead.

Kade's tracking ability soared, and the emotions weaved into his connection with Evelyn tugged from the fortress—she was there; he could *feel* it.

Something plush pushed against his shin. Between his legs, Maxie stared up at him, eyes begging him to hold her. The edges of Kade's lips tugged into a smile, and he obliged. She pranced from his forearm and climbed his chest, positioning herself across the back of his shoulders. Her purr vibrated down his neck. Her yellow eyes stared straight ahead like she, too, sensed Evelyn.

Kade rallied his breath against the wind, and down the bond he whispered, "We're coming, love."

Chapter Twenty-Nine

K ADE WAS CLOSE.

Evelyn *felt* him.

His beastly strong-yet-kind touch vibrated through the barrier blocking her magic.

Evelyn's magic danced at his proximity, flared in greeting. Their bond held power. Stronger, braver than the dark magic encompassing Evelyn's or the distance between them. It pulsed and ignited, letting them caress the other.

I'm coming.

A faint whisper traveled down the bond. Not words. A feeling. Weaved with love, promise, and *restlessness*.

It mirrored her own state—the rage to escape this tower and reunite with him.

Soon. His promise ached through her bones, her entire being alight with his energy, the feelings of his soul. Goddess, he—

"Evelyn, are you alright?" a sweet voice pulled her back to the present, severing her connection with Kade.

When he'd reached out to her, Evelyn had stooped against the sofa, their bond so strong she lost her knees. Her knuckles had gone white as she gripped the back cushions for balance, a dizziness settling over her.

She blinked, and Belle's ringlet curls came into focus. She held a stack of books close to her chest, chin resting on the top one. Her freckles scrunched together as her face pinched with concern.

"I'm..." Evelyn hesitated.

She trusted Belle. To an extent. She'd taught her magic and explored the secrets of the castle with her, but she wouldn't risk Kade's safety. She hid her shudder at the thought of Riven ever learning he was near.

"It's the nausea, from the bracelets," she said. "It still hits me from time to time."

"Oh dear," Belle said, setting the books down. "I'll be sure to grab you some tea for that the next time I visit."

Evelyn offered her a grateful smile and sauntered over to the books. The chrome titles glinted from the light of her fire. Evelyn thumbed through tabs and clips bookmarking pages and sections. "Did you pick up some light reading?" she asked.

Belle giggled. "Goddess, no. Ingrid's been watching me closer than ever before, so I grabbed a handful of books and went off to my room. She'll be none the wiser, believing I'm occupied for the night."

"Does she not spend time with you?"

Belle's gaze snapped to the stone floor as she said, "She and Visha are quite in love. She spends time with me when she can."

A solemnness laced her tone. A pang of sadness went through Evelyn. She had considered the witch was lonely, but with Kade so close and escape at the forefront of her mind, she'd yet to consider Belle's fate once she left. The castle was no place for the young witch. Could she risk getting them both out? Did Belle even *want* to leave?

"So"—Belle ran her fingers down the spines of one of the books, her eyes downcast—"I've been following Riven the last few days."

Evelyn's blood ran cold. "What?"

Belle shrugged. "Not following him exactly, but watching him. He uses passageways and tunnels, too. There's one he travels more often than others, and I'm fairly certain we can get there from the passage here in your room."

"Through the abandoned servant's quarters?"

Belle nodded.

Evelyn debated. Kade had felt close, the closest since they'd been separated. It wasn't lost to her that he could already be in Drystan, hours or a day away from entering the castle. Did she continue risking herself searching for answers? The servant's quarters were passed the fighting rings, and it had been the closest she'd come to crossing paths with a vampyr other than Tala.

Trailing Riven's path and learning more about him was a greater risk. Sure, she had Matilda Moore's knowledge, etched words from the scribbled prophecy, letters she'd yet to open, but what did it all mean? It felt like nothing, not enough to defeat the darkness once and for all when she reunited with Kade. And if he was close, time was running out to find more. This might be her last chance.

"Alright, let's go, but let's be quick."

The servant's passage was as eerie as it had been before. Worse, in fact, despite the brighter daytime gray streaming in from the high windows, shedding light on the bones, dried blood, and destruction Evelyn and Belle tiptoed around. Death gripped the space, and Evelyn fought a shutter. She didn't need her magic to know something dark and wicked had happened in this part of the castle.

They were silent as they continued on, and this time, Belle veered them left. Broken foundation and piled beams fell into the stones of a tunnel. The temperature dropped as they climbed farther down. Evelyn ran her hands over the rock, some of it smooth, like water had weathered it, while other sections had been cut and broken by tools. Rubble crunched under their boots, the only sound in the empty tunnel.

Ahead, light flickered from a small, weathered hole. Both she and Belle slowed the closer they came, careful not to disturb the loose stones. Evelyn peered into the hole first, anticipation prickling at the back of her neck.

Below, a small humble cavern had been lit with hundreds of black candles. At the center lay a rectangular slab of stone, carvings etched onto its sides that bled into the dais it sat on. Rusty stains seeped into the center.

Blood.

"It's..." Evelyn squinted. "An altar."

Cold washed over Evelyn, and her magic grew flighty. Movement caught her peripherals, and both she and Belle cursed, ducking out of sight. Boots echoed in the cavern. Belle tucked her knees into her chest, eyes wide as a doe. Evelyn grabbed her hand and squeezed it in comfort and laid a finger over her mouth. She rose, slowly and to the side. Back flush against the wall, she strained her neck and eyes.

Prince Riven used the talon of his right hand to slice open his right palm. Blood dripped like the trickle of rain as he knelt, bowed, and laid his forehead against the dais. Crimson seeped into the stone, blood rushing through the crevices of the carvings. With arms splayed out ahead of him, Riven's back shook as he murmured like a madman into the stone. What in the Goddess was he doing?

Evelyn swallowed, sure to not make a move, not a sound as she tried to listen to hear *anything,* even a single word to pocket and study. Nothing happened aside from the howling air in the tunnel and the swaying flicker of candles.

"*Answer me!*" Riven bellowed.

His cry was so desperate, so loud, it rattled the bones in Evelyn's chest. Belle flinched, her curls and the layers of her velvet dress shaking along with her.

A chilling, raspy laugh echoed here, elsewhere, everywhere. A woman's. It vibrated in Evelyn's ears. The fire in her veins flared to the surface, heating her blood.

Steam rose from the carvings, Riven's blood bubbling and seeping into the floor. An offering. A summoning. When he lifted his head, his eyes had gone black as ink. His head twisted, snapped, and tilted, as if something had taken over from the inside. As if something was *in him*.

Evelyn was too far away, too high to hear every word.

"Do you... trust...?" The woman's voice came in and out.

Riven's head snapped to the left, eyes blinking back to the color jade. Spittle fell from his lips. "You know—"

"*Don't lie.*"

Like nails, the voice grated against Evelyn's skin. Belle clamped her hands over her ears. *Shit.* The poor witch was petrified. Evelyn bent to her knees, losing sight of Riven and focusing on Belle.

"We're going to be alright." She barely spoke, barely whispered. "Remain still and quiet."

Belle nodded. Red blotched her cheeks, and sweat matted her ringlets.

Evelyn rose, watching Riven again. He struggled, thrashing as he tried to regain control. His voice came out pained, ragged as he said, "I trust you. I only fear the plan."

Did he mean the spell, walking in the sunlight, or breaking the curse? Which *part* of the plan did he fear?

His head snapped back this time, eyes bleeding back to black. He snickered—no, someone else snickered. "You have her, yes?"

Evelyn's stomach backflipped. Whoever spoke through Riven meant *her*. There was no doubt they talked about the spell, and Evelyn listened, trying to grasp onto every word.

"I have already told you I have!" Riven said with frustration.

With black eyes again, he stilled. A slight nod. A twitch of the fingers. Evelyn covered her mouth, holding back the contents of her stomach as he licked and lavished his palm and sucked the blood clean off.

"Cast... cast in... cast in red, cast in red, cast in red."

Wait. The words from the scribbled lines—Evelyn's heart thumped, and she fought a gasp. *In red* had been carved into the wood, a word missing after *land*. Was that word *cast*? Was this woman, this voice filling in the gaps? How in the Goddess did she know those words?

Riven, with black eyes, continued to chant the lines over and over. "Trust the timing. Trust the power. Trust the Blood Moon, prince. Please me, grant me what I seek, and you'll get what you've lost, what your heart beats for. *Walk in the Light.*"

The candles whooshed out, casting the cavern in shadowed darkness. Riven retched and collapsed to the ground, his hand over his heart, grasping it like it may beat out of his chest. That's when Evelyn noticed—the absence of his bloodstone necklace. He crawled out of the cavern, cries of agony and fatigue splitting from him. Sad. Ragged. *Broken.*

Evelyn almost pitied him. Almost.

Belle tugged Evelyn's sleeve. "We need to get back."

Evelyn nodded, a tad numb from the experience. As a child in the summer months, her parents had whispered ghost stories and tales of the ancient faerie around a fire while she and her sisters listened, huddled under blankets and giggling against their parents' passionate theatrics. Some stories, though, entranced Evelyn so much, the frightening tales left her wide and hollow, haunting her.

The voice had done that, the ancient darkness a sound she'd not soon shake. It rattled her senses, left her so uncertain she bobbed in an endless sea of questions.

She and Belle walked on the pads of their feet back through the tunnels. A hurriedness had bled into their steps, like the voice followed, moments away from appearing. In the shadows. In the stone. In the silence.

You have her.
Cast in red.
The Blood Moon.
What you lost.
Walk in the light.

Evelyn gripped the memory like she may lose the fragments. They came and went, filtering through her mind as she tried to make a connection. She replayed the words over and over, round and round up the tower steps. Why was *cast in red* so important? Wait, did a Blood Moon have that effect on the land? Is that what the voice had alluded to?

Evelyn furrowed her brow, her theory on the tip of her tongue, ready to share it with Belle as the hidden passageway door clicked open to her room. She collided right into the young witch's back.

Straight ahead of them, three figures stood. Sneering with arms folded, Ingrid, Visha, and Tala waited for them.

"Isn't this a lovely surprise?" the princess said.

Tala stepped forward, face void of emotion. "I think it's about time you visit the dungeons, witch."

Fucking flames.

CHAPTER THIRTY

T OVI

T OVI GRITTED HER TEETH as she pulled her hood closer around her face and flattened herself against an alleyway wall. She peered down the line of werewolves following her—Eldrick, Kade, Bétar, and Todd.

Bloody hel, stubbornness had to be a werewolf gene. Or at least, a *male* werewolf gene. Yennifer hadn't batted an eye when Tovi suggested they stay behind on the ship while she met with her contact. Kade had downright refused to stay on the ship a minute longer than he had to, and Todd had whined he'd never seen a vampyr village, and it wasn't fair if he had to wait. Bétar had agreed. Eldrick, on the other hand, hadn't said a word, but by his ticking jaw, she'd known he didn't want to let her go alone either. Perhaps their recent fresh start held him back from saying anything, but nonetheless, he'd joined.

Thank the Goddess it was day. The few who possessed a bloodstone resided in court, while those in the village kept their days as nights and nights as days. Linx, too, had mimicked the enchanted necklace Blair had crafted for Kade, masking each of their werewolf magic a tad.

It didn't hide Eldrick's delicious spearmint scent though. Any slumbering vampyr would awaken if they got a whiff of it. Tovi gritted her teeth harder, molars grinding as she imagined another vampyr feeding from him. She shut her eyes, pushing the horrid image from her thoughts. It elicited an anger inside her she didn't want to diagnose. She also didn't want to linger on the mysterious fact she could smell *him*, despite his necklace, unlike the others.

At least the Alpha, along with his youngest brother and the Gray Fenris's second-in-command, prowled through the village like a pack of hunting wolves—stealthy and as swift as the mists kissing their cheeks. Their tact called to Tovi's own inner beast. Todd, on the other hand, clinked like the poor werewolf was made of steel, not wearing it.

"You are as loud as *caillte* in a herd of cattle," Tovi hissed.

"I came prepared," Todd whispered. "Can never be too careful."

"Weapons will get us nowhere if half the village awakens. Quiet, or I'll send you back to the ship."

"Can't say I remember the way. You wouldn't send me back alone now, would ya?" he asked with a playful smirk.

Tovi rolled her eyes. "No. I'd send Bétar back with you."

The second hit Todd in the shoulder. "I think not. Keep it together. I can't brag to my mate I saw the village before her if I'm dismissed by the princess, now can I?"

Tovi doubted the archer cared.

Bétar continued to argue with Todd, the banter somewhat endearing, like that of a family. Her gaze snagged with Eldrick's, a small, toothless smile playing on his lips. She smiled back, and, for a moment, lost herself in his stare while the others bickered.

Except for one.

"Tovi, where to next?"

Kade's question snapped both Eldrick and Tovi from their dazes. She blinked a few times, peering behind the Alpha to address Kade. He too wore a small smile. A smug one. Tovi turned before he could see the rouge blush spread across her cheeks.

"Two more blocks to go," she muttered and darted onward.

The others followed, mimicking her path. Luckily, the human borough was south down the river, and they headed north. Foot traffic would be light, but not nonexistent for those who still lived during the day. Loyalty to her or Riven extended to both humans and vampyrs. She'd done a considerable amount for the rights and treatment of humans over the years. Any human they encountered could keep silent out of loyalty to her. But loyalty couldn't compare to the pile of coins Riven could produce for any information on their whereabouts. Anyone who'd spotted her in the village could make a tidy sum, and she wouldn't fault them for it. Humans stuck in Drystan had their own trials against the curse, and Tovi sighed her sadness away. Getting Evelyn back, challenging her brother, breaking the curse—she'd do it for all of those who called Drystan home.

Tovi slunk into the thin gap between two clay-packed buildings. There was no step, no lightness of foot to silence the pebbled alleyway. At least water trickled down a drain and drowned out some of their advance. The larger building of the two had dark timber beams lining its foundation while clay—once white but now green with age and mold—filled the in-between. A wooden door sat at the center. Tovi knocked three times, paced a breath apart, and finished her knock with four rapid hits of her knuckle.

Nothing stirred on the other side or in the village, aside from the mists slithering their way over and atop buildings.

One of the werewolves moved, but Tovi held up her hand to be still.

Past the door, Tovi's sense of hearing caught wooden floorboards groaning under the weight of someone's boot. The door eased open, no one but darkness on the other side. The first bit of whoever answered the door emerged as the tip of their crossbow. Inch by inch, the silver tip of an arrow flashed as it reached the low light.

Small, dainty, but with the temper of a bear, Lou Foret stepped outside her home. Behind large-rimmed bright-red glasses, her brown eyes landed on Tovi, and she lowered the crossbow in an instant.

"Goddess, Tovi!" Lou said. "I smelled werewolf and, bloody hel, I almost shot you. Wait, who the hel are they?"

She leveled the crossbow up again.

Praise the Goddess, none of the werewolves moved an inch.

Tovi held her hands out, putting herself in the line of fire. "Lou, I—*we* need a place to stay."

Lou narrowed her eyes, not daring to lower her crossbow. "But who *are* they?"

"The name's Todd!" a boisterous, jolly voice echoed in the alleyway.

Bloody hel.

Everyone rushed a shush. Tovi winced and shut her eyes. Goddess, help them. She peered over her shoulder and—

She shook her head, blinked, certain she'd seen it wrong. Did Todd consider that a smile?

Thankfully, Kade intervened, shoving his weapons master back. Tovi dared a breath of relief. Kade was always calm, collected. Well, aside from when he stressed over Evelyn.

"I am Kade Drengr, Son—"

"No." Lou cut him off. She lowered her crossbow and pointed a finger at Tovi. "Absolutely not."

Lou shut the door.

Tovi cringed. She really should've fought harder to come alone. Or at least warned Kade his title wouldn't get him anywhere.

"What did I do?" Todd whispered.

"You opened your mouth!" Kade said.

"I think it was a poor attempt at flirting," Bétar grumbled.

Tovi scrunched her nose like she smelled something foul. "Moons, I hope that wasn't flirting."

Eldrick nodded towards the door. "I take it she's not a fan of werewolves."

"I am most certainly not!" a voice shouted from inside.

"We really don't have time for this," Kade said, pinching the bridge of his nose.

The door swung open again. Lou's dark hair had a slight tint of red, and though she was as pale as any vampyr, her cheeks heated crimson.

"Don't have time for this? Such a werewolf thing to say!" She shut the door in their faces.

Tovi's hope fizzled. Kade appeared ready to shift into his werewolf form and head to the castle himself. Not a good plan. Bétar was worn. They all needed rest. Todd frowned, looking confused. Nothing new.

Eldrick had his arms crossed and his attention elsewhere. Until his emerald-green eyes snapped to her, and their stares connected. Tovi's breath hitched, heart pounded.

"Why do we need her help anyway?" Eldrick asked. "Why not use the woods?"

"Because Lou has access to tunnels into the castle," Tovi muttered.

Before Eldrick could ask the questions swimming in his green eyes, Lou swung the door open.

"Why do you need to get into the castle? You're the princess."

Tovi shared wary glances with the team. "Haven't you heard?"

Lou's face fell paler. "Is Riven king?"

Tovi stepped back, shaking her head. "No, well, I don't believe so, but..." *No.* If Riven were king, the village would know. *Sorin* would know if he'd succeeded in the spell and assumed the throne. Caught off guard Lou hadn't heard the news, Tovi's brows pinched so fiercely she'd have a headache later. It wasn't that she didn't trust Lou with the news of Evelyn, Tovi trusted Lou with all their lives, but she'd expected her brother to have paraded his victory through Drystan court and village.

"I don't understand. Riven captured Evelyn weeks ago," she said.

Lou blinked, grip on her crossbow relaxing. "He has her for her blood, doesn't he?"

Tovi nodded. "To allow vampyrs to walk in the sunlight."

"Bloody hel," Lou hissed.

Tovi shook her head, droplets of the mists clinging to her hair. "You're certain there's been no whisperings of her in the castle?"

"No," she said. "Other than Riven returning home, there's been no news."

Eldrick shook his head. "Does that not strike you as odd?"

"Yes." Both Tovi and Kade said.

She didn't miss he'd turned stiffer, *tauter*.

"Why not tell his people he was working on the spell?" Bétar asked. "Wouldn't he want to boast?"

Tovi racked her brain, schooling every ounce of fear and worry out of her expression. They didn't have time to debate this. She didn't have the energy to evade questions that might arise.

"One would think, yes," she whispered. "But my brother is naturally secretive. He may be a pompous ass, but he's also smart. The less who know, the less information gets out to jeopardize his plan. Regardless, the tunnels are our best way into the castle."

Lou's lips fell in a thin line, eyes searching the group. She sighed.

"Alright. I hope you have a plan, princess."

Tovi had a plan. That wasn't the issue. It was convincing the werewolves of it.

CHAPTER THIRTY-ONE

"WALK US THROUGH THE plan one more time," Linx said, a mischievous glint shining in her eyes.

The moment explosives had been mentioned, the Gray Fenris's healer had been glued to Tovi's plan on infiltrating the castle. Eldrick, though, didn't need Linx's contraptions to burst with objection.

Lou Foret owned a renowned bakery in Drystan Village. Sacks of flour and jars of sugar lined every inch of free space in the basement pantry. The scent of fresh bread seeped into the terra-cotta floors beneath Eldrick's boots while he stewed in the corner as Tovi went through her plan for the third time. A map of the underground tunnel system covered a workbench, and bread-shaping baskets cluttered the perimeter. Lou had supplied a marker for the fighting ring's location, deep in the underbelly of the castle.

"It's a good plan," Kade whispered beside him.

"I know," Eldrick muttered, crossing his arms.

It wasn't a *bad* plan. It was *her* plan. Instead of lashing out verbally, he battled the two warring concepts internally.

"And how exactly will you get us into the rings?" Bétar asked.

"We will have to investigate that part in the coming days," Tovi said. "I know somewhere we can get that information."

That part of the plan also had his wolf howling at the notion. They'd freed five werewolves from slavery days ago, and Tovi wanted to throw two of them into the fighting rings as a part of getting Evelyn out of the castle.

"We'll need a distraction," she'd declared.

That distraction called for Kade and Bétar to be smuggled into the rings as fighters while Todd and Linx were stationed under the cavern. Yen would remain in the woods, manning the team's exit. They'd give the signal to alert everyone else the plan was in motion. They'd keep the vampyr court busy while Tovi and Eldrick got Evelyn out of the castle.

"How do you plan to get her out of the castle?" Kade asked.

"I..." Tovi paused. "Have someone in the castle I can trust." She and Lou shared a knowing, wordless glance. "I'll get in contact with them immediately, now that we've arrived here."

Eldrick grinded his teeth and shifted his stance up against the wall. It was a good plan, and with the access to the tunnels the bakery possessed, they had the advantage. But it didn't take away the fact Tovi had numerous secrets, ones she chose to unveil when the time was right for her. Tovi may not have had the allies to win the favor of her people, but she had a network of supporters in Drystan Village and apparently also the castle.

It didn't sit well with Eldrick, not knowing everything there was regarding the princess. Except he was being unfair. Drystan was her home. If the roles were reversed, he'd be no different in Drengr Village.

Leading.

And doubted.

The ire her people felt for her unsettled him, too. Perhaps because he could sympathize. It was something they had in common—an unbending desire to lead a people, some of whom doubted them. She the rightful queen, he the Alpha. Why did he have such difficulty accepting it?

"What about us?" Siv asked.

She and the other werewolves had lingered to the side. Eldrick hadn't missed how their eyes shined with excitement and promise when Tovi discussed the plan. He admired their bravery, even after the weeks they'd endured.

Tovi sighed, relaxing against the table. "I think it's best we get you all home."

"But we can help," Sam said.

Kade pushed off from the wall beside Eldrick. "We know it. You've all been brave these last few weeks. I'd gladly add you to the Gray Fenris if I had a spot open. But this mission will require stealth, and we need low numbers."

Tovi nodded. "Kade's right. I have a way to get you all home by the evening hour, but it'll require you to trust a vampyr to guide you."

Erik crossed his arms. "Do you trust this vampyr?"

For a moment, the princess considered. "Yes, I do. He'll follow through."

He'll.

Eldrick stiffened and pushed off the wall.

Lou beat him to the question. "You can't seriously be considering the captain."

"If I ask, Flynn will make sure they get home." Tovi avoided everyone's stare, but Eldrick caught the stiffness in her shoulders and her stone expression, something she did when she was hiding something.

Lou shook her head. "It won't be a favor, Tovi. He'll want something in return."

Eldrick's blood heated, and his wolf growled below the surface. "This Captain Flynn, is he a part of the underground pirates?"

"He *is* the underground pirate, the one who runs it all." Lou tsked. "Tovi—"

"If it's a hefty payment, the Drengr pack can help with the fee," Eldrick said, making eye contact with Tovi.

She blinked, and a pink blossomed on her cheeks.

Lou shook her head. "It won't be payment he asks for, you know it—"

"Agree to whatever he asks for, Lou. The werewolves deserve to return home." Tovi returned her attention to the map. A finality rang in her tone, ending the conversation.

Mouth open and brows pinched, Lou looked like she wanted to argue.

Their conversation on the ship about suitors and marriage filtered through Eldrick's mind, and his inner wolf growled. She'd not give her hand in exchange for these werewolves she barely knew, would she?

Eldrick dug his nails into his arms, focusing on the pain and not the anger flooding through him. He withheld the urge to object and demand a better solution, but in front of everyone else, he couldn't demand something he himself couldn't explain. Why did he care so much about what Tovi sacrificed? Besides, the werewolves—*his* people—needed a way home.

Siv walked up the table, resting her hand over her heart. "If you trust this captain, so will we. Thank you for getting us this far, Princess."

The werewolves inclined their heads and said their goodbyes to the rest of the Gray Fenris. Lou escorted them out of the basement, and Tovi, Kade, and Bétar continued running through the plan.

"What of this contact of yours inside the castle?" Kade asked.

"Leave that to Lou and me," Tovi said with a curt nod. "In the meantime, we'll need to figure out the best way into the rings. Tonight, I'll scope out who runs them and where they deliver new werewolves."

"I'll come with you," Eldrick blurted.

Everyone whipped their attention to him, eyes wide. He hadn't meant to sound so urgent, so eager, but he still didn't want to let Tovi out of his sight. Eldrick might've kept his mouth shut about the plan, but that didn't mean he couldn't still scope Tovi's intentions and behaviors.

Tovi nodded. "Alright. Fine by me, but Linx will need to check your cloaking necklace. It doesn't help against your scent like the others, and where we're going, we can't afford vampyrs who bite first and ask questions later to get a whiff."

Todd leaned into Eldrick and inhaled. "I can't smell him. Necklace works fine."

Tovi blinked, brows pinching. "It must be my vampyr senses then."

The basement bristled with static and unsaid words as the team shifted uncomfortably. Eldrick's mouth went dry. Everyone knew Tovi's bloodstone hid her vampyr scent, yet he'd kept the fact he could smell past it entirely to himself. Yet, it appeared she smelled him, too. Despite magic. Despite cloaking. Which begged the question—

Kade cleared his throat. "Okay, Tovi and Eldrick will learn more about the fighting rings tonight. What about the rest of us?"

"I'd rest," Tovi said. "If we find a way into the rings, there's a chance you and Bétar are headed into the castle tomorrow."

Kade crossed his arms and nodded.

Discussion continued, but Eldrick stood frozen by the table only half listening. He dismissed the earlier awkwardness. Even when he caught a glimpse of Tovi's bloodstone and smelled violets and plums, he refused to linger on what it all meant.

He battled wariness and trust. Kade had asked him for the sake of the team and mission to put his quarrels with the princess to rest, and he had. He hadn't even objected to her plan when it clearly put his brother in danger. *Moons*, he'd drank far too much wine the other night with her, and his attention kept falling to those damn lips of hers. As he let his guard down, the less he saw her as a vampyr, as the enemy.

In fact, the more Eldrick considered her efforts, he was starting to see her less and less as a vampyr and more as a worthy ally.

Chapter Thirty-Two

Eldrick, alone, sat in a booth, wedged into the corner of Lou's bustling bakery. Leg bent, arm resting on his knee, he waited for Tovi to arrive as they set out to learn more about the fighting rings.

The evening hour reminded Eldrick of the same foot traffic as the morning hour in the Drengr Village, as the days in Drystan were reversed from the Vadon Mountains. Vampyrs, none the wiser he, a werewolf, observed them, grabbed breakfast, breads, and desserts. Some dashed out the door, while others lingered to chat with those they knew, enjoying their steaming cups of coffee over an evening chat.

Warm, inviting, with sugar and yeast bubbling in the air, Lou's bakery challenged every notion of vampyrs Eldrick had. They dressed differently than werewolves back home, with satin and silks replacing wool and furs. The vampyrs moved differently, too, light on their feet, a slight prowl or slink. Yet, they came and went, laughed, chatted, and ate like a werewolf would before heading to their posts in the early hours.

Robin's-egg blue tile and maroon painted furniture decorated the space. Behind a counter, Lou's eyeglasses matched the red leather booth Eldrick sat in. She paid him no mind, running her shop as though a handful of werewolves, a mage, and the rogue princess weren't staying in the hidden passageways and tunnels of her secret safe house.

A lithe frame glided through the open door. Tovi wore the same emerald cloak, hood up, as she had when she'd left a few hours ago. Where she went, she hadn't said. An odd trust had settled over the Gray Fenris toward the princess, and yet Eldrick couldn't help but be curious. Where had she gone, and why had she slipped out like a thief in the night?

She weaved her way through the bustle, her gaze snagging his. It kept happening. Chaos ensued around them, but with a single look, a chanced glance, they'd connect like a thread pulling taut. The bakery fell away. The grating of forks, laughter, and clattering cups muted. A stillness, a constant grounded Eldrick. The sight of her jade eyes calmed his wolf.

Tovi broke the connection as she slid into the booth across from him. She dropped her hood back and—

"Moons, what did you do to your beautiful hair?" Eldrick asked.

Tovi's eyes went wide, and embarrassment flushed through him. *Beautiful.* The word burst out him. She did that to him—made him speak without thinking, made him act without looking, made him feel without caution.

He couldn't let his growing trust of Tovi lead him away from rational decision making and into the burning realm of want. Because he wasn't sure he could control his desire for Tovi. His wolf growled, a hungry beast pacing to be let loose.

He cleared his throat. "I mean... you dyed it."

Tovi's once snowy blonde hair, the color that reminded him of a dove, had an auburn hue. The red undertones heightened the green in her eyes, and Eldrick pushed down his yet again growling wolf.

"The hair is sadly a Verena trait. I'd be spied a mile away. Linx helped me with the color. She suggested a green to match my eyes but," Tovi shrugged. "I reminded her my goal was to be inconspicuous."

"I see." Eldrick relaxed farther into the booth.

There was little Eldrick understood about Linx. Why and when she'd left the mages of the east or who she was amongst them, for example. But what he didn't understand the most was his friend's ease with change. How she took pieces of herself and morphed them into something else entirely. And now she'd done it to Tovi too.

"Do you think your brother suspects you'd try and free Evelyn?"

Tovi shrugged. "He considered me a threat enough to bury me in a box while he captured her."

"He what?" Eldrick whispered, a deadly calm trickling over him.

"He buried me, miles outside of Callum. I'll always be a threat to Riven, seeing I was the twin born earlier. He also knows I love Evelyn. But Riven—"

"Underestimates you and your influence in Drystan," Lou said. She placed numerous plates of pastries, sweet and savory, onto the table. "Always has."

Herbs, custard, lavender, and a sharp cheese filled Eldrick's nose, eliciting a grumble from his stomach. As interested as he was in the promise of breakfast, he was far more interested in what Lou could reveal about Tovi.

"What do you mean?" he asked.

Tovi tucked a stray strand of dyed hair behind her ear. "Lou." A warning sat in the single word. Was she afraid Lou would reveal secrets?

The baker didn't falter, pushing her red glasses up her nose and crossing her arms.

"Riven cares about those who fund his pockets and make his court happy. He forgets there are vampyrs in Drystan that aren't lords and ladies, vampyrs like me who didn't have a name or centuries to earn a place." She waved her hand around. "None of this would've happened without the efforts of Tovi."

"Your bakery?"

"No," Lou said, rolling her eyes. "The village. Along with many others throughout Drystan. Cursed as it is, Tovi made it better, made it bountiful."

"*Lou.*" Tovi's one word this time was a plea. A slight downturn to her pink lips, a pinch between her brows, hands clasped so tightly on the table, her knuckles whitened.

Tovi was embarrassed, but Eldrick couldn't understand why.

"Hate hearing it all you want, princess, but it's the truth." Lou pointed out the door. "You'll find vampyrs and humans living in harmony here. There're laws against harming humans." She pointed back at Tovi. "We have her to thank for that, too."

With that, Lou sauntered off, leaving an awkwardness twisting in the air with the steam rising from their food.

Eldrick tried to rack his brain. "Why haven't you mentioned anything before?"

"About?" Tovi stabbed a fork into a golden crisp pastry filled with stewed apple.

Eldrick gestured towards the line at the door. "What you did for your people."

"Because I didn't do it to gain favor." She peered up at him, lips pursed. "Not from my people or potential allies. I did it because it's what's right."

Eldrick stilled. His stomach roiled, but not from the sweetness cloying the air but guilt. He'd misjudged her. An apology sat on his tongue. Perhaps it was pride. Perhaps he was worried feelings pushed him to say it. He couldn't muster the courage.

The true issue was, Eldrick's logical side whispered that admitting his desire for a woman like Tovi—brave and smart, loyal and fierce—would be no weakness. How could it be, vampyr or not? And that *terrified* him. What would he do if his feelings and thoughts mirrored the other when it came to a woman like Tovi Verena?

Perhaps it wasn't his judgment he didn't trust, but himself.

CHAPTER THIRTY-THREE

WHILE DYEING TOVI'S HAIR with magik, Linx had claimed she'd tinkered with Eldrick's necklace. Whatever the mage had done, it hadn't worked. Now more than ever, as they weaved their way through Drystan Village, on their way to learn more about the fighting rings, Eldrick's spicy, fresh scent invaded Tovi's senses. She focused on the excitement of her home instead. Humans and vampyrs milled about. Farmers pushed wagons. Shop owners hollered from their doorways.

Lou had been right. Tovi had helped build this village. She'd painted the chairs red in her friend's bakery. She'd chopped and hauled the logs across the river for the library. She'd situated the human borough down the river, nearest the bridge. And yet, Tovi couldn't see past the mists clinging to the rooftops and weaving between their legs and boots, a lingering resident of Drystan. She spotted the rigid walks of vampyrs fighting the curse, the darkness laying in every crook, crevice, and puddle.

Darkness had its wicked claws in her people's home. How could she look at the scant prosperity her people had built for themselves and think it enough? All of it was a fight, a struggle. All Tovi saw was what held them back, their robbed potential.

Beside her, Elrick's jaw was tight, his gait rigid as he matched her step for step. She'd hated seeing the shift in his gaze back at Lou's. Yes, she wanted him as an alley. She needed to gain his trust, but she wanted her current efforts to speak loud enough. With chin high and a pounding heart, Tovi wished she didn't have to give him a history lesson of her efforts. Why wasn't *she* enough?

It didn't help that her history was tied up with shame and running from someone she wished she'd never been. Her efforts now weren't so different from back then. She was trying to demonstrate she wasn't that spoiled, bratty princess. She'd already revealed her darkest mistake, failing Iona and Oliver. He hadn't judged, hadn't ridiculed her in any way. She had to let current efforts not her past help gain his favor.

Angst weighed her boots to the stone. As she sighed it all away, their destination appeared as they turned the corner.

Eldrick lost his footing and cursed as he gathered himself. His eyes widened, mouth parting. "Where in the moons are their clothes?"

Tovi burst out laughing. He scowled, and she covered her mouth with her hand to hide her smile.

Up ahead, the dance house stood three stories tall. Each level possessed a balcony. Women, dressed in lacy undergarments, feathers, and sheer robes beckoned those that walked by. Reds, purples, dark greens—the moody shades set the tone of the dark and alluring building. A slow, lazy, seductive tune trilled from the open doors and windows. The dancers twisted and turned, showing off their bursting breasts and bare legs.

"They are in fact wearing undergarments," Tovi said.

"Undergarments aren't clothes. They go *under* them," Eldrick said through gritted teeth.

"I had no idea werewolves were such modest creatures," Tovi murmured.

"We aren't." Eldrick's jaw ticked.

"Ah." Tovi grinned, a playful wickedness flushing through her. "Perhaps it is you who is modest. Is the sight of a little flesh your undoing, wolf?"

Eldrick stepped ahead of her, halting her tracks. They were toe-to-toe, nose-to-nose. The heat in his eyes warmed her belly, and Tovi hid a swallow.

"I'm quite familiar with flesh." He snatched her waist, pulling her closer. "I enjoy how it shivers, the taste of it, the burn of it against my own." He leaned into her ear, and Tovi thanked the Goddess he held her waist to keep her stable. "But I prefer to be alone with whoever's flesh I touch, lost in the darkness and shadows of the night where no one might hear the sounds I'm able to elicit."

He released her, set her free from his delicious scent and proximity. It took all of Tovi's strength not to lose her footing as they continued towards the dance house. She kept her eyes ahead and averted from Eldrick's gorgeous build, refusing to imagine the flesh against flesh he'd made her envision. Damn him, the thought made her *shiver*, and she swore a hint of male pride played in his smirk.

Tovi veered them down an alley. The establishment had been carved into a cavern, some of its onyx rock curving over to the adjacent building and connecting it all. Holes created from time and weather acted as windows to the gray sky above. The alley ended, but nestled behind the last rocky bend, and unseen to those walking the streets, a wooden door awaited them.

Tovi knocked, the same tempo she had at Lou's door. On the other side, laughter and feminine voices fell silent. The door's bolts, three in total, rattled one at a time until it swung open, revealing a beautiful pale woman. Cherry-red hair tumbled over her shoulder, curled and luscious. The color red continued to her attire. A bloodred garment covered her torso and barely covered her breasts. Lace trimmed the edges, and fishnet molded to her legs. High ruby heels were stark against the cold gray alleyway.

"Bloody hel, Tovi, it really is you," the vampyr said. "Hardly recognized you with that hair."

She smiled. "It's good to see you, Juliette."

"Get out of the cold." She opened the door wider, ushering them both in. Her yellow eyes shifted over Eldrick for a second, but her focus stayed with Tovi.

They entered a narrow galley full of tulle, dresses, mirrors, and makeup. Other dancers, vampyrs and humans, sat and painted their lips ruby red, powdered their eyelids with a smoky shade of makeup, and fixed their hair in gilt-framed mirrors. Some familiar faces smiled at Tovi and waved. A few glanced at Eldrick, interest piqued. Tovi ignored them along with the hot anger that shot through her.

Dancers came and went through a set of red curtains. Some had blood stains marking their lace ensembles. Next to Tovi, Eldrick tensed as a human hurried by, puncture wound fresh and blood trickling down her collarbone. Wine and blood and music filled the air, and Tovi blinked away splendors she'd once enjoyed.

"I take it you didn't visit for a quick tumble, did ya, Princess?" Juliette asked.

"No," Tovi laughed. "We came by to see if you knew anything about the fighting rings."

Juliette placed a hand on her hip. "We know all about them. They were competition for a little but," the vampyr shrugged, "nothing beats blood and sex."

"Any idea who runs them?" Tovi asked.

Her friend blinked. "You haven't heard? It's your sister, Visha."

Tovi swallowed. She rarely thought of her sister, hardly regarded her as one. The two had never had a loving, kind relationship. Her sister was the worst of the worst in court. But still, surprise froze Tovi in place. She couldn't believe Riven had let their youngest sister create such a thing.

"It befits her," Tovi finally said. "She's always been the most violent one."

"Where do you rank?" Eldrick asked, brow raised.

Before Tovi could answer or gauge if Eldrick had been joking, Juliette sauntered over to him and danced her dainty fingers over his shoulder and down his arm.

"If you're not biting, Tovi, perhaps you wouldn't mind if I do," she said.

Tovi hissed, fangs elongated as she snapped Juliette's arm away. "He's off-limits."

Juliette's attention jumped between her and the alpha. She smirked. "Oh my, what fun."

"Anything else you can tell us about the rings?" Eldrick asked.

Tovi made sure not to look at him. She wasn't entirely sure what came over her. An animalistic, territorial urge egged her on. It'd been a Goddess-sent miracle she hadn't ripped Juliette's arm off. What in the bloody hel had gotten into her?

"Sadly, only that it's run beneath the castle. If you want to learn more, I'd suggest you hang around. You know how the lords and ladies like to talk." She sauntered over to the curtain. "It's a shame you two aren't already entangled. It was always the most fun, Tovi, when it was a party of three." She winked as she left.

Crimson stained Tovi's cheeks as dark as a passing dancer's breast bite. Tovi wasn't embarrassed of her past entanglements, as Juliette put it. They'd been fun, she'd enjoyed them. The issue was she'd also enjoy a night here in the dancer hall with Eldrick. After he'd whispered such horrendous things in her ear, she craved a taste of the alpha standing next to her.

But she didn't even acknowledge him as she moved towards the curtain, peering out into the dancer's hall. On the main stage, dancers performed a choreographed routine. With each twirl and dip, a piece of clothing fell off. A beat drummed as each pretended to inch their lace underwear down, breasts already out in the open. A hungry audience cheered them on, and as it appeared they'd relent, the stage's lights went dark, ending the routine. The crowd cheered and hollered, loving the tease.

A presence, strong and lean, moved behind her. Tovi fidgeted, but Eldrick didn't move away. His breath tickled down her neck.

"What are you looking for?"

"Anyone important."

"Like?"

"A lord. Pompous. Arrogant. Gaudy." She scanned the crowd and sucked in a breath.

The perfect lord sat alone at the bar, drinking a wineglass full of thick blood. Red stained his lips and teeth, a droplet caught in the wires of his caterpillar mustache. His slicked-back black hair shined with grease under the chandeliers hanging from the cavern rafters.

Lord Oziel.

Arranged lunches, chaperoned walks in the castle garden, forced dances at celebratory balls. Her mother had practically shoved her into his path, like dangling raw meat in front of a demon. To her father's dismay, she'd refused his hand for decades. Riven had been the only one to see him for what he was—a slimy excuse of a vampyr. She exhaled, fighting the dread creeping up her spine. He couldn't have her. Never would.

"Who is he?"

Eldrick's guttural words tickled the shell of her ear, sending a new shiver down her spine. One she welcomed, one she certainly preferred.

"No one."

The dismissal came out quicker than she'd intended. With bite, too. She clamped her eyes, shook her head, and left the curtains to devise a plan. It didn't matter who Lord Oziel was. Only his status in court mattered, only his vile nature. They meant he most certainly had answers regarding the fighting rings.

Eldrick moved in front of her. "That is not the impression I gathered."

Tovi didn't like him continuously stepping in her way, blocking her path with werewolf height and lean physique, and she didn't like the glint in his eyes. Interest. Curiosity. Wonder. Those were dangerous, standing the hairs up the back of her neck in warning bells.

"It doesn't matter." She stepped left, but Eldrick countered her retreat. Like she'd predicted. The moment his foot stepped left to mirror, she swiveled back and right, far too fast for him to block her path again.

Behind her, he cursed.

"You did that thing."

Tovi halted outside an empty dressing room and turned to him. "What thing?"

Without her hood up and under the bright lights of the galley, Tovi felt exposed, out in the open as Eldrick's emerald eyes zeroed in on her. He took two long strides towards her until they were toe-to-toe. Before, out in the village, they'd had the frigid Drystan air between them. But here, the hall was too tight, too small for both of them this close. Tension and *want* vibrated between them.

"It's your eyes."

Suddenly, Eldrick wasn't looking at her, he was looking *into* her. Deep into her eyes, emerald clashing with jade, burrowing in and leaving a mark. Tovi didn't like it. It felt as if she stood naked in front of him, bare and open for him to see every scar or wrong deed etched into her skin like a cursed tattoo.

"When you're rehearsing, withholding something, there's no shine in your eyes."

Tovi couldn't breathe. Whatever churned in his eyes drowned her in false promise. She felt sucked in, being pulled deeper into the center, turning and turning, and off kilter. She didn't like that she'd become such a subject of his attention, he'd began to notice small things like that. Tovi's stomach roiled. What else did he see? What else did he judge?

"And sometimes," Eldrick said. "I think it's not secrets you're hiding, but yourself."

She stepped back—the words were so on the nose; it was like he'd cut her at the knees, exposing her in this ridiculous dance they'd entered. Her attention fleeted past his shoulders. Lord Oziel still sat at the bar. A dribble of blood trailed down his chin. Tovi blinked, centering her focus on the waiting alpha ahead of her.

What harm did it do to tell him?

Tovi inhaled. "He was one of my most-eager suitors. He's also one of the most influential trade merchants in vampyr court. His deep pockets made him my parents' favorite choice. But let me make myself clear, he is *no one* to me."

Eldrick stiffened, whirling in the direction of the bar. "Did he hurt you?"

Aside from his rather possessive hold on her while they danced— "No."

Eldrick's stature vibrated with tension, his hands tightened into fists at his side. Tovi swallowed, denying the territorial similarities between them. If Eldrick felt the same as she had with Juliette touching his arm—which was an absurd notion—he wasn't going to like the next part of the plan.

Tovi stepped backward, one foot in the dressing room, one out. Eldrick's head snapped to her.

"What are you doing?"

"Getting ready to dance." Tovi darted into the dressing room and slammed the curtains shut.

"*What?*" Eldrick growled behind the wall of red.

Chapter Thirty-Four

ELDRICK

ELDRICK LEANED INTO THE curtains. "Do you mind keying me into this plan of yours?"

Tovi rustled about on the other side. Clothing fell to the floor, possibly her cloak by the sound of the weight. Her boots went next, clattering across the room. Zippers cried open, buttons popped, and more clothes fell to the floor. Heat, scolding and maddening, traveled up his neck as he imagined her beyond that curtain, her pale flesh glowing in the yellow light.

Eldrick looked away.

It felt wrong to imagine. It felt wrong to think about it.

For so many, many reasons. All of them rational, all of them based on fact.

Yet, no matter how many Eldrick sifted through, his baser instinct grew hungry for the vampyr princess readying herself on the other side.

"Tovi." Eldrick's tone came off gruff and direct.

She pulled the curtain aside, and he reared back, heat now searing through his entire being.

A lilac-purple mesh corset molded to Tovi's torso. The color complimented her pale skin and drew out the green in her eyes. They shined like mystic stones.

Eldrick fought a growl as he caught sight of her breasts, swelling atop the corset. Tufts of fabric created black and lavender roses sewn in a snaking pattern. More roses traveled the corset lines above her strong, slender thighs. Lace stockings with rose stitching stretched over her legs. Layers of tulle piled high and stitched to the back of her corset were a wicked concept of a *very* short skirt. She'd let her hair, still auburn, down, and shaken the roots to create a tousled, wild look. The light caught the dip and curve of her bare, muscular arms.

Stars above, she was the most breathtaking beauty he'd ever seen, the most frightening figure of death.

"You're not wearing that."

The words fell from his lips without any forethought. With her standing there like that, thinking wasn't possible. Whatever warm, hungry sensation swam in his belly led him on.

Tovi scoffed, placing a hand on her hip. "I wear what I want, wolf."

Eldrick fumbled with his words, trying to grasp onto reason. Why did it matter what she wore? Why did he care? And why had he made her think he did?

Eldrick shook his head, grounding him back to the present. "Again, what is the plan?"

Tovi ignored him, passing under the curtain.

He grabbed her arm and dragged her close.

Surprise flushed Tovi's face. They both stared down at his hand gripping her arm. Eldrick let go, hand going cold without her skin against his. He didn't have the energy to step back, his body tightly wound.

"I can't wait here while you go dancing in that," he said. "Especially if your plan involves him."

The jade in Tovi's eyes softened. "We need to learn how to get Kade and Bétar into the rings. Lord Oziel might know a thing or two."

"That's a wild guess. He might also recognize you up close."

Tovi grabbed something over Eldrick's shoulder. A mask. She put it on, the black shell covering a majority of her face aside from her chin, lips, and eyes. With the black marring the brightness in her eyes and the auburn hair, she didn't look herself. Not unrecognizable, but at arm's length, perhaps she'd have a chance. Determination tightened Tovi's jaw, and Eldrick sighed, his instinct telling him he'd not convince her otherwise.

"How can I help?" he asked.

Tovi pointed upward. "Do you see up there?"

Eldrick followed her line of sight. Past the chandeliers and draped curtains, he caught the sight of a grid of scaffolding and wooden beams. Some appeared to have banisters like they were walking paths to and from the other side.

Without another word, Tovi dragged him into the small fitting room. He collided into her frame, and they tumbled into hanging garments, tossing and turning in tulle and feathers.

"Stars above," Eldrick cursed.

Tovi hissed, showing off her vampyr fangs. "Hush."

She pushed aside the hanging garments and revealed a wooden ladder built into the stone wall. Up, up, and up it went to the dark and empty scaffolding above.

"While I'm out in the hall, you can keep watch up there. I'll lure him to the alley. Once you see me heading to the galley, meet me outside."

Eldrick let his gaze slide up and down the length of Tovi's body once more. Her seductive outfit, her authoritative tone—the combination almost brought him to his knees.

But she was a vampyr. Maybe not his enemy any longer, but that didn't matter. Eldrick had to ignore the temptation trembling through his muscles. "Alright, solid plan."

He tightened his hands on one of the ladder's railings, and with each climb up, he left the wicked thoughts in the fitting room below.

Chapter Thirty-Five

Tovi slipped past the velvet curtains into the throngs of laughter and song. Musicians dressed in all black played in a pit beside the stage. Violins and cellos whined in a sultry tempo as a show atop the stage went on, six dancers bending and swaying to the slow beat of the music.

Other dancers mingled amongst the guests. Goblets of blood tickled Tovi's nose, and she ignored the ache in her gums as her fangs begged to be released. She had to fight the baser instincts of being a vampyr. Sex. Blood. Pleasure. Pain. It all gripped her in one giant haze of need and standing in the proximity of the alpha back in the galley had nearly driven her mad.

She'd witnessed the want in his eye, the undeniable *heat*.

It was dangerous; they wanted each other. That much was true now. But he hated her kind despite forming some sort of trust with her, and she had an alliance to make. Sleeping with him would do her no favors, no matter how hungry she was for the werewolf.

She set her sights on Lord Oziel. His greasy, vile aura turned her cold quicker than the Drystan wind, freezing over any warmth Eldrick had elicited. The lord's bony hands tightly gripped the stem of his goblet—the hands and grip that had once plagued Tovi's hips or hands during forced dances. Tovi's feet turned to lead as she weaved through the thicket of dancers and vampyrs, but the promise of intel regarding the rings propelled her forward.

The closer she grew to Lord Oziel, the sharper the creep climbing up her back became. Tovi knew if she turned and searched she'd find Eldrick in the rafters, but again, she kept her focus ahead. He'd already learned her discomfort when it came to the vampyr lord. She refused to let him learn the anxiety thrumming through her veins, too. Or at the very least, cause him to drop from the rafters and intervene.

Tovi exhaled, dismissing the disastrous notion, and sidled onto one of the bar's stools, two away from Lord Oziel.

"Wine," she said to the bartender, using a higher pitched tone and accent from the southern part of the continent. Lord Oziel had met her a handful of times, and she had to play the part of someone else to ensure her mask and hair did their job.

The petite human eyed her with suspicion, but thankfully didn't say a word as she slid a wineglass over to her. A new creep crawled up Tovi, but this time it screamed *threat, threat, threat* like some monster watched her. She paid it no mind, sipping her wine and playing absolutely aloof.

The trick worked like flies to honey. His chair skidded across the floor, and a shadow fell over her as he approached, so close she could smell the blood on his breath, iron-like and fresh.

She turned, mocking innocence and widening her eyes. "Oh my," she gasped, using her fake accent.

Lord Oziel smirked, stained fang jutting over his lip. "Are you new? I've tasted every female in this hall, but never the delights of you."

With a sip of her wine, Tovi swallowed her disdain. "Tonight's my first night."

He blinked, tilting his head as he drank her in. His focus lingered on her eyes, and he trailed a hand up her arm. Tovi fought the urge to slap his unwanted touch away. He hadn't asked, and she hated his forwardness, the keen possessiveness.

"You remind me of someone I know," he whispered.

Tovi remained calm, ignoring her fear. Though she hated it with every fiber in her being, she fell into his touch, encouraging it.

"Someone you want to fantasize about?" she whispered.

Lord Oziel's hand fell to her hip, and he grasped hold and tugged her closer. Rough and dominating. Tovi's heart raced, and she wished another male held her, one with sun-kissed skin and gems for eyes.

"It might be your first night, but not your first time, I take it?" he drawled.

Tovi leaned into him, her chin hovering over his collarbone as she whispered, "You're right, and in my experience, it's best you and I go somewhere more private."

Lord Oziel's eyes widened a fraction. His bottom lip fell open, and Tovi swore drool dripped out. "Eager, aren't we?"

Tovi stood in one swift movement, leaving him alone at the bar steps away. "Let me show you eagerness."

He sneered. "Lead the way."

Tovi outstretched her hand, and Lord Oziel snatched it. She faced forward, hiding her eyes and fear as she headed towards the galley. She stepped behind the curtains, hurrying to another passageway that ran parallel to the galley of other dancers. Unseen, she and Lord Oziel hurried down the hall. Dancers giggled on the other side. Ahead, the door to the outside promised open air. Tovi rushed towards it, opening the door and embracing the cold mist as she tugged Lord Oziel with her, hoping no one saw as the door slammed shut.

She hadn't even a moment to exhale with relief when her back slammed against the cavern's rock. His tall, lanky body leaned over her, pushing her against the wall, *hurting* her. Tovi couldn't help it—her instinct took over, and she bared her fangs, hissing.

Lord Oziel only laughed, the sound echoing off the stone walls eerie and evil. "Do you take me to be a fool, Princess?" He ripped her mask off.

Her revealed face stung in the cold. She rushed forward, but Lord Oziel pushed her back. A fool—she was a stupid, reckless fool who'd forgotten a weapon.

"Did you really think fake hair and accent would deter me?" Lord Oziel hissed. "I've dreamt of your mouth around my cock too many times for you to hide from me."

Tovi shook. From rage. Fear. *Revulsion.* "Get your hands off me!"

Scream. She should scream for the other dancers or anyone nearby, but what good would they do? *This* was a lord. He outranked them, overruled them, and if Tovi made more of a scene, she'd attract more attention, which risked her brother discovering she was in Drystan.

Instead, she'd fight back. Tovi elongated her talons and swiped before he could push her again.

"Do you plan to play first, future wife?"

Silver shot through the shadowy space between them—an axe pressed to Lord Oziel's throat, and a furious, heaving werewolf pressed against his back, gripping the blade's handle so tightly, his knuckles were bone white.

"What is the meaning of this!" Lord Oziel shouted.

Eldrick snarled, leaning into his ear. "Say another unwelcome, foul word and I'll slice your head off."

Lord Oziel squirmed a fraction until Eldrick's blade kissed his skin. The vampyr hissed as blood beaded onto the blade. Pure beastly energy radiated off Eldrick. Outwardly, he seemed calm, lethally so, but Tovi felt his wolf in the air. He was seconds from snapping. Tovi inhaled a breath. It was all too much—Lord Oziel's vile touch, that he'd discovered her, and Eldrick's whiplash of emotions. But—

"You're going to answer some questions," she said, crossing her arms.

Lord Oziel—the pig—had the audacity to ogle her bursting breasts. Eldrick growled, throwing him to the ground.

"Don't look at her!" he said. "On your knees."

Lord Oziel obeyed. Eldrick kept his axe at the ready, and the lord sat between them. Escaping both down and up the alley was now out of the question.

"Do you attend the fighting rings?" Tovi asked.

Lord Oziel scoffed. "Well of course, every lord and lady attends." A haughtiness rang in his tone. It made Tovi's insides twist.

"Do you know who the Lone Wolf is?" she asked.

Eldrick's gaze flicked to hers, gratitude shining in them.

"No." Lord Oziel's gaze darted towards Eldrick's axe. "Though I can't smell it, your weapon is a dead giveaway, wolf. I hear they're your kind. I haven't dealt with them personally, but they've supplied my fighters."

"Your what?" Eldrick stepped closer, jutting his axe under Lord Oziel's chin.

Lord Oziel bared his fangs. "My fighters. Young werewolves. *Your* kind. Sadly, my last two died. I punished them for losing their previous fight and refused to feed them, and then... Well, I forgot entirely. Shame really." The vampyr shrugged.

"You bastard," Eldrick said, pushing his axe forcefully against the lord's throat.

"I'd gotten wind that a new shipment was arriving today."

Tovi stilled Eldrick's arm. Lord Oziel deserved every ounce of the alpha's ire, but they still needed answers.

"How do you enter new werewolves into the rings to fight?" Tovi asked.

Lord Oziel studied her, mouth set in a thin line.

"Answer her."

Eldrick pushed his blade dangerously deep into Lord Oziel's skin. The single blood drop turned into many, blooming together into a thin, red line.

"I said answer."

The stone of the alley seemed to shake with the werewolf's rage.

Lord Oziel sneered. "There's a back entrance into the cavern on the east side of the forest. Everyone's fighters are locked away there."

"You're lying," Eldrick said.

Tovi wondered the same. She and her family had built the castle into the lopsided mountain—tunnels and caverns weaved through the rock like an ant hill. Yet, she'd never known an entrance in the east side. Unless, it had been carved to accommodate the fighting rings.

"I'm *not.*" Lord Oziel shook his head. "I've delivered my fighters there myself."

Tovi and Eldrick shared a glance.

But Lord Oziel laughed. "Whatever your plan is, it won't work. I'll tell Prince Riven you're here. I swear it."

Tovi shook her head. Fear shot through her, but she tamped it down. She didn't have time to worry about how her brother would retaliate.

"No. If you utter a word of my presence, I *will* kill you."

Lord Oziel smiled, fangs flashing. "You won't have a chance. In exchange for the information I will provide the prince, he will finally agree to make you my wife. You'll marry me, Princess Tovi, and finally be mine—"

Metal sang, and then Lord Oziel's head bounced on the stone ground.

Eldrick flicked his axe, blood flying through the air and landing in the forming puddle of crimson. Death darkened Lord Oziel's vacant eyes. Spidery black veins spread across his pale skin, hardening him into a shell of cracked marble. His headless body dropped with a thud to the hard stone.

For a moment, silence stretched in the alleyway. Tovi's heart hammered in her chest, her gaze jumping between a very dead Lord Oziel and a very calm Eldrick Drengr. She opened and closed her mouth, struggling to find words.

"You killed him..." she managed to say, gaze landing on Eldrick.

"He threatened you," Eldrick whispered with such a level of calm, like the break of silence during a storm before thunder boomed.

"Yes, but—"

Eldrick took a step towards her. "He touched you."

"Eldrick."

"He *hurt* you."

Tovi shook her head, a foreign feeling swimming in her gut. He'd killed Lord Oziel because he had touched her. *Touched her.* Yet, why did that matter to Eldrick? Why did he care?

They stood so close, their breaths mingled. He'd killed for her, slaughtered a man, and she wanted to fall farther into him. His gaze robbed her of breath. He may have appeared calm, but war raged in the gem green of his eyes. Shoulders taut, muscles quivering, axe at the ready.

"I had also promised if he said another unwelcome, foul word, I'd slice his head off."

Bloody hel, Tovi recalled the threat, but hadn't taken Eldrick seriously.

Reality rolled through her. "You killed a well-known, prominent lord. Do you have any idea the mess we now have on our hands? He will be missed."

Eldrick sheathed his axe back at his side and nudged Lord Oziel's dead body with his foot. "I actually have a plan for that."

Tovi blinked. *He* had a plan. Had they reached a part in their truce where he moved without her and filled her in later?

"Do you mind keying me into this plan of yours?" Tovi used his words from earlier, crossing her arms.

Eldrick smirked as if he too remembered. "Of course."

Chapter Thirty-Six

KADE

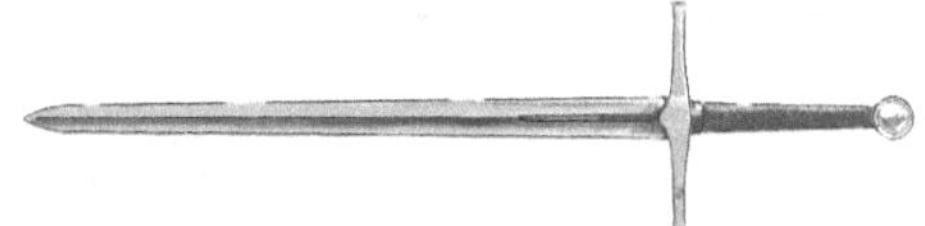

A QUAINT, IVY-COVERED COTTAGE sat on the Drystan River's edge. The churning of its waterwheel broke the forest's silence, resounding louder than fast-rolling rapids. It appeared abandoned with the smokeless chimney and blur of mildew in the windows, entirely unassuming, when in fact, an underground tunnel ran from here to Lou's bakery.

A safe house.

Because whatever Tovi and her few allies—who Kade had gathered resided mostly in the village—had faced, there'd been enough resistance to have called for one. He wanted to ask what and why, but the princess and Linx were still inside the cottage, the mage's magik an opal glow in the kitchenette window as she manipulated her healing abilities to shift the vampyr's features yet again for part one of their plan to gain entry into Drystan Castle.

This far southwest from the village, not even the mountain it sat on could be seen through the army of spruce and pine trees. Slow, tranquil and delicate, snow lollygagged its way from the gray sky. The land held a bit of peace, a softness even Kade's wolf couldn't ignore in the precipice of so much risk to come.

By his side, Eldrick assessed the forest, too. After he and Tovi had learned more about the fighting rings—as well as killed a high-ranking lord, and it was still not blatantly stated *who* had killed him, but Kade's guess was his brother—the princess had rushed to meet her contact in the castle, alone.

Evelyn's been placed in the dungeons. Tovi's earlier news whispered in the back Kade's mind, and his anger became as sharp as his wolf's claws and teeth, his determination steely like the sword he wouldn't bring with him. Nothing was more absolute than his focus to set Evelyn free.

Eldrick turned, his green eyes, so bright like their father's, drank him in. "She'll be alright, Kade. Evelyn's strong."

Kade nodded. "I know."

When he'd asked his brother about the deceased lord, Eldrick had muttered something along the lines of "he deserved it." Kade didn't doubt it, especially when he learned the bastard had bought and used werewolves as fighters, but his usually closed-off, reserved brother buzzed with more emotion than he'd ever had in his thirty years.

Days ago, Kade had kept a tight lip about his brother's complicated relationship with the vampyr princess. He'd envisioned waiting, sharing a pint with his brother at the Shield-maiden *after* they'd rescued Evelyn and returned home, but in the stark contrast of the forest's peace compared to the unknowns shadowing the hours to come, it felt as though the moment was now.

"You know," Eldrick said, "Mother would've loved a mission like this."

Kade, despite it all, found it in him to smile. "*Moons*, you're right."

It was true. His mother relished in risk, danger—the chance to infiltrate their enemy right under their nose. Her battle cry seemed to carry on the wind.

"Have you written to Claus?" he asked. He'd never understood his brother's closeness to their uncle, but when Kade had found his purpose, his ability to move past their mother's death, Claus had supported Eldrick.

His brother raised a brow. "Not about the plan, but regarding our progress north and the missing werewolves."

Kade braced himself, evening out his tone. "What have you told him of Tovi?"

His brother swallowed. "Nothing of late."

"Nothing?"

"What is there to share?" Eldrick asked. "She has proven, so far, to be an ally. She wants to free Evelyn as much as the rest of us."

Kade scoffed, shaking his head. "Is it so hard to admit that to our uncle? To Father, even?"

The pace of the falling snow quickened around them. His brother's jaw ticked, but his eyes softened as they connected with Kade's.

"I have a hard time admitting it to myself, let alone inking the words to paper."

The truth, the *emotion*, was so unlike his brother, Kade paused. He searched for the right words.

"I wrote a letter to you in Callum, detailing how I had found Evelyn."

Eldrick's brows furrowed. "I never got a letter."

Kade laughed. "Because I never sent it."

"Why?"

Kade shrugged. "Whenever I came back to the letter, time and time again, it wasn't, well, accurate. Maybe in the beginning. I *had* found her. But after weeks of spending time with her, I don't think the letter was the truth anymore."

His brother stilled, silent. So much so, the slight crinkle of flurries landing around them could be heard.

The door to the cottage swung open, and Linx poked her head out. "She's ready."

Before the others joined, Kade leaned closer to his brother. "Don't worry what others think of your assessment, Eldrick. Listen to what your gut is trying to tell you. As your brother, I support you. No matter what."

Green and amber locked. Two werewolves. Two brothers. In the land of their enemy.

"Thank you," Eldrick said.

So much weight in a two word sentence.

Kade gave a curt nod and joined the others. The Gray Fenris, Lou, and lastly, Tovi emerged from the cottage. The princess's cheeks had sunken inward, a scattering of freckles over her now thinner nose.

"Will it work?" Kade asked.

Lou nodded. "It will. Tovi looks like Visha. Frightening actually. No offense, your sister is the worst."

Linx handed Tovi a truffle of some kind, weaved with herbs, nuts, and magic. "Eat this when the time comes, and you'll be yourself again."

Tovi nodded. "Is everyone ready?"

The team murmured their agreement and faced Kade.

"Let's pray to the stars above this works," he said.

The Gray Fenris said their goodbyes to Kade, Bétar, and Tovi. His mated team members lay their foreheads together, eyes open and soaking the other in. An ache spread across Kade's chest, and he turned away from the intimate moment. Tovi and Eldrick barely acknowledged the other, and the team split, the plan finally in motion.

Silence, fog, and what lay next stretched between Kade and his companions as they headed north. They trudged through the thicket of the forest. Brambles and ferns dotted the pathways closer to the rocky mountain where the castle sat. Past the tree line, stretching hundreds of feet above, its shined like icy onyx. The snowfall thickened, too. The ooze of dark magic, of something ancient clotted the air.

Yards away from the base of the mountain, Tovi held up her hand, and all three of them crouched behind a fallen tree.

"It's time," she whispered.

She rummaged in a sack and set chains and two sets of bracelets on the forest floor. With Linx's help, they'd removed the dark magic from the bracelets, but the vampyrs wouldn't be any the wiser. Kade's wolf's hackles rose, knowing the chains and bracelets had been used against his own and were *still* being used in the depths of the castle.

The three of them shared one last, stern look. The tension in the air shifted. It was like the morning of battle, the singing of swords as they unsheathed, the taunting of muscles as one readied to defend. Bétar and Kade shared a silent conversation, and with a single, determined nod, they each shifted into their werewolf forms. The bracelets followed, and Tovi whispered apologies as she attached the chains. As one, the three moved closer to the castle.

Snow collected in Kade's fur. He didn't feel the cold. Instead, with each step, he grew closer to Evelyn, he could feel it. Not the bond, but the mirror of his heart.

In the distance, two vampyr guards dressed in Verana purple stuck out against the green, gray, and dark landscape. Specks at this distance. Kade's heart quickened, fisting his claws at his sides. *Moons*, they were so close—

"Aye! Who goes there?" someone called.

Bétar stumbled into Kade's back as both he and Tovi stilled. Their gazes connected, and the princess gave a slight shake of her head. His nervous breath clouded in the cold air, the furs on his back rising.

A vampyr guard, hand on the hilt of his sword, plodded through ferns. Blood dribbled over his chin. Past him, a limp body lay on the forest floor. Red flashed through Kade's vision, and he stepped forward only for Tovi to yank him back with the chains tied at his wrists. He shot her a glare, baring his teeth.

She sneered back, fangs out, but her eyes screamed, *Don't.*

"Oh my!" The vampyr guard kneeled and bowed his head. "Princess, I did not see it was you."

Kade and Bétar each relaxed a fraction.

"What are you doing away from your post?" Tovi asked in a pitch that grated against Kade's spine.

The guard flinched as he rose. "I needed to feed. Have you brought more werewolves for the rings?"

Tovi pulled the chains connecting Kade and Bétar. The two stumbled forward, a growl rumbling through Kade's chest. He didn't miss how she not only dragged them closer to the guard, but also down so they were obscured by the forest hills, out of sight of the other guards in the distance. It didn't matter. Every muscle in his warrior being warred against the chains attached to him, riling his wolf. He tried with every ounce of control to remind himself it was for Evelyn. A slight brush of Bétar's arms by his side was a reminder, too.

One foot in front of the other.

"I have." Tovi held her nose in the air. She smirked, a single fang glinting over her bottom lip. "Aren't they perfect? They belong to Lord Oziel."

The guard's eyes flashed in recognition. "Excellent. Have you sampled a taste?"

This time, a growl rumbled from both Kade and Bétar. He charged, but Tovi's grip on the chains tightened. She laughed, drowning out their protests.

"It would be rude of me to touch what is not mine," she said.

The guard smiled. "Of course—wait, when were you granted a bloodstone, princess? Are congratulations in order?"

This time, Tovi stilled, the *clink* of a chain resounding in the forest as she lost her grip for a moment. Kade fought the urge to turn and assess her expression. Did her sister not have a bloodstone? Had that been a detail they overlooked? Kade's muscles quivered. One guard and a measly necklace stood between him and Bétar entering the rings. His insides raged. For weeks they'd traveled, journeyed to this moment, and all Kade could do was stand and do *nothing*.

"I... *borrowed* one from my brother again." She giggled. "How about you and I keep it our little secret?"

The guard scoffed. He stepped closer to Kade, hungry eyes raking over his frame. They landed at his neck, and the bastard sniffed and licked his lips.

"Let me have a taste of the new fighters, and I won't say a word."

Bétar moved, and Kade growled for him to stay back. He bared his teeth at the vampyr. His wolf dared the vampyr to try, itching for a fight.

"How dare you?" Tovi hissed. "I am the *princess*. You rude, pathetic—"

"Precisely. You are the princess. You disobeyed the prince and soon-to-be king. I have every right to turn you in."

Kade snapped. Fear eclipsed his patience, and he drove his claws into the soft, malleable belly of the vampyr. He choked and grunted, blood gurgling from his wide, shocked mouth.

"Stop!" Tovi hissed, grabbing Kade's arm.

Kade grunted and drove his other set of claws into the vampyrs throat. Crimson splattered onto the snow, and he threw the vampyr to the ground.

"Goddess, Kade!" Tovi shook her head. She knelt by the dead guard. "You damn Drengrs, killing now and asking questions later. I swear to bloody hel—"

"What happened here?" someone shouted.

The three of them whirled. Two more guards ascended the hill, blades unsheathed.

"Fuck. If you wanted any chance of getting Evelyn, not another move," Tovi breathed.

She pulled something gold off the dead guard, and as she walked by, dropped it into Bétar's trouser pocket. Before she reached the two new visitors, she threw her hood up and pushed her hair over her shoulder, covering her chest and bloodstone.

The guards sauntered over as blood dripped from Kade's claws. He bared his teeth but stilled his rage. *Moons*, he was a fool. The energy inside him surged, threatening to unleash. Kade closed his eyes. He thought of Evelyn's steely blue stare. Her resolve. Her bravery. Her ability to do what needed to be done, no matter the emotions battling inside her. Kade grasped what he admired about his mate and embodied it, prayed and tried to play along with whatever Tovi said next.

"Princess," they both said and bowed.

"He shifted into a *caillte*," she said, gesturing towards the guard. "Attacked me and Lord Oziel's new fighters."

"It appears this one killed him," one said.

Tovi threw up her hands. "I'd rather it be him than me!"

The other glared at Kade, leveling his sword. Black spidery veins slithered around his eyes.

"He needs to be dealt with," the other said.

Tovi's chest heaved. Kade waited, holding his breath and chanting his mate's name over and over. He'd waited so long to get Evelyn back, shoving his desire to barge in after her behind the need to wait for the opportune time. This was supposed to be that time, and this moment... he'd ruined. His fate rested in Tovi's hands now. Evelyn's fate.

"He will be," Tovi said. "In the rings like Lord Oziel requested. Now, if the both of you don't mind, I'd like to get them into a cell immediately. This one," she pointed at Kade, "fights tonight."

CHAPTER THIRTY-SEVEN

EVELYN PACED HER CELL.

An *actual* cell.

After Ingrid had reprimanded Belle, Tala, without a word, had grabbed Evelyn with such force, her bicep bruised. She'd escorted Evelyn far from the tower and straight to the damp, dark, miserable dungeons. Other prisoners moaned in the distance, and by their desperate cries and hisses for blood, Evelyn guessed them to be vampyrs.

She shivered, unable to see into the other cells in the limited light. Water trickled, her breath puffed in the air, and the scent of mildew turned her stomach. *Fucking flames*, this *was* far worse than the tower.

Evelyn had tried everything to get out. She'd had nothing, aside from the bolts and screws in the hinges of the door, which she'd failed to grasp and remove. Instead, she'd tried to wedge herself through bars, but after all her efforts, she'd been left with bruised shoulders and restless magic raging in her chest.

So, Evelyn paced.

She was angry—angry at herself for getting caught and being so reckless in the first place. This need to prove herself, this drive to earn forgiveness was blinding.

Kade had felt close, so close, and she'd gone and possibly ruined his plan. Down here in the dungeons, she was also away from the intel she'd gathered. Matilda's books and journals. The scribbled words. At least she had witnessed the exchange between Riven and some haunting voice, but that wouldn't help Kade rescue her. It would be more difficult for him to reach her deep in the dungeons of Drystan Castle.

White rats with red beady eyes scurried along the edge of her barred cell. They paused to sniff and carried on, free to roam the depths of the castle, too small to be noticed. Evelyn gritted her teeth, jealous of their freedom. The rats veered between the bars two cells down. In the flicker of the sconces, their white bodies appeared on the adjacent wall and disappeared into the crevices below. Evelyn scurried to her own wall, running her hands across the seams where the stones of the floor met the bricks. Her hand came across a few divots, far too small for her to fit through. But it was something. Evelyn fell to her hands and knees, laying her ear closer to the crevices. Wind rushed underneath, and the trickling water grew louder. She peered into the cracks. A faint light glowed with promise.

She began to dig. Her fingertips split and bled against the sharp rock, but still, she pulled and pried at the loose rock. Determination to escape swelled within her, and Evelyn didn't care how much she injured herself. She scraped across the cracks in the brick, over and over, until one stone gave way. Evelyn blinked and stared in disbelief at the hole big enough for her arm to fit through.

Fucking flames, perhaps she had a chance.

She flattened against the ground as much as she could, peering down into the hole. Her heart thudded against the castle's foundation. Candles. Hundreds. Flickering light. The dungeons were above the altar she and Belle had found. Evelyn backed away, the wrongness and darkness of the space seeping into her cell. In her haste, she pushed her hands against the jagged rock, slicing her sore and worn palm. A single bead of blood ran down and dropped to the cavern below.

It landed on the stone in silence. The same stone where Riven had placed his own blood. It faded. Soaked into the carving until it no longer existed, sucked into nothingness.

The cell rattled. The stones shook. Evelyn braced as debris and dust showered over her.

The shrill voice of a woman cried, "*You.*"

Evelyn scrambled from the hole. Her dress's skirts tore, her hands and elbows cut against the rocks. Mist clotted the air, ice entered her lungs.

"You dare wear the blood of my brothers and sisters when you call upon me?" the voice boomed.

Evelyn swallowed, searching for where the voice came from, mind racing. *Blood of my brothers and sisters.*

The words jarred Evelyn's memory. The bloodstone—Riven hadn't worn his when he'd visited the altar. Had that been intentional?

"I... I didn't know," she whispered. "I don't know what it is."

The echoing voice hummed, thoughtful. "It hides what you are, *who* you are. It can hide a curse. Hide magic of any kind. In, in, in. All of it goes in, shielded by the blood of fallen gods and goddesses."

Evelyn stilled, the voice's earlier words coming to the forefront of her mind. Did the altar belong to a deity? She'd never considered it. There were few left, lost to time. Evelyn had visited one in Cirrillo to pray for her magic to return, but it had been grand, looked after, golden and bright.

A reflection of the goddess it had been created for. The caverns. The castle. The ooziness in the air. This was darkness.

"Who are you?" she asked.

Laughter, cruel and piercing, grated against her skin. The other cells had become lost past the mists, the darkness in hers frosting the bars. As her breath came out ragged, it puffed in the now freezing air. Her fingers began to ache.

"I am the Goddess of the Deep and Darkness. I am named after what you gave me, little one."

Gave.

An offering. Like Riven had—blood. Evelyn racked her brain, tried and tried amidst the cold to recall her teachings where a Blood Goddess had ever been mentioned. Never. Not once. The Moon God, the Sun Goddess, the Earth Goddess. Never had she come across such a name.

"How about I show you my power?" the voice echoed in the cell. "How about I show you those of my making?"

The mists began to twist and turn, morphing into people, places into things. The shadows up and reared their heads like serpents and plunged into Evelyn's being, her mind held by an iron claw of the past.

A young woman sobbed over a motionless body. A man beside her, tears running down his face, stared out into the distance, chanting to himself. Their clothes weren't of this time. Wear and tear clung to them both. Blood marked them all, too, but not as badly as the blood seeping from the woman, bleeding into the stone of the altar. No candles, no light.

"Father."

Evelyn sucked in a breath, her heart twisting. She knew that voice.

Tovi—younger, thinner, an innocent sheen in her eyes, different—peered up at the man. *Father.*

"Mother is gone."

"No!" the man bellowed. "She is not. Someone will listen!"

Fragments of Evelyn's friendship with Tovi twisted like roots reaching for water. Her friend was in pain, and she felt it like her own. Not from whatever goddess possessed her mind or the dark magic seeping into her cell, but from the bruised love she still carried for her best friend. This was her family. Before she'd changed. Or turned?

The scene snapped from existence. The voice, the darkness. All of it vanished like evaporating mists. Evelyn blinked—the cell remained the same. No dust, debris, or broken rock. Just the hole she'd dug and her bloody hands. As if she'd imagined it all.

Someone approached through the dungeons, boots echoing off the walls. Their steps hurried than hesitated. Slowly. Creepily. Had a vampyr snuck down to the dungeons to sample the Daughter of the Goddess's blood? Evelyn peered around the bars of her cell, trying to make out whoever it was.

A small figure passed under the lone sconce, and the features of a friendlier face had Evelyn doing a double take.

"Belle!" she hissed. "What are you doing here?"

The beautiful witch's cerulean eyes roamed over Evelyn as she rushed to her cell's door. "Are you hurt? You're crying."

Evelyn shook her head, wiping away tears she hadn't known she shed.

"I'm alright," she said, throat raw.

"Good, because I'm breaking you out." Belle retrieved a key from her dress pocket and unlocked the cell door.

"What?" Evelyn asked, disbelief making her words breathy.

Belle had been helpful but so timid Evelyn had discredited her ability to be brash. A warm feeling spread through her as she eyed the sweet, gentle witch.

"Thank you," she whispered.

Belle gave her a weak smile. "I couldn't leave you, not when you've been so kind to me. But we don't have much time. Most of court is headed to tonight's scheduled fights. Rumor has it that a high-ranking lord supplied new fighters, and the buzz is immense. If you want any chance of surviving Drystan, we'll need to get the bloodstone off."

We'll.

Belle opened the cell's door, and a red smudge on the witch's blouse caught Evelyn's attention. She grabbed Belle's hand, dragging her close.

"Goddess, you've been bit."

Belle pulled away, a blush creeping up her cheeks. "It's nothing. Henri, a guard, and I have had a few months of fun, but I've never... you know." She averted her gaze to the bite on her neck. "But tonight, I let him."

"You what?" Evelyn choked.

Belle shrugged, so indifferent. "Vampyrs are practically sedated after they drink blood and have sex. It was the best way to grab the keys."

"You didn't have to do that."

"No, I didn't, but I wanted to. And don't worry, being bitten is actually quite lovely. Under the right circumstance of course." Belle pulled her from the cell and tugged her down the hall. She spoke so casually, as if they were talking about breakfast or the weather and not about being bitten by a vampyr.

The door at the end of the hall became visible. They crept closer, and Belle held up a finger to her lips.

Evelyn nodded, mastering her breathing and treading her steps lightly against the stone. Belle eased open the metal door, the hinges a low whine in the dungeon's silence. Together, they crept up the stairs, taking two at a time. At the top, more light flickered from lanterns on chains and sconces on the walls.

Outside a cracked door, Belle hung the dungeon keys on a hook. As they passed, Evelyn swore she spotted a sleeping guard, armor and uniform littering the ground. She almost felt bad for him.

Almost.

"Now what?" Evelyn whispered as they entered the main hall.

"We head to the library. My sister made your necklace, and her supplies are there."

"So, you know how to get it off?"

Belle's brows pinched together. "Well, not exactly."

Evelyn opened her mouth and then snapped it shut. "We'll figure it out."

Trying was better than not, and Evelyn's resolve matched the warmth and light of her flame, giving her the boost she needed to keep moving forward. Belle was right. If she had any chance of escaping and finding Kade, she'd need her magic back.

Ten agonizing minutes felt like an hour, and sweat beaded at Evelyn's temples, but eventually the library's archway came into view. They ducked behind the pillars and kept to the perimeter of the library, hunkering low against the bookshelves. Through the slits between leather-bound books, Evelyn tried to make out anyone else in the library.

No witch. No vampyr. Not even a human servant.

Only her and Belle, scurrying along unseen, like the rats in the dungeons. She motioned for Belle to follow, and together, they dashed through an array of desks.

Potions bubbled away in boiling flasks, black gunk sat unused in a beaker, and fur, hair, and twigs lay taped to an open grimoire.

"Is this Ingrid's?" Evelyn asked. The magic surrounding it was oozy and thick, like that of the White Lady. The newer pages had weathered with age far quicker than that of the earlier ones, tainted by the dark magic written into the pages.

Belle nodded, flipping through them. She shivered, face flinching as she did so.

"Wait, is it hurting you?" Evelyn asked, grabbing her wrists.

Belle blinked, shaking her head. "Sorry, the dark magic in it is ghastly. I don't know how my sister stomachs it."

Evelyn swallowed. "Here, let me flip through it. Maybe since my magic is snuffed down, I won't be able to feel the effects as much. Point me in the right direction."

Belle shut her eyes and nodded. "Alright." Her eyes sprang open, and she exhaled, pointing to a particular section where a raven's feather stuck out of it. "You'll find notes on various items there."

Evelyn turned to the section, expecting a wave of dark magic to hit her. She braced, but instead of pain, something slick and cold slithered over skin, like snakes coiling up her arms. Not painful. Unpleasant. She flipped through the pages, ignoring the sensation and focusing on Ingrid's notes. She'd label the section Objects, and numerous drawings within depicted the various subject matters waiting beyond the page.

"There," Belle whispered.

Snug between a bat's wing and hemlock, a pencil-shaded bloodstone alluded to the gem's sheen when hit by the light. Her swirly penmanship below read *Page 133.*

Evelyn flipped through the grimoire, the slithering dark magic tightening around her the farther she went, but she gritted her teeth and kept on, the promise of getting out of this wretched, cursed place worth the discomfort. When she landed on the bloodstone's passage, both her and Belle cursed. Ingrid's notes spilled over the pages. Not a blank space had been left. By the dates, it was a year's worth of study, detailing the what, where, and how of the bloodstone.

"We don't have time for this," Belle whispered.

"No, we don't," Evelyn agreed. "But..." She considered the goddess's words earlier. "I don't think the bloodstone itself is bad. Your sister placed dark magic on it, and that's what we need to get rid of. You can do that with your water brotannas."

Belle stared at her. "Wait, you want me to use my water, not my innate magic? Evelyn—"

"You can do this."

Doubt and fear contorted Belle's face. It soured the air, engulfing Evelyn in a place she'd been not too long ago, a scared, soul-tired witch.

Belle struggled to find her words. "I don't know, I mean, my sister's magic is probably strong—"

"You're stronger." Evelyn's words were softer than a whisper. "Use the power, your light against it. I believe in you."

The young witch's shoulder snapped straighter. "Alright. Fine. I'll give it a go."

She hovered her hand over the bloodstone. Nothing happened for a moment, the two witches stared at the other, waiting, until—

The metal casing glowed, dark shadows rising and disappearing into the air. Evelyn's magic flared to the surface and met no resistance, hovering at the ready. Hot. Fiery. *Alive.*

"You did it!" she said, face splitting into a wide smile.

Belle jumped. "Did I really?"

Before Evelyn could assure Belle, her magic sensed darkness, a heavier, slicker sensation than Ingrid's grimoire. Boots quickened across the stone floor, growing louder as they approached. Ingrid waltzed into the study area. Her bob swishing back, she stopped abruptly as she spotted them.

"Belle, what are you doing here?" Her lip lifted in disgust. "And you!"

The sisters stared at one another as the youngest's chest heaved up and down, her mouth open in a surprised O. Evelyn tamped her magic down, hoping Ingrid didn't sense it was no longer blocked. She still wore the bloodstone, and from the way it looked to others, her magic was still snuffed. She didn't want to use it, not yet. She didn't want to cause any sort of commotion and risk her escape.

"Are both of you going to just stand there? How are *you* even out of the dungeons?"

She stepped closer to them, fingers flexing at her sides. Evelyn's flame itched to ignite, ready to defend, ready to fight—

Tala stepped out from between two bookshelves, her uniform pristinely pressed, an axe hanging at her right side.

"Because I was instructed by Riven to escort her to the fights tonight. Belle and I ran into one another earlier, and when she learned Evelyn would be at the fights, she asked for us to meet her here. Isn't that right?"

Belle swallowed, blinking a few times before she stammered, "Tala's right. I figured Evelyn had been lonely in the dungeons, and so I wanted to keep her good company at the fights."

Ingrid's brows pinched together, and her gaze narrowed. "Absolutely not. I told you to stay away from her."

Evelyn side-eyed her vampyr guard. Why was Tala intervening? Attending the fights did not help her or Belle escape, and it would put her directly in Riven's path. Unless, escorting her to the fights had actually been his request, and Tala had found her cell empty. If that was the case, why wasn't she saying anything of the sort to Ingrid?

Was she helping them?

Ingrid approached the table, and Evelyn didn't miss Tala's hand reach for her axe. *Fucking flames*, Evelyn grasped her magic, her power fiery hot, like her resolve to get out of here.

She had to.

Ingrid grabbed her sister's wrist, dragging her close. "How many times have I told you to stay in your room at night?"

"I know!" Belle hissed, anger blooming on her cheeks for once instead of embarrassment. "Everyone else in this castle is so mean and drab. She's my only friend. I hate it here, and all you ever do is spend time with Visha. It's like I don't even exist anymore, so please let me have one night of fun."

Evelyn gritted her teeth, trying not to smile at the witch's performance. Belle was not the demure witch Ingrid believed her sister to be—or who Evelyn had believed her to be—no, there was fight in her, and Evelyn's magic danced at the small victory as Ingrid's stern face softened.

Ingrid swiveled to Tala, black cloak swishing in the air, then turned to Evelyn. "We should walk together then, shall we?"

Tala's golden eyes met Evelyn's, and she couldn't detect the emotion swimming in them, but they widened a fraction, as if egging Evelyn to agree. She hid her rippling confusion, clearing her throat.

"Of course," she said. "Let's all go to the fights together."

Belle winced, but Evelyn averted her stare down, hoping Belle didn't push. Ingrid's bloodred lips tilted in a sly smirk, and she whirled and headed towards the exit.

"Go," Evelyn mouthed to Belle, and she followed close to her sister, hands clasped ahead of her.

Tala and Evelyn fell in step together and once Ingrid reached a respectable distance, Evelyn breathed her next words so only the vampyr could hear. "What are you playing at?"

Tala spun in front of her. "Listen, I like you, I swear, but you're an absolute pain in my fucking ass, witch."

Evelyn stepped back, blinking a few times as she recovered from Tala's insult. Her tone suggested an endearment, a friendly vexation. Evelyn tried to remember all the times she'd been around Tala these last few weeks. The kindnesses, the *small* things. They flooded through Evelyn, leaving her off kilter. Because Tala was a vampyr close to Riven. She had to have heard her wrong.

Tala inhaled, shoulders rising and falling. "If you want tonight to go as planned"—she emphasized the last word—"stay close to me. When we enter the rings, stay to my left, and make sure Riven doesn't see you."

"Wait, what plan? Who's plan?" The possibility Tala *was* helping had her tripping over her own feet. Why would the vampyr help her? *How* would she?

"Are you two joining us?" Ingrid called across the library. Under the arch, she stared intently at Evelyn, the malice and darkness wafting from her magic rearing Evelyn's flame so close to the surface, her skin prickled with a powerful warmth.

Tala cursed underneath her breath, and Evelyn gasped. The vampyr's golden gaze connected with hers, and she shook her head once. A clear message—*Don't say a bloody word.*

Evelyn didn't need to be warned to remain quiet, though. The one little hissed cursed had shocked her entirely into silence.

Because she was fairly certain Tala had hissed "Moons."

CHAPTER THIRTY-EIGHT

VAMPYRS HURRIED DOWN THE castle hall leading to the fighting rings. Wine and blood sloshed from their goblets, staining the floors crimson. Mildew, tannins, and iron hung in the air as cheers echoed from the lower levels, the growls of werewolves muddled against the snarls of demons. Tala weaved far behind Ingrid and Belle, letting the current swallow them up.

At the last second, Belle's doe eyes connected with Evelyn's, and she gave her one committal nod.

"Get out," she mouthed.

Sweat trickled down Evelyn's temples, prickles traveling down her neck. She didn't want to leave Belle. *No.* Not in this wretched castle surrounded by the court of vampyrs. There had to be another way. But she had no other choice at present. She and Ingrid veered right towards Riven while Tala turned left.

It was so different at this level. Louder. Harsher. More brutal. Evelyn tried to tune out the fighting below and the cheering of vampyrs, but Visha's screeches of glee snagged her attention.

The princess wore white, and blood ran down her chest and exposed cleavage, bleeding into the fabric of her low-cut bodice. Next to her, a body lay motionless, the glassy and vacant eyes of a dead servant staring straight into the fighting ring.

Evelyn's flame wrestled in her blood. Her heart hammered in her chest, lips inching upward into an angry snarl. *Fucking flames*, she was so furious, so done with Visha and her hatred and malicious ways. She stepped away from Tala. She had her magic back. She'd end this—Evelyn halted. In the row above Visha, Riven sat between two lords, his attention focused on their conversation. Not the fighting. Not his sister. Not even the sisters seating themselves a few rows over.

Evelyn retreated, the chorus of chaos around her snapping her back to reality. Visha was *one* vampyr. A horrible, terrible one. But there was more at stake than the vicious princess. Despite Evelyn's blood coursing hot and hurried through her, she couldn't fight back. Not yet. She couldn't risk being thrown into her cell again and not reuniting with Kade.

She fell into step with Tala, who angled her body aside Evelyn's, shielding her from anyone that passed. Tala tugged her into a seat obscured by a column in the second to last row at the top of the stadium. Evelyn lost sight of the others, but if she couldn't see them, they couldn't see her.

At least she hoped.

She turned to Tala. "Are you ever planning to tell me what is going on?"

As Evelyn asked, the horns signaling the next fight drowned out her question. She knew Tala heard with her vampyr hearing, but she ignored her, attention riveted on the fighting rings. The war adviser swallowed, a flash of recollection fleeting through her golden eyes, and Evelyn followed her line of sight.

The gates to the ring screeched open, revealing a golden-brown were-wolf stalking inside. Evelyn's heart hammered louder than the cheering crowd around her. Her entire being turned ice-cold. The blood in her veins, the weaved tendons of her soul, her very essence soared, plummeted, and burst.

Kade. Her fated.

In his werewolf form.

In the fighting ring.

The air underground turned humid and thick, and Evelyn couldn't breathe. The beat of her frantic heart matched the surrounding drums. She clutched her stomach, afraid she'd be sick. Her other hand gripped the bench, her nails digging into the wood.

Who had captured Kade? Had Riven done this? Visha?

She'd kill them.

Below, Kade roared, and Evelyn shut her eyes. Her heart pounded. Once, twice, a third time. The sound of his beast reached to her bones and soul.

She willed her eyes open again, and the next moments slowed as the madras entered the ring from the other side. The arena's cheers fell away, the cavern unnaturally silent. The only echo was her own ragged breath. The demon's prowl inched step by step as it circled the perimeter. She sucked in as it charged.

Her flame—wicked, angry and protective—pushed and pushed to be released. To protect her fated. Her love. Her heart.

"*Don't.*"

Tala's commanding tone snapped Evelyn to the present. She blinked, focusing on the vampyr blocking her view of Kade.

Kade. Kade. Kade.

She couldn't stop thinking, couldn't sit here and do nothing. Evelyn had to protect him. She'd burn every last vampyr in this arena to get to him.

"Evelyn, don't. You will ruin everything."

Tala's words were absolute, so stern they bordered harsh. Her golden eyes bore into Evelyn, begging, relenting— Wait, not golden, *amber.*

Evelyn's world spiraled, her mind reeling. She shifted her gaze between her fated and Tala. The same eyes. The same look. The familiarity.

The likeness, the eyes alone pulled at her soul, a piece of her mate.

His mother.

"But that's not possible..." She spoke her thoughts out loud, unable to contain her shock. No. She had to be wrong. "You can't be. You're... dead, right? I mean." Evelyn shook her head again. She'd never met Alpha Nadia Drengr.

How could she be certain? "Are you...?" She trailed off, unsure if she was right or absurd.

Tala's features softened—and Goddess, right then and there, she learned where Kade had gotten his kindness from. "I am."

The two words filtered through Evelyn like a gust of wind, leaving her off balance. For weeks, she'd been guarded by Kade's mother.

A vampyr. A member of Riven's council. Someone she believed to be the enemy.

Evelyn swallowed and refocused on Kade. "Why is he down there? Did Riven capture him, too? Has he been here this whole time?" Her questions tumbled out of her as she tried to keep tabs on Kade's fighting werewolf form. Seconds ticked by like hours as he swiped his claws, and the demon bared its teeth. Jaws snapped. Two canine-like creatures fought. Bits of the bench peeled under Evelyn's fingernails, her lungs ballooning.

She still couldn't breathe.

"No, Riven didn't capture him. The prince doesn't even know that is Kade. No one does. It is part of the plan to get you out, and you must remain calm for it to work."

A sense of suspension, like falling or sitting at the edge of her seat, bound her in place and threatened to speed her heart faster and faster in her chest, but Evelyn remained calm, grasping a sense of Tala's words.

The plan to get you out.

Kade had come for her, and Evelyn begged, tugged at their fated-mate bond, sending her warmth and light his way as he fought the demon.

Kade muscles tightened as he rose above the madras demon and delivered a deadly swipe of his claws. The demon dropped to the sands of the pit. Kade lowered slowly, vertebrae by vertebrae back to all fours and turned, amber eyes locking on Evelyn.

A small sound, a whimper, escaped her. Relief. Hope. Love. For a fraction of a second, the torment of the last month dissipated like mist when the sun came out. Her light, her fated, the man who held her heart was yards away, and the promise of their reunion filled Evelyn with blazing determination.

And then the world exploded.

The east wall of the fighting ring blew to bits, destroying rows of the arena on the farthest side instantly. Above them, the cavern shook, debris and loose rock falling. The column closest to Evelyn and Tala groaned, hairline fractures splitting across its surface.

Vampyrs screeched and cried out, fangs bared and eyes wide with horror. Another explosion shook not just the cavern but the foundation of the castle. Evelyn fell off the bench, Tala tumbling with her. Vampyrs around them scrambled to escape, silk skirts covering Evelyn in layers of darkness. A heel pushed into her belly, and Evelyn groaned. She grabbed the vampyr's cold, bony ankle and jerked them off her. Chaos and light warred with the other as she regained her wits.

The howls of werewolves silenced the fleeing vampyrs. Everyone in the arena stilled for a moment, an unease, an impending beastly energy filling the cave. The howls grew louder, the growls fiercer, and Kade's roar, the loudest of them all, joined.

Evelyn pushed her way through legs and limbs and rubble, pulling herself upright on the bench. She had to get to Kade, fight by his side. Someone grabbed her wrist, fierce and strong, pulling her the opposite way.

"Evelyn, we must go," Tala said.

She peered at the vampyr. "I am not leaving him!"

"Kade has his part in the plan, and you must follow yours."

Evelyn fisted her hands at her sides. "I can't let him fight alone!"

"You can and you will. This is a distraction while I get you to the meeting point. Besides, he isn't alone."

Evelyn turned back to the arena, and *Goddess*, werewolves from the fighting rings emerged with a deadly vengeance, chains off and teeth bared. Smoke passed over the opening created by the first explosion, figures approaching from a tunnel. Evelyn swore she saw pink hair and a tall man glinting in enough knives for an entire army.

And arrows began to fly, hitting their mark every time—square into vampyr hearts.

"Evelyn." Tala tugged her wrist, and Evelyn, despite her fated-mate's instinct, followed. Her heart raced, threatening to burst from her chest. It felt wrong to leave Kade, to abandon him in such chaos, especially when Riven was here, but she had to trust the plan, had to respect his decision to enter that ring. She'd escape, and they'd be together again.

Evelyn swore it. Her belly fluttered. Her limbs tingled. Her soul beat hope down her bond with Kade, singing the promise of seeing him soon.

None of the vampyrs paid mind to her and Tala as they pushed their way to the exit tunnels. The entire time, Evelyn searched for Riven. As they reached the east tunnel back to the grand hall, the column at the center of the arena crumbled. Shouts to save the prince and princess gained the attention of vampyrs around them and some turned. Reassurance rushed through Evelyn, fueling her steps forward.

At least the destruction of the arena separated her and Riven.

She and Tala sprinted through the grand hall. Evelyn followed close behind, forming a blind trust with the vampyr. She didn't have all the answers, but her instinct told her not to doubt Tala and to keep going. Tala led her to the southeast side of the castle, the stone halls led to ones with carpet. Passing guards barely acknowledged them, swords in hands and heading towards the booms shaking the bones of the castle.

At the stairs in the tower where her old room was located, up and up they climbed, an icy sensation coating Evelyn's throat as she broke into a sprint to keep up with Tala's frantic pace. They entered her room, the space frigid; the fire in the corner had died. Out of her pocket, Tala retrieved something small and slender. She placed it in Evelyn's hand, closing her fingers around it, the familiar smoothness of bone drawing out her protective instinct.

"This belongs to you. I'm afraid I couldn't save all your things. Riven dropped your muince necklace into the depths of the Sapphire Sea, afraid your coven would discover where he brought you."

Stunned, Evelyn found her dragon bone staff in its hairpin form. She elongated it, magic brimming at her fingertips as it grew to its full size. It was a light and welcome weight in her hands. She'd used it last against the White Lady, and it felt good to be reunited with a piece of herself. But for only a moment before she shrank it once more and tucked the pin inside her pocket.

"I..." Her words trailed off. Near the bathroom, Tala fiddled with the hidden door. It gave way to the passage beyond.

"You knew that passageway existed this whole time."

Tala sighed and nodded. "That's why I chose the tower. An escape route if we needed." Her gaze ran up and down Evelyn. "I never imagined you'd find it and start exploring, especially with Ingrid's sister, of all people. Rather reckless."

"Why didn't you try and stop me?" Evelyn asked.

Tala paused. "Because it kept up your resolve. You take risks, Evelyn, but you're also very brave."

Evelyn swallowed. Tala—no *Nadia's* words, *Kade's mother's* words bloomed warmth through her belly. She wanted to fidget, to hide from Tala's assessing stare.

"You saw me that night, didn't you?" Evelyn whispered. "Across the arena, you saw me in the rings."

"Yes." Her edges of sternness had softened, the light of her eyes glowing in her every movement, in every angle of her body.

Evelyn shook her head, her confusion paralyzing her. "Why didn't you say anything? Why not be honest with me?"

"Tovi and the others hadn't made contact yet. They hadn't arrived in Drystan. Until I knew—"

"I don't understand. What does Tovi have to do with this?"

Tala pushed open the hidden door, a draft gusting into the room. "We don't have time to discuss everything. She is waiting for us."

Evelyn's heart fluttered in her chest. She wasn't ready to face Tovi, not yet, but if it meant escaping, reuniting with Kade, she'd make do. Before she stepped towards the passageway, she rushed towards her bed.

"What are you doing?" Tala hissed from the doorway.

"I'm not leaving without what I've discovered." She retrieved her notes, Matilda's journal, and the unread letters shoved under her mattress, hands shaking with adrenaline. Evelyn folded them and secured them beneath her undergarments.

Tala's lips pinched into a thin line. "So bloody reckless."

They descended the stairwell. Explosions continued, sending slight tremors through the castle. Dust shifted and fell onto Evelyn's shoulder while her bones rattled. They slunk down the stairs until they reached a dead end, their breathless, winded faces reflecting in the still, sludgy water.

"I actually forgot to ask," Tala said. "Do you know how to swim?"

Evelyn grimaced and fought the urge to pinch her nose. "Yes. In that, no."

Tala laughed. "It's our only option. Not deep is a doorway into the abandoned part of the castle where Tovi's waiting."

Evelyn sighed and tapped into her magic. She conjured her flame and created a sphere of swirling light—Goddess, it felt good to wield her power again. She dropped the light into the water, and it sank. Magic kept it alive, and the swirling ball cast a glow onto the dark rectangular shadow of a door.

Not deep at all, like Tala had said.

"You should go first."

Evelyn nodded and tapped her side, sending a protective enchantment onto the books and letters hidden there, refusing to lose them. With that, she dove. The water's cold bit at her exposed skin like tiny needles. It stung her eyes, her vision blurring to a tinged green. Evelyn swam deeper and straight ahead, reaching for the dark silhouetted doorway. She kicked and pulled her way forward, using the door's stone frame to propel herself through it. Her vision flashed bright as her lungs screamed.

She surged up and gasped, air filling her lungs. A moment passed, bubbles popped, and Tala sprang out of the water and joined her.

Tala had told her Tovi was waiting, but that hadn't prepared Evelyn for the sight of her friend standing there. Nothing could have prepared her.

Dressed in gray fighting leathers, Tovi stood at the center of a partially flooded set of stairs. She had a dagger strapped to her thigh and her snowy hair braided and pulled over her shoulder. The two friends locked eyes, steely blue snagging jade. The betrayal Evelyn had felt all these weeks scorched sharper than ever.

Because the woman before her wasn't her friend, but a well-armed vampyr princess.

A boom quaked through the castle, this one far bigger than the rest. The water rippled and lapped against the steps. Tovi's head tilted as she listened. Two more booms followed, and Tovi nodded to herself.

"That's the signal," Tala said.

Tala swam to the stairs, and Evelyn followed. She shivered, not from the cold but from nerves. She pushed them down, buried them. It'd been some time since she'd worn her stoic, aloof mask, but Evelyn placed it on, letting it absorb her nerves and shield her from the pain squeezing her heart. The fact was, Evelyn feared Tovi's betrayal more than anything.

The two regarded one another.

Tovi swallowed. "Look, Evelyn—"

"Save it. I assume if that's the signal, we need to move." She didn't recognize the sound of her own voice—lost, angry. It belonged to the witch she'd sworn to have left behind.

Pain flashed through Tovi's eyes, and her mouth hung open. Evelyn knew she was being childish, avoiding the conversation, and she hated the hurt in her friend's eyes, but now wasn't the time.

"She's right. You both need to go."

Evelyn whirled. "You're not coming with us?"

Tala nodded once, her golden eyes forlorn and lips down turned.

"But why?" Evelyn hissed. "Come with us. Kade—"

"I can't. I'm the only contact in the castle that can keep tabs on Riven."

"What if Riven learns you helped?"

"He won't," Tovi said.

Evelyn shot her a glare. "She's your spy."

The more Evelyn learned and connected the dots, the more it stung. She added her fated's mother's life onto the never-ending pile of things Tovi had chosen to withhold.

Tovi stepped towards Evelyn, arm outstretched.

She recoiled, her stomach twisting. "Please don't touch me."

Her friend—*betrayer*—flinched, brows pinching in pain.

Another tremor shook the castle, dust and flakes of paint falling from the weathered ceiling.

"Go," Tala hissed, swimming back toward the submerged door. "Now."

The urgency in her tone awakened Evelyn's magic, and it sensed darkness approaching. Tovi' nostrils flared, and the two communicated with only a look.

Run.

Tovi led the way, running up the grand staircase that bled into a destroyed hallway. Ripped tapestries whipped in the wind filtering through the shattered windows. Something crunched under Evelyn's flats—her soaked heel had gone straight through the eye socket of a skull. She shivered, shaking her foot loose of the broken bone, and keeping up with Tovi.

No light lit their path aside from the glow of the overcast clouds outside the windows, painting the darkness a silvery gray. Tovi's leathers blended into the haunted hall, and Evelyn felt silly in her days-old dress, soiled with dungeon mildew, old water, and fearful sweats.

She sent out her magic, and it recoiled from the nearby darkness, but she heard no one approach. No one followed down the hall, and the castle had been still from tremors for minutes.

Tovi and Evelyn rounded the corner. They skidded to a halt and grabbed the other for balance. Ahead of them, a stern, cold witch waited, hands outstretched, wind magic upturning dust into twisters, dancing at her feet.

To Evelyn's left, Tovi crouched, hands flaring to talons. Evelyn couldn't fight her shock, couldn't fight the slight amazement at her friend's transformation.

"Move aside," Tovi snarled.

Ingrid didn't move, but the twisters at her side grew. "I don't think I will, *Princess.*"

Wind tunneled through the hall. Their clothes billowed, tapestries swung in the air, and shards of glass chimed against the stone. *Fucking flames.* Evelyn grabbed her staff, elongated it to its full length, and braced as Ingrid struck.

Her attack hit both Evelyn and Tovi like the winds of a storm. And yet, Evelyn's flame, starved from weeks of captivity, flared to life. Mighty, strong, and unbending. It spread across Ingrid's wind, the magics flush against the other.

Tovi gritted her teeth. Held her stance. And turned from the heat of Evelyn's magic. Ingrid's magic stilled, and Evelyn attacked. She shot fire at Ingrid, spheres of flame flying through the air, lighting the dark, abandoned hall in an orange glow.

Ingrid braced, throwing her hands up and diverting Evelyn's attack with a gust of more wind. Fire shattered the windows and dissipated into the cold of night.

Tovi stepped forward, dagger in hand. Evelyn was momentarily stunned from her speed. She moved with an unnerving yet beautiful fluidity. She'd held a blade before, the weapon an extension of each of her advances.

Evelyn joined Tovi, and together they fought Ingrid, two against one. Ingrid unsheathed a weapon of her own, a long, slender staff, equally sized from tip to tip. It shined the same onyx black as the setting around Evelyn's bloodstone.

Dark magic threaded the wind Ingrid wrapped around it, the little light in the hall dimming further. Licorice seeped into the air, clotting it with overly sweet anise.

Gritting her teeth, Evelyn advanced closer and thrust her staff towards Ingrid. The witch met her head-on, both staffs colliding. Light and dark magic battled the other. Power built in the air like crackling static.

Tovi skidded across the stone floor, dagger slicing across the back of Ingrid's knees. Her gaze snagged Evelyn's and time became suspended. Not in a hundred years would Evelyn have imagined fighting alongside her well-dressed and poised friend. Betrayal still lingered, but so did a sense of rightness. It was uncalled for, uncomfortable for Evelyn to accept, though warmth spread through her chest, a kind that calmed her.

As if this was where both her and Tovi were supposed to be.

Ingrid cried out, breaking Evelyn from her thoughts. The dark witch's knees buckled, and Evelyn delivered a blow to her head with the end of her staff.

Ingrid fell, face smacking against the stone. She growled, a horrific hiss of anger vibrating from her. She reached for her staff, but Evelyn wedged it into place against the stone using hers. She gripped her flame, driving the power of light downward. There was no *fucking flames* way she'd let Ingrid succeed or spend one more godforsaken hour in this cursed castle and away from Kade.

She drove that hope, the promise into her magic. Flame danced down the dragon bone and traveled to Ingrid's weapon.

Evelyn destroyed it.

Anger contorted Ingrid's face. Blunt hair amiss. Cloak tattered. Blood streaming from her shaky legs. She rose.

Along with every piece of rubble in the grand hall, hovering in the air from the strength of her dark magic.

"Evelyn!" Tovi cried.

But the onslaught never came. Tovi pushed her aside, grabbing her by the waist as a wave of water surged from behind them. Another magic—a bright lively kind that skittered like spring rain across her flame in greeting. Ingrid's eyes flared wide, and the water crashed into her, washing her away down the hall.

Belle stood at the other end, arms shaking as moisture glistened her eyes.

Tovi and Evelyn pulled apart, not daring to look at the other as Evelyn stepped closer to one of her allies in the castle.

"Go," Belle whispered. "Guards are coming."

"Come with us," Evelyn said.

"What?" Tovi hissed behind her. She grabbed Evelyn's arm, forcing her to look at her. "We can't wait or take—"

"No," Evelyn said far calmer than she felt. She knew this was a risk—one that jeopardized Kade's plan in getting her out, but if anyone else understood being protector, knowing what it meant to defend others, he would know most of all. Evelyn's next words came out shaky as she said, "She saved us, Tovi. We have no idea what consequences she will face from her sister or even Riven. I won't abandon her."

Tovi flinched, Evelyn's message clear. Guilt wormed in Evelyn's gut. Was she being cruel? Too harsh? But she was so angry, so hurt, she didn't care. She faced Belle.

"You don't have any time to decide," Evelyn said. "Come with us and escape the castle, but we leave now."

A choice. Because as much as her instinct screamed to protect Belle, especially after the kindness she'd shown her while trapped in the castle, she also had to escape and reunite with her fated.

Belle nodded. "Alright. I'm coming with you."

Footsteps echoed, moments from turning the corner. Everyone glanced at each other, decision made as tension weighed in the air. Evelyn grabbed Belle's hand and dragged her along as Tovi led them through the next door, continuing their way deeper under the castle.

CHAPTER THIRTY-NINE

Tovi

Thе tunnels under Drystan Castle held two things—memories and darkness.

Both clung tightly to the crooks and crannies like the claws of the slumbering bats, rustling in their dreams. Belle, with her golden-spun curls and wide turquoise eyes, kept close to Evelyn, turning Tovi's dearest friend's hand white as bone with her death grip.

Evelyn's steely gaze met hers. The two stared at one another for a tense breath, and then Tovi cut the connection by turning down the tunnel. Stalactites jutted from the ceiling like rocky teeth, and she crouched down as she led them onward.

This far below, Tovi couldn't feel the aftershocks of Linx's explosives, couldn't know for certain that things were going to plan or not. She tried to find relief that Nadia had successfully brought Evelyn to their meeting point, and they'd face no challenges getting this far, but her friend's appearance caught her off guard.

Tiredness clung to Evelyn, and she'd lost weight. The dress she wore hung off her tall bloody-and-bruised frame. Her standoffish demeanor soured Tovi's sense of success, too. Not that she'd imagined a happy, joyous reunion, but the way Evelyn had looked at her made her want to retch.

How you're seen is what you are.

Tovi clamped her eyes shut, bracing her hand on the tunnel walls and pushing forward. Her mother's voice was fiercer in the home they'd built. She didn't want to imagine what Evelyn now saw. A vampyr, a princess, a liar. It didn't help that the tunnels held so many memories of Tovi's past. She'd been made immortal on this level, her rebirth place beyond the bend. She and her family had become the first of the first, the Verena dynasty planting itself like pine, rooting itself into the rock of the mountain. Their hold had twisted in marvelous ways. It had decayed and split in others, too, its branches basked in green glory while its core rotted away.

She had been rotten. Ravenous. Wretched. Mischievous.

Here, she'd metamorphosed into the monster she wished to destroy, and yet the curse held strong, like a fungus spore, far too small to brush away and too strong to pluck out. The memories didn't help either, lingering like ghosts in the shadows of the underground.

The tunnel widened into a cavern, and the air dropped ten degrees. Their breaths puffed into the air, Belle's rapid and quick while Evelyn gave her a reassuring squeeze of the hand. Tovi swallowed. She and Evelyn used to comfort each other like that at times. In an attempt to drown out the past and eeriness of tunnels, Tovi cleared hear throat.

"Eldrick, Kade's brother, is waiting for us at the edge of the tunnels. It'll lead us to the safe house. We're almost there."

Her friend opened her mouth, and then clamped it shut. An awkwardness stretched between them, the silence filled with the water dripping from the stalactites. Tovi tried to manage a small smile, but Evelyn averted her gaze, teeth grinding so hard Tovi heard it.

She sighed and crossed the cavern, the path turning rocky. Belle let go of Evelyn's hand as they used their arms for balance, placing their steps slowly on the slippery rocks.

When they scaled to the top, it opened into the cave where Tovi's new life had begun. Dark candles glowed in the space, the light stinging her eyes. She blinked away the pain, both from memories and the candles.

Evelyn and Belle were hesitant behind her. She turned to assess them, catching recognition on her friend's face. Evelyn studied the carvings as they moved past the altar. Tovi blinked away the image of her mother's dying body on it and the memories of her father's frantic chants.

"Why didn't you tell me?" Evelyn's voice cracked, and the sound broke Tovi's heart. *Goddess*, she wished she could take it all back. All of it.

"I didn't want to lose you," she said.

Evelyn scoffed, brushing away her tears before they fell. "I think you did that anyway."

Tovi sucked in a breath, and that small part of her, the one from centuries ago, the angry princess no longer seen by her parents, judged by people, and ogled by males reared its ugly, angry head.

"That may be the case," she said. "Trust me for the time being—"

"What?" Evelyn hissed. "You lied to me for years! Was our friendship even real?"

It was as if her friend had slapped her. "How can you say that?"

"What am I supposed to believe?" Evelyn charged towards her. "You're not only a vampyr, Tovi, you're the princess. I feared your father my entire life, and he isn't even alive. You have a brother and sister, and there's rumors you killed your sister-in-law and nephew—"

"Stop."

Tovi gritted her teeth. Stupid, hopeless, and a fool. Why had she not anticipated this? Why had she expected Evelyn to learn so much and not care? It always hurt more from someone she loved, someone she cared for. Judgment.

It sank its inky claws into her and hung on. The only way Tovi knew to shake it off was to hurt and lash out and rage against it.

"I made a mistake, Evelyn. One I regret deeply. But don't you dare throw your hurtful words at me. You are no saint. You're the one who ran. From your people, homeland, sisters, duty, and even your betrothed."

Tovi's words hung in the air between them, so much truth and hurt mixing with the cold of the cavern.

Evelyn's face fell, something flashing in her steely eyes. She shut them, blinking back a bit of moisture and exhaled. "As I recall, you encouraged me to run. I wonder why."

Tovi stewed, haste and frustration warring within her. She hadn't meant to throw Evelyn's decision as a weapon, because her friend was right, she'd told her to go. And for good reason. *Bloody hel.* She'd made everything worse.

Evelyn traced a shoe across the dais's carving. Her brow furrowed, the way it did when her friend was deep in thought.

Confusion rippled through her. "Wait, have you been here before?"

"Yes." Belle's timid response made Tovi jolt—she'd forgotten the witch was even there.

Evelyn continued to study the carvings, dropping to her haunches to inspect the cross between the moon and sun, the two spheres overlapping the other.

"Belle had seen Riven use passageways that led here. When we scoped it out, we stumbled upon him visiting the altar. He"—Evelyn swallowed—"talked with someone." Evelyn's stare bore into Tovi, asking a question, but she gave Tovi no clues to help her answer it.

The cavern's temperature dropped, the candles flickered, and the shadows shifted as if the underworld crept from above. Tovi teetered foot to foot, a creeping sensation crawling up her spine. Her skin tightened with the cold.

She shuddered a breath as she asked, "Did he ask for something? From her?"

Evelyn's brows furrowed, and concern, not fear, flashed across her face. "No, but she promised him what he lost, what his heart beat for."

Tovi shut her eyes, fighting both the pounding of her heart and the tears stinging her eyes. "Bloody hel."

"I assume you know about the spell?"

Tovi nodded.

"It seemed he was doing the spell in exchange for something."

A boom so big rocked through the cavern. Candles whooshed out and some toppled to the ground. The vibration was like an omen, shaking through Tovi.

"We'd better keep moving." Tovi's throat went dry as she forced the words.

She was tired, *too* tired to dive any further into what her brother fought for or wanted. She had an inclination, and an ache bloomed across her. She'd been the one to take it from him in the first place. If Riven fought for what she feared, he would fight until the ends of this world to get it back.

Even if it was a lie, a false hope.

But Evelyn wasn't following behind. She'd stayed at the altar.

"She showed me a memory," she said. "Of you."

Tovi stilled—the candles flickered in a wave of light. Her friend's stare dug into her back, but words turned into ash on her tongue.

"Whatever you saw, it was not real," she whispered. "Let's go before a real threat finds us."

Neither said another word as they hurried onward. The last bit of cold from the tunnels was overshadowed by a promising fresh-yet-spicy scent. Tovi's baser instinct rose—a calming reassurance settling over her. A familiar handsome face came into view, and the world stopped. Jade connected with emerald, and the chaos inside Tovi's mind ceased. She swore Eldrick's usually stoic expression relaxed.

"Stars above, the plan worked," he said.

"Why do you always doubt me, wolf?" Tovi said, her voice coming out far more cheerful than she intended.

Eldrick rolled his eyes and grunted.

Such an alpha response. Tovi smiled, a warmth in her belly, one so fierce it spread down to knees to elbows, made her feel like she might melt into a puddle. Now was certainly not the time. They had to keep moving and—Tovi halted. Standing beside her, Evelyn's brows had risen so high they almost touched her hairline. Her head swiveled back and forth between them, her mouth gaped open. *Goddess*, she'd noticed.

"Evelyn, this is Eldrick, Kade's older brother," she said.

Eldrick smiled. "It's good to finally meet you."

She nodded. "It's good to meet you, too." She tugged Belle behind her and turned down the bend of the tunnel. Eldrick turned to follow, but stopped, eying Tovi's angled body.

"What are you doing?" he asked.

"I have to go back and do one more thing," she whispered.

"No." Eldrick's alpha tone echoed in the tunnel. "That wasn't part of the plan."

"I know, but I need to know if I'm right about something." She shook her head. "If I am, Riven is the threat we have feared."

Eldrick searched her face, jaw ticking. "If you go see him, you might not make it back out. It's too much of a risk."

Sincerity coated his every word. Not accusation. Not judgment. Concern for her.

He gestured around them. "You got Evelyn out, *you* got out. Let's go before—"

Tovi took one mighty step towards Eldrick, the urge to do something she'd wanted to do for days propelling her forward.

She grabbed his breast plate and tugged him down into a kiss.

Their lips crashed together, a heat zapping between the two of them. After a second, Eldrick's shock passed, and the two sighed into the other. Their lips moved together, so in sync it was like both had imagined it enough times, it really wasn't their first.

Two beings blissfully intertwined.

Eldrick's hands fell to Tovi's hips, pulling her closer. Tovi groaned, the taste of him like a forbidden fruit—sweet and wrong and delightful. She put everything into her kiss, the way she moved her lips with his... she was telling him, assuring him, getting drunk off him.

I'm coming back.

Eldrick's lips were needy and hungry against hers, his hold on her hips almost painful, demanding. Tovi had thought his gaze made the world fall away, but this kiss, them coming together, was unmatched. It transported them to a different dimension, one filled with whispers.

You and I.

Tovi's memories and sense of wretchedness fell away. It was only Eldrick. She and him. Lips molding together, gasps, and their flesh searing against the other. As they broke apart, breathless and wide-eyed, courage swelled within her.

"Trust me," she breathed against Eldrick's swollen lips.

He shut his eyes, shuddering. "Alright."

With that, Tovi left him, running through the tunnels, determined to return from her mission to set her people free, and back to the werewolf alpha.

CHAPTER FORTY

Tovi

RIVEN STOOD OVER A small dusty bed.

A canopy made of tulle had been eaten by moths and was dotted with tattered holes like windows to the golden threaded quilt beyond. Untouched for centuries, the bed held the memory of the brightest joy Drystan Castle had ever known. Stars and constellations shined through the dust, reminding Tovi what her brother had called his son.

My whole universe.

It hurt. No memory, no reminder, no thought of her nephew ever undid the guilt of what she'd done. Not his bright smile, his curious thoughts, or bubbly laugh.

For some time, Tovi had suspected her brother had been promised this—to bring back the dead. A promise similar to one their father had been granted with their mother. And yet, Tovi hadn't said it out loud, as if whispering the words on the wind gave the possibility power. She also hadn't wanted to face the sickening truth. Riven would not yearn for his wife and child if she hadn't been so selfish. Her own mistake threatened to destroy their homeland.

"You're a fool if you think she'll bring them back, Riven. She won't," Tovi whispered from her hiding place.

Riven didn't flinch, didn't give any indication she'd spooked him at all. "You don't know that." He trailed a bony finger across the bed's dusty frame.

"Riven." She emerged from behind the curtain, saying his name like a plea. "You know she's manipulative. She did it to Father and all of us."

"She's shown me them, Tovi," Riven said, still not looking at her.

"It isn't real."

He whipped his attention towards her. "What if it is?"

"Is it worth destroying our homeland, our people for?"

"You wouldn't understand. You've never loved anyone."

Tovi clutched her chest as if a dagger had pierced her heart. She set her shoulders back, stretching against the hurt of his words.

"That isn't true. I loved them, too. I still love you, after everything."

Riven tsked. "You didn't love them. If you had, you wouldn't have forgotten about them, and they wouldn't have died."

Tovi shut her eyes. "I'm sorry."

Her apology shuddered out of her. She'd already said it so many times. Even then, when she'd been a terrible version of herself, her heart had broken for her sister-in-law and nephew. She'd never meant to hurt them. Never meant to fail them. "I can't undo what I did. I can't bring them back, and you can't trust her to do so either."

Riven remained silent and still, eyes burrowing into his son's empty bed.

"I don't trust her," he whispered. "But I can't let that get in the way of the slightest chance I can bring them back."

Tovi tried to find the right words, tried to tread carefully in Riven's emotional state. "Even if she did bring them back, what's to say they'll be the same? Resurrecting the dead is dark magic, Riven. You—"

Riven growled and whirled, prowling towards her. "Aren't you listening? *I don't care.*"

She did hear him—she saw a lost, heartbroken man poisoned by false hope. Like their father.

"I won't let you do this," she said, shoulders back, head held high.

Riven chuckled. "You think freeing Evelyn will stop me? I will hunt her down. I will kill anyone and everyone protecting her. Her blood is *mine*."

Bloody hel, he meant it.

The curse, thick and oozy, turned the air humid. It stuck to Tovi's skin, raising the hairs on the back of her neck. It crept up and up like the beast she'd been afraid to turn and see.

Her brother was lost.

She hadn't wanted to accept it, that his efforts weren't to become king and break the curse. *That* was a fleeting, frivolous goal she could dissuade him of, but she could never ask him to not wish for his wife and son to be alive again. Her soul squeezed for her brother. The divide between them stretched farther than ever before.

As if it agreed, the walls of the castle shook, the canopy above the bed wavered, and Riven had to grasp the bed frame. Tovi crouched into a deeper stance, keeping balance as the tremors continued.

She and her brother's stares connected, and Tovi leaped as Riven charged. He growled, fangs bared as he chased her through the room.

"She may have escaped, but I won't let you," he hissed.

He appeared ahead of her, fast as ever, yet Tovi had always been light on her feet. She sidestepped and jumped, grabbing hold of the curtain as she swung into the window, shoulder first. She barreled through it, letting go of the aged fabric as she met the cold night air. The cracked glass rang with Riven's monstrous cry.

"Sorry, brother," she whispered, her farewell filtering into the wind.

Tovi fell, fell, and fell, the last of her emotional connection to her brother snapping as she somersaulted and landed on her feet. The force boomed, dirt ricocheting in a circle. She ran, headed south, not looking back at the home she so desperately wanted to save.

Chapter Forty-One

L IGHT BLINDED EVELYN AS a hatch opened above the tunnel.

The scent of bread, sugar, and butter overtook the mildew and dirt of the darkness as Eldrick pulled her free.

Evelyn panted from running what felt like miles, and as Eldrick closed the tunnel, she tried to even out her breathing. She stood, half expecting to find Kade, but the space was empty aside from a female vampyr with red-rimmed glasses, staring at her intently.

Evelyn backed up a step, but Eldrick squeezed her shoulder reassuringly.

"This is Lou. She's a friend of Tovi's and helped us get you out of the castle."

"Oh." Evelyn swallowed. "Thank you."

"Think nothing of it," Lou said. "Nice to finally meet who's been causing all the fuss."

Aside from her paler complexion, the vampyr didn't dress or carry herself like the vampyrs within the walls of Drystan Castle. In fact, she was reserved, wearing a simple tunic and trousers, while a kindness shined in her eyes.

She sized the three of them up. "Wait, where is Tovi?"

Eldrick gritted his teeth. "She had something she needed to do."

Evelyn assessed Kade's older brother. He looked much like Kade, but that's not what riveted her. She was more interested in his reaction to Tovi earlier. She'd seen her old friend's reaction around the werewolf, something she'd never seen in all the years she'd known her. Usually, Tovi ignored the opposite sex unless she desperately needed a night of release. Even that was rare.

"I don't recall another witch being a part of the plan," Lou said.

Belle stepped closer to Evelyn, her shoulder bumping against her elbow. The usual rosy glow of her cheeks had spread farther, exertion coloring the freckled bridge of her nose. Her blonde curls matted to her forehead with sweat, and though they'd sprinted for their lives from Drystan Castle, Belle already appeared better, brighter outside the stone walls.

"Sometimes plans change," Evelyn said, using her body to shield Belle from the vampyr's perusal, friend of Tovi or not. "Belle is here to stay."

Lou chuckled. "Alright, Daughter of the Goddess, no need to bring that flame of yours forth. Not yet anyway."

Not yet.

What else did their plan entail? The day's events weighed on Evelyn. She wanted to see Kade. To have him hold her, to run her hands through his hair and beard. She felt useless, unaware of the plan. A stone dropped in her belly, her heart thudding in her chest like a series of war drums thumping to impending doom. She couldn't wait any longer, couldn't stand and do nothing as the walls of whatever cottage they'd stumbled into closed in around her.

"We have to go back."

Eldrick whipped his head around. "No."

The simple, stern tone seemed to be a Drengr trait, and it riled an angry heat through Evelyn's blood.

"I'm not going to stand here while Kade fights—"

"Listen to me," he said. "I know you want to go to him, I know this is driving you insane. But Kade waited for the right precise moment, almost driving himself mad before he could get into the castle. He waited, you can do the same. Trust the plan, trust him."

Evelyn's fingernails dug into her palms as she fisted her hands. She hated every second Kade wasn't here, but Eldrick was right. She couldn't jeopardize the plan, not when it seemed so many had risked their lives to make sure it all went well, and she'd trusted Kade since she'd been thrown into the carriage in Callum and stuck on that ship in the Sapphire Sea.

Evelyn swallowed and nodded. "Alright."

A small smile spread across Eldrick's clean-shaven face. "It's truly good to finally meet you, Evelyn."

"And you," she whispered.

Evelyn half expected anger or annoyance from Kade's brother. Yet, the eldest Drengr brother seemed pleased to see her, excited even. His eagerness threw her off guard, the right words lodging in her throat. The only ones that came to mind were apologies, and they left her deflated.

Luckily, Eldrick gave a roguish grin. "When we leave Drystan, I want your account of Kade as Cyrus Skender the huntsman."

The playfulness in Eldrick's tone relaxed her taut muscles, and she smiled. "He was rather unbearable."

Eldrick's small smile stretched into a full-blown one, and he laughed. "Oh, really? Did you hear that, Lou? Unbearable."

"Doesn't sound like the story he's been telling us," the vampyr said with crossed arms, leaning against the cottage's whitewashed brick walls.

Evelyn wanted to ask what Kade's version was, but her name on the wind outside caught everyone's attention, averting their gazes out the front window. Evelyn's heart skipped. Anticipation thrummed in her veins.

"Evelyn!"

Her name was a cry that boomed—it gripped her soul and *tugged*. She moved, running towards the door and ignoring the protests behind her as she sprinted into a wintery forest. Her breath plumed like clouds of smoke in the frigid air as she whirled around wildly, searching for Kade.

"Evelyn!" he called again.

Evelyn spun, snow crunching under her useless wet flats.

Through the trees, Kade ran towards her. Evelyn released a sob. Shirtless and bloody, she'd never seen him so worn, so tired, and yet so wild. Half his hair had been tied away from his face, but a few strands stuck to his forehead with blood, sweat and dirt. His strong muscles pulled and pulsed through his frame, as if he ran through battle to get to her. All the while, his amber eyes never left hers, the warm whiskey sending heat through her even at this distance.

"Kade!" Evelyn moved without thought, without thinking. She only wanted to be with him—*needed* to be with him. Snow caught in her eyes, tangled in her hair, and burned her cheeks as she ran. Her shoes slipped off in the snow, but it didn't matter. The icy forest poked and froze her feet—that also didn't matter. She was so close. He was so close.

She ran, ran, and ran until they reached one another, and Evelyn launched into Kade's outstretched arms.

Her heart thumped. *Raced.* Beat in tandem to its twin.

Everything she'd been through crashed into her. It hit her in waves. One after the other. Uncertainty, worry, devastation. Everything she'd kept at bay during her time in Drystan Castle. All of it rocked Evelyn as she clung onto Kade, desperate to feel, to smell, to see the man she considered home. Evergreen and rain filled her lungs, calmed her heart, and swelled her soul.

Kade was here. He was here. He'd come.

For a moment, they held each other, letting their souls be one, centered together. She buried her face in his neck as she cried. Kade held her close, one arm around her waist while his other hand weaved through her hair. His heart hammered so quickly in his chest, Evelyn felt the rapid thumps through her breastbone.

When they pulled apart, tears stung against the cold as they traveled down Evelyn's cheeks. Kade appeared pained, brows pinched and eyes narrowed. That brave, wild warrior had shifted to a man in anguish.

"I got you, love," he said. "It's alright."

They leaned their foreheads against each other. Evelyn sighed as peace floated through her. The forest was still, and flurries descended around them in silence.

"I always knew you'd come," Evelyn she said so low it was a mere breath.

Kade pushed her hair out of her face, drinking in every inch, his amber eyes leaving a caress across her skin wherever they roamed. "I'd fight the gods and goddesses to have you by my side again, Ev."

Ev.

She could burst.

Evelyn shut her eyes, letting Kade's words sink into her bones, reaching her soul and cementing what she already knew of their bond. She kissed him. Kade met her fierceness like a starving beast hungry for her, but there was also something else, something deeper. As his lips molded to hers and Evelyn held him close, their kiss vibrated through them like a declaration, far deeper than a homecoming.

When they pulled apart, tears at the corner of Kade's eyes collected like beads, and Evelyn ran her thumbs under them, smiling and laughing through her own tears.

Being together again was a magic within itself.

PART III

Chapter Forty-Two

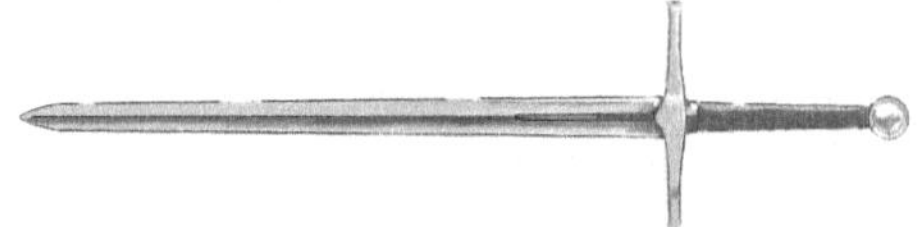

KADE'S HEART SWELLED AND soared with Evelyn at his side. He refused to let her go, his hand intertwined with hers as they entered the cottage, safe and sound.

For now.

The Gray Fenris were waiting with Eldrick as Tovi slipped up from the cottage's hatch last, joining Lou. They discussed something in hushed voices. Before Evelyn's boot hit the cottage floor, Yennifer pulled her out of Kade's grasp and into a tight hug. A pulse of power echoed in his core, but he fought the irrational protectiveness. It was Yen, one of his oldest friends. He knew this, and yet, an animalistic, primal urge to pull Evelyn back into his arms and keep her there safe overcame him.

A strong hand clasped his shoulders, and Kade blinked away the haze of his inner wolf.

"You mentioned she was brave and courageous, but you failed to mention how beautiful she is." Bétar wiggled his bushy red brows.

A growl rumbled in Kade's chest. Heat flushed through his tense body. Yet, his warning only made Bétar's face split into a wide devilish grin.

"Territorial already? This shall be fun."

Bétar, the bastard, took Evelyn's hand and laid a delicate kiss on it. Kade saw red, perhaps the future of Bétar's blood on whitewashed walls except—

No.

This was Bétar. His second. His friend. He tried to focus on Evelyn and remind himself as the Gray Fenris introduced themselves, that they weren't a threat. Yet, the pounding in his ears, the ringing, his vision tunneling in and out of focus, the power in his chest thumping along with his heart... Growing, it manifested into an energy he couldn't control.

"Kade."

A soft hand rested over his heart while another cupped his bearded cheek. Kade blinked, his eyes focusing on Evelyn's stare. That blue he'd dreamed about for weeks marred with concern, and her left brow, as always, pinched as she thought deeply to herself.

"It feels silly to ask this," she said, "because I know you're not okay. I know I'm not entirely okay. But..."

Kade understood, and he pulled her in close, planting a kiss on her forehead. "I'm fine, just not ready to let you go yet."

Evelyn sighed, lowering her hands to grasp his and running her thumbs over his knuckles. Her touch, her stare, her entire disregard for the blood that painted his face, hands, and chest as she soothed him—all of it reminded him she needed his touch as much as he needed hers. They belonged to each other.

"I'm not going anywhere, and if it makes you feel any better, right now I need you close, too." She squeezed his hands, dropping one and intertwining her fingers with another. A shudder went through him. Kade didn't know what she'd gone through inside the castle.

She was paler, cheeks less rosy, and she'd lost a bit of weight. He detected iron in the air. Her blood. He peered down at her feet. Crimson smeared the stone beneath them. He growled, the earlier haze threatening to return.

Evelyn shifted, squeezing his hand. "It's alright—I did it to myself running to meet you. I..." She shook her head, blinking away tears.

Kade used his forefinger to tilt her chin up. "Talk to me."

"I really hope this is real," she said.

He lowered his lips to her ear. "Later, I'll show you how very real this is."

Evelyn peered up at him over her lashes, sucking in her breath. He felt her heart skip a beat and the slightest pink warmed her cheeks.

"You better not dare tease me, huntsman," she whispered.

Kade smiled, his old nickname spreading a welcome warmth and familiarity he'd missed.

The small cottage brimmed with a giddy edge. The steps Kade and his team had taken these last few weeks had led them to this moment. The distressed brick walls of the main floor weren't strong enough to contain Kade's euphoric, disoriented self. Out the window over the kitchenette's sink, the glow of the moon passed through the blanket of clouds and painted the rapids silver. The sight of his God's power slowed his heart and rallied his breath, allowing him to size up his team. Across the way, the hatch leading to the tunnels jolted, and a mass of fiery fur sprang free.

"Maxie!" Evelyn's voice cracked as she cried her familiar's name.

A resounding meow greeted her as the cat launched into Evelyn's arms. Kade's heart squeezed when a shuddering sob released from his mate. She buried her face into Maxie's thick coat. Her familiar's purr was like a gentle hum, and her tail swooshed side to side, the first time he'd seen her so lively in weeks.

He ran a hand down Maxie's forehead. "She's been with me ever since..." Kade didn't dare mention the specifics of what happened that day, not when a tiny voice in his mind threatened to say he *lost* her.

Evelyn wiped away her tears. "Has she been alright without me?"

"Maxie's one of us now," Linx said from across the room. "She fit right in."

"Really?" Evelyn asked. "I thought werewolves didn't like cats."

"They don't," Kade said. "And don't be fooled, it took a few days for the team to warm up to her. But for the most part, Maxie fared well. We think it's because of the bond."

Evelyn's brow furrowed, and her silvery gaze jumped between him and Maxie. "Oh, our bond?"

Kade nodded. "It was suggested since both your souls are connected, and ours are too, Maxie and I might share a slight bond."

Evelyn smiled, big and wide. "*That* would explain a lot of what happened in Callum."

Kade agreed, but the town name dried the words on his tongue. That's where he'd lost her. But they were *here*, at the safe house. They'd made it. He didn't want to waste time thinking about that wretched day. Not with Evelyn at his side, Maxie in her arms, and everyone back in one piece.

Everyone including someone new. A witch he'd never seen before stood with Yennifer. The witch's energy was at least calm and bright, but Kade's restless wolf didn't trust her.

"Who is that?" he asked.

"That's Belle," Evelyn said.

"Why is she here?" Kade didn't hold back the gruffness in his tone.

"Kade, be nice. She was kind to me in the castle. Her sister is rather cruel—"

"Did she hurt you?" Kade's wolf paced beneath his skin.

Evelyn shut her eyes, rallying a deep breath. "Not in the way that you think. Ingrid's the one who gave me the necklace that blocked my magic."

Kade caught the glint of the red stone pendant around Evelyn's neck for the first time.

She laid a hand on his cheek, making him look at her instead. "Stop worrying. Belle broke the dark magic, and I have my powers back. It's useless now."

Kade tried to search her face, to find some relief, but they'd spent weeks away from one another. Not knowing what she went through made his skin tingle, palms sweaty.

"The other werewolves in the fighting," she said, breaking him out of his trance. "Were they set free?"

"Yes," Bétar said. "Thanks to Tovi, who slipped me a key, I was able to get each of them out. There at Lou's bakery now, readying to travel with Captain Flynn's crew. We were able to save twenty werewolves."

Twenty-five if they counted the ones they'd set free on their way here. Kade nodded at both Bétar and Tovi. A solemness seeped into the air, though. Forty-one had been taken from the Vadon Mountains. None of them would forget the lives they weren't able to save—the ones lost to the cruelty of their enemy.

The thought had Kade peering down at Evelyn, his worry resurfacing. "How did you know there were other werewolves?"

Evelyn pulled out of his hold and approached an empty worktable. She released Maxie on top of it. With free hands, she rummaged under her dress and retrieved something. She set a pile of folded parchments onto the table. "I may have been Riven's prisoner, but I did a bit of exploring while I was in the castle."

A glint shined in her eyes—one Kade had never seen before. It unnerved him. As did her lack of self-preservation. But did he expect anything less? Of course, Evelyn would search for answers. He didn't want to argue or allow his frustration with her rather courageous efforts to dampen their reunion. Not when he wasn't really sure how to voice his worry without sounding like an absolute overbearing, controlling ass. Kade had no intention of being that kind of man in their relationship, but how did he control his need to protect her?

One foot in front of the other.

The others moved closer to join Evelyn at the table, and the realization clicked again—their plan *had* worked. They would need to come to terms with their time apart, but they needed to move forward, too. Whatever items Evelyn had brought from the castle would help with that, would ground them in what came next.

Kade joined her side. "What did you find, love?"

Pink returned to Evelyn's cheeks, but she focused on unfurling her parchment from a weathered journal. Notes, letters, and etches of random words. The stack brought Kade back to Callum, late nights around Evelyn's kitchenette table, investigating the murders. *Moons*, he loved this woman's mind and drive.

"It's all a bit of nothing and something." She turned to Tovi. "I assume everyone is aware of Riven's plans?"

Everyone nodded.

Evelyn leaned over the table, arms outstretching over her findings. "Well, for starters, Riven does in fact have allies. After searching his study—"

"You did what?" Kade's hands turned clammy.

Evelyn waved him off, far too excited to notice his reaction. "Specifics don't really matter. I read some of his letters. He has contacts, one in Nūa who used a flower symbol but never a name. The other was positioned in the Vadon Mountains and went by a code name—the Lone Wolf."

Eldrick cursed, and the others bristled.

Evelyn looked up from the table, left brow pinching. "Does that name mean anything?"

Kade joined her side, relishing being in her orbit. "We don't know who it is," Kade said. "But we've confirmed they're a werewolf and responsible for supplying the werewolves for the fighting rings."

Evelyn crossed her arms, nibbling her lip as she thought. "His letter said something about a plan that involved phases. He mentioned the missing werewolves caused unease and predicted loss of faith would follow."

The cottage fell deadly silent—so much so, one heard the ting of snow against the window's glass. He and his brother shared a glance.

"This doesn't look like a werewolf trying to make a profit anymore," Eldrick said.

Tovi shook her head. "No, it sounds like someone trying to create a rift amongst the werewolf packs."

"It makes sense," Yennifer said. "The werewolf packs have been at peace for centuries and are a formidable force when they band together. If Riven succeeded in allowing vampyrs to walk in the sunlight, he'd want to weaken the biggest army he faced. We've been patrolling and containing the Void for decades. Divide their forces and Riven and his allies have an unguarded crossing into Sorin."

"Any idea who this werewolf might be?" Evelyn asked.

Everyone shifted on their feet, bitterness and frustration leaping into the air.

"No," Kade said.

"We'll need to let Claus and Father know," Eldrick said. "If the Lone Wolf is amongst us, they should be warned."

"And we can still learn more while we're here," Tovi said.

"We're staying in Drystan?" Evelyn asked, rearing back from the table.

Kade moved closer to her, placing his hand on her lower back. "Only for a little longer while we wait out the unrest."

"Riven is most likely scrambling to put his castle back in order," Tovi said, "as well as hunting you down, Evelyn. He'll expect us to be on the run instead of hiding nearby."

"Alright." Evelyn swallowed, hesitant as she met Tovi's stare. "Are you able to get a letter to Nūa?"

Tovi regarded her. "Yes, I can try my best. Why?"

Evelyn assessed the group. "The other contact is in the city of witches. Now, I'm not certain they're a witch, but they supplied my sister Blair's address. Riven and Ingrid threatened her life if I stepped out of line."

Kade's fist tightened at his side, knuckles popping from the force.

Tovi hurried a nod. "I'll get a letter out to her and Mirella."

"Thank you."

A silence seeped into the air, a static buzzing between the old friends. Kade witnessed the unease in Evelyn's stare, blue scarred with hurt. He'd seen it before—betrayal. Tovi had been like a sister to Evelyn, but moons, he hoped she'd see what Tovi had done to get her back.

"What else did you find?" he asked.

Evelyn splayed out handwritten notes. One had lines sectioned together and in blocks. One was a list of words, random at best. The others were words etched from the lead of a pencil, outlining the indention of a what appeared to be a scribble. Something familiar grabbed Kade's attention, and he reached out his hand, hovering over words he'd heard since boyhood. They tickled the back of his mind—words that had influenced the man he was today.

"That's our prophecy," he whispered.

The team gathered closer, reading the words to themselves.

"I know, but, Kade, it wasn't alone." Evelyn pushed the parchment with the lines towards him. "It was a stanza among others. Some words I was able to make out. Most don't make any sense, except for this, *land...in red*. Riven communicated with"—she paused, glancing up at Tovi—"a deity I believe—"

"*What?*" Kade's tone came out far harsher than he intended. His fear had leaked through, the pressure in his chest pulsing. He didn't know which to process first, Evelyn spying on Riven, or a goddess or god having been present.

To her credit, Evelyn didn't balk, but continued on. "Belle and I found Riven at an altar. She, the goddess I think, spoke with him about something called the Blood Moon. She also whispered these same words but more, *land* cast *in red*." Evelyn pursed her lips, as if she had more to say, but didn't.

Tovi shook her head. "I've never heard of the Blood Moon before."

Eldrick crossed his arms. "But the land cast in red suggests an eclipse."

Kade nodded. "He's right. There's one a year. Scholars claim the land comes between the sun and the moon. Werewolves usually celebrate that night, the symbol of transition into the winter months."

"Winter?" Evelyn asked. "Any idea when this season's will be?"

Bétar shrugged. "I think a week or so."

Evelyn's brows furrowed, and Kade's instinct screamed to reach out and touch her, to take her away from this discussion and let all the unknowns be problems for tomorrow.

"I think," Evelyn said, "that's the night of the spell, when Ingrid or whoever planned to follow through with the White Lady's plans. If the Blood Moon and this eclipse are the same, the night would be a rather powerful time to conjure magic." Her eyes grew distant, thoughtful. "I'm also curious if the land blocking the sun from the moon has anything to do with it, as if the Sun Goddess would be her weakest separated from the Moon God."

Tovi crossed her arms, lips pursing. "It makes sense. Lou can ask around, learn more about if and when this eclipse occurs. I think for now, we proceed believing the Blood Moon and the spell is a week away."

"We'll need to leave Drystan before then," Eldrick said. "The more distance between us, Riven, and his witch the better."

"That should be plenty of time for us to recoup and start our journey," Tovi said. "We should reconvene here tomorrow and discuss preparations."

A timeline for the spell. They hadn't one since embarking on this mission, and having one gave Kade solid ground. His restlessness settled, as if the timing and date gave him even ground to navigate.

"Until then, we lay low," Kade said. "Evelyn and I will stay here in the cottage, as planned. I know the signal if we need to head south."

The team said their goodbyes. Tovi and Evelyn regarded each other, but in the end, neither said a word as Tovi undid the hatch and jumped below, Eldrick following close behind. Evelyn whispered encouraging words into Belle's ear, who offered a sweet smile. She handed Maxie to her. Evelyn's familiar willingly curled into the witches arms, eyes shutting as she fell asleep. Kade didn't miss Todd standing close to the witch, but he didn't say a word as Linx ushered her along.

It felt like hours, and it felt like mere minutes—Kade and Evelyn were finally alone.

When she averted her attention back to him, he sucked in a breath. The brick of the cottage melted away and the crackling corner fire tuned out. Kade's heart beat like a steady crescendo drum. He couldn't stand it, the distance. After all this time, being in the same room feet apart was too far away.

He charged towards her, one, two, three steps, and grabbed her face in his hands. Evelyn groaned as their lips clashed. He kissed her with a fever. Her touch was scorching. It traveled to ever bit of his taut, ravenous being. Smoke and sweetness. She tasted like burnt vanilla on his tongue.

When they parted, Evelyn gasped, blinking against the haze.

And Kade said the three words he'd hadn't said out loud, the words he'd felt and meant more than anything in his entire life.

"I love you."

CHAPTER FORTY-THREE

EVELYN'S BODY THRUMMED WITH electricity. A smile broke across her face, so wide it hurt. The edges of her eyes stung, yet a floaty sensation came over her. Light. Warm. Airy. She'd known Kade loved her, had *felt* it through their bond, but hearing him say the words had the power to buckle her knees.

"I love you," he said again. "And the gods know I wish I'd said it sooner. That morning in Callum I should've said it back. I've loved you since that day in Castle Connacht. Fuck, I think I might've even loved you sooner, the moment I saw those eyes of yours in the commissioner's office." He grabbed her hand, laying it over his racing heart. "*This*, my heart, beats for you, Evelyn. I love you with every fiber of my being."

Kade's eyes shined more gold than the sun, and an unwavering truth swam in them. She grabbed the nape of his neck, threading her fingers through his longer hair, the waves twirling around her digits and pulled him in for another kiss. Something passed between them—something deeper than fate or the whims of gods or goddesses or the whispers of ancient prophecies. It was them. It was love. It was a choice.

And Evelyn had made hers.

Somehow, Kade had backed her against sacks of flour. Her ass landed at the edge, and Kade caged her with his arms and more kisses. She broke away first, breathless and hungry and too desperate for what she needed to continue on without it.

"Kade, I want you. *Need you.* All of you."

She needed him to know, wanted him to know. Wanted *him*. She'd been ready back in Callum, ready for this moment, this binding.

His amber eyes brightened, his mouth falling open. His chest rose and fell as he stared at her, eyes roaming over her with such a level of intensity, it was like his gaze caressed her skin, laying promise to the delightful moments to come. He tucked a strand of hair behind her ear, a strikingly gentle contrast to the heat between them.

"It is binding for werewolves and their mate," he whispered.

Not a warning, but honesty—always thinking of her, respecting her.

Evelyn smiled. "It's the same for witches and their fated."

Kade swallowed and placed his lips on Evelyn's. Hesitant. Slow. The opposite of what his body and eyes screamed. Evelyn opened her mouth to him, and Kade dipped his tongue against hers. She groaned, falling farther back against the flour. He shifted, pushing against her as he savored her lips and made her see stars with a mere kiss.

Evelyn tugged his trousers, hands cupping the manly bulge pushing to be freed. Kade's hands traveled up her legs, fingertips burning her pebbled flesh. She hissed and broke their kiss as he gave her thighs a squeeze. Not gentle. Not harsh. Just right.

The world spun as Kade picked her up and moved them to a taller stack of flour. There, he laid her down; naturally, her legs spread wide and wrapped around his hips, and she dragged him to her level.

His amber eyes never left hers as he ran two fingers against the fabric blocking her sex, and the growl he emitted shook the entire cottage. "You're soaking."

"For you," Evelyn breathed.

His stare was beastly, terrifyingly hungry, it made Evelyn's toes curl and her core heat.

She pushed up, and Kade shared the same mind because in one swift movement, together they pulled her tattered dress off and threw it to the ground. Evelyn tore her undergarments holding her breasts in place, too, and hissed as her nipples met the air. Kade hooked his fingers through the sides of her underwear and tugged. Between his appraisal and the friction, her sex throbbed with heat. Inch by inch, he pulled the lace off her body, leaving her bare and exposed.

He placed his hands on her knees and spread her legs, opening her sex to him completely. His gaze dropped to it, eyes darkening.

"Show me," he said, tone absolute. "Show me how you like to be touched so for a lifetime I can pleasure you right."

Evelyn's breathing turned rapid. Kade's amber eyes locked with hers, and the desire, the hunger in them—she bit her lip. Never had she wanted to be so intimate, so bare with someone.

Only for Kade. Forever for him.

With one hand, she traveled slowly down her body, moving between her breasts, down her stomach, dipping her fingers through her folds. Her other hand gripped her breast, pinching her nipple as she plunged two fingers into her core, gasping as she soaked herself.

Kade's jaw ticked, his nostrils flaring, but his eyes watched as she began to draw circles around her sensitive nub. Slowly, deliberately. Evelyn took her time. Molding her breast, repeating the pattern with her two fingers. She watched Kade all the while, his body covered from battle, blood, muck and floured handprints.

He was beautiful and beastly, and he *loved* her, and she was his.

Kade's grip on her knees tightened when she dipped her fingers inside. She was so wet. So ready for what was to come. At the thought of Kade and his muscle atop her, letting his inner beast come out, she gasped, quickening the circles, but Kade snapped.

He snatched her hand away and pinned it above her head. Evelyn whimpered as his fingers took over, quick circles the way her body craved.

"Like this?" Kade didn't break eye contact.

She was breathless, and the tension built inside her as her heartbeat thudded like drums to her undoing. All she could do was nod and mewl.

"I need to hear you say it," Kade said, peppering kisses on her cheek, chin, jawline, down her neck.

He ran his whole hand down her folds, pressing his palm into her sensitive spot.

Evelyn writhed, pushing against Kade's other hand where it still pinned her arm above her head.

"Yes." Her word was breathless and small, a plea for more.

"Yes what?"

"Yes, like that, Kade."

His circles had become slower, taunting and cruel, as Evelyn sat on the edge of shattering. She was at his mercy, at his touch. He increased his pace, her breath shuddered and then slowed again. Evelyn's back bowed.

"Should I go faster, Ev?"

Goddess, that nickname.

"*Yes.*"

Kade tilted his head, a hungry gleam glowing in his eyes. "Tell me exactly what you want."

His tone. His beastly energy. She'd do anything this beautiful man asked.

"Please, Kade. Please go faster."

Kade did. He worked her, pumping his fingers into her, drawing rapid circles over that spot, and when Evelyn called out his name, he quickened his pace. Kade finally released her wrist, freeing his hand to palm her breast, to suck and tug at her nipples with his teeth. Evelyn's sight tunneled, the tension in her core rising in a wave of ecstasy, hovering, waiting to crash. And when it did, she cried out, every sensation overtaking her legs as they clamped around Kade. She shuddered as she came down, and Kade kissed her slowly.

He smoothed back her hair, and Evelyn's bones turned to liquid. When Kade picked her up, she wrapped her legs around his middle and her arms around his neck, never daring to let his face out of her sights. He carried her upstairs where more sacks of flour and sugar filled the room, but at the center, a humble cot and wool blankets waited for them. An empty hearth sat in the corner, and with the snap of her fingers, Evelyn lit it. A small fire crackled, warming the room, but it didn't compare to heat flowing between them.

Kade sank to his knees and lowered Evelyn to the cot, the floorboards creaking underneath their weight. She blinked and his trousers were gone, his length ready and needy. Evelyn reached for it, ready to taste him, to shatter him like he did her, but he moved over her.

"No," he said, aligning his hips over hers, his length slicking through her soaked folds. "I want all my pleasure to be when I'm inside you."

Evelyn whimpered. Kade lined himself up at her entrance, and she threaded her fingers into his hair, pulling him closer. Nothing had ever felt so right, so good compared to this moment. His tip pushed against her, the tease and promise unbearable.

"Kade, I need you," she whispered. "Please. *Now.*"

His lips crashed to hers, and in one single thrust, he entered her. They cried out as their bodies joined, and Evelyn's back bowed, her entire being coming undone. Kade shuddered, shoulders shaking as he pushed further in, stretching her in a glorious way.

"Stars above, love."

He grasped behind her knee and hiked her leg up and over his waist, the angle perfect for one final push and Kade was buried to the hilt.

Stretched, full, whole. Evelyn's body relaxed to the glorious size of him.

"I love you," Kade said, laying his forehead onto hers.

Then he began to move, slow, deep, and long. Every lovely inch of him sent tingles of pleasure through her. She panted. Breathed his name. Fell into bliss. All over again, tension built in her core.

Evelyn ran her hands up Kade's back. Blood, dirt, flour, and sweat coated her fingers, and love vibrated between them in the firelight of the small room in a land covered in winter.

They kissed. Sweetly. Hungrily. Kade's pace grew faster, and Evelyn lost all sense of time and place. There existed only her and him and their pleasure.

She was so close to shattering again.

"Evelyn." He whispered her name like a prayer, smoothing back her hair and cupping her face.

She came undone from the look in his eyes, the pure love and adoration shining in them. Kade unraveled, too, shuddering and growling into the place where her shoulder met her neck. He climaxed, body turning taut as his hips slowed and he filled her so fully. He muttered her name with various curses, and Evelyn found herself crying out his name again, the pleasure all too much.

When their bodies stopped moving, they didn't stop looking, drinking the sight of one another in—sweating bodies, panting lungs, loving hearts in their eyes. Time stood still, suspended, and the tethers of their souls reached and connected, weaving together, becoming one.

Wolf and flame.

The fated-mates bond complete.

Tenderly, Kade kissed Evelyn and pulled out of her with care. He lay on his side, dragging her close. They lay there, dazed, and their breathing slowed. The effects of two climaxes still vibrated in Evelyn's knees, her toes numb. Kade trailed his fingers over her body. Across her collarbone, around her breasts, down her stomach. She did the same, tracing his new and old wounds decorating his wide, muscled chest. Neither said a word—their bodies had said enough.

Not soon after, they drifted into peaceful sleep.

Together.

Chapter Forty-Four

ELDRICK TOSSED AND TURNED in his bed.

The village had been brimming with guards when they'd arrived back at the bakery. Lou had encouraged everyone to rest. No one had objected, and certainly not him. The angst of the mission had tired his muscles and thoughts of the Lone Wolf and their mystery of an identity raced through his mind.

Yet, it was a kiss, the single taste of a vampyr princess that kept him wide awake. She'd been sweet, slightly sour, like her ripe stone fruit scent. Plum sat on his tongue, and his wolf howled for more. Never had a female lingered on his mind for so long. Eldrick hadn't been numb to the effects of want though. He'd had his casual fun before and a few serious courtings here and there, but this was different. Feelings haunted him, one's he couldn't put a name to.

Or perhaps he was too frightened to.

Eldrick had thought feelings would be like a cage holding him back, and yet his blood rushed through his veins, his wolf jumping deep inside him. Energetic. Buzzing. Wild. The inability to grasp control *did* frighten him.

He rose from bed, stretching his spine as he did so, as if he could squeeze these feelings from his lean body. His feet pattered against the floorboards but stopped midway to the window, hearing another set of footsteps echoing from the hallway behind his door. From the heavy fall of the soles, it was clear they wore boots, and when he opened the door, he caught a glimpse of Tovi descending the steps at the end of the hall.

The memory of her lips against his, the tantalizing sounds she made and the responsiveness of her body, came back to him. Suddenly, this coming and going in the night didn't sit right. After such an intimate moment, did she not trust him enough with this secret? The notion she didn't *want* him to know ate away at him. It made him all the more curious, so much so, Eldrick dressed for the cold, and in a moment's time, he was slipping out into the night.

He caught Tovi's distant figure turn down a street. He veered left, a few blocks back. During the times he'd left the bakery to scout the village, he'd learned which ones intersected.

Fog lingered like the town's ghosts, rising and falling around the squat buildings. It wrapped around passing vampyrs and clung to scampering humans. The slow, dreadful kind of rain soaked the roads. Eldrick used it all, letting the grayness shadow him as he trailed his target. Like he'd hoped, Tovi crossed the road, darting down the alley across the way. As he passed by it a few yards later, he swore plum invaded his wolf's senses.

He kept straight, flexing and unflexing his hands, unable to fight the urge to touch his now tainted lips. Would she linger on him for the rest of his days like the fog in Drystan?

In the tunnels of the castle, Eldrick had fallen into the kiss before he even knew what had happened. He'd caved into her, grasping at reality as his world spun out of control. And now, like some beast in the night scouting its prey, Eldrick realized he didn't regret it.

Not one bit.

The notion had him hurrying his steps, and through the alley gaps between buildings, he caught sight of Tovi's weaving figure. Too focused, Eldrick collided into someone. He muttered an apology, but the figure, a woman by the shape, didn't turn or stop. A hood concealed her face, and she strutted by and disappeared down an adjacent street and into the engulfing fog.

Every sense linked to his being became alert—he knew that woman. Eldrick halted on the road and shook his head, not trusting the foolish notion.

No, there was no way in the stars above. He stepped forward, but movement in his peripheral halted his advance. Tovi's plum cloak passed by a block away. He fell back into step with her, not daring to lose her wherever she went.

Eldrick turned at the last minute and flanked against the brick of an alleyway. The path between buildings opened to the street Tovi walked up. Eldrick exhaled a puff of his nerves, his cloudy breath floating in the cold air. Boots clicked and clacked against the cobblestone street. Eldrick peered around the corner, skin prickling at the possibility the boots belonged to a guard.

But it was the same hooded figure from before, the one he swore held a familiarity. Her pale hand clutched the edge of her hood, keeping it close to her cheek. Eldrick couldn't make out her face or her features, aside from a dark strand—

Eldrick stepped out from his hiding place, chancing a closer glance. His inner wolf raced in his blood. The female vampyr had the darkest shade of brown hair, like Lorkan's.

Like his mother's.

Moons.

No.

Eldrick retreated down the alleyway as she approached a courtyard with a frozen fountain. Laundry hung from twine between buildings, soggy blouses, tunics, and britches curtaining his view. He tore his gaze back to Tovi who was yards away. He kept his sights on her, shaking the ridiculous hope.

There was absolutely no possibility. It was coincidence. The fog was playing tricks. His mother may have had the same dark hair, but that was not his mother.

She was dead.

Because of him.

Yet again, feelings got in the way. Emotions, grief, sadness, hope, all of them wormed themselves through him, and he buried them down and down—

Tovi turned onto the same street as the other woman, parting through the hanging clothes and getting swallowed by fabrics. Eldrick froze in place. The frigid wind blew by, blowing the clothes out of the way until he could clearly see Tovi meeting the woman at the fountain. Was this her contact?

His heart stopped dead in his chest. A thin nose, high cheekbones, eyes the color of honey. It was as if a soul from the underworld had grabbed ahold of Eldrick and tugged him forward against his will. He moved on shaky legs, treading toward the two women and their meeting place.

His heart, his sanity. Eldrick had to know he was wrong, had to get a closer look. He knew his mother was dead. In his soul, ingrained in his memory. He'd watched as vampyrs overtook her. He'd witnessed her death. And yet, Tovi spoke with his mother.

Fierce. Beautiful. And alive.

Eldrick clutched his chest, unsure if his heart was ripping in two or if he was going to be sick. What were they discussing? Why was *Tovi* with his mother?

"What..." He shook his head. "What in the hel is going on?"

Both Tovi and his mother whirled. Their eyes went wide. Tovi appeared stricken, and his mother blinked back tears.

"Eldrick," she whispered.

That's when he noticed. Fangs peeked out as she spoke. A bloodstone sat on her chest—she, too, wore the magic to block her vampyr scent. His head grew heavy, his world tilting and his heart tearing.

"You're..." He couldn't say it. Couldn't stomach it. "No." He refused to believe it. "This isn't possible. I watched you die. This isn't real."

His mother flinched, and Tovi approached him with hands out as if he were some wild beast about to unleash.

"I—*we*—can explain," Tovi said, taking a step towards him.

We.

Eldrick saw red, charging towards her. "You knew? You've known all this time that my mother has been alive!"

Tovi held up her hands, but his mother stepped between them. "I know you have questions, but we can't afford to attract attention to ourselves."

Eldrick blinked, trying to grip reason or sense, but every fact he conjured rallied a wave of emotions he couldn't handle. His mother was alive, but she was also a vampyr, and Tovi had met her here. Eldrick shook his head, the realization dawning on him.

"My mother's your contact in the castle."

Not a question, a fact.

Neither disputed it, and before Eldrick had the time to ask questions, a horn blared through the village. Guards shouted commands. Tovi and his mother shared a look.

"You should go, Nadia," she whispered.

"What?" Eldrick roared. "You're going back into the castle?" Panic laced his every word. "But if you helped get Evelyn out, doesn't that put you at risk. Stay with us. Come home."

His mother grabbed his shoulders, golden eyes burrowing into him. "I can't yet."

"What about Father?"

His mother blinked back pain. "Your father will understand. I love you, son. Always have and always will. I am so, so proud of the man you've become. I know you don't want to hear this right now, but trust Tovi. I swear it, Eldrick, she is on our side."

His mother kissed his cheek and then hurried past him, vanishing through the clothes and down the path. Eldrick moved to follow her, his heart refusing to let her go after all these years, but Tovi grabbed his arm, stopping him.

He snatched out of her hold, turning to her. "Don't you dare touch me!"

"If you go after her, you risk my brother discovering who she is. He will kill her and hunt you and your brothers down next. It's why she never found you, never told you she survived. She did it to protect you."

Eldrick stilled. The finality in Tovi's words rooted him in place. He'd never risk his mother's life again, not even when emotions warred inside him to find her and demand answers. So many questions left him off balance, his heart dropping like a stone in his belly.

Because his rational side understood. If his mother was indeed a spy, the decades-old secrets made sense. *Moons*, he even understood Tovi's motives, her reasoning for keeping her contact in the castle coveted information. But the issue wasn't that Eldrick didn't recognize the facts or reasoning.

Tovi wasn't the problem.

He was.

His feelings were always far too big. It was why he had to work so hard to tamp them down in the first place, ever since that dreaded day when his mother—or so he thought—had died.

And to learn she was alive was too much. How could he possibly grapple with his years of guilt sparring against relief? It was as if everything he'd felt, done, worked toward had been a wasted effort. All for nothing.

Tovi stepped towards him, but Eldrick countered it by stepping out of reach.

"I was beginning to trust you," he whispered. "I was beginning to—" Eldrick stopped himself, and Tovi sucked in a breath.

"I didn't mean to hurt you, Eldrick," she said. "I swore an oath, a promise that I would not tell you, or your brother Kade, for that matter, that she was a vampyr. I'm so sorry—"

"Sorry?" Eldrick held out his arms, gesturing at the emptiness of her apology. "Sorry!" he said it again, but this time as a hiss. His anger, disbelief. All of it surged like some wave, his control trembling.

The village closed in on him, stone by stone, building by building. The truth, his fear, wedged a darkness in his heart thicker than the fog itself, and anger won.

"How can you live with so many secrets? You're like poison," he said.

Tovi stumbled back. The sadness in her face hardened to fury, and this time she charged him.

"I do have secrets, Eldrick Drengr. Ones that I am most certain, undoubtedly sure you will never deserve to know." She pointed back at where his mother had been, tears now long gone in her cutting stare. "That secret was not mine to tell."

"Save your apologies and bullshit excuses," he said. They stood so close, their noses almost touched. Eldrick's next words were venom. "From here on out, every time I hear your voice, I'll regard it as lies."

He pushed past her, knocking his shoulder into hers. Even with the truth that his mother was alive, Eldrick couldn't shake the sense he was grieving the loss of something else with each step back to Lou's bakery.

CHAPTER FORTY-FIVE

K ADE WOKE WITH EVELYN in his arms and her scent wrapped around him. He shifted their entangled bodies, so he lay flat on his back, and Evelyn stirred a little, sighing into his chest as he pulled her closer and weaved his fingers through her hair. It fell from his fingers like delicate spun silk.

They'd only been asleep for a few hours. The fire had gone out aside from the specks of embers dotting the scorched timber. Early morning cast the room in a grayish purple, painting Evelyn's naked body in a lovely light, drawing the pink undertones of her skin and the blue in her dark hair. As if his staring had tickled her, she roused from sleep, blinking up at him.

Hello, she said, rather lucid but through their mental bond.

Her greeting was crisper, sharper than ever before. And not because of the little distance between them, but because of their stronger, fully mated bond. Wolf and flame now threaded Kade's being, his soul newly woven. He and Evelyn were finally one, and nothing had ever felt so right in his existence. So pure, bright, and fierce.

Hello to you, too. He tucked loose strands behind her ear. Their earlier activities had left her hair tousled and wild, and Kade's insides warmed at the sight.

He liked seeing Evelyn a little messy, a little unraveled because of their intimate time together. It made him smile and took his breath away all at once.

"I can... feel you," she whispered, a sense of wonder glimmering in her eyes.

Kade nodded. "Is that to be expected for fateds?"

Evelyn nibbled her bottom lip. "I think so. I know ones souls ties to the other, and I can most certainly feel your wolf. It's so..."

"Beastly?" he asked.

Evelyn laughed, leaning into his chest. When she peered back up at him, she rested her chin on him, silvery gaze drinking him up. "That's precisely it."

"Your magic is warm," he whispered. "Like a summer's evening."

Evelyn hummed. She trailed her fingers across his abdomen. "We should probably bathe."

Kade's injuries had healed since their attack on the castle, but dirt and blood remained, along with the numerous floured handprints. The same covered Evelyn—*his* handprints—as well as muck and scrapes. At the sight, Kade's hold on her waist tightened, but Evelyn wiggled free, rising to her full height. Her skin glowed like the surface of the moon, her eyes the blue of a clear sky at witching hour.

"Please don't worry," she whispered. "My injuries are healed."

Kade disagreed. Bruises remained on her legs and day-old yellow ones on her wrists—she shouldn't have bruises with her witch's magic, so why did she?

Evelyn held out a hand, stalling the unsavory questions on his tongue.

Kade could never deny Evelyn, especially not when she stood beautiful and bare for him, breasts peaked, and his scent left on her sex. He took her hand, and together they found the washing room. The cottage, thank the gods, had working plumbing like Lou's bakery. The two showered in silence, washing, touching, and kissing the other every so often as dirt and crimson swirled down the drain.

Kade had half a mind to turn Evelyn around, arch her ass out and take her from behind. The image was tempting, especially when he thought of their last time in a shower, Evelyn on her knees, looking up at him. He grabbed Evelyn's waist, tugging her to him.

Rose and honey soap created plumes of perfumed steam, droplets gathering on her lashes like tiny jewels reflecting the silver in her eyes. He smirked, letting his heat and desire into every inch of his stare. Evelyn smiled, giddy and pleased, until—

Her stomach growled. Both of them stilled, and it rumbled again, louder than the running showerhead.

"How dare my body betray me," she said.

Kade laughed. "When was the last time you ate, love?"

Evelyn said nothing, pulling out of his hold and exiting the shower. She passed him a towel and began to dry off with her own. The shower had done her wonders, but it didn't undo the tiny bit of weight she'd lost. Kade had been so eager, so hungry for her hours ago, he had almost forgotten she'd been in the dungeons.

"Evelyn," he said.

She brushed her hair out and wrapped the towel to stay in place, again ignoring his question.

"Do you think they left food downstairs?" she asked.

Kade sighed. It was clear she didn't want to talk about it. *Stars above*, her evasion of what she endured these last few weeks made him want to talk about it more. The need to demand answers bubbled up in him, but Kade bit back the words. He repeated his mantra, *one foot in front of the other*. Find food. Rest a little more. Yet, something else stilled his words. Kade couldn't put his finger on what, though.

Downstairs, they found fresh clothes on the kitchen table. Yennifer had left Evelyn a few pairs of trousers and tunics, their heights similar, but Kade didn't miss how she grabbed an extra one of his tunics. It swallowed her lean frame, hitting right at her maddening, muscular thighs. She didn't appear inclined to dress in anything else, and Kade's chest swelled with male pride.

She opened a neatly folded box, gasping at the sight of the contents inside.

"*Fucking flames*, these look divine," Evelyn said.

Kade laughed, peering into the box. Pastries, eggy custards, and a few breads bursting with the last of autumn veg waited for them.

"Lou happens to be a talented baker." He pointed to the slice of eggy pie. "That is called a quiche."

"It smells like cheese and heaven," Evelyn murmured.

"It tastes better than it smells, if you can believe that."

Evelyn nibbled her lip. "This Lou, she's a friend?"

Kade shrugged. "I've only known her for a few days, but she's been more than helpful in our efforts to get you back. She housed my team and me, and her bakery connects to the underground tunnels, like the one you used to travel here. She is, though, Tovi's friend."

Evelyn stiffened at her friend's name and closed the box.

"What's going on in that head of yours?" he asked.

Evelyn gave him a smile, but not a real one. "Debating if I should have a coffee now or if I'll take a post-pastry nap after eating these."

She rummaged in the cupboards, and when she secured a jar of the beans she needed, her decision had been made as she prepared the items to make two cups. Unlike in the shower, Kade didn't hold back.

"You'll need to talk with her eventually," he said.

"Oh, she and I already spoke." She turned to look at him. "Tovi and I said plenty in the caverns under Drystan Castle. Not sure there's much else to say now."

A kettle whistled under Evelyn's touch as her magic heated its copper exterior. Some metal contraption sat on the counter, and Evelyn got to work grinding the beans. She was busying herself—Kade recognized the tactic. He'd done it so often in the past, distracting himself from unfavorable topics and focusing on something else. This didn't feel like a subject they could ignore. Tovi was now their ally, even he'd dare say, a part of his team. They needed her to get home and against anything else they faced in the coming weeks.

"She has done nothing but try to free you, Ev," he said. "Ever since we left Callum—"

"Why are you on her side?" Evelyn said, freezing in place. She shot him a look, and Kade softened from the hurt flashing in her eyes.

"I am most certainly not on her side."

"Then be angrier," she muttered as she poured hot water over freshly ground beans.

Kade joined her at the counter, holding the mug in place. "I was angry. *Moons*, I almost killed her because of my anger, but she cares about you. I don't think she'll ever forgive herself for what she did."

"She lied to me for years, Kade. *Years.* I thought she was my best friend, and she played me. How can I be sure that everything that happened wasn't as much of a lie as what she is?"

"Perhaps what she is was the only lie and everything else was the truth. I say that as a man who was in a similar position once."

Evelyn blinked a few times, shoulders drooping. "I'm not ready to talk to her. But I assume she'll be a part of getting out of Drystan?"

Kade nodded. "She's trying to gain the Drengr pack as her ally against her brother."

"To become queen?"

"Yes."

Evelyn tsked. "Alright, she'll be a regular presence. Splendid. I know how to be cordial, but she's not my friend anymore. For the sake of everyone else, I'll be on my best behavior."

Kade had heard that tone from her before. It rang with an absoluteness, nothing he'd say would sway her. When she handed him his coffee, his attention caught the yellow bruises at her wrists again.

"How did you get those?"

Evelyn followed his line of sight and sighed. "Kade—"

"I need to know."

His tone was desperate and shaky, like a starving man barely able to contain his hunger.

For the name of who he needed to kill.

Evelyn leaned against the counter, clasping her mug with both hands. Her silvery eyes drank him in, leaving his skin tingling, his wolf howling.

"They were bracelets forced on me by Riven. They bound my magic, but they underestimated the level of darkness within them and"—she swallowed—"it was too much. That's why they gave me the bloodstone, altered it to block my magic, but in a way I wasn't so severely bound."

"You're holding back the full truth." His grip on his mug threatened to shatter the clay.

Evelyn palmed his cheek, making him look at her. "When the sun fully rises, Kade, I promise to tell you about my time in the castle, but for the few hours we have left, I want to savor us, *this*. Being together again. Nothing else matters to me right now. Please."

The plea in Evelyn's tone made Kade pause. He softened under her touch, exhaling away his pent-up muscles and rigid posture. She was right—moving forward, being in the present and not letting the past outshine their time together was more important.

The two headed upstairs and, with the blankets and cot, created a makeshift breakfast picnic. They ate in contented silence, sipped their coffees, and enjoyed being together again as the gray inside the room turned brighter and lighter.

Bellies full, Lou's boxes empty, and caffeine thrumming through their veins, Evelyn and Kade had grown closer, lying on their sides and staring at each other on the cot. Evelyn brushed his hair back and combed his beard as he trailed the tips of his own fingers down her thigh, reaching higher and higher with each brush.

"I missed you," she whispered. "Every minute of every day, there wasn't a time I wasn't wishing to be with you again."

He swallowed, words thick. "I missed you, too, Ev, and this. *Being* together, in the same room, breathing the same air."

She shifted, goose bumps forming on her skin as his hand drew circles on her hip bone.

"I'm still hungry." Her words tickled his lips.

He chuckled. "I'm sure Lou left more food downstairs."

She ran her thumb over the scar on his eyebrow. "Not for food, Kade." She said those words out loud, but the next were in his mind, *I'm hungry for you.*

Static bristled with each touch, their strengthened bond pulling and tugging them closer, eliciting the same hunger deep in Kade he wasn't certain he'd ever satiate.

"I want to know what you thought about," Kade said, voice guttural.

"When?" she asked, but knowing heated her stare.

"When you touched yourself, tell me what you were thinking."

Evelyn shifted, lying on her stomach, never breaking their stare. *You, taking me from behind as I screamed your name into a pillow.*

Evelyn sent images into his mind, not words. She sent him what she wanted, what she craved. He felt her hunger, her *need* for him like he felt his own.

Wild. Unapologetic. Eager.

Kade growled, shifting to his knees in an instant. Evelyn screeched as he lifted her hips and knocked his knees against hers, widening them. He pushed up her tunic, revealing her glistening, wet sex. She arched her back, creating the most delicious curve and raising her ass perfectly in the air. Kade shuddered, threatening to come undone at the sight like some teenage boy.

He ran a hand through her folds, eliciting a whimper. She'd straightened her arms ahead, hands gripping the edge of the cot. So needy, so wanton.

"Like this?" he'd said.

"Yes," she breathed. "You gave it to me hard and rough."

"Fuck," Kade growled.

He'd chosen trousers but thank the gods he'd not tied the laces. He fisted his hard and ready length, setting it free against the fabric. He ran it through the slick of Evelyn's need and spread her legs even farther. Evelyn was so responsive, sighing into the position and pushing her hips back. His tip edged her entrance, but he stayed still, teasing her with promise.

"Kade."

His slap against her ass echoed in the tiny cottage, and as Evelyn cried out, he entered her in one, strong thrust, straight to the hilt, drawing out an even louder, pleasure-filled cry from her. He set one hand on her back, the other gripping her hip. Kade rocked into her, one, two, three times as he adjusted to Evelyn's tightness. He chased the sensation of her sex squeezing his length. The feel of her and her breathless cries built a mounting need for release in him. He gave her what she imagined, a pace so different from hours ago, his beast sitting at the surface.

Rough. Deliberate. Hard.

And Evelyn took everything he gave, screaming his name over and over into the cot, like she'd imagined, until they were both riddled and undone, climaxes wrecking them senseless and spent.

CHAPTER FORTY-SIX

IT TOOK EVERY OUNCE of Evelyn's willpower to leave their room and not spend the rest of the day exploring all the wicked ideas she had in store for Kade. Now that her flame was intertwined with his wolf, she couldn't get enough of the *feel* of it. The warmth, the wildness.

Kade, too, had seemed reluctant to leave the bliss they'd found. His eyes had darkened to a molten amber when she'd removed his tunic and set her sights on an outfit Yennifer had left. But he'd blinked it away and donned appropriate attire as well. Clothes didn't help. She felt, more than ever, the desire to undress him. He pulled half his hair and twisted it into a bun, the rugged, wolfish look heating her core.

Yet, the sight of his eyes drew Evelyn back to something she'd forgotten in the haste of escaping the castle and bliss of being with Kade again.

His mother.

Evelyn's insides twisted. She felt rotten all of the sudden, selfish. How could she have forgotten? The need to tell him coursed through her so wildly her head spun. Even if it hurt and he grew angry with her for waiting, Kade deserved to know. She'd be there for him, however he decided to process the news.

He appeared at her side, grabbing her elbow so she looked at him. "Moons, what's wrong? I can hear your racing heart across the room. If you need more time to rest before we discuss what's next, stay here."

Evelyn shook her head. "No, there's something I need to tell you."

But how did she tell him this? How did she admit something so altering?

She stared at her fated's handsome, beautiful face. Brows pulled together, amber eyes searching her up and down. Evelyn, too, had lost her mother. And father. Time never allowed her to forget the loss, and their absence and death etched a scar of grief on her heart, one that throbbed time to time. It never got easier, Evelyn learned the pain and how to lean into it.

This was different for Kade. Her parents were gone, she knew that, but if she didn't, how would she want to learn such heavy news?

This involved Kade's heart, and the desire to hold it with care overcame her like the gentle warmth of an evening sun. She stepped towards him, mustering the courage.

"You're scaring me," Kade whispered. "Is it something that happened in the castle?"

"I'm sorry." When Evelyn reached him, she grabbed his hands in hers and met his stare. "What I'm about to tell you isn't easy, but I want you to know I didn't mean to wait. With everything... it didn't slip my mind, I... the right moment hadn't made itself known. I'm with you in this, whatever you need, I'm here."

Kade's brows pulled together even more, but his eyes searched her face, and he breathed, "Okay."

Evelyn inhaled. Her words came out soft and kind. "Kade, your mother is alive."

His eyes widened, and he squeezed her hands tighter. His mouth opened and closed, expression slackening. "How?" was all he asked.

Evelyn shut her eyes and shuddered. "I don't know. Your mother was my guard, she's also in Riven's council. She's the one who brought me to Tovi."

"Tovi said she had a trusted contact in the castle... Whoever they were, they were a part of the plan of getting you out."

She nodded. "When I look back at the last few weeks, I'm remembering the small acts of kindness. I never thought her an ally though. When I was caught with Belle exploring the castle, she suggested I be thrown in the dungeons, but honestly, I think she did that on purpose. She wanted me somewhere far away from the rings when the plan came into place."

Evelyn didn't have the energy to add she'd possibly derailed that plan when Belle broke her out of the castle dungeons.

"I'm sorry I waited to tell you," she said. "It wasn't intentional, and I feel awful for not telling you sooner—"

Kade grabbed Evelyn's shoulders. "Please don't apologize for the most memorable, blissful hours of my life. I love you, Evelyn, and I trust that you told me when the time was right."

Evelyn sighed, softening into his touch. "You both have the same golden eyes."

Kade blinked away tears. "We do."

"And kindness. It all clicked when I saw you in the arena. My heart saw a little bit of you in her from the beginning." She caught one of his tears before it fell. Her chest ached from the sight of his pain. "Do you think there's a reason Tovi didn't say anything?"

Kade sighed, and the two of them headed towards the door. Voices resounded on the main floor of the cottage, loud enough to indicate the entire Gray Fenris had returned.

"I'm sure she has her reasons," Kade said, lips downturned. "But if she hasn't told Eldrick yet, I fear for the princess's well-being."

A hole in Evelyn's heart festered. In the tunnels, her conversation with Tovi had only reopened the wound she'd cut. Her words had torn the little healing Evelyn had done these past few weeks. Evelyn knew she'd run from home. She recognized her flaws. But she'd meant what she'd said. They were no longer friends, and despite that, Evelyn's heart raced like a trapped bird. She didn't want to, but she feared for her friend should Eldrick discover Tovi's secrets.

As they joined the others filing in from the tunnels, it turned out Eldrick had already discovered his mother was alive. Unlike Kade though, his eldest brother's feelings toward the matter weren't as telling. He barely muttered a word about Tovi, too, but when the vampyr princess entered through the cottage beside Lou, a tension vibrated in the air, threatening to shake the cottage's foundation worse than any of Linx's explosives.

At least Lou had brought her bakery's offerings, defusing the tension with food. The table became a spread of pastries, breads, and cured meats, engulfing the cottage in morning breakfast. The questions about her time in the castle began, and Evelyn jumped into a more detailed account about what she'd discovered.

She started from the beginning, arriving at the tower and meeting Belle for the first time before discussing Matilda's journal. She proceeded with the secret passageway in her room, leading to Riven's study. They'd already covered the Lone Wolf and witch contact, so she glossed over those details and jumped to the destroyed room. Everyone was silent and attentive to her story, and as her time in the castle spilled from her, she hoped they didn't see some frightened witch locked away, but one who'd done all she could.

Evelyn paused. Kade's knuckles had gone white as he gripped the table. Unlike last time, he hadn't interrupted with questions, but he bristled with tension. She swore the wood groaned, but why would he react in such a way? They'd stood here before, discussing over a table with notes spread out, investigating darkness. The difference in Kade unnerved her, but she ignored it and continued on.

"As I mentioned last night, Riven was visited by some deity," she said. "What I didn't mention was that... *Goddess* visited me when I was in the dungeons."

Kade's jaw ticked. "Excuse me?"

Evelyn set her shoulders back, not letting Kade's far-too-calm exterior rattle her. "Yes, a goddess. It was only a voice. She referred to herself as the Blood Goddess, saying her namesake was after what had been given. Riven had offered his blood when he visited the altar."

Yennifer shook her head. "There's never been any goddess of that name before."

The team murmured their agreement, sharing bewildered expressions, mirroring Evelyn's own.

She sighed, glancing at Tovi. "I know."

Indecision warred within Evelyn. Answers about the prophecy, the spell, Riven's motives—it all pointed to that instance at the altar with Tovi and her parents. She'd seen the look in Tovi's eyes when they'd visited the caverns, noticed how quickly her old friend had wanted to hurry through it. But she'd also seen Tovi *there*, a vision of her from years ago. The haunt. The chill. The memory still fresh on Evelyn's mind.

"What did she say?" Kade asked. "Did she show you anything?"

Evelyn fleeted one more glance at Tovi, giving her the chance to say something, because the truth was, Evelyn didn't have it in her to call Tovi out. Not when her once friend sat back from everyone else, shoulders slumped as if she carried a thousand pounds. The tension, the static among the team had shifted in light of Nadia Drengr being alive, and nothing sat well with Evelyn adding more ire, more hurt to the situation.

It wasn't her place. No matter the pain she harbored.

"Mists and memories," Evelyn said, "but none of it made any sense. If we find out more about the Blood Goddess, then we might learn more about the spell or Riven's intentions."

"Where do we start researching a deity no one has ever heard of?" Bétar asked.

Eldrick splayed his fingers onto the table. "We write to Lorkan—"

"You have all never heard of her because she was banished by the other gods and goddesses. She is lost to histories. Lost to this world."

The cottage fell silent, every gaze turning to Tovi. Outside, the snow stopped, the river appeared to slow, and the gray in the sky lessoned a fraction.

Kade leaned into the table. "How do you know who she is?"

Tovi set her shoulders back, settling her jade gaze on each one of them until they connected with Evelyn's only. "Because she is my maker."

CHAPTER FORTY-SEVEN

"**W**HAT DO YOU MEAN?**"** Evelyn whispered.

Kindness. *Hope*. It flickered like silver in Evelyn's eyes.

Tovi's heart pounded in her chest. The truth of her past, her making, peeled back a curtain to who she was, who she'd been, and she hated the vulnerability of it. Standing out in the open, at the cusp of a cliff, ready to descend into the depths of what she tried to forget. She didn't enjoy being watched as she fell, fell, and fell to a place she didn't want to return. She shivered, like a cliff's breeze hugged its cold embrace around her shoulders.

But Evelyn had seen Tovi at the altar, and yet Tovi said nothing. She'd refrained. Nadia's secret hadn't been her own, yet *this* was. Evelyn was giving her a chance to own it. Despite not believing she deserved her friend's patience, it lit a warmth in her belly.

Besides, what else did she have to lose? Eldrick already didn't trust her. Telling the truth didn't compare to how she was already hurting. And more importantly, the team needed to learn everything to know what they were up against.

Goddess, she wished she had a glass of wine. Resolve. Something to hold onto as she entered this dangerous path. She grasped onto hope of her own instead. Like the hilt of a dagger or grip of a bow.

She ignored the sadness seeping into her centuries-old muscles and swallowed.

"I'm originally from Callum, you know. My family and I used to live on a farm, ten generations strong. Back then, my parents along with a few other families, didn't agree with the persecution of witches. When the Great Burnings started, they began hiding witches in their home, keeping them safe, and then assisting them on getaway ships. I was nineteen then, as was Riven, both at the cusp of adulthood. I remember clear as day helping witches in the night, the scent of burning flesh in the air. It was a dark and dangerous time for Torren, for humans and witches."

Tovi exhaled. She could still smell death over the spring grass, clotting the air. It didn't compare to the now cheery Callum.

"One night, we were leading a notoriously violent coven through the harbor when persecutors intercepted us. Half the coven perished in the chaos, and those who'd attacked didn't care who they killed—witch or human. We barely made it out alive, fleeing on a ship and heading west without anything at all. No belongings, no money. Merely ourselves and three other families. We hoped to reach Sorin and find refuge with witches we had saved in the past."

The team remained silent. A single emerald stare bore into the side of her face, but she ignored Eldrick.

"A brutal storm hit, veering us farther north than we anticipated. On the third week, tired, worn, and food stores running frighteningly low, we landed on the shores of what we call today Drystan. The land was beautiful, but harshly cold compared to home. We began our new lives and started a settlement." Tovi scoffed, memories fit with cold and snow. "Riven was shit at farming, but he tried. He'd been studying to be an artist in Callum, but those dreams were long gone. I, on the other hand, didn't care for books or sitting and had been a hunter in our old village. The skill came in handy during the colder months."

Tovi shifted in her seat, the chair's frame creaking in the cottage's silence. She recalled the whine of her taut bow, how snowflakes landed on her nose, the rush when the arrow pierced her target, and the shine of pride on her father's face when she returned with a kill large enough to feed their entire settlement. That pride had frozen over in the years to come.

"It seemed we'd made a life for ourselves, and we dared hope that was our new home. Until the coven we'd failed found us. They arrived with a vengeance, believing we had led their sisters and brothers to their deaths on that horrible night. Nothing we said swayed their blame, and they burned our settlement to the ground, a year's worth of work gone in an instant." Tovi paused, the flames of that night merging with the flicker of the fireplace. "We were defenseless against their magic, and they killed anyone who tried to fight. Desperate, a handful of us fled, retreating into the tunnels of the mountainside, but my mother had suffered grave injuries, and death clung to her.

"My parents, our family for that matter, didn't have a lick of magic weaved into our souls, but I do believe my mother and father were made for each other. Soulmates. My father couldn't bear losing her as she bled out. He succumbed to a maddening chant. Calling to faeries, the ancient kind of our homeland, any gods and goddesses he knew. For days, he and his mutterings filled the corners of the tunnels."

Tovi couldn't sit still. Memories fleeted through her mind and quickened her heart. She had to move, to do *something* other than sit idle. She rose from the table and stared out one of the windows. Tovi crossed her arms against the chill seeping through the seams, focused on the snow blanketing her people's land.

"I don't know if it was fate or bad luck, but out of all the places we could've retreated, we stumbled onto the altar of a particularly wicked deity, the Blood Goddess. Her history is so old, I think even the gods and goddesses we know forgot about her. During their reign, her greed and power grew, different and darker than the others. Her cruelty and destruction began to threaten the future of this world, so the gods and goddesses went to war. In the end, they succeeded, vanquishing her from this realm into the depths of Hel."

The pines swayed against a mighty gust of howling wind, as if the deity herself cried out against Tovi mentioning her name.

"What happened?" Evelyn asked in the tiniest whisper.

Tovi shut her eyes. "While my mother's blood seeped into carved runes, my father prayed to whatever being that would listen. Between his chants, love for my mother, and the blood offering, his calls were answered. The Blood Goddess gifted us the ability to save my mother and become strong enough to fight the dark witches. She made us in her likeness, immortals in the living realm."

Someone fidgeted and cleared their throat. "There has always been one constant in the story of vampyrs," Kade said. "Witches bones. Where does that play into your story?"

Tovi sighed, turning to her audience. "Our creation, our *making*, was a gift from the goddess in exchange for the bones of witches as well as agreeing to rule over her lands. Desperate, my father agreed. He was the first vampyr. He turned our mother to save her life, immortality in his venom, and then they turned us. One by one, whoever remained of our settlement became a vampyr. With our new heightened abilities, we tracked down the witches, slaughtered them all and brought their bones to our new goddess, our first promise fulfilled to the deity we called maker."

Yennifer, blue eyes wide, shook her head. "It's similar to the Moon God giving werewolves the power to shift in his likeness or the kernel of power in witch's souls from the Sun Goddess's light."

Bitterness coated Tovi's tongue, and she scoffed. "At first glance, it may seem that way." She began to pace, her story pushing to be released.

"For a time, my father ruled Drystan as a fierce leader as the Blood Goddess wished. The humans who traveled to Drystan and desired to be turned into vampyrs were. Our kingdom grew. Every hibernal solstice, the longest night of the year, we celebrated the Blood Goddess and embraced the magic of darkness, thanking her for everything she gave us."

Tovi grimaced. Those celebrations had been filled with wine, pleasure, and the party princess her people resented and judged. *Goddess*, she prayed her people would recognize her efforts and she'd become the queen they deserved.

"A full century after witches had settled in Sorin, we decided to invite them to that year's feasts. During the celebrations, my parents took part in a great hunt with the other founding families and our guests. Yet, that night, a pack of madras demons surrounded the hunting party. The witches weren't used to the beasts of Drystan like we were, and their fear created chaos. Amidst the fighting, a witch shot their magic towards a madras, their aim far too close to hitting my father. My mother jumped in front of the blast, saving him, but sacrificing herself."

Tovi and her mother had drifted apart over the decades, but the loss of her had still left a scar on Tovi's heart.

"My mother's death destroyed our father, riddled him into a broken and withered man in a matter of moments. He died of a broken heart. With his death, our prosperous kingdom crumbled. Unlike your gods, the Blood Goddess didn't gift us anything. We bargained for it, and in my father's death, he ceased ruling the lands as promised and broke that bargain. She *used* my father as a vessel."

"With the bones of the witches, she made you all immortal," Evelyn whispered, "but with the broken bargain, she was able to curse you and your people. The darkness, it changed all of you."

Tovi nodded. "Insatiable hunger, the inability to walk in sunlight. The curse twisted our natural tendencies and made them wicked. Not to mention, her bargain was also directly tied to the land, casting it into darkness is a part of the curse."

Kade shook his head. "Do you have any idea why the Blood Goddess did this?"

Tovi shrugged. "I imagine it's to return to this world. Revenge against the gods that banished her perhaps. Darkness feeds off darkness, right? In the passing centuries, the Void has grown. Not because more demons are entering, but because more of my people have fallen completely to darkness."

"Caillte," Evelyn said.

"Precisely," she said. "What better way to grow power in this realm than to create a people infected with her darkness."

"It's allowing her to grow stronger." Evelyn squeezed her eyes shut and shuddered.

The weight of her friend's words fell over the team. A lightness had settled over Tovi, but her tale had cast a shadow over everything they had known, *believed*. Eldrick caught her stare, but he snapped the connection

Why did she get a sense unburdening her truth had meant nothing to the alpha?

Chapter Forty-Eight

Evelyn shook her head. Thank the goddesses she sat, because she wasn't sure her legs or wits could handle hearing more of Tovi's tale. The small cabin was silent, so much so, one could hear the snow as it landed and blanketed the forest outside, a delicate chime.

"I can't even begin to make sense of it." She looked at Tovi, risking a bit of pain to see if she could find answers in her eyes. "But the Blood Goddess said 'a land cast in red' while that same phrase was etched next to my and Kade's prophecy? How are the two related?"

The vampyr princess shrugged. "I only know the one stanza like the rest of you, the truest of unions between the third-borns. I have always believed the darkness meant her presence in our realm, not vampyrs themselves. But how these other lines comes into play, I haven't the slightest idea. I am only certain about Riven's motives."

The team tensed, and a creep crawled up Evelyn's spine. "Is it to bring back his wife and child?"

Tovi swallowed. "Yes."

"Are you suggesting it has nothing to do with becoming king?" Eldrick asked.

"No," Evelyn said, before Tovi could finish. "I encountered Riven enough to know he cares more about resurrecting what he lost."

Belle approached the table and laid out the letters Evelyn had found in the mysteriously wrecked room—the ones she hadn't had a chance to read herself yet. Open against the wooden table, the words whispered to Evelyn's curious mind.

"I read through them this morning," she said. "I think they could help us."

Evelyn pulled the letters closer to her, scanning the words. "How?"

"They're love letters between a man named Odin and Matilda."

"Matilda Moore?" Evelyn asked.

The werewolves and vampyrs blinked, but Linx said, "Matilda Moore is an infamous witch scholar."

Evelyn nodded. "Witches study most of her texts and anthologies during school, but Belle found her personal journals in the Drystan Library. She had researched vampyrs extensively, but I've never seen this information formally printed before. Do these letters give any indication who Odin is?"

"Other than her lover, he was a guest at Drystan Castle."

Everyone turned their attention back to Tovi.

"Does anyone by the name of Odin ring a bell?" Kade asked her.

Tovi shook her head. "No. Do the letters have a date?"

"Yes, 1894."

Tovi leaned back in her chair, shaking her head slightly. "That was before the curse, and I wasn't very present in court at that time. I was either running from a suitor or getting drunk and partying."

Tovi had always been one to open a bottle of wine or drag Evelyn to some dimly lit bar in the Nūa, but she'd been poised and collected, even with a few glasses in her. *Drunk* and *partying* weren't two words Evelyn would've associated with her once friend. She sank deeper into her seat, memories of laughter and late-night talks with Tovi blurred into lies. She fought the urge to clutch her stomach or throw up. So much of her past felt like a lie, she couldn't help but feel sick.

"The letters also mention his sister, Opal, a few times."

"Opal?" Tovi asked.

She moved closer, and Evelyn's body went taut. Tovi didn't seem to notice as she peered at the letter over her shoulder—like so many times before when they'd pored over pamphlets, books, or newspapers. Her voice was too loud in Evelyn's ear, too familiar and close to the sound of what Evelyn once associated with someone she loved like a sister.

"Opal was my younger brother's lover. She was a witch if I recall correctly."

"What happened to her?" Bétar asked.

"I'm not sure exactly, but it was believed she died the day the curse fell. Sven left and created his estate farther south, away from court. He's never returned since. I think the memories are too difficult."

"If Opal was a witch, it suggests so was Odin, Matilda's lover. Does it indicate why they were guests in the castle?" Evelyn asked.

Linx shrugged. "Not directly. She mentions a few times his haunting thoughts and hopes he and his sister will find comfort in Drystan, away from the chaos of Nūa."

"Hopes and thoughts?" Evelyn turned to Tovi. "Was Opal a seer by chance?"

Tovi shook her head. "If she was, my brother never mentioned it, but Sven has always been guarded, a recluse."

"Why do you think she was a seer?" Kade asked, leaning across the table.

"The prophecy was scribbled into the floorboards of the room I found. I'm going to take a wild guess and assume the room was Odin's, seeing his letters were found there. Haunting thoughts also suggest he saw things he didn't want to see. I've only ever met one seer, and visions ailed her at uncontrollable times, leaving her withdrawn for days after what she saw."

"Uzoma?" Tovi asked.

Evelyn nodded, a small smile breaking across her face at the name of her well-respected tutor, the one who'd shown her kindness. "Seers are rare amongst witches, and in most cases, they are in sets of twins or triplets. Uzoma, for example, has a twin sister. If Opal was a seer, there's a chance her brother was, too."

"Triplets?" Linx pushed the second letter towards Evelyn. "There's a mention of another sister, Orla. From what Matilda writes, it seems she may have died."

I pray to the Goddess you do not succumb to the same fate as your dear sister, Orla.

Evelyn had searched for this—a connection, a source, a starting point, something or someone to answer her tumbling questions. Back in Callum, she'd experienced the same when she recognized the missing body parts or on the Guard when she'd figured out the type of demon wreaking havoc on a village. She'd wondered what the scribblings in the room had been. A poem, a song, or—

A prophecy.

And Evelyn had a wild and frightening thought.

"What if Kade and I are one part of the prophecy?" she whispered.

Kade leaned over the table. "What do you mean?"

"I don't think it's a coincidence our prophecy was etched along with these other stanzas, and in the abandoned room of a haunted seer, I'm tempted to believe there is perhaps more to the prophecy than we believed."

Tovi nodded. "Actually, that's an interesting thought. The Blood Goddess said, 'cast in red,' right?"

Evelyn nodded.

Tovi pointed to some of Evelyn's notes. "Land *cast* in red fills in the gaps of this one line."

"Exactly," Evelyn said. "Don't we think it's a little odd she whispered a line from the writings of a seer?"

Yen crossed her arms. "A land cast in red would also relate to a Blood Moon."

"Aye," Bétar muttered. "Has that effect some years."

Evelyn was close to answers, and it excited her, energized her muscles and broadened her mind. While her heart raced, her body and magic begged to keep going and discover more. Recharged and light, an idea sparked.

She turned to Tovi. They were eye to eye, as if a vast distance of betrayal didn't separate them.

"How much of a recluse is your brother?" she asked.

Tovi settled into the seat beside her. "Very. Why do you ask?"

"I wonder if he'd be open to a visit. Unless he's on Riven's side, perhaps he could supply some of the missing pieces in all of this. Maybe he remembers Opal's or Odin's visions."

"Absolutely not," Kade said.

The room fell still and silent—more so than when Tovi told her tale. Evelyn blinked, trying to understand Kade's words or read his expression. It was stone, so different from his earlier warmth and tenderness.

"I'm sorry?" she asked.

"We head home. That is the plan."

Evelyn laid her hand on the table, steadying her rising magic. It heated, riling with frustration. She'd finally gotten *something*, and Kade's dismissal threatened to tug it out from under her.

"I'm not suggesting we don't head home, but we should consider learning more about this. If there is more to the prophecy, it might help us defeat the darkness. After all, that should be our top priority."

Evelyn wanted to return home more than anyone else, but her resolve to learn about their enemy, about the curse had actually grown steelier, stronger since she'd left the castle. Not only had she learned more about the Blood Goddess, but she also had a connection, *someone* who might know more about Matilda and this Odin and why she and Kade's prophecy had been scribbled with other stanzas, lost behind paint. Reuniting with Kade, being at his side again, as well as having the promise of a team around her had given her the sense they could figure it out. She could get the answers to breaking the curse and return home with something of worth.

"She has a point," Eldrick said.

"I agree," Yen said, offering Evelyn a small smile. "Why not learn what we can while we're here?"

Kade peeled off the table. His shoulders straightened, and at first, Evelyn believed his relaxed demeanor suggested they'd gotten through to him, but his next words riled her more, her flame rising to the surface.

"Visiting Sven is out of the question. End of discussion."

Evelyn reared back. This wasn't the Kade she'd experienced in Callum—the *partner* she believed him to be—and hurt rocked through her.

"End of discussion? What happened to us being a team?"

Kade's jaw ticked—she'd never seen him like this, so wound up he might combust.

"This is my team. I'm the commander—"

Evelyn rose from her chair, the screech of the legs drowning out his words. Tears pricked in her eyes as her nails bit into her palms. She couldn't believe Kade was speaking to her this way. In front of everyone.

"Do I answer to you now? Is that how this works? I know we haven't had a little formal chit chat about our titles, *Commander*, but I don't take orders well. I also never expected you to be so dismissive."

Evelyn.

He begged, no chastised her, using the mating bond. Rage shot through her. How dare he use something so special, so strong against her.

"Don't," she said out loud. "We were partners in Callum, Kade."

He searched her face and sighed. "Can everyone give us the room?"

"No. Absolutely not." She flung his earlier words back at him. *Fucking flames*, she was hotter than the fire blazing in the corner. "I'm not some child you get to belittle behind closed doors. If you have something to say, *say it.*"

Kade growled, raking his hand through the hairs falling loose from his bun. "You're being reckless."

"Excuse me?" Evelyn stumbled back.

"Exploring the castle? Visiting the fighting rings? Spying on Riven? You could've gotten yourself killed!"

"Riven needed me alive for the spell. I knew that wouldn't happen."

"Is that supposed to bring me comfort? You trusted the whims of a lunatic prince who'd dared to bind your magic. Again, reckless!"

"What was I supposed to do?" Evelyn shouted. "Sit around and wait for you to rescue me?"

"Yes! I told you I was coming. I promised." Anguish rippled through her fated's golden stare.

Evelyn lowered her voice, hesitant. "Kade, if this is about me not trusting you or doubting you, I never did. I knew you were risking your life, all of you were." She glanced at the rest of the team, even Tovi. "I couldn't sit around and do nothing."

Kade pinched the bridge of his nose. Evelyn waited. The silence in the room was thick, the team's stares like pinpricks against her skin. She'd never imagined this. With Callum's salty sea wind whirling around her at the docks, she'd thought they'd return home a team. She hadn't expected things to change, for Kade to change. Even last night, huddled around the table, she had fallen into something that no longer existed—a partnership. But there was none. She was exposed, bare, alone in wanting *damn* answers for how to break the curse.

Finally, Kade placed both hands on his hips. His eyes landed on her, full of a warrior's resolve. "Our mission was to get you back. We've done that. It's now time we return home, out of enemy lands."

"These lands have answers."

Kade tapped the pile of papers and notes. "You got answers. This is more than we've ever had before. It's time to go home, Ev."

She didn't trust the plea in his tone or the use of her nickname. "It's not enough."

Evelyn hadn't meant to say the words out loud, but the truth flew out of her. Kade assessed her, his body relaxing as if he finally understood—saw through her intentions and why she was desperate, so willing to do what needed to be done.

"Getting you home is enough," he whispered. He turned his attention to the group. "We leave tomorrow at dawn. Rest and be ready to travel south."

Please, Ev, he said through the bond.

Evelyn didn't wait to hear more of Kade's plans. She headed for the stairs, feeling his gaze lingering on her back as she retreated.

Anger drove her forward, but so did hurt.

CHAPTER FORTY-NINE

SNOW FLURRIES FELL IN thick sheets, silence blanketing the forest of pine trees. The white powdery dust collected on Tovi's cloak and horse. She tried to inhale the last remnants of home, unsure when she'd experience Drystan's winter magic again.

But she couldn't breathe through the tension gripping the entire group.

The snow, beautiful as it was, made it difficult to see far ahead, and the horses trudged through the inches growing taller with each passing hour, putting the Gray Fenris on edge. Eldrick had barely acknowledged Tovi's presence since he'd learned his mother was alive—even after she'd admitted her last secret. Ahead, though Evelyn sat snug with Kade atop Bleu, a static of unsaid words surrounded them, and had since their fight at Lou's cottage.

The baker followed behind. Despite Tovi's shattering secret, Eldrick had offered Lou safe refuge in his village after helping them. Everyone feared for her friend's life. It wouldn't be long before Riven discovered the tunnels leading to her bakery, and no one wanted her to suffer all the crimes alone. It had taken some convincing, but when Todd rattled off about his Aunt Lucy's tavern and a possible job for her, she relented.

Guilt ate away at Tovi. Something had been forming between her and the alpha, and yet Eldrick was giving her the silent treatment. Evelyn couldn't even look at her without shuddering. Kade had been short with her, too. The rest of the team still talked with her, but there was a hesitancy in their words and gazes she didn't miss.

She'd thought coming clean would've made things different.

Tovi had been wrong. Since secrets came so naturally to her, she never once thought about the consequences. Even when she tried to reason she was honoring her friend's wishes, she saw the excuse. And what kind of friend was she really when she had lied to Evelyn, her *best* friend, for years? Besides, if she were in their shoes, would she have trusted her timing or motives?

Yet, Tovi hadn't been concerned with the alliance when she'd told them of the Blood Goddess and bargain. Not once.

Instead, so many what-ifs played in her mind. She couldn't have told Eldrick about his mother weeks ago—it would've jeopardized the entire mission to get Evelyn back. Though, she could've told him the moment they got to Drystan. Telling him wouldn't have hurt the plan then. But he might have lost trust with her when they were forming a truce. Tovi bristled. Her mind was going in circles, and like their snow-covered journey, there was no end in sight. No reprieve of the trudge they'd put themselves in.

A branch snapped in the distance, bringing Tovi out of her miserable, spiraling thoughts. Eldrick must've heard the movement, too, because he stopped his horse and held up a hand for everyone to stop.

They waited in stillness and silence. Tovi tilted her head to the wind, but aside from Eldrick's scent and the freshness of snow clinging to ferns and pines, she didn't detect a vampyr or demon.

"Let's keep moving," Kade said, kicking Bleu into action.

The rest followed. Tovi's and Eldrick's horses met up, and she sighed away her pent-up energy and mustered some courage. "Eldrick, eventually we're going to need to discuss what happened."

He reared his horse around so suddenly, Tovi's own veered left to avoid colliding with the huffing beast. His eyes were focused on her.

Hatred. Malice. Disappointment.

All emotions Tovi had been on the receiving end of before, but they were somehow so much worse coming from his sharp green eyes.

"Discuss what exactly? That you're the liar I said you were?"

Tovi winced, tightening her grip on her horse's reins. Everyone else had heard the commotion, halting their travel. Kade called from ahead, and Lou's horse whined from behind.

"Eldrick, calm yourself," Bétar muttered a few paces away.

Tovi wished she'd kept her mouth shut. She veered her horse to go around him, but Eldrick charged his forward, cutting her horse off the path.

"What—" Tovi glared at him as she tried to calm her horse down. She barely made it out of the way, attempting to reverse the horse back, but Eldrick urged his horse forward, jarring her off course. "Eldrick, stop it!"

He didn't, matching her retreat step for step.

"Now you're being a child!" she said.

"What are you two arguing about now?" Kade roared.

Eldrick ignored his brother. "I stopped being a child the day my mother died."

"*I didn't kill your mother!*"

"You're right. Your people did, the ones you're so hell-bent on saving from the Blood Goddess. Perhaps they deserve her darkness."

Ancient anger, putrefying deep in Tovi's soul, rose its hideous, thorny head.

"Let me remind you that your mother is a vampyr, and the curse most certainly applies to her, too."

Eldrick blanched, the tan of his cheeks fading to a sickly white. By his wide eyes and sheer shock, he hadn't considered this. *Bloody hel*—she'd gone and made everything worse.

Something whistled behind Tovi, and thank the goddess for Tovi's vampyr sight. A thin, wooden arrow flew through the air, its tip pointed in Eldrick's direction. With no time to warn him, she charged her horse towards his. It sidestepped. An arrow whizzed past them and thudded straight into the trunk of a pine tree.

Frozen in her saddle, her heart skipped. She hadn't heard anything, smelled anyone. No one had. Time slowed, minutes suspended in time as she blinked and met Eldrick's shocked stare.

The whiz of more arrows brought her back to reality, and the team erupted into commands and battle cries.

The arrows descended towards them, flying from various directions. Through the pines from the left. Between the evergreens to the right. Above, falling from the canopy like deadly fallen stars, their tips glinted in the low light.

Eldrick grabbed the reins of Tovi's frantic horse, but it was no use. The beast was spooked. As it stood on its hind legs, Tovi lost her balance. She fell with a bone-rattling thud.

"Tovi!" Eldrick dismounted and swung from his horse.

"Stick together!" Kade said.

But the attack continued, separating Tovi and Eldrick from the rest. He dragged them under the canopy of clustered trees. Arrows got lost in the chunks of snow clinging to the pines. He lifted her onto his horse and followed her atop the saddle. His arm snaked around her middle, keeping her close as he kicked the horse into a gallop.

"Eldrick!" Kade said.

The rest had ridden yards ahead, snow kicking up under their retreating hooves.

"Protect Evelyn," Eldrick called. "Go!"

Tovi peered behind them, trying to see their attackers, but they were lost in the falling snow, hidden out of sight in the winter-covered brush. She felt eyes on her though, gazes creeping up her neck like some venomous spider waiting for the perfect patch of flesh to sink its teeth into.

An arrow whooshed past, Tovi's hair flicking upward. Eldrick hunkered both of them into the saddle, their bodies growing so close they moved as one. The path snaked into an army of lone pines sprawling for a hundred yards. No ferns, underbrush, or thick evergreens.

No cover.

The team rode on, sprinting to the next thicket of forest. Two sickening thuds popped behind them. Their horse thrashed, arrows stuck from its left thigh. It collapsed as its back leg gave way. Eldrick growled as he held Tovi tighter around the waist and pulled them free of the horse's saddle before they crashed to the ground with it.

They tumbled. Cold clung to Tovi's bruised muscles as ice and snow crunched beneath her. Her ears rang as she righted her fall. Through the leaves of a fern, the eyes of an attacker connected with hers. Axe raised, murder in his eyes, he charged.

Towards Eldrick.

She cried his name and jumped to her feet. Her dagger was in her hand one moment, the next it was hilt deep in the chest of the attacker. Eyes wide with death, he collapsed onto the snow. Crimson blossomed into the white.

Voices resounded behind them. The team rushed back. Hurried and frantic. Arrows fell from the sky again. Tovi dove left, Eldrick right. He jumped over a fallen tree, the spineless branches like the spikes of a weapon.

Another attacker sprang from a hiding place, twin axes at the ready. Others emerged with him—blades, brawn, and beards in common. The Gray Fenris entered the fray. Water, fire, and steel fought back.

"Eldrick!" Tovi tried to warn him, but he was stuck flattened against the trunk, arrows raining down on him.

She ran, barreling into the one with two axes. They rolled. Her fist made contact with his nose. His chin next. He ripped her hair. Snow, ice, and dirt joined their fight. Tovi flopped to her back, panting. Metal sang as it impaled the frost, inches from her cheek. She scrambled. Hands grasped her ankles, dragging her back. She cried out, clawing at anything—a fern, a branch, a root.

A ball of flame descended on her assailant. He screamed and writhed, running into the forest, crying out to the gods. Kade countered his retreat in two strikes. One across the belly and the next down his spine. The attacker dropped dead.

Evelyn's face came into view, dark hair wild in the wind. She grabbed Tovi's hand, helping her stand.

"Are you hurt?" Sincere concern pinched her brow.

"No." Tovi shook away the pain of her recent fight, knowing she'd heal in minutes.

Evelyn nodded, and the two friends regarded the other, chests heaving.

"Moons, come out and fight us, you cowards!"

They both whirled in Eldrick's direction. Dozens of arrows stuck from the tree, a few by his legs. They didn't stop.

And they didn't land anywhere near the rest of them.

Evelyn gasped. "It's like..."

"He's their target," Tovi breathed.

Her mind reeled. Who would want the alpha dead?

Goddess, the arrows finally stopped. But two-dozen attackers popped free of their hiding places and advanced. Tovi ran, Evelyn in pace behind her. A distant growl suggested Kade followed, too.

With the ease of wind, Tovi grabbed a bow and arrow off a dead man. She skidded to a halt, boots sliding through the snow as she reached the tree.

"You need to take cover," Eldrick said through gritted teeth.

"Shut up."

Nocked and ready, the bow groaned with tension. Tovi let go. It sang. And popped, embedding straight into an opponent's eye. She readied another. Released and hit her next target. One, two, three. Her victims dropped like the fallen tree she shot behind.

The descending snow kissed her cheek. The wind blew past, carrying her arrows farther. Tovi's homeland reached out, threads of cold and strength reaching the tendons of her heart. She almost wept. Centuries-old memories blurred with the present. She was mortal again, nocking her arrow to bring down an elk. Drystan seemed to sing, reminding her she was a fighter. What she used to be hadn't been all bad.

Resilient. Strong. Fierce.

Only her breath existed. Her beating heart. And the tickle of snow.

Tovi released the last arrow. She'd gotten rid of half the numbers, and their team charged.

But Eldrick stayed, breathless. Haggard. A pinch between his brow so sharp, it narrowed his eyes. Those gems cut through her.

"Come on, wolf," she said.

Fighting rang in the forest. No Riven. No Visha. No witch, either. Not a single vampyr, in fact. Belle and Linx worked in tandem. Splashes of water to the face left their opponent blinded, an opening for Linx to swipe and end with her blade. Todd danced with his two daggers, slicing left, right, and up. Bétar was brutal, his axe crunching into bone with one deliberate blow. Kade and Evelyn fought back-to-back, the moon and sun in perfect balance. Yennifer wielded her sword with the same ease and calm she possessed when she held her bow.

Promise bled through Tovi. She dared to hope.

Behind her, Eldrick snarled. A fierce protectiveness overcame her as her sights tunneled. Feral. Animalistic. Down to her core. But nothing to do with the darkness of the Blood Curse.

An arrow pierced Eldrick's shoulder—his body was angled closer to Tovi, as if he'd stepped in the way to take a hit meant for her. He stumbled back, clutching the wound. Tovi caught him as he sank to his knees.

"Fuck," he said through clenched teeth.

Kade called out commands. He and Bétar rushed into the trees. But Tovi's world spun. Blood seeped from Eldrick's wound, his breath ragged.

"Tovi, look at me."

That fierce overprotectiveness was eclipsing her. A darkness encroached. Like the vines of a thorny plant it climbed, a twine wrapping around her heart. Tovi's baser instinct called to the curse, inviting it in. And Eldrick's blood. She wanted to taste it. For two very warring reasons.

"*Tovi, look at me.*"

Eldrick's repeated command sucked her back to the present.

"I'm alright," he whispered.

CHAPTER FIFTY

"ALRIGHT? THERE'S AN ARROW in you!" Tovi said.

She knelt at his side, holding him upright. Snow fell between them like the ticking of minutes.

Eldrick laughed and winced. "It's not deep."

She inspected the wound, frantic almost, and sucked in a breath. "*Goddess,* you're bloody lucky. The prongs of the arrow didn't go past your leather vest, but you're still hurt."

"See?" he said, relishing her embrace. "There's nothing to worry about—"

A man cried out, screaming like a fox in the dead of night. Kade dragged him through the snowy brush, Bétar at his heels, axe dripping blood.

Kade threw the man into the center of them all. "Who the fuck are you?"

Eldrick had to admit, even though he knew his brother, sword in hand with a blood-spattered face, Kade was a terrifying, unnerving sight, beastly and rugged. His brother tugged an arrow free from the snow along with an axe and shoved them into the man's face.

"These are werewolf weapons. Where did you get them?"

Eldrick stilled, zeroing in on the weapons his brother held. During the fray, he hadn't noticed. The axe's shaft and the curve of the blade was similar to his own—werewolf ruins carved into the wood. But the man on his knees wasn't a werewolf or vampyr, but a human.

Despite his bleeding and bruised face, the man held his ground. He spit into the snow. "Kill me and be done with it."

Bétar tugged the man's braided hair back, exposing his neck to the sky. He lay his axe against the flesh. "Tell us and your death will be swift rather than painful."

"Did Riven send you?" Kade asked.

"Who the fuck is Riven?" the man asked.

The team shifted on uneasy feet, sharing bewildered expressions.

The man's wide gaze landed on Tovi for a fraction of a moment then on Eldrick.

"Kade," Evelyn called, snapping everyone's attention her way.

Gritting through the pain lancing his shoulder, Eldrick turned and found the Daughter of the Goddess inspecting a dead body, pulling at a necklace. "Some of them *are* werewolves."

Tovi stiffened beside him, and Eldrick sniffed the air.

"There's herbs," he murmured.

"The same herbs Linx and Blair used to hide werewolf magic," Kade said.

Eldrick's chest heaved, arrow still in his shoulder. "It's why we didn't sense them approaching."

His brother nodded, his usual bright eyes grave.

Linx and Todd pulled from the pockets of the dead bodies. Evelyn's eyes went wide at the coin they threw towards her. She shared a look with Tovi who swallowed, throat thick.

"What?" Eldrick asked.

"That's coin from Torren," Tovi said.

Bétar moved his axe to the man's shoulder, the blade angled into the soft muscle where his shoulder and neck met. Steel kissed skin. Not a death blow, but a painful one.

"Are you a human mercenary?" Kade asked.

The man flashed a smile. "Aye. Got paid handsomely for the job."

"Can't bring money with you to the underworld, can you?"

The reality of Bétar's words rang true.

"How about this," Kade said, standing over the man. "Answer our questions, and we'll let you go. You can take your chances with the demons and vampyrs."

The man's brows knitted, and he pursed his lips. "Fine."

"What was the job?" Kade asked.

He jutted his chin towards Eldrick. "Him. Kill him, only him. The witches and white-haired princess were strictly off-limits."

Eldrick had half a mind to disagree with Kade's proposition to the man, and by Tovi's taut posture beside him, it appeared she, too, disagreed. She glared at the mercenary like a lioness zeroed in on her prey.

"Why?" Kade asked.

The man shrugged. "I don't know. My lot gets a name, a target, and we don't ask questions. The werewolves with us talked about the unrest it would cause, that's all. He's an alpha's son if I recall."

"That sounds like the letters Evelyn found in Riven's study," Eldrick said.

Kade nodded. "And these other werewolves, who were they?"

"Don't know. They found us in Morrow, proposed the job, supplied the weapons and then we were off scouting your lot in this cold shithole."

"Morrow was on the coast," Evelyn said. "Did witches help you travel?"

The man nodded.

"That sounds like Riven and Ingrid were involved," Lou said.

Snow kissed Tovi's cheek, but she didn't say a word. She and Riven stood on rocky ground, but why target Eldrick specifically? A cold realization washed over him.

"Do you think Riven learned about my mother?" he said.

Tovi's head snapped towards him. "No. If that were the case, he'd not send assassins. He'd not hide behind the fact he wanted you dead. With consideration to the alluded unrest, perhaps the Lone Wolf was involved. It explains the werewolves and the weapons."

"Is that a name you've heard?" Kade asked the man.

"No. Look, the bunch was secretive, alright. They used coin from Torren for a reason. They didn't want to be discovered."

"He's right," Yennifer inspected an arrow. "They're generic. No colors or feathers to indicate what pack they came from."

Kade's jaw ticked. He grunted and gave Bétar a curt nod.

The second released the man, who scrambled into the wood. A stone sank in Eldrick's gut. He wasn't one to shoot a man in the back, but as the mercenary disappeared into the forest, his wolf couldn't shake a terrible feeling.

His brother's boots crunched in the snow as he approached. "We need to get that arrow out of you and move out."

"I'm aware," he said. "This Lone Wolf sounds like a right bastard, but why kill me? Unless—*fuck!*"

Eldrick reared forward, his sights landing on the arrow no longer lodged in his shoulder. Tovi held it.

"What in the stars above?" he asked.

"That's for being an ass earlier." Tovi rose to her feet and threw the arrow aside. "We need to find an inn and rest. If Riven does come for us next, we won't have a fighting chance tired and wounded." With that, Tovi stormed off from the group, Lou following after her.

Eldrick rose on shaky legs, staring after them. The gazes of the group bore into the side of his face, but he didn't need to see their expressions to know they agreed with Tovi.

Because she was right. He *was* an ass.

Moons, he'd been taking his anger out on her. How had he been so unaware, so cruel even? Eldrick shook his head, stomach twisting into knots.

Despite it all, she'd *saved* him during the attack, putting herself at risk. He recognized the fear in her eyes when the arrow had pierced his shoulder. He recognized it so easily, because it mirrored his own fear—the all-consuming kind that washed over him when the first arrow had been shot and Tovi'd fallen off her horse, exposed as they fell under attack. Or when one had been aimed at her back, the one he'd stepped in the way of and taken the hit with; a decision, a choice that had almost been instinctual. Eldrick could no longer dismiss that he cared for the vampyr princess, his wolf rumbling in agreement.

He stared after her again, not losing sight of her lithe frame as she grew smaller in the distance, hair blending in with the snowy forest.

Regret for everything he'd said and done washed over Eldrick. More regret lay on the horizon if he didn't make things right with Tovi soon.

CHAPTER FIFTY-ONE

THE OWNER OF THE closest inn turned out to be an old friend of Tovi's, but at present, she regarded her as more of an enemy since the woman had only a few rooms to spare.

So few rooms, Tovi and Eldrick had to share one.

Along with a bed.

Behind Tovi, the door of said room clicked shut. A single, damning beat solidifying her fate above the stables.

She averted her gaze from the bed pushed up against the western wall and ignored the stare of the alpha werewolf piercing between her shoulder blades. She hadn't been able to meet his eyes since they'd left the inn's main building and the owner escorted them to the stables. To Tovi's dismay, Eldrick hadn't uttered a word, not even a grumble of protest.

A fire raged on the eastern wall, making the space far too warm. The heat closed the four walls around Tovi, and she abandoned her cloak on the desk. A door leading to the bathing chamber beckoned her. Perhaps she could hide out there until sleep beckoned, then she'd crawl into the bed after Eldrick. Tovi's plan to avoid him evaporated. The bathing chamber was the same size as a broom closet with a pitiful copper pot for a toilet and a rusty old sink.

Tovi shut her eyes and said a small prayer, bracing herself for the night to come. She turned, which was a mistake. Eldrick had already begun to undress. He wore no shirt, his tanned muscles glistening in the light of the roaring fire. The desire to dig her nails into those shoulders or run her hands over his chest overcame her.

Until she caught sight of the swollen red wound festering above his left peck. Blood still oozed from it. She charged towards him as he sank onto the edge of the bed.

"For fuck's sake, Eldrick." She inspected the wound and sniffed.

Poison.

Not only had it overtaken the scent of his blood, but it'd also stopped his healing.

"Why didn't you say anything?" Her hands went clammy, and she rose to her feet. "I'll get Linx. She can heal it—"

"No." Eldrick grabbed her wrist.

She ignored the heat searing her skin. "The arrow was laced with poison. If I don't get Linx, it might get worse."

"If Linx comes, Todd will join her, and if he comes, so will Bétar, and then Yennifer. Before you know it, the entire Gray Fenris will be in here. I need a moment of peace. Please."

Tovi's heart hammered in her chest. Her throat had gone dry. Eldrick's voice had cracked with such vulnerability it hurt to hear. Space. Time alone. She understood what he meant, respected it. She'd been there, too.

"If I get the supplies from Linx, will you let me tend to it?"

Eldrick's green eyes studied her face, brow to chin. When his gaze flicked back to hers, air whooshed out of her lungs. That green wasn't fair. It sank its emerald powers into her and stole every ounce of will and wit she had.

"Yes."

Tovi blinked a few times, trying to register his response. She rose to her feet, wringing her hands together. "I'll be right back."

It only took her ten minutes to find Linx, get the necessary herbs, and return. She thought the Gray Fenris healer would argue and demand to see Eldrick herself, but the pink-haired mage had handed over what Tovi needed and given direct instruction. As Tovi left the inn, she swore Linx and Yennifer shared small smiles laced with mirth, but Tovi was too nervous to care.

When she shut the door to their room, Eldrick was where she'd left him—shirtless, seated at the edge of the bed, shoulders curved downward. They said nothing as she prepared the materials. She filled a bowl with hot water, grabbed a cloth from the humble bathing chamber, laid out the herbs on the bed beside his thigh, and saddled a small stool between his legs.

Their gazes connected as she sank onto the stool, and Tovi swallowed. The small room grew tighter, warmer. The fire crackled behind her, and the two became entangled within each other, yet they weren't even touching. A hair's thinness lay between their legs and less than an arm's length stretched between their chests.

"Are you ready?" Tovi's voice came out thick, as if her thudding heart had lodged its way into her throat.

Eldrick nodded, and she got to work. She cleaned off the blood from Eldrick's skin first, his tight and strong muscles like solid stone under the washcloth. Tovi, for a moment, wished the washcloth didn't come between her and his tanned skin but dismissed the ridiculous thought. Soon, her bowl of warm water had turned scarlet.

Eldrick flinched when she dabbed the washcloth over the entry wound. Laced with some sort of oil, Linx had said it would sting, but it would also stop the bleeding. Tovi had forgotten to warn him, cursing to herself.

"Sorry," she whispered.

"It's alright," Eldrick said, his words tickling her nose. She was hunched under his chin, and even though she could not see his face, she knew he looked at her, felt it like a touch against her neck. "Will you tell me about her, how it… happened."

The fire popped behind them, and the wind howled against the walls of the stables. In this small room, tucked so tightly together, telling him what happened to his mother was the last thing Tovi wanted to do. No—that wasn't it. She wanted to tell him, but she wasn't sure *how* to tell him.

Yet, she heard the desperation in his voice and felt his nervous shudder under the wash cloth when he'd asked. A warmth, a desire to be kind and honest, swelled within her.

She sighed. "I haven't always been a believer in the prophecy or the fates. To be honest, I despised the gods and goddesses because of what they allowed to happen to my people. While Riven was concerned with appeasing the lords and ladies in court, I kept my attentions on our people, making sure they got by against the curse. But that didn't mean I didn't sympathize with Sorin. I'd often visit after a demon or *caillte* attack, blending in to offer aid."

She paused, blinking past the fog of memories. "It was the attack at Morrow, and the day felt... different. Fate seemed to be pulling me through the destruction, until I stumbled upon your mother. I didn't know who she was at the time, only that she was a warrior, clinging so strongly to life, and so I asked her if she wanted to live. I don't know why. I'd never turned anyone before. Not once. It's a sacred act. And yet, I asked her. She only had moments before she said yes, the underworld already had its grasp on her soul, and yet she kept telling me yes. Over and over yes.

"Even when I told her about the curse and everything it meant to be a vampyr, she wanted to live."

"You gave her a second chance," Eldrick whispered.

Tovi didn't dare meet his stare. She'd began stitching his wound, Linx's oils numbing the area, so he didn't feel the thread or needle weaving through his skin.

"Does the transition change someone? Is she different than before?"

Eldrick's question surprised Tovi into silence for a moment. She hadn't known Nadia before she'd turned, and Tovi knew that becoming a vampyr did change more than the physical. Indecision wormed through her. She couldn't speak directly to the things Nadia knew about herself, but that wasn't what Eldrick was asking, was it?

"What was she like?" she asked. "How do you remember her?"

Eldrick sighed then swallowed, his throat bobbing in Tovi's peripheral. "My mother was equal parts fierce and kind. When I was a pup and the summer storms raged, she always held me to sleep, soothed my fears, and sat with me in the darkness. But by day, she was a warrior, sharper and stronger than any steel blade. She walked into a room, and you felt her presence, a good presence. She made any place she went better."

Tovi listened as she pulled the final stitch across. "Your mother hasn't been a warrior for some time. Well, not the warrior you think of, but I can tell you she is one of the kindest people I've ever had the privilege of knowing and her fierceness is something to be admired."

"And she's your spy?"

"She's not *my* spy. Your mother fights for the prophecy. She sits on my brother's council along with other lords. Their titles and uniforms are equivalent of children playing dress up. The access, though, allows her to be privy to important information that may threaten the entire continent. Since she's a female, the other lords overlook her."

"But your brother looks past the fact she's a female?"

Tovi nodded, saddened all of a sudden. "As awful as he is right now, he's never disparaged females. His wife was his equal. If it wasn't for his efforts against my parents, my future would've been a lot different."

Eldrick huffed. "And what sort of information has my mother learned that helped fight for the prophecy?"

"When Evelyn and Kade's lives were threatened, for one. Your mother feared Riven would attack their wedding. It's one of the reasons I encouraged Evelyn to run."

Tovi didn't warn him when she ran the newly oiled cloth against his stitches. He growled through the pain, and Tovi gripped his arm to steady him. The skin-to-skin contact sent heat through her hand, reaching deep within her belly and surging a hunger through her that had nothing do with food or blood. Tovi most definitely didn't dare look in Eldrick's direction.

"Your brother, he doesn't suspect anything?" he asked.

"No. We have a habit of taking things from one another, and he believes he stole a friend of mine."

"You used his pride to your advantage."

"Pride and competitive spirit. It's been that way since we were children, long before we became vampyrs."

Tovi wasn't used to being so open, her energy depleted. Silence stretched aside from the crackling fire.

Eldrick swallowed. "Did you keep her from us?"

Tovi stopped, slowly pulling back her hand. She knew this question was coming, it was one of the reasons she didn't want to have this conversation. Her heart lodged deeper in her throat, and she squirmed in her seat. Not because she was afraid of the answer, but because of what it would do to Eldrick.

"No."

Eldrick shoulders snapped back, and his brows furrowed. "What?"

Tovi shook her head. "Staying away was your mother's choice. I gave her the option, told her we could make it work. But in the end, even after she mastered her feeding and hunger, she refused."

"Why?" Eldrick asked.

Tovi sighed. "Remember when I told you I admired her? One of the reasons is because she taught me about the importance of—"

"Duty." Eldrick stared past her, the orange of the flickering fire reflecting in the green of his eyes. His lips thinned and his jaw ticked, a mixture of sadness and understanding marring his face.

"Yes, duty. Your mother was a protector, and she believed in the prophecy. When she learned about the curse, she believed in her purpose even more."

"She chose the prophecy over us."

Tovi shut her eyes. Her gut twisted at the hurt in his voice, and she focused on the final salve. She layered it over the stitches.

Still not looking at Eldrick, she said, "Your mother loves you, Eldrick, and when she became a spy, revealing herself or returning home would've put you all and her mission at risk."

Eldrick snorted. Tovi's curiosity ate away at her and stilled her hands. She couldn't resist searching his face, his reaction so uncharacteristic of him.

Eldrick wore a small smile, but it wasn't pleasant. Forced and frustrated.

"Are you angry with her?" she asked.

Eldrick sighed, green eyes clashing with hers. "I don't think so. I think I'm angry at the possibilities of what could've been." He studied her face, and Tovi turned away, anchoring herself in the dressings she needed to bandage his wound with.

He exhaled, his breath tickling the nape of her neck. Her teeth ground together so hard, Tovi feared her molars would crack.

"I'm sorry," he said.

Tovi stopped, her heart skipping in her chest. She folded, one, two, three layers of the bandage before she lay it over his wound. "For what?"

Eldrick swallowed, staring at the floor. "For getting so angry—"

"I lied to you. You had every right to be angry."

"But you honored her wishes. You kept her, and us, safe ."

It wasn't far from the truth. She had to protect Nadia's true identity when she was so close to Riven, but she hadn't even tried to find a way to tell Eldrick. Right then and there, Tovi could've left it at that, crawling back into the comfort of her secrets and allowing their familiarity to be her armor, but she shook it all way, refusing to hide behind them any longer.

"No," she breathed. "I think I kept telling myself it was what your mother wanted, but then I wanted the alliance, and I was selfish. I should've told you, and I'm sorry."

The scent of the herbs was thick in the air underneath Tovi's handiwork. Eldrick's skin on his chest had already returned to its usual color, and her job was done. She stood, moving to back away, but Eldrick's hand snatched her wrist. She snapped her head up to ask why and wished she hadn't.

Eldrick's green eyes drank her in, fully, unabashedly, hungrily.

"Don't look at me like that."

Eldrick cocked his head. "How?"

"Like you want me." Her voice wasn't a whisper, but a mere breath.

"And what if I do?"

Tovi retreated back a step, but Eldrick pulled her closer than ever. She stood over him, and he peered up at her. She knew that look, had wanted that look. She couldn't bear it. Except she was so ensnared by this werewolf, this maddening desire for him, she couldn't move.

Tovi shook her head. "You can't."

"Why not?" Intent had overtaken his face. He wanted this. He wanted her.

"Eldrick."

"I know you want me, too," he whispered. He lowered one hand to her waist, giving it a gentle squeeze. Oh, damn the Goddess, his touch was torturous, even through her tunic.

"You sound so confident," she managed to say.

A strand of hair dropped and curled over his forehead. Dangerous thoughts of weaving her fingers through his golden-brown hair drove Tovi mad. She tried to blink them away, tried to regain control of her wants and needs. The alliance, her people, the curse—she had to stay the course and not become distracted.

"I've seen women in my village look at me the same way you're looking at me now."

She snorted, pushing him away. "You cocky bastard."

Eldrick held firm. "Perhaps. But it's different from those other times. Then, I was never consumed with never-ending wicked thoughts. Now I am. And you're in them, Tovi, and I can't stop them."

No. No. No.

Doubt screamed in her head. Tovi stepped back. Eldrick let her, yet he followed. He stood up, tall and proud. He matched her step for step as she walked backwards from the bed.

"Eldrick, we can't." Tovi shook her head, the movement stiff as it contradicted her body's desires, knowing her words went against what she wanted.

"Why?" he asked as if he didn't already know.

She was a vampyr. He was a werewolf. She was the princess, and he was the alpha. It was already so complicated.

"You're going to regret this."

"I don't care."

"Eldrick." This damn room was far too small, and Tovi's back hit up against the wall.

"Do you not want this?" Eldrick whispered. "Say the word, and I'll stop, dove."

Stop.

He would, she knew it. She didn't want to stop, but it didn't matter what she wanted. It didn't matter that she craved the werewolf looming over her so fiercely, it was maddening. She needed an alliance. What if he judged her after?

"I don't want you to hate me," Tovi whispered.

Eldrick took her in, looming over her with a hunger that vibrated between them. Chests flush together, Tovi felt his heart racing.

He brushed his knuckles over her cheek. She shut her eyes, relishing his touch. It was scorching, radiating through her, and he barely laid a hand on her. Her eyes snapped open as Eldrick gripped her chin, making her look at him. Her breath hitched at the severity of his stare, and she was thankful for the wall behind her, because she'd lost her knees, her entire being melting at the possibility of what came next.

"I've tried to hate you, but I can't." Eldrick removed his hand from her chin, sliding it to her neck before threading his fingers through her hair. With a slight tug, he angled her face up, and their lips almost touched as he continued. "The gods know I've tried, but it isn't possible. I want you, and I'm tired of denying it."

Tovi searched for the chink in his usually unemotional armor, but he'd unraveled before her. He'd become a different man, a different werewolf. He wasn't desperate, he was yearning, and she was, too. Their hearts were hammering in sync together as the inevitable beat between them.

"I can't afford a distraction," she whispered.

She wasn't saying no, and Eldrick nodded as if he understood. "Alright." He moved an inch closer to her, and anticipation trickled through Tovi like the heat and cold of fire and ice colliding. "No feelings," Eldrick said.

His ask. His need in this—Tovi understood.

"No feelings," she repeated.

"No distractions."

"Okay."

"Okay.

A breath passed, and then their lips crashed together. They became a frenzy. Tovi grabbed her trousers and shimmied them off along with her undergarments. She gasped against Eldrick's mouth as her wet sex became exposed to the warm air. Eldrick worked at his britches, and along with his belt, they both dropped with a thud, and he released a groan as his cock sprang free.

Goddess. So long and thick. Tovi whimpered.

Eldrick didn't stop kissing her, their lips and teeth hitting as they kissed. His strong hands cupped her bare ass. He lifted her in the air. On instinct, Tovi's legs wrapped around his waist. Nothing was between them as Eldrick's cock slid between her wet folds. She was breathless. Ragged, desperate and needy.

With one movement, Eldrick slammed her up against the wall and slid into her, straight to the hilt. They both released a cry as they joined, weeks of tension, wanting, needing, finally being met. They stared at each other. Eldrick's breath was hurried, his eyes hooded. Tovi melted around him, getting used to his size and length as it stretched her in a delicious way.

Then he moved, and she came undone.

His pace was hungry, hurried, but beautiful. She tipped her head back, crying out with each thrust in a way she never had before. The pleasure of him, the feeling of him inside her sedated the hunger that had built for weeks.

Eldrick released one hand from her hips and tore open her blouse. Tovi gasped as her breasts came free, and Eldrick growled. *Growled.* Her nipples had hardened with arousal, sensitive to the air and friction of Eldrick's chest. He didn't lose pace. She had one foot in reality, the other teetering into oblivion. He fisted one of her breasts, threaded his fingers around her nipple. Pinched and squeezed. Tovi cried out his name, the pleasure of his pace and the pain too glorious to hold back.

"These are beautiful. You're beautiful. Look at you, taking me so well."

The build within her mounted to an aching state, and Eldrick's words almost sent Tovi over the edge. She needed release before she combusted, melting into the wooden walls of the stables and shattering into nothing.

Eldrick pulled out of her, leaving her empty and wanting. She whimpered, then gasped as Eldrick turned her around. Her feet hit the ground as he lined her hips to his. Her pebbled nipples crashed against the wooden wall, the friction curling her toes. His cock brushed against her ass. Tovi shuddered. With one hand he grabbed both of hers and held them high against the wall. His other kept her steady.

She was at his mercy

And she loved it.

They both cursed loud enough to awaken the forest as Eldrick slid into her wet sex again. He moved at a slower, torturous pace. Tovi felt every inch of him.

This angle. This position. She could stand here for hours and take this pleasure he gave, but she needed release.

"Eldrick, please."

"Are you begging?" He picked up his pace and then slowed again.

Tovi hadn't meant to, but a groan escaped her, and she pushed against him, giving him her answer.

A laugh rumbled from him, and his pace turned tortuously slow. "You have no idea how often I've imagined this," he whispered, his words tickling down her spine. "You up against a wall, like this, taking it. Taking me. Fuck, Tovi, I've only just had you, and I don't know if I'll ever stop."

He increased his pace, and Tovi took what he gave. Every beautifully paced thrust. Eldrick released her hands, giving her freedom to elongate her back and arch into him more. He growled and snaked an arm around her waist. She cried out when he found her sensitive swollen clit. Two of his fingers slid up and down over it, the direction and speed her body needed.

Oblivion stretched its blissful hands and held on. Never had Tovi been with someone like this. Their bodies called to each other, craved, wanted, knew.

"Come for me, dove."

If his words were a command, her body obeyed—Tovi fell. Her knees buckled, her core quivered around his cock, and she was certain the cry of release she unleashed reached the rooms at the inn. Warm tingles stretched to every inch of muscle and tendon of her being. Soon after, Eldrick found his own release, shuddering and cursing as he held them both steady against the wall.

They melted into it, two spent, sedated bodies finding their breath as they came down from what they could never undo. As their gazes met, Tovi didn't want to admit it, but like Eldrick, she wasn't sure if she could ever stop.

CHAPTER FIFTY-TWO

EVELYN UNDRESSED AND READIED to bathe. As her clothes dropped to the wooden floorboards, jitters pricked her skin. The day's events had unnerved her, and she still couldn't shake her and Kade's argument days ago. Pressure rested on her chest. No matter the deep breaths she tried, nothing shook away the worries and fragments of unresolved hurt. She couldn't stop thinking about it, the shift in him, but when she decided to address it, words died on her tongue. Fighting felt like a waste of time after being apart for so long. *Goddess*, she was so content with being with him again, she hadn't had the courage to bring it up.

She hissed when she dipped her toe into the steaming tub. As she sank farther into the warmth, her body finally exhaled. She heated the water more with her magic, the temperature so lovely and scolding. Pent-up, tired, she rested her head on the tub's edge and thought of home.

The chance to reunite with her sisters sent a thrill through her, and Evelyn couldn't deny the slight comfort in knowing that past the Void back in Sorin, she'd be farther out of Riven's reach. With the threat of the spell looming, Evelyn couldn't deny it was the wise choice, the less risky one—or as Kade would put it, less reckless. What Evelyn had discovered in Drystan *was* something. Right?

Evelyn swallowed and fidgeted in the tub. The unknowns regarding the prophecy were like haunting shadows, following her each and every mile to Sorin, one's she was certain she'd carry into her homeland. A sense of unfinished business nipped at her heels, too. Torn, Evelyn remained silent amongst the team.

The suds popped as Evelyn traced them with her fingers. She feared she'd do the same—pop the peace if she made her case. When she rehearsed it in her head, each word dripped with a sense of ungratefulness, like Kade and everyone else's efforts hadn't been enough. She sank deeper into the tub, focusing on the heat of the water and not the frantic beat of her worried heart.

It didn't help Kade was also pent-up in a way she'd never seen. There was an edge to him. An extra tick in his jaw. Sharper shoulders. Keener focus. Evelyn knew werewolves became territorial after they mated, but this felt different, like there was something he wasn't telling her.

The door whined, and Evelyn found Kade leaning against the door frame with his arms crossed. The candlelight illuminated the rivets of gold in his amber eyes, and it brought back memories. In the Runaway Radish, with the rows of whiskey behind him, she'd experienced that warmth, the kindness, and power that stare had over her for the first time.

Unlike then, Kade wore a forlorn expression as he drank her in. His jaw was rigid underneath his beard, his eyes marred by thoughts he didn't share. Evelyn didn't ask for them either, too afraid to fight.

"Let me wash you," he whispered.

Evelyn only nodded, her throat and mouth going dry. Kade's strong, beautiful muscles moved underneath his tunic and leathers, and his attention never left her as he strode towards the tub. The dim lighting, the warm water, her naked body tingled under his stare alone. Evelyn's stomach bloomed with a delicious heat.

He knelt behind her. *Knelt.* Commander Kade Drengr, Son of the God and fierce werewolf warrior, had knelt behind her. He dipped his hands into the water, trailing her arms with the tips of his fingers. His touch sent goose bumps through Evelyn, the friction of cold and warm curling her toes. He placed a kiss on each of her shoulder blades and withdrew his hands from the tub.

Cinnamon perfumed the air as he lathered his hands with the bathing chamber's soap. He cupped water, wet her hair, and began washing and massaging her scalp. Evelyn almost groaned, her eyes fluttering shut as Kade's gentle, meticulous touch relaxed the tension out of her shoulders. He scrubbed the grime from the crown of her head to the nape of her neck. He didn't leave a strand untouched, bubbles of goat's milk falling into the tub and surrounding Evelyn in a fresh aroma.

"I can never tell if your hair is black or blue." Kade's whisper tickled the shell of Evelyn's ear, making her sigh. "Sometimes, it's as dark as a raven's feather, but when the light hits it just right, it's a summer's night sky in the Vadon Mountains, the deepest shade of navy."

Kade talked like he was reciting poetry, and Evelyn had to remind herself he was talking about *her*. She heard the adoration and wonder, and the warmth in her belly shot to other parts of her body, tingling her elbows and knees.

She gasped as a sponge came in contact with her breast. Kade had moved from behind her and knelt on the side of the tub. He trailed the sponge underneath her breasts, outlining the female curves of her chest. Evelyn tilted her head back, and rested it on the rim of the tub, meeting Kade's eyes in the haze of tantalizing sensation his gentle touch gave. He ran the sponge over her collarbone, scrubbed her arms, and dipped the sponge back between her breasts, inching closer and closer to the apex between her thighs, the very spot Evelyn's body screamed for him to touch.

At the last second, he veered to the side, following the lines of her hip bone down her thigh. Shivers shuttered through Evelyn's entire being, her legs jolting from his touch.

With each brush up and down, he said, "These legs drive me mad, Evelyn." He moved to the next leg, wetting his tunic and not caring as he reached across the tub. "Your strong thighs, such muscle." He abandoned the sponge in the water, gripping her thigh with his hand. Evelyn gasped. Somewhere between gentle and possessive, he guided his hand from knee to hip, massaging her sore muscles from horseback riding and sending that belly warmth to her core.

Evelyn turned into a puddle, and her eyes hooded, anticipation and relaxation warring within her. She'd never been afraid of *wanting*. She relished in her body's needs, and with Kade, she'd never hold back. The want swimming in his whiskey eyes was as fierce. By spreading her legs a tad, Evelyn indicated what she desired.

"Is there somewhere you want me to touch you?" Kade asked, the slight tilt of a smirk playing on his lips.

Roguish. Handsome. *Beautiful.* Between his jawline, beard, smile, and eyes, Evelyn was done for with this man.

"Yes." It was all Evelyn could manage.

"Here?" Kade moved his grip to the inner thigh, his thumb at the edge of her folds. One maddening inch away.

"Higher."

The bastard moved up half an inch away and to the right. Again, his glorious hands gave her thigh a squeeze, sending more heat to her core.

"Here?" he asked when he bloody well knew it wasn't where she wanted.

Evelyn may not be afraid of wanting, but she wasn't one for begging. She relaxed, elongating her body. Her breasts peeked over the suds, her thighs rising out of the water like mountains in a lake. Her sex far more visible to Kade, and yet she didn't say a word.

Kade had gone very still and taut, the werewolf inside him at the edge. His grip on her thigh tightened, far more possessive than before, as he moved higher and higher—

Her body bowed as his thumb ran back to front in her wet, aroused folds, drawing a circle over her most sensitive spot. Kade touched her right where she wanted, but he didn't watch her body. His eyes connected with her eyes, a touch that grasped Evelyn's soul.

"*Shit.*"

Evelyn was already so close, the lead-up to his touch *there* so wonderful and calculated, the heat growing in her belly had her already on the wave, teetering above release.

She grabbed his hand, stalling his movements. "Join me."

Kade's eyes darkened as he stood, stripping off his leathers. The tub was big enough for two, and he sank into the other end. The water barely hit his chest, while his arms rested on the porcelain edge. Evelyn crawled to him, straddling his waist, but not seating herself full onto his ready length.

His jaw ticked. "I'm sorry."

Evelyn stopped, searching his face.

"I was wrong the other day to dismiss you like I did, and the truth is"—a breath shuddered out of him—"I'm terrified of losing you again. I can't."

Something in Evelyn cracked—his vulnerability painful.

She cupped his face. "Kade."

"I need you like air. When you're not by my side, I'm half dead inside, Ev. When you finally told me all you'd done in the castle, I couldn't think straight. I hadn't been there to protect you. You'd been alone, and I..." He swallowed, and something flashed in his eyes she couldn't put a name to. "When you suggested we continue searching for answers, that we stay in Drystan, I panicked."

Evelyn's chest ached. She loved him and hated seeing him tormented, but they weren't any mated couple; they had obligations, a prophesied destiny.

"There will be risks we must take," she said. "There's the prophecy, our titles, our duty to Sorin—"

"I know." He studied her, not her nakedness, but deeper. "I also know you better than anyone else, and I'm terrified you're on some mission that won't be worth it in the end."

Even in Callum, Kade had recognized her doubt before he fully knew her. There was no running from this, even if Evelyn wanted to. Kade read her regrets and shame like they were tattoos on her skin. She said nothing, did nothing, and waited for the moment to pass, yet her mistake rose like a wave of flame and crashed down.

"You're trying to make up for ever leaving."

Evelyn tried to back away, but Kade locked his arms around her, holding her firm to his torso. She was stuck above his knowing amber stare, and *fucking flames*, he saw right through her. She squirmed from the perusal.

"You have nothing to prove," he whispered.

She clamped her eyes shut. Fought tears. She had *everything* to prove.

"You're wrong. My sisters—"

"Love and miss you and will forgive you if you ask, but I don't think they expect an apology."

"They deserve it," Evelyn muttered. Tears stung in her eyes. She wished for her sisters' laughter. Their hugs. A shared breakfast for dinner. She'd missed them so terribly these last two years, and when she did see them again, she wanted something in hand, a tangible thing that said, *Look, see what I did!*

"Then offer one when you see them, but do not sacrifice yourself to prove to anyone what and who you are. Brave. Smart. Kind."

"But I ran away. I made a huge mistake, and I don't know how to undo it unless I—*we*—defeat the darkness."

"Yes," Kade said. "You made a mistake, but you cannot sit in the past. We have to move forward. Chasing forgiveness, being reckless, is not worth your well-being."

Evelyn sighed into his hold. She wasn't reckless. She was facing her fears, not running from them. She wanted answers—they *needed* answers—ones that led them to breaking the curse. Belief strong and wild danced within her like a new magic. Evelyn had a firm grip on it, ready to use it.

"I don't disagree that visiting Sven or staying in Drystan is a risk, but in Callum, you let me enter Castle Connacht, the Gray Wood, and even into the temple to face the White Lady. I love you with all my heart, Kade, but we can't hold each other back, no matter how much it scares us."

Kade weaved his fingers through her wet hair. "My intent is to not hold you back, it is to protect you."

Evelyn swallowed. *Goddess,* down their bond his need to protect her was fierce, as strong as steel and as wild as his wolf. Her flame mirrored his need to protect, but reality settled over her shoulders, too, her gut twisting.

She placed a palm on his cheek. "There may be things we can't protect one another from. Fate is tied too tightly to us."

Kade's beastly energy thrummed under her hand. His jaw tightened, the gold in his eyes darkened to a bronze.

"That is not good enough for me," he said. Calm. Deadly. Power, his wolf perhaps, pulsed in his chest. "But you're right, holding you back is wrong. Nothing has changed since Callum. We're partners in this, always."

Evelyn traced the scar through his brow, adjusted herself over his hips. "I love you."

Kade leaned towards her and brought her into a bruising kiss. Their lips molded together, and she felt his length harden again. They broke apart, heat buzzing between them.

Against her lips, Kade said, "I love you, too."

Evelyn kissed him, melting from the words. She fisted his length, lined it against her entrance, and sank onto him. Kade cursed. Evelyn threw her head back, gasping his name. He gripped her hips, encouraging her to rock against him. Evelyn found her pace, relishing at how deep he was inside her.

Kade watched, mesmerized. "Beautiful."

With hands on his chest, she moved. Her tempo built. Water sloshed in the tub. Pressure throbbed at her core. Kade's fingers brushed and circled her nub.

She was so close, and his *damn* fingers kept the same course. A wave threatened to crash down. His length throbbed—he was close, too.

As they reached the crest of their wave, it all receded, and she whispered his name.

"Kade."

He silenced her moan of release with a kiss. It shuddered through her body, wave after wave of ecstasy. She rode the pleasure tingling down to her toes and locking her knees. Kade's own filled her, her name, like a prayer, emitting from him.

Panting and wet, the two lay in each other's arms, the small washing room brimming with their love.

CHAPTER FIFTY-THREE

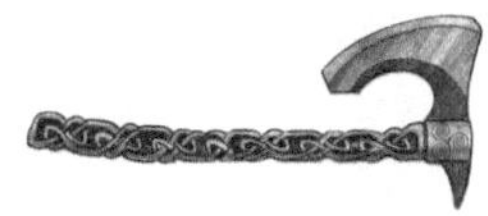

THE TEAM TRAVELED WEST instead of south.

Over fresh biscuits and sour gooseberry jam, Kade and Evelyn had asked Tovi how far out of the way her brother's estate was. As it turned out, Sven wasn't out of the way at all. A smile had etched across Eldrick's face at the glint in Tovi's eyes. Mirth. She'd known, and by Kade's heavy sigh, he'd guessed it, too—Tovi had led them in her brother's direction all along.

"How did you know Kade would change his mind?" Eldrick asked.

He and Tovi walked side by side as he guided their horse. Shin-deep snow covered their particular path in the forest, making it difficult to ride with two. The others had followed suit, trudging through the powdery terrain.

Tovi sighed. "I didn't, but hoped he might. Sven might have answers to this entire prophecy. That is too vital to pass up. Even if we returned to Drengr Village, we'd eventually have to come back."

The promise of home rippled through him. An ale at the Shield-maiden. Lucy would have pumpkin beer brewed by now. The horizon lined with snow-capped mountains, not a slant of shale in sight. Blue birds sang as the sun rose, even against the morning frost.

Eldrick brushed his knuckles against Tovi's fingers. She reciprocated the touch, lacing a finger with his. Between the thoughts of home and the touch of her skin, a lightness spread across his chest. He'd introduce her to the pumpkin beer. Perhaps she'd enjoy it a little more than the sour blueberry one. When spring came, he'd take her to the waterfalls west of the village and admire the snow's seasonal melt.

Maxie pranced through the snow, occasionally pouncing mound to mound, her orange fur becoming lost in the crater of soft snow she created. During the fifth time, Evelyn's familiar underestimated the depth of the snow up ahead. She jumped and fell through three feet's worth, her orange coat disappearing. A desperate meow disturbed the peace of the snowy forest, and the Gray Fenris laughed at Maxie's unfortunate predicament.

Thankfully, Todd strode past, dipped down and dragged Maxie to freedom. Her golden eyes landed on every team member, half-slits that gave the impression she plotted against them. Her tail, though, swaying side to side, gave away her playful spirit. Todd plopped her atop his horse's backside, and there she stayed.

Tovi sidestepped a few inches, leaving an empty spaced between their hands. Eldrick followed her line of sight. Up ahead, Bétar wiggled his brows at them while Yennifer flashed a smirk in Tovi's direction.

"Goddess, does everyone know?" Tovi whispered.

Eldrick chuckled. "Why? Embarrassed?"

"What? No!" She shook her head. "I was hoping, I don't know. We were in the stables, perhaps they hadn't heard us."

Eldrick held back another laugh. Her cheeks burned red, and he didn't want to increase her embarrassment. "I'm sure being in the stables helped with our noise, yes, but that doesn't mean they don't know."

"What? How?" Her eyes were wide, searching the team.

Eldrick scratched his chin. "I thought vampyrs had a keen sense of smell, too."

She blinked, shaking her head as she reared back. "We do, but we don't go around sniffing for who someone slept with."

"I don't recall us doing a lot sleeping." Eldrick winked.

Tovi slapped his shoulder. "Eldrick Drengr, this isn't funny."

"What? The fact you two *finally* released all that tension that's been building the last three weeks?" Linx had appeared from thin air, and she annunciated the word *finally* with such dramatics Eldrick rolled his eyes. Tovi, on the other hand, stared with her mouth open and eyes wide.

Bétar didn't bother turning around when he said, "About bloody time, you two!"

"This is mortifying," Tovi whispered.

Eldrick leaned close to her ear. "Don't worry about it too much. No distractions, remember?"

Tovi narrowed her eyes to slits. "No feelings, remember?"

"Precisely," Eldrick said. "You can't be mortified."

Tovi glared, but before she objected, Kade and Evelyn stopped up ahead. As the rest of the team joined them, the Daughter of the Goddess pinned Tovi with a hard stare, but Eldrick detected a hint of a smile. Tovi stiffened, and her jade eyes didn't know where to land.

Todd whistled, the high-pitched sound cutting through the awkwardness between friends.

"Now, that's an estate," he said.

The group congregated outside a set of iron gates. Through the bars, a black bricked home large enough to compete against Lār stood amidst a winter-touched garden. The shapes of hedges, bushes, and fountains were blanketed by snow, and around the bend, a man emerged, his hair the winter twin of his snowy surroundings.

Shovel in hand and shirt unbuttoned to his navel, sweat and exertion clung to the vampyr. He readied to plow snow on a path when he stopped, attention fixating on the newcomers waiting in silence outside his gate.

Tovi approached the bars in her usual businesslike walk. The siblings assessed each other. It wasn't tension strung tight between them, but apprehension. Years of it, prickling the air. Sven tossed his shovel to the side and headed towards them. Strong, well-built, the vampyr was accustomed to labor and work. Mud covered his leather boots, and dirt covered his hands. His Verena hair was cropped short, out of his face and neat.

"Sister," he said a step away from the bars.

"Brother."

Eldrick's wolf sat at the surface, guarding Tovi from afar. Sven unlocked the gate. It wailed as it swung open. With nothing separating them, Tovi and Sven assessed each other briefly once more, and then her brother dragged her into one of the fiercest hugs Eldrick had witnessed.

Still, he stepped forward, hand resting on his axe. His wolf paced under his blood, uncertain of the new vampyr in their company, but his chest swelled with a warmth as Tovi held her brother back.

When they parted, she held his face—an older sibling marveling at the younger.

"You look well," she said.

"You look like you've made a lot of new friends." He smiled at the group. His nostrils flared and eyes narrowed. "Some are werewolves I see. Witches, too. Why have you visited, Tovi?"

The shift in Sven's tone had Eldrick gripping the eye of his axe tighter. The group noticed too—Evelyn's fingers twitched at her sides, Kade caressed down Bleu, reaching for his sword, and Todd hid a dagger in his hand.

"They're here to see me, of course," a woman said in a songlike voice.

Sven shut his eyes and exhaled.

Behind him, an airy vampyr stood barefoot in the snow. Copper hair blew in the breeze. Her eyes, entrancingly too large for her face, unnerved Eldrick's wolf.

Tovi's jade eyes popped, her mouth going slack. "Opal?"

CHAPTER FIFTY-FOUR

Long neck ducks, burly goats, pepper feathered chickens, and curly-haired cows milled about a farm behind Sven and Opal's estate. Sliding doors revealed a fresh layer of hay in the black painted barn. A few animals slept, forms lost to the piles of warmth. Ducks quacked as Maxie chased them through the snow. Opal threw out feed, encouraging the goats and chickens to follow her while Sven scratched under the chin of a blissed cow. Both wore matching wedding rings, a bloodstone at the center of each.

A hundred questions rooted Tovi in place, but she managed at least one—the most demanding of them all. "Forgive me, but I thought Opal died the day of the curse," she said.

Sven shrugged. "She did die, technically, but not in the way that you may think."

Todd crossed his arms. "I think we should make a list of those we *think* are dead and triple-check. I'm beginning to notice a trend."

Belle giggled beside him while the rest remained silent. Her brother and his *mate* moved with the animals in a dance. Opal possessed a lightness, like she floated step to step, the same kind she'd possessed the few times Tovi had met her. She twisted and turned at times, the layers of her dress and apron spreading like a blooming flower. Sven had a roguish air to him; he seemed unburdened and happy as he never had at court, like he spent most of his days like this. Outside, under the endless gray sky, tending to his land and livestock.

"You turned her?" Tovi asked.

It wasn't the fact he turned her, but more so he'd kept her a secret. By technicality, Opal was a princess as his mate, but perhaps that explained his actions. He'd protected her from court, perhaps even from Riven. The setting only made the stark difference between her younger brother and her twin more obvious, leaving her off balance, shocked even. It was as if she were seeing Sven not only in a new light but meeting him for the first time.

"He did," Opal said. "The same day as the Blood Curse. The timing was unintentional, of course."

"Mother and Father didn't approve of Opal and I. Riven didn't disagree, but he never stood up to them for me like he did you. Visha, well, you already know. She can't be trusted. Her version of fun and games can be deadly. And well, you were nowhere to be found. I decided to take Opal away in secret, let her transition away from court and the castle. At first, it was frightening—the curse befalling us all hours after I'd turned her, but I decided to use it to my advantage."

"You kept her a secret all this time. Why?" Kade asked.

Tovi shared the same question, but shock dried her words on her tongue. For once, Tovi herself understood the marks secrets left. No matter the reason, they stung.

"Because vampyr court is a wretched place," Sven said. "Neither of us belonged there."

It confirmed Tovi's suspicion. "But—"

"Mama! Papa!"

Tovi whirled in the direction of the manor. Two children sprinted from the open back door and ran in the cleared pathways in welly boots too big for their small, unsteady legs. As well, they wore knitted wool sweaters, wide grins, and bloodstone necklaces. A boy and a girl, a few years apart, shared Opal's copper hair and had Verena jade eyes.

Tovi sucked in a breath. A knife pierced her heart.

Children.

Someone grabbed her hand and gave it a squeeze. Her heart thumped. Skipped a beat. She blinked away tears and found it was Evelyn holding her hand. Tightly. Reassuringly. A sheen coated her friend's eyes. Tears of her own. The two said nothing. Only a shared look. Like the ones they'd shared for years. *Thank you.*

The children sprinted into their parents' arms—the daughter into Sven's and the son into Opal's. Their wide smiles and bright eyes outshined the dreary gray of Drystan, and for a moment, the land no longer seemed cursed with their giddy presence. Tovi held her friend's hand, certain without it she'd crumble from happiness.

"Would you like to meet your auntie?" Sven said, bouncing the little girl.

Bashful, she buried her head into his chest, peeking out at Tovi. "Is she the one who took down the elks?"

Tovi let out a broken cry, and Evelyn kept her steady. Eldrick drew closer to her. The other team members sent small, reassuring smiles. Her heart almost burst.

Her brother laughed, eyes landing on her. "Yes, Tovi is the huntress."

"Hi, Tovi!" the daughter said.

"What are their names?" she sniffled.

"Juni and Bryn." Sven kissed his daughter's cheek. "Why don't we give everyone a snack in the house, Juni? Mom needs to talk with your aunt for a moment."

The little boy, Bryn, mumbled about wanting to meet a werewolf, and Sven took his hand and led the rest of the Gray Fenris indoors.

"I'm a werewolf," Todd said.

"Wow!" Bryn's childish excitement lightened the chilly air.

Tovi leaned into Evelyn's ear. "Thank you."

Evelyn nodded and pulled away, falling into Kade's side. Eldrick placed a reassuring hand at the small of her back. The four of them stood with a wide-eyed Opal. She removed a handful of carrots from her apron's pocket, and the bells around the cows gonged at a faster tempo as they hurried towards the sweet treat.

"Go on then," she said. "Ask your questions, I will not bite."

Tovi gave Evelyn an encouraging nod.

"Was your brother a seer?" she asked.

"We were all seers."

"All three of you?" Tovi asked.

"Yes," she said. "We were all plagued with horrible visions from a young age. They were worse for Orla, and on her twenty-second birthday, she jumped from the cliffs in Morrow to rid herself of them forever. Odin and I feared we'd one day share the same fate if we did not find a remedy to rid our minds of them."

The farm dropped in temperature, the coolness of Opal's tone icy.

"Whisperings of immortals began to trickle into Nūa's underground. They were rumored to have been touched by a goddess, changed into something anew. Odin's lover, Matilda, set off on a mission to learn more. She became a visiting scholar for the vampyr royals. She soon won enough favor for them to hear her request. Turn Odin and save him from the visions that plagued him.

"But vampyrs hadn't turned anyone but humans. There was worry it would not work on one already touched with the magic of a goddess. Could any soul handle the power of two, or would one cancel the other? In the end, which one would prevail?"

The four of them stood, listening as the cows took turns nibbling to carrots.

"Odin and I were both invited to the castle to stay as guests. Drystan was quiet, different than the growing city of witches. I found a sense of peace here in this land, and I also met Sven. Odin found comfort, too, but he struggled with his decision. If he turned, he would one day outlive Matilda. She begged him to choose peace. In the end, though, Odin didn't make his decision in time. They placed us in the guest wing of the castle atop the human servant's quarters. When the curse fell, it became a bloodbath there. No one survived the vampyrs who fell to bloodlust immediately, not even Odin."

"He died that day?" Kade asked.

"Yes," Opal said. "And from what I know, Matilda vanished into thin air."

Evelyn nodded. "Your visions, did they stop after you were turned?"

"Yes." She forced a smile, eyes downward. "Sven gifted me with a life of peace. I'm no longer plagued by sights, new visions, or the whisperings of past, present, and future, but when your mind has been connected to the in-between for over two decades, there are things you never forget."

A heaviness spread through Tovi's chest while the cold tingled across her skin. She and the others sat at the precipice of answers, the fall a breath away. Her heart hammered to the impending beat.

"Opal, we believe Evelyn found notes that might've belonged to your brother," Tovi said. "I know the past can be painful, but will you look at them for us?"

Her brother's mate nodded. "I can try."

Evelyn reached into her cloak and retrieved the paper she'd used to draw out the stanzas. She handed them to Opal with shaky hands. "Do these words mean anything to you?"

Opal smiled to herself. She held the meek notes and began to walk and weave her way through the gathered animals. Then, she began to recite words like they were lines of poetry.

> *"As frost bites trees and ferns, whispers*
> *of Gods and Goddesses travel on the wind.*
> *The banished One reaches from Below,*
> *grasping the hope of a heartbroken mortal.*
> *A bleeding bargain struck, weaved with*

trickery, and the tendrils of immortality.

But when true love dies,
it'll be the land's demise.
Not until the land is cast in
red, a new dawn will rise.

The age of curse, a crack in the land, the
seep and sorrow of death, darkness, and rot.
Her children cast in night, whilst a
hunger for blood will be their blight.

After a storm between mistaken enemies,
the wolf and dove, the clash of the light and night,
those of these lands will unite.

A sowing of seeds, a journey to the beneath where
life and death meet. A king and queen will emerge,
with the seeds sown from elsewhere, life
to rid the shade and make way
for the Prince to walk with Light.

With bones an old friend now set free,
and the blade of the ancients
the truest of unions between the third-borns of
the Sun and Moon will defeat the darkness."

Her too-wide eyes landed on them all. "I'll never forget *these* words."

A chill, not from the winter, trickled through every one of Tovi's tendons, muscles, and bones. She tried to grasp the words, their possible meanings, but thoughts didn't connect as the weight of what they learned descended over her.

"Evelyn and I are not the only ones mentioned in the prophecy," Kade whispered.

The wolf and the dove.

Panic laced through Tovi, and she turned to Eldrick. His usual stony expression cracked with concern. His nickname for her. His magic. Both had been stated in the prophecy as if—

"There are others," Opal said, turning to Evelyn. "It was your eyes the most I saw in my visions. They were the brightest sight against the horrors my mind whispered."

Eldrick stepped forward. "But who exactly are the others?"

Opal shook her head. "You don't understand. I did not know who Evelyn was until now. I did not see full faces. Only glimpses. Symbols. My siblings and I saw so much, so many, it all blurs together. I cannot make sense of these words. I do not know who or what these words belong to."

Eldrick shook his head. "How can that be? You've seen visions, you recited them!"

Tovi held his arm, pulling him back.

"I'm a vessel, a messenger. What it all means, I can't tell you," Opal said.

Eldrick shook his head, raking a hand through his hair. "We need to return home, get this to Lorkan, the scholars. It needs to be studied."

Kade and Evelyn nodded their agreement. Both third-borns had paled, growing tauter together as if the words threaded them closer. Tovi agreed, too—returning to Sorin, outrunning her brother and the Blood Moon, and getting the prophecy to those who could study it had to come next. But a small part of her grew unnerved by those lines that hit too close to her and Eldrick. Unlike him, she was in no hurry to learn their part in the prophecy, no hurry to learn how much her future was not her own.

Not when so much was on the line.

Especially her heart.

CHAPTER FIFTY-FIVE

THE WEIGHT OF ALL they learned left Evelyn floaty, as if a burden had been lifted from her shoulders. No—they hadn't learned exactly how to break the curse or defeat the Blood Goddess, but the entirety of the prophecy was something worth returning home with.

She and the team stayed the night with Sven and Opal. One glance at Tovi holding her niece and nephew, and Kade had suggested it. No one felt inclined to take her from the new family she'd met, the green in her jade eyes the brightest it'd been since Evelyn had met her.

That evening, they'd sat around the fireplace on cushions and blankets with Opal's wild mushroom stew and Sven's brûléed custard. They laughed, told stories, and played music. Tovi's brother had the voice of a deep sea siren, captivating everyone with tales of shadows and lost loves.

It wasn't long before the estate's clock chimed midnight. Juni and Bryn had fallen asleep on Tovi, and through Evelyn's drowsy haze as Kade led her to their room, she swore her once friend didn't appear ready to leave them.

As Evelyn fell asleep in Kade's arms, she thought perhaps light against darkness came in many forms. Family, love, *forgiveness*. The very thing she hoped to earn with her sisters. Her tangible effort sat on the bedside table. Folded neatly,

Opal had written the prophecy down for her. She brushed her fingers over it, the inked words the most coveted finding.

Hours later, a red tinge roused her from sleep. Lids heavy, muscles aching, Evelyn hadn't slept for long. When her eyes sprang open, red lit their room in an eerie glow. Past the night overcast, the moon, now glowing a brutal crimson, burned in the sky. Darkness, horrid and wrong, clawed against Evelyn's magic, hissing.

The Blood Moon.

"Kade!" She pushed him awake, springing out of bed.

"What?" He blinked awake, eyes widening at the room drenched in red. "Shit. Wake the others."

But Kade and Evelyn found the others had already risen. Sven and Opal's estate turned into madness as the team hurried outside. Every inch of snow had shifted from white to red, painting Drystan in the likeness of the Blood Goddess's namesake. The winter winds had weakened, leaving the air far too still.

Evelyn exhaled, her breath blooming like clouds. The pines tilted, and loose snow twirled upward. Dark magic and licorice invaded her senses and prickled her skin. Her stare met Belle's, the only fellow witch among them who might've felt it, too.

"Kade—"

A force blasted against them all, and Evelyn flew. She landed with a thud in the snow. Her vision blurred. Her hearing rang. Someone roared her name. Ahead of her, something pink and small screamed. Evelyn blinked, her sights focusing on Linx. A vampyr held her by the throat.

"Remember these, mage bitch," he hissed.

He held one of Linx's explosives in an outstretched hand—one that must've not gone off during their attack on the fighting rings. Linx writhed and clawed at his grip, her face turning an awful shade of blue.

Evelyn rose and flared her flame, reaching a tendril of fire straight into the vampyr's back. He screeched in pain, dropping Linx. The mage's eyes ran with tears, but she grasped the explosive out of his hand. He didn't care. He was too concerned with his cloak engulfed in flame. Frantic, he tore it off, but his tunic and flesh festered a painful shade of red where Evelyn's flame had reached.

Around them, the rest of the Gray Fenris fought other vampyrs. Sven cried to Opal to get the children inside. Lou ushered to help. Arrows punctured the chest of a vampyr fighting Bétar, the Gray Fenris archer unseen, but her shots landing true. Evelyn's heart raced in her chest as she searched for Kade.

Linx, Todd, Bétar, Tovi...

She counted some, but *fucking flames,* where was he?

There.

Eight feet of furred, rippling muscles stalked a vampyr into the corner. Eldrick paced by his side, unshifted, axe drawn. Fighting ensued, and the Drengr brothers worked in sync as they slayed vampyrs.

Wind howled through the clearing, unfurling Evelyn's hair. Red dust fluttered and flung in a twister. Riven and Ingrid stepped through the estate's gate, and the prince's sights landed on her. How had he found them?

Evelyn pulled her staff free of her bun. It elongated in her hand, flushing against her palm in beautiful familiarity. She cast her flame up it, power dancing and twirling from the ancient bone.

She tilted her head, egging Riven to attack. Adrenaline thrummed through her as she widened her stance, facing her foe head-on. They weren't in Drystan Castle. She was no longer his prisoner, and she'd make sure she killed him before he could threaten anyone else she loved ever again.

Riven unsheathed a black metal sword, the power of the weapon ringing through the clearing. More dark magic. Rage unleashed through Evelyn, and she bellowed a cry. For Kade. For her sisters. For herself. Riven readied for her attack, and his blade reflected the snow like silver against charcoal.

Evelyn unleashed a wave of flame with her staff. Riven deflected her blow. One after the other. His sword matched her ferocity, the magic weaved in the blade an equal against her own. She aimed a fiery blast at his feet. Snow steamed as it melted near his boots. Riven *moved*. His vampyr speed propelled his steps left to right over and over, Evelyn's attacks missing him by inches. He turned and slashed his sword. The metal rang through the air as she pivoted, the whoosh of the blade leaving her cold and breathless.

Dragon bone collided with Riven's blade. Evelyn pushed, and Riven's boots slid through the snow. A boom like the crack of thunder rocked through them. He faltered. Evelyn spun, advancing this time harder, swifter. She hit the center of his sword while he still regained his footing. He was off balance, distracted, and blasted backwards into the snow.

Wind tickled Evelyn's ankles, and she deflected a wave of power from Ingrid. She locked eyes with Evelyn and blasted a wave of wind, throwing her through the air. Her flame went out as she landed hard, yards away. Her staff clattered out of her hand.

Righting herself with one foot behind her, the other out front, Evelyn stood her ground in a lunge, fighting the pain. She forgot her staff and splayed her fingers, letting her flame come forth again. In the proximity of Ingrid's encroaching wind, it danced and twisted to overshadow the dark with light.

She inhaled, exhaled, and attacked.

The witches sparred, ribbons of wind and flame tangling together. Each winced against the blows, the magic reaching to their souls feeling the impact of each attack.

A blast from Ingrid pushed Evelyn back, her boots skidding in the snow. No. She refused to lose. Fire, anger, resolve burned in her so hot and fierce, her eyes shined with it. She launched. Evelyn's power ballooned and spread against Ingrid's burst of wind. The witch held true until—

A blast of water, ice, and snow collided into her, throwing Ingrid into the air. Belle stood at a distance, hands open and splayed, the water around them bending at her will. Pride shot through Evelyn at the sight, and she nodded towards Belle.

Around them, fighting continued. Tovi and Eldrick battled side by side, a refreshing sight. The Gray Fenris held firm, but blood still painted the snow—drenched Sven and Opal's acres of peace in darkness. And vampyrs blocked Kade's path to Evelyn, his face contorted with rage.

"Surrender, Evelyn, and maybe I'll let them all live." Riven dragged his blade through the snow.

Ingrid rose, glaring at her sister. She wheeled her hands in the air. Wind picked up and up to reveal a glimpse into another place—a *danu*. The darkness of the Drystan dungeons waited on the other side.

Not until the land is cast in red, a new dawn will rise.

Opal's earlier words tickled Evelyn's memory. She didn't have the faintest idea how the prophecy worked or what the words meant, but if they had even the slightest chance of figuring it out, she couldn't let Riven capture her again. She'd never let that happen. And perhaps, a new dawn that rose could be of her choosing, not the Blood Goddess's.

All Evelyn had was hope and belief. It ran through her veins, fiery, hot, and *powerful*. And this resolve to face her fears fueled her spirit and lit her soul. The next time she set foot in her homeland and saw her sisters, they'd know it. *See* it, too. Because she wouldn't let Riven win. Not now, not ever.

Riven's desperation to succeed slid across her skin like the dark magic Ingrid wielded.

Magic.

A wild, reckless idea sparked inside Evelyn.

Their plans. The spell. Allowing vampyrs to walk in the sunlight. *Her* blood. They needed the magic in it. Not her exactly.

The prince advanced, and Evelyn swiped one last mighty wave of flame. He screeched, dropping his sword and clutching his right eye. Steam and the scent of burning flesh wafted in the air.

Evelyn dove left, her insides flipping backwards. The idea. Her anxiety. *Reckless.* Perhaps, but in the end, the Blood Goddess's wishes hinged on the light in Evelyn's magic. What if she robbed them of the possibility?

It hides what you are, who you are.

She grasped the bloodstone she still wore. The light of her flame disintegrated the remaining setting Ingrid had created, leaving only the red stone. The power of fallen gods sang to her soul.

It can hide a curse. Hide magic of any kind.

"What are you doing?" Ingrid shouted.

Evelyn tightened her hand, crying out from the pain. She gritted her teeth, ignored the sweat prickling at her brow.

In, in, in.

She chanted, she sang. She cried to the Sun Goddess for help and will and strength, pushing her magic, her flame into the stone to hide it from those who wished to use it against her.

"No!" Ingrid's cry almost broke through her maddening attempt.

Then her soul ripped. A knife, red and glossy like the bloodstone, reached and snatched a tendon of her soul and sucked it into the enchanted gem. Blinding pain seared through her.

Evelyn screamed.

CHAPTER FIFTY-SIX

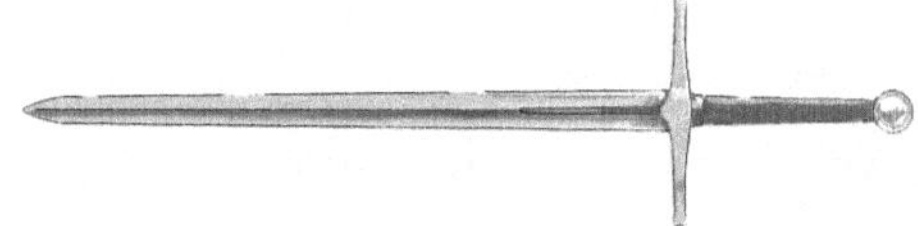

ANGUISH TORE KADE'S SOUL in two.

He spun around, and the intense fear that washed over him brought him to his knees. He shifted out of his werewolf form. His bones snapped, his muscles stretched, and the growl and roar that unleashed from him was half man, half wolf.

Yards away, Evelyn screamed. Her back arched against the snow. Her hands had curled at her sides and sweat trickled down her brow. She was hurting, and Kade felt the pain like his own. What in the stars above was happening to her?

"Get to her!" Eldrick cried. "I can handle them."

He swung his axes at a vampyr. Metal clanged against metal as Kade raced towards his mate. The Gray Fenris fought around him. Arrows flew. Bétar howled. Pink hair and buckled leathers worked in sync in Kade's peripheral. Black talons swiped as Tovi tried to make her way to Evelyn, too.

Everything else around Kade became mute aside from her anguish-filled screams.

Sword at the ready, he aimed to cut down the witch leering over her. He swiped down. Metal rang as he hit something hard, the force ricocheting through his arm. Kade held true, gritting his teeth against the strength of another. He roared as his attacker pushed him back, separating him from Evelyn. The tall, slender figure obscured his view of her, the Verena green of the sibling Kade had learned to hate.

Riven.

The prince peered down his nose at Kade. A fresh burn glistened and blistered across his face, right eye clamped shut. A snarl thundered out of him, and he attacked. Fast and fluid, Riven moved as one with his sword. Kade met him blow for blow. Left, right. Backward, forward. The two danced with blades, both with the strength of the night.

Except the power of the moon—*that* had been the energy building inside of Kade. The light he yielded was of his god. It swelled in him like the strong, unbending power of gravity, pulling the tides.

Riven lost his footing over a fallen vampyr, and Kade backhanded the hilt of his sword into the prince's jaw. Bone crunched and blood sprayed across the snow. Riven wiped his split lip and smirked, red painting his fangs.

"You played into my plan so easily, it wasn't even fun." Riven twirled and brought his sword down. Kade deflected, the swords screeching as they ran against one another. "A measly letter about your sick father dying, and you believed it without a second thought."

It was Kade's turn to lose his footing. His heart skipped. Raced. Sweat quickened at his brow. Riven stepped in front of him and charged. A second almost too late, Kade sidestepped and countered. He and Riven roared at each other, nose-to-nose, while the prince's eyes danced with delight.

Kade growled, body tensing. He refused to let Riven win. He gripped his sword tighter. His chest rose and fell, his heart beating for Evelyn.

He pushed Riven back. His new power rose to the surface, building and building inside his chest. His strength only angered Riven, and the prince hissed as he drove his heels into the ground and held.

Their swords crossed. Both of them shook. Kade's muscles screamed in agony, his boots sliding against the snow.

Riven sneered, his words like a knife to his heart. "You don't deserve her. She sacrificed herself to keep you safe—"

Metal echoed as Kade silenced his words with a shoulder-shaking blow. The prince rose, laughing.

"And you're about to lose her all over again."

Kade lost his focus. A slight truth rang in Riven's words, and he faltered. The fraction of a moment was enough time for Riven to turn his sword downward and knock Kade's out of his hand. A blast of air hit him at the side, and Kade skidded across the snow.

He panted, his heart skipping and racing. He turned. Evelyn reached for him. Her skin had gone ashen. The silver in her eyes dimmed.

"Kade," she breathed. Her eyelids fluttered, and she passed out.

Pain and turmoil filled her one word, and Kade bolted. The distance between them tugged at Kade's soul. His anger and fear reached his inner wolf, and he shifted as he ran. His strides grew longer, his footing in the snow firmer. His arms pumped at his sides, claws cutting through the air. Another blast of dark wind boomed between them, throwing Kade off course.

The branches of pine trees blew in the wind, snow whipping into funnels shy of Evelyn's unconscious body. Tucked between the trees, the air whirled in a continuous circle, brimming with magic. Through it, Sven's estate no longer existed, but a different place, as if it were a doorway. With walls of gray stone and at the center, waiting, Prince Riven stood with his arms behind his back.

Patient. Stoic. Inside a dungeon.

Kade's mind lost all thought and reason.

The drumming of his heart beat to the build of his mounting power. His vision tunneled. Time slowed. Sounds echoed and warped. Vampyrs entered the forest from the castle, focused on Evelyn. Kade roared. On his periphery,

Todd flanked his left. Bétar and Yen, in their werewolf forms, weren't far behind. Arrows soared overhead, aimed at Riven and his guards.

The prince held Kade's gaze.

You're about to lose her all over again.

"Kade, wait!"

His team shouted his name, but he didn't listen. Didn't care. Turned on her side in the snow, Evelyn was serene against the white, but the streaks of red from tears and blood splattered on her hands and leathers painted a different story.

Someone joined his side, but his focus never left Evelyn. One step closer to her. His mantra built the in tempo of his power. The pressure overtook reasoning. He couldn't think, couldn't grasp this newness, this chaos inside him. It pulled and pulled, like the gravity of the moon. His emotions ebbed and flowed like a wave, until they receded farther and farther from the shore of control.

Kade lost his hold on his power.

A sonic boom emitted from him. The light of day sucked from the sky and traveled to the light emitting from his being. It stretched far beyond the estate, past the trees, and over the snow in a pearly blue. His power rumbled like a beast on the prowl, and the ground shook. When he blinked, pressure pushed against his chest as he clutched it. It felt empty there, like he'd emptied *himself*, hollowed himself out. Exhaustion gripped him.

But he was paces away from Evelyn. She groaned awake, fumbling to right herself. Kade crawled to her, catching Evelyn as her arms gave out. She fell against his chest, clutching him as sobs wrecked through her.

"Evelyn." Tears thickened his words. "You're alright. You're safe."

The *danu* had closed, and Riven was gone. Vampyrs still fought behind them, the screech of talons against iron still close.

"No!" someone cried.

Kade and Evelyn scrambled, their breaths hitching. Yen, Bétar, and Linx bent over someone. The rest, Eldrick, Tovi, and continued fighting.

"Todd! *Todd!*" Linx's frantic words punched Kade in the gut.

They ran to them, and Kade collapsed to his knees. A single gash ran hip to shoulder on Todd's side, like a giant blade had opened his weapon master's torso. Pearly blue magic smoldered from the wound. Kade's stomach roiled, and Evelyn grabbed his arm for strength. Guilt crept up his spine. *He* had done this.

Yennifer's hands covered her mouth, tears streaming down her face while Bétar's usually ruddy cheeks had gone white as sheets.

Linx applied pressure wherever she could, blood seeping through her fingers. "Somebody get my bag! Please!"

"Linx," Kade breathed.

"No!" his healer hissed. "You don't get to make orders right now. You did this!"

"Linx." Yennifer dropped to her haunches, grabbing Linx's shaking shoulders. "It's alright. You can heal him."

Could she? Everyone's silence mirrored Kade's terrible thought. Todd's usually tanned skin had paled a shade close to death. And the gash. It was deep. So much blood.

"I have it!" Belle rushed over and fell to the ground. She sifted through Linx's satchel, thrusting ointments and oils through her search. "Yarrow root?"

"The greenest jar." Belle passed it to her, and Linx's hands shook as she tried to open it. She sprinkled the dried herb over Todd, but it was no use. Blood soaked the ointment like a sponge, giving it no time to take effect.

"Fuck," Linx hissed. "We'll have to cauterize it, but we don't have time to build a fire. Evelyn, will you help?"

Kade turned to her, but her bottom lip trembled. Tears streamed down her face.

"I... I can't," she whispered.

He grabbed her hand. "You might cause him pain, but this will save him."

She shook her head, tears so heavy her words came out thick. "No, you don't understand. I *can't*."

Evelyn opened her fist. She'd been clutching her hand, bloody half-moon cuts from her fingers stained her palm. Steaming against her skin, the bloodstone necklace reflected orange, no longer red. The black metal setting was gone. Kade's magic pulsed, recognizing what ebbed and flowed within the gem. His heart cracked and sank to the depths of his gut.

"Evelyn, what have you done?" he asked.

CHAPTER FIFTY-SEVEN

TOVI AND ELDRICK FOUGHT together like lovers danced. In sync, tempo, and as one.

She bellowed, her next hit with her talons harsher than the last. The vampyr screeched. Spittle dripped from their fangs. Black veins rimmed their eyes. The curse sat in the air, clawing at Tovi. Talons unsheathed, her beastly shift called to the darker side weaved into her blood and heart. She ignored it, trying to fight as hard against it as she fought against her opponent. She lunged, slicing the vampyr's shoulder open. Blood coated her talons, the liquid warm as it ran down the creases of her palm.

Riven—the coward—had left, abandoning two vampyr guards. Tovi's animal instincts detected the shift in the team, grief gripping them all. Something had happened. But she had no time to check, not when Sven's family had run to safety and she'd sworn to protect their home the moment her twin had arrived. Beside her, Eldrick sidestepped and handled his own. The metal of his axe hit the iron of a sword, clanging between them.

Tovi didn't avert her attention his way either. Her heart hammered. Her breath came out ragged. The spin of her boot against the snow kept her fluid, *moving* against her attacker.

She stepped back, pivoted and twisted, trying to outrun the eerie whisperings in the back of her mind. Blood seeped into the snow. Friend, foe, enemy, *his*. The droplets and sprays sang to her, whispered sweet nothings, and reached the part of her she kept buried.

Tovi blinked, and talons whipped across her face. She reared back, the glint of black hovering a hair's thinness away from her nose.

Death lingered all around her.

It clung to Tovi's skin like a parasite, spreading the darkness of the curse. It's fungus-like web dug its roots into her heart and mind, feeding vicious images. Blood on her tongue, dripping over her chin, streaming down her cleavage. Hunger raged in the pit of her belly.

Tovi couldn't think, the blood curse whispering like an evil sprite on her shoulder.

Hunt. Kill. Drink.

A heartbeat echoed in Tovi's ears. Her fangs ached to be released, to bite and suck the first drop of blood she could get her mouth on. Inky black began to spread up her arms. Her sight faded to red.

Goddess, she was on the edge of bloodlust.

Eldrick growled in pain. She whirled. The vampyr had swiped the back of his leg, and he'd fallen to his knees. He swung to counter a final blow, but he was flailing. Tovi's limbs shook. The skin on the back of her neck rose.

No.

Everything turned red. The curse, along with *something* deeper, rose to the surface. Adrenaline pumped through Tovi's veins, and she sprang forward. Her talons swiped against the fleshy neck of her opponent and blood showered her face. She didn't wait to watch as the vampyr dropped dead.

She lunged with a territorial cry at the vampyr delivering another blow to Eldrick. Her talons caught his sword before it fell. A snarl bubbled out of her. Her vision went in and out with each pulsing push of her sharp fangs. They unleashed. Longer, sharper, deadlier. The tips pierced her bottom lip, and her own blood sent a maddening thirst through her, liquid ecstasy driving her to a place of darkness and compulsion.

The whisperings had turned to chanting. A sweet melody of darkness. Thorns pricked her heart. Dark magic thickened the air. But the color of emerald flashed against the red. The need to protect Eldrick eclipsed the need for blood. The two wove together. His attacker became her prey, and Tovi's caged beast broke free.

She swiped. Up, down. Across. Each blow made contact. Each shredded flesh. Each felt *glorious*.

Panting, hungry, liberated, Tovi's chest heaved as the vampyr slumped back, thudding into the snow. She'd done it. Tovi had protected her ma—

"Tovi."

Her name sounded as if it tunneled through a vacuum. It came and went, loud and soft.

She blinked. Red, black, and green tinged her sights. The scent of blood—a minty spice—increased her hunger. A growl rumbled through her chest like a lioness.

"Tovi."

A hand landed on her shoulder, and she spun, squatting into a defense. Talons splayed, fangs bared, she hissed. Eldrick fell back, his green emerald eyes widening in horror—he wasn't afraid of her.

He was *petrified*.

The sight caused Tovi to stop. Shame washed over her. The sight of him stalled her bloodlust. The red haze dissipated, the green of the forest coming into view, but it only reminded her of Eldrick's emerald eyes.

He blinked a few times, swallowed.

"Eldrick." Tovi tasted blood on her tongue when she said the word. She stepped towards him, but he retreated on his elbows. She froze, her own reflection in his eyes stilling her in place. Her talons had turned black, spidery veins rimmed her eyes.

No.

The curse retreated back into her as she fled his judgmental stare, black melting into her pale skin. Something cut across Tovi's heart. An open wound she couldn't close.

Understanding flashed across Eldrick's face and he rose, running his hand threw his golden-brown hair. He reached and grasped the back of his neck.

"Fuck—Tovi... I didn't mean to—I'm sorry."

Pity and unease.

Both wafted off him worse than the scent of blood. Tovi's biggest fear came to fruition. He'd seen her for what she truly was, and he couldn't accept it. Gone was the want, the intent he'd shown in the room above the stables. Tovi turned away, unable to handle the tightness in her chest, refusing to admit what she felt. This wasn't pride or hurt feelings. It was far more than that. A man she—

Goddess, she loved him.

Tovi's world stopped. She'd had one task—to gain an alliance—and she'd allowed herself to get distracted, putting herself on display for him to judge. Like they had in her court all those decades ago. Hurt surged into anger, and Tovi hadn't the energy to rein it in.

"There's nothing to be sorry for."

She moved to walk around him. She needed space. Air that wasn't filled with blood. A stare that didn't threaten to break her heart more than it already had.

Eldrick grabbed her elbow. "Wait."

Except Tovi's ire had been lit, and she bit back, spinning towards him. "Did you think I would actually hurt you?"

He winced. "You don't understand. I—"

"I understand perfectly. You'll never see me as anything other than a vampyr."

"You *are* a vampyr!"

Tovi's heart tore to smaller pieces. She loved a man who only saw her for what she was not who. None of it had mattered. Not her efforts. Skills. Expertise. It was like she stood across from her parents again, begging them to see what she'd built with her own hands, not the promise of an alliance she'd secured by wearing a certain dress or attending some dinner. But it was her own fault. She'd gotten distracted. She'd dropped her poised, proud princess act around him and let him in. And for what? He hadn't seen her any differently. It had never been worth showing him the real her.

Eldrick shook his head. "All my life, vampyrs have been the enemy. They *are* my enemy. Your brother attacked us, Tovi!"

"Yes, you've made your hatred of me and my people clear. Despite every effort I've made to gain your trust, to show you that I am not like my brother, to make you fucking see that I'm different. After everything I've done, the things that I have sacrificed..." Tovi shook head, tears unwillingly spilling down her face. "I fought by your side! I guess that means nothing to you. It's clear your opinion of me will never change."

Anguish rippled through his emerald eyes. "I'm an alpha, Tovi. I have to hold onto the facts. When I saw you... I wasn't thinking. I never meant to hurt you—"

Tovi shook her head, tears rolling down her cheeks. "Stay the fuck away from me. Whatever this is"—she waved her hands between them—"this stupid, sick game between us is over. I'll get my alliance with the werewolves without you. *Stay the fuck away from me.*"

Tovi headed towards the others.

"Tovi!"

He shouted her name into the wind, into the cold and cursed land. She ignored him, refused to face his judgment again, not when her heart was torn to shreds.

PART IV

CHAPTER FIFTY-EIGHT

THE TWO DAYS AFTER Riven's attack passed in a blur. They had rushed south without stopping to ensure they reached the Drengr Village. Linx, with the help of Belle, had stabilized Todd's injuries, but Kade's weapons master had fallen into an endless sleep, his wounds grave.

The return home hadn't been the joyous affair Kade envisioned.

Bétar and Yennifer had excused themselves to return home. Eldrick had headed straight for Lār while Tovi headed in the opposite direction towards the Shield-maiden with Lou. Kade had walked through the motions of introducing Evelyn to his father and uncle, but then they retreated to his own cottage in the woods, away from the village and the weight of the last two days.

Night ascended over the forest outside the window. Kade grew restless. Upstairs, Evelyn washed the grime and dirt away, and by the emptiness in her eyes, Kade knew to give her space. She'd placed her magic into the bloodstone to protect everyone from the possibility of Riven ever using it. Kade's heart ached for her sacrifice. They didn't understand the gravity of it, yet. Could she get it back? What did this mean for the prophecy? He hadn't the capacity to broach the subject, not when he partly blamed himself. He hadn't gotten to her in time, hadn't protected her.

In fact, he'd harmed his teammate, someone he loved, in the process.

The fire in his cast-iron hearth dwindled to cinders, wisps of smoke traveling unseen through the pipe leading outside the roof. Burning pine tickled Kade's werewolf's sense of smell, and the shrinking flame reflected Kade's misery. He sank further into his chair, stewing.

Evelyn's feet pattered in the bedroom upstairs, the floorboards creaking above him. He tried to grasp some calm, grounding himself in the fact Riven hadn't succeeded. Evelyn was with him, safe. Kade should've been upstairs with her, but how could he when his efforts had harmed Todd? This power, this energy, made him lose control, and Kade *never* lost control. Purpose. His mission. His title. *Duty.* Kade had always grounded himself in those things, and he should've felt grounded with Evelyn, his mate, finally home.

Yet, he was restless. Why?

Perhaps it was because his newfound power still grew within him. His use of it had barely dimmed its strength, and it was building again. The more he thought of everything he faced—Evelyn's pain, Riven's threat, hurting one of his own teammates—the quicker the energy pulsed and grew.

Outside the kitchen window, he couldn't make out the stars past the evergreens, but a glint of hazy silver followed the curve of the waning moon.

Evelyn appeared at the bottom of the stairs and sauntered to him. She wedged herself between his legs, running her hands through his beard and making him look at her. She wore one of his tunics. It reached below her knee, and by the way it fell over her chest, he guessed she wore nothing else underneath. Any other time, he'd delight in taking his time peeling it off her gorgeous body.

Her silvery stare locked with his, yet something dark and vacant muddled the blue. "If you're worried about Todd, you should go and see him."

At his teammate's name, Kade hung his head. "I don't know if I should."

Evelyn brought his face to her chest and wrapped her arms around him. Kade's body relaxed into her hold, and he inhaled his mate's sweet, warm sent as she dragged her fingers through his hair. She was so strong, so kind—despite cutting out a piece of her soul.

"It was an accident," she said. "You didn't mean to hurt him."

Kade shut his eyes and gritted his teeth. Evelyn wasn't wrong. He'd never hurt Todd willingly, but it didn't negate the fact he had.

"It's happened before."

"Your power?"

"Yes, a few times. It's new, and I don't know how to control or wield it. Everyone told me to learn it, but..." Kade couldn't manage to admit he'd been too worried about her. He didn't want to *blame* her. That wasn't it. Instead, he couldn't sort it all out. *One foot in front of the other*, and yet his boots had been filled with stones.

"Why didn't you tell me?" Evelyn asked.

"I think I was ashamed." The words rang true, but hurt, nonetheless.

"You never need to be ashamed of anything. Not with me," she whispered. "I, more than anyone, know what its like to struggle with power or an ability. Talk to me, Kade. I'm here for you, always."

Love weaved with her words and brimmed between their mated souls. Even with her magic gone, their hearts still beat in tandem with each other, the mating bond intact. That magnificent certainty had the power to bring Kade to his knees, and relief washed through him, enough he revealed his fears to Evelyn.

"What if I hurt someone else? What if I hurt you?" He studied her face.

Evelyn cupped his cheek and peered down at him. "Do you remember what you told me in Callum?"

Kade shook his head.

"We'll figure it out," she said.

Kade blinked. Those hadn't been the words he'd expected to hear. Not at all. He wanted to tell her how much he appreciated her, but his tongue seemed as tired as the rest of him, and he couldn't form a single word.

She interpreted his silence as agreement—she kissed his forehead and untangled her hold of him. "Go to the infirmary. Sit with him. No one will hate you for it."

"I don't want to leave you alone," Kade said, grabbing her hips. "Not after what happened."

They studied one another. There was so much to discuss. Her magic. What they'd learned from Opal. Riven's relentlessness. And yet, Kade couldn't focus on any of those things, not with the pulsing in his chest. He *had* to figure that out. He knew that now, and perhaps seeing Todd was the first step.

Evelyn sighed. "I think I'm ready to talk to Tovi."

A breath whooshed out of him. If Evelyn had mustered the courage to talk with Tovi, he had enough courage to enter his village and sit with his teammate.

"Alright," he said. "Let's go."

CHAPTER FIFTY-NINE

EVELYN FOUND TOVI SITTING alone in a bustling tavern Kade had called the Shield-maiden.

She'd hesitated for a moment, tucked out of sight by the entrance. Werewolf warriors mingled as froth dripped over the rims of their mugs. A few cheered as they played a game she'd never seen before with stones and bones in the corner. Others hollered and hummed as a man, tall like Kade and burly like Bétar, played a stout, bulbous guitar. He sang of shield-maidens and the wonders of winter.

Circling her finger around the edge of her own mug, Tovi paid it all no mind, her jade eyes lost in thought.

Evelyn's heart—now absent her magic entirely—hammered inside her chest. It gaped open, the wound still fresh and bruised. Her magic sat, twisting and turning inside the bloodstone around her neck. She hadn't taken it off since they'd left Sven's estate, too nervous to do so. She couldn't help but worry that if she let it go, she'd lose it forever.

She wasn't sure she hadn't already lost it forever.

Reckless.

The moment she'd ripped her flame—her magic, a piece of her soul—out of her body, she'd regretted it. She'd realized then and there, broken in the snow, she'd made a grave mistake. Worse than the one she made two years ago. Both

"

mistakes were similar in a way—she couldn't go backwards and undo what she'd done.

Evelyn inhaled, mustering the courage to face Tovi, and made her way to friend's side.

"Is that beer?" she asked. "Never thought I'd see the day. Always thought you preferred wine."

Tovi's head shot up. Her red, swollen eyes grew wide. She'd been crying, a rare thing for her friend. *Goddess*, the sight of Tovi hurting only reminded Evelyn of the many times Tovi had been there for her. Lies aside, she couldn't forget that Tovi had always had her back. Through every heartache, loss, and laugh. She still felt Tovi's arms around her when she'd sobbed after losing her parents, could still remember Tovi's open, understanding eyes as she listed her worries about Mirella and Blair. The urge to drag Tovi into the biggest, tightest hug overcame her, but she refrained, blinking back into the present.

"What are you doing here?" Tovi asked.

Evelyn rummaged under her cloak and slid a bottle of red wine across the table. "Found this stashed in Kade's cottage."

Tovi peered between her and the bottle, not saying a word. Evelyn tingled with nerves, throat growing thick. Did Tovi not want to talk? Evelyn had been rather difficult to navigate the last week, so she didn't blame Tovi for her hesitancy, but Evelyn had already made her decision.

"Look, I know a bottle of wine won't fix what happened, but I think we should talk," she said. "And I figured we could try over a glass."

Tovi smiled with no teeth, but the twinkle in her eye made Evelyn's heart skip.

"I'd like that."

It took some convincing to secure a corkscrew and suitable glasses, but when Evelyn introduced herself to Lucy, the owner shifted her tone and even offered them the "usual" spot for the Gray Fenris team, tucked back from the rowdiness.

At first, they drank in silence. The ripe currants and black pepper shot straight to Evelyn's knees. She'd imagined the conversation on the walk over here, letting the evening air fuel her muster. Yet now, sitting across from Tovi, the alcohol left her dizzy, and all the words she came up with turned her palms sweaty.

"I'm—"

Both of them spoke at the same time. Evelyn smiled, sheepish, and Tovi forced a laugh.

"Let me go first," Tovi said, pulling her hair to the side, "since I owe you an apology." She inhaled. "I'm sorry I never told you. I have my reasons, but out loud, they're shitty excuses. I should've found a way, but not saying anything, waiting for the prophecy seemed easier. I never imagined Riven would try and take you. I knew he was up to something, I... never thought he'd strike like that."

"Why not tell me in Callum?" Evelyn said. Their reunion. Chats over dinner. Visits to the Runaway Radish. The murders had been steeped with mystery and familiarity, and Evelyn couldn't forget the many opportunities Tovi had ignored in those weeks. "You had to have had your suspicions about Riven."

"I did, but he's clever. Nothing ever traced back to him except McKenna's death. I knew they'd been lovers, but that sort of subject between my brother and I is a tense one. I *am* the reason his wife and child died, and I witnessed a similar pain in him after McKenna. I couldn't bring myself to discuss something that hit so close to home." She swallowed. "You were also happy, Evelyn. For once in years, you weren't faking it."

The wine floated thick on Evelyn's tongue. She *had* been happy in Callum. Despite the murders, she'd begun to make a life—a home, a job, and a relationship that changed her forever. The smell of rain still awakened her muscles, a deep-seated reminder of the new beginning she'd created there. The days following when she discovered who Kade was swam through her mind. Tovi's tenderness and honesty. She remembered her friend *caring*—suffocating the apartment with it.

"Did you know who Kade was?" she asked.

Tovi sipped her wine. "Not at first. Blair's necklace worked, so I couldn't even smell he was a werewolf. But when he took an obvious interest in you, I grew suspicious, and then when he started looking at you like he was falling for you, it was his eyes that gave him away."

"Nadia's eyes," Evelyn said.

Tovi nodded. "Yes. The moment I realized it, I don't know. I couldn't make my decision, and then you figured out who he was on your own. You were in love, and I kept coming back to the prophecy, thinking that perhaps this was it. Once you told me he was your fated, I knew it was you and him."

And then Aster had died. Evelyn's heart grew heavy. Her sweet bubbly friend. Tovi had been there for her then, too. At her side during the burial. The time had been hasty and chaotic, and she didn't blame Tovi for not telling her then—it hadn't been the right time.

"Did you befriend me because of the prophecy?" Evelyn sank into her seat, trying to ignore the sting at the corner of her eyes.

Tovi gripped the table, eyes downcast. "Yes and no. I never intended for us to become friends. Nadia feared for your life because Riven knew what your blood could do, and so I bought a place in Nūa, enrolled in some of the classes and kept tabs on you. That was it. And then one day we sat next to each other, and I noticed everyone staring at you. I've been there, the center of unwanted attention, and I had to say something. And then..." Tovi shook her head.

"We became friends."

"Yes," Tovi said. "None of it was a lie, and I think because it was so real, the harder it was to tell you. I was afraid that once you knew I was a vampyr, I'd lose you."

Evelyn swallowed, wiping away a tear. She'd feared that the most, and to finally hear it aloud as well as the truth in Tovi's words, a weightlessness overcame her. "What about now?" she whispered. Another worry, another fear.

"Now?"

Evelyn shrugged. "Well, I know who you are, the truth of vampyrs and the curse. You don't need to keep tabs on me anymore. You don't need to..." She trailed off, the words stalling on her tongue. Saying them aloud seemed to make them too real.

"I love you like a sister, Evelyn," Tovi said. "I hurt you, and I'll never forgive myself if I lose you as a friend, but that is ultimately your decision, and I'll respect it either way."

A breath shuddered out of Evelyn, her chest cracking. She'd made her decision long before she found Tovi at the Shield-maiden. She'd made it, lying in the snow, with the ache of another mistake rocking through her—she'd understood then what held her back. Shame was a brick wall, and regret was the chain that tied her to it.

"I forgive you."

Tovi straightened and blinked, eyes wide. "What?"

Evelyn leaned back. "I put my magic in the bloodstone."

"I know."

"While I was Riven's captive, I wanted to find something, *do* something that showed my sisters I've changed. When I saw them, I didn't want them to see the girl that ran away two years ago. Maybe if I did something good enough, *brave* enough, it'd be like I never left. I put the magic inside the bloodstone so Riven didn't have the light for the spell, but my desperation to do anything drove me too far."

"We'll get it back, Evelyn. *You* will. If anyone can, it is you."

She smiled, fingers lingering over her pendant. "I plan to. After I gave it up, though, I realized it wasn't about my sisters at all, it was about me. I didn't have the ability to forgive you, not until now because I couldn't even forgive myself. Yes, you lied to me and made mistakes, but our mistakes and past don't define us. I thought I could undo mine. I didn't think you could undo our years of friendship, but the notion held me back from forgiving you."

Tovi tilted her head, a sheen coating her eyes. "You made the best decision at the time, Ev."

Evelyn nodded. "I believe that. I think our present efforts matter, of course, but even the harshest sacrifice doesn't change that I ran. I accepted what you did, and now I don't want to lose you as a friend. I can't. I—"

Tovi moved closer in the booth, grasping Evelyn's hands. "You won't. Thank you for forgiving me. I, too, realized efforts matter, but acceptance is equally important. Because sometimes efforts aren't enough."

"What do you mean?" Evelyn moved closer, and it felt like old times. Seated on her couch, bottle of wine open, talking late into the night. Though, she'd never seen her friend so distant, so sad. Something wormed in her belly, knowing it had nothing to do with them.

"If this is about your efforts in getting me back, they were enough. I'm sorry for being hurtful—"

"I love him."

Evelyn reared back. It was perhaps the most vulnerable and honest Tovi had ever been, and pain laced all three words. She'd suspected her friend had feelings for Kade's brother. That had been a shock all on its own. But the fact it went so deep rooted Evelyn in her chair—she wasn't going anywhere. She'd sit right there and support her friend like she had for years.

"What happened?"

Tovi exhaled. "He witnessed me touched by the curse. It was only a brief moment, but it was enough to see what I'd always feared."

A stone dropped in Evelyn's gut. It was jarring to remember the curse lived in all the vampyrs, even her friend.

"You're more than a vampyr, Tovi."

"I know that now. I didn't try to get you back to gain forgiveness, but a part of me hoped you'd notice my efforts, judge them for what they were, and I hoped the same for Eldrick. But I'm exhausted from trying to show everything I am."

She laid a hand over her heart. "I know who I am and why I do the things I do, and that's enough."

Evelyn swallowed, words thickening in her throat. She'd recklessly placed her magic into the bloodstone. A foolish, rash idea. She too had wanted to be seen, affirmed for her efforts. In the end, it hadn't been worth it, not when she had her reasons for leaving two years ago in the first place. She accepted those reasons and her decision. She'd found forgiveness, enough grace to do so, but not before she cut herself open and ripped something away.

Yet, at her friend's words, warmth trickled through her. She clamped her eyes shut. Evelyn meant what she said—she planned to place her magic back where it belonged, and despite that missing part of her, her heart thumped.

With hope.

She peered at Tovi, sipping her wine. "Have you told him?"

Tovi scoffed and grabbed her own glass. "Goddess, no. But it doesn't matter. I have to focus on securing an alliance with the werewolves."

"That doesn't mean you can't talk to him."

Tovi stared into the maroon in her glass. "What's the point? In the end, I am the Princess of Drystan, and he is the next in line alpha of the Drengr pack. Nothing can come of it. Besides, there are far more important matters. Bringing vampyrs and werewolves together is merely one small feat."

Evelyn sipped her wine. Her eyes grew heavy. Tovi was right, in a way. She hated seeing her friend hurt, but Riven might strike again. At least, they'd evaded the Blood Moon, but there was still an entire prophecy to understand, and a curse left to break. Tiredness clung to Evelyn's bones. They still had so much left ahead.

She reached for Tovi's hand. "Whatever comes next, we're in this together."

Her friend clasped her hand. "Together."

Chapter Sixty

Kade

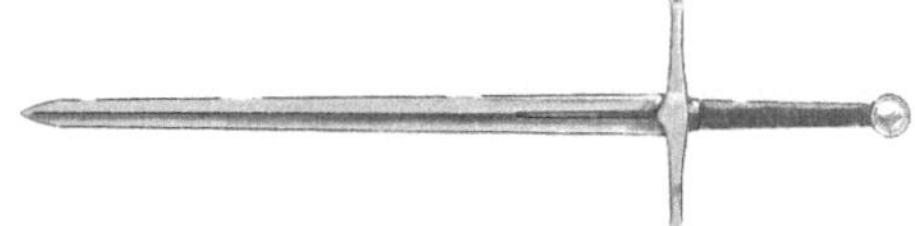

L̄ar's infirmary was in the west wing. The warrior training grounds leading to it were as empty as the night sky, not a cloud in sight. The distant stars twinkled above, twisting and clustering to create the shapes and stories Kade's parents had told him about as a child, their loving voices whispering late into the night.

Lanterns lit the stone hall, the master healer nowhere in sight at his desk as Kade stepped into the building. A center fire crackled on the right, and smoke and embers traveled up and out of the skylight above.

Vacant beds, aside from two, lined the front wall. Linx slept on one, her pink-haired buns bobbing up and down with each breath. Todd lay on his back, still as stone. Ointment bled through the bandages wrapped around his chest. Herbs and oils perfumed the space.

Sleep and home had done Kade's teammate wonders. Color had returned to his cheeks, and the dark circles waned around his eyes. Not that Kade could find any relief. Todd's injury still haunted him.

He rounded the bed, hoping to sit beside his friend but stopped. Yennifer sat against the wall, a bottle of whiskey between her feet. Her wheat hair was unraveled from its usual braid, gold and honey catching the light of the wall's lantern above. The scent of Bétar wafted off her shirt, an oversized tunic borrowed from her mate.

"Couldn't sleep either?" she asked.

Kade sighed. "Not in the slightest."

He squatted to the floor and sat against the bed next to Todd's. His teammate's chest rose and fell so slightly, more worry wormed its way through Kade. His friend's heartbeat thudded away in his chest, his shallow breath ruffling against his wool blanket.

Yennifer handed him the bottle of whiskey, and Kade swigged a shot. The liquid burned down his throat and tickled the hairs in his nose. He coughed and winced, almost losing his eyesight.

"Moons, Yennifer. What is this?"

"Bétar's homemade brew. We like it strong."

"You don't say," Kade whispered.

They sat in silence. The fire hissed, embers retaliating against the cold night. Linx's soft exhale filtered past Todd, and Kade's inside flipped. Her words from a few days ago echoed so loudly the infirmary wasn't silent at all.

Yennifer sighed. "We all know you didn't mean to. It was an accident."

Kade said nothing, a hollowness widening in his chest. They sat in continued silence. The walls closed in on him, and Kade craved to release the shame inside of him.

"I don't know how to do this," he whispered.

"Do what?" Yennifer asked.

"Love her so fiercely and put my duty first. I *can't*, Yennifer. I keep trying to put one foot in front of the other, but I don't know how when all I can think about is protecting her. Sometimes, I think about stealing her away from all of this, but I know that's not who we are, so I keep trying to move on, looking forward to the future we can create together. But then I worry about losing her again... I never want to feel that ever again. I thought staying focused on the future, like I always have, would help me get her back. And now—" Kade gestured towards Todd. "Now, I hurt someone else I care for. I don't know how to handle whatever's growing inside of me."

"Wait, is that what you think? That you lost Evelyn?" Yennifer asked.

Kade stilled, a breath whooshing out of him. He hadn't said that out loud, had he? He wasn't certain he'd even said it to himself in that way either. He remembered the salt on the wind and wooden grooves of the dock, and his declaration to get her back. No matter what. Had he been harboring blame this entire time?

"I don't know. I feel like no matter how many steps forward I take, there's three more to tackle."

Yennifer hesitated, her light-blue eyes softening. "Perhaps it's because you haven't paused and made peace with what happened."

Kade ran his hands through his hair. "I can't sit in the past. I don't want to get stuck. After my mother—"

"I say this lightly, Kade, but your mother's death was different than this. There was a finality to it all. I know you busied yourself with training and missions, but this mission was steeped in the consequences of what had happened on those docks and in the hours prior. With your mother, you *had* to move forward. There was no back. But with Evelyn, perhaps you needed to understand those past moments and come to terms with them before you could move forward at all."

Kade considered Yennifer's words. "What if I can't get this power under control? What if I had left to look for Evelyn five minutes sooner? None of this would've happened. What if I'm not worthy enough to love her?"

"I think those are all valid questions to ask yourself. Of course, you're right. The what-if cycle can be endless. Trust me, Bétar and I used to do plenty of it."

"What do you mean?"

Yennifer sighed. "We'd always talk about *what if* we'd been honest with one another when we realized we were mates. *What if* I hadn't been so stubborn?

What if Bétar had had the courage earlier? We talked through those things, found honesty within our reasons. We stopped looking at the past as a waste of time but lessons to be learned for the future. Reflecting doesn't always have to hold us back, Kade. It can give us peace."

Kade's heart skipped a beat. "I think deep down perhaps I had blamed myself for Evelyn's capture, but I know we were both tricked with Riven's forged letter about my father's death. I can accept the reasons for what happened that day, and in the end, I got Evelyn back, we're together again. Yet, if I linger on my duty, my loyalty is tugged in too many directions. I don't know what guides me anymore, Yennifer."

She sipped her whiskey. "When you came home, you told us what we needed to know for the mission. The details, the land, the threats, our end goal. You never specified a why."

"She's my mate." The words rushed out of Kade. He thought the why was so obvious.

Yennifer tsked, moving closer to him and resting a hand on his. "I know she is Kade, and as another mated werewolf, I know that bond is strong, but its deeper than that. We may be your team, but we're also your family. Tell me about her. Tell me something good, something about your time together in Callum."

Tiny moments flashed through his mind and pulsed against his soul, like they'd been etched into his heart. Her furrowed brow. Those silvery-blue eyes. That laugh she made when she didn't care who heard. How she was thoughtful and kind to others and refused to back down in a fight—magic or not. But Kade didn't land on anything related to her title, witch, Daughter of the Goddess, mate, or otherwise.

He recalled one of the first things he ever learned about *her* and smiled.

"She's not a morning person," Kade said.

Yennifer's eyes went wide with horror. "Oh, dear. I said tell me something good. Not something you'd loathe."

A laugh flew out of him. "It is good."

"What? You've never slept past dawn a day in your life, Commander. How have you handled that?"

"I love it."

Yennifer pulled away, mouth agape. "Love it?"

Kade leaned against the bed, running his hand through his beard. He shrugged. "She slept in, and I made the coffee and the breakfast. It all seemed to work."

Yennifer's shoulders relaxed, a soft smile spreading across her face. "You made breakfast?"

"Pancakes to be exact."

"Stars above." Yennifer smiled and handed him the whiskey. "What else?"

The whiskey burned less fiercely the more Kade sipped, the warmth comforting now. "Evelyn and I worked naturally well together, but she also challenged me. *Moons*, she didn't even want to work with me in the beginning, which was maddening. It made no sense. But when we did work together..." Solving the murders, investigating, talking things through, doing things not as Son of the God or Commander, but as Cyrus Skender.

"Perhaps it's not a matter of duty," Yennifer said. "There's been one constant these past few weeks, even as you've talked about her tonight."

The answer dawned on him. That moment in the commissioner's office. The first time they met. Or in Castle Connacht. The first time she'd admitted to being a witch. He'd said so himself days ago to Evelyn.

He loved her, and it was his heart that lead him forward.

Nothing less, nothing more.

Neglecting the past had manifested itself into physical anxiety, creating a war inside of Kade despite how severely he believed in his duty. Because it was so much more than that, wasn't it?

Love.

A weight slipped from Kade's shoulder. The word, the feeling was a better, more powerful thing to grasp, especially when they had so much ahead. As strong and unyielding as a Vadon Mountain blade, Kade grasped hold onto it and anchored himself.

"I forgot how wise you are, Yennifer," he said, lips turning upward.

She laughed. "Well, here's more wisdom for you: learn that power of yours. I also think you have an excellent teacher to show you the ins and outs of a magic like that."

Evelyn.

He'd be honored if she taught how to use this power, but they'd need to set course on getting hers back.

"As long as you promise not to use me as target practice again," Todd grumbled from his bed, "I also suggest you learn that power. Speaking from experience, it really packs a punch."

Kade scrambled to Todd's side, leaning over his friend. "*Moons*, I'm so sorry for what I did."

Todd chuckled, wincing slightly as his chest shook. "Don't worry about it. Now I can brag about this impressive scar and how the Son of the God gave it to me. Ladies will love it."

"Ladies would never believe that story," Linx said, yawning as she sat up. She tiptoed from her bed and checked under Todd's bandage. Her shoulders relaxed slightly as she put the bandage back in place. "Haven't you read the papers? Kade does no wrong."

Linx's usual sarcasm rang in her in her tone. Her perusal landed on Kade, and he gave her a small smile.

"The issue there is," Bétar called from the infirmary's doorway, "is that Todd can't read."

Todd squirmed on his bed roll, fighting to sit up but slumped backed down once he realized he didn't have the strength.

"I can read, thank you, and on the contrary, Kade does wrong on occasion."

"*Stars above*, Todd!" Yennifer leapt to her feet. "You don't need to rub it in."

Bétar joined her side, pulling his mate towards him and planting a kiss on her temple. He whispered something in her ear, too low for anyone to hear, and Yennifer relaxed against his chest.

Kade locked eyes with his weapons master. "Todd's right. What happened was my fault, and I'm sorry for it."

"I'm sorry, too, for what I said," Linx whispered.

Each pent-up muscle in Kade relaxed. He gave Linx a soft smile. "It's alright. We were all frightened."

Todd nudged Linx's elbow and wiggled his brows. "Don't worry. Yennifer gave him a proper chat about matters of the heart."

Yennifer cursed. "Were you listening this whole time?"

Todd huffed. "How could I not? The two of you are absolute shit at whispering."

Bétar barked out a laugh and slammed his mouth shut as Yennifer's eyes narrowed, shooting him a look as sharp as arrows. "What? You whispering? That's funny."

"Oh dear," a small, but sweet voice said from the doorway.

The entire team turned. Belle stood, basket in hand. She wore fresh clothes, werewolf-style tunic and trousers, while her hair had been pulled to the side and tied in a loose braid, ringlets sticking out every few knots.

"I hope I'm not interrupting a team meeting." She lifted the basket, a blush climbing up her neck. "I thought I'd come check on Todd—I mean you, you're awake. To give Linx a break of course. That's all. Oh! I also brought soup and some bread. If you're hungry, that is."

The team fell silent, not a joke from a single one of them. Kade peered at Todd, but his dark eyes were locked on Belle, transfixed. Linx shared a knowing smile with Kade, and the two fought back laughter.

"That is a lovely idea." Linx rose, gathering her things. "Todd is an exhausting patient, and I need my rest."

"As do I," Yennifer said.

"Actually, I think you came at the right time," Kade said, backing away from Todd's cot. "We were all headed out."

Belle beamed, a radiant smile brightening her face. She sauntered over, taking Linx's place. Todd and Belle stared at each other, and Kade caught himself glancing backwards three times as they left.

"Bétar, I think your brew is a little too strong," he said.

His second bumped his shoulder. "Nothing wrong with my brew or your sights. It appears the witch is smitten with him."

"Do you think he'll notice?" Linx hissed as they headed out of the training grounds and into the bustle of village nightlife.

"Kade only cut him open. He didn't blind him," Yennifer said.

Kade threw his head back, praying to the stars above. "I'm never going to hear the end of this, will I?"

"What sort of team would we be if we didn't keep you in check?" Bétar said.

All four of them laughed, and Kade threw his arm around his second, inhaling the promise of what was to come, and finding the peace in yesterday.

CHAPTER SIXTY-ONE

ELDRICK BLINKED AGAINST THE sun. Not a single cloud drifted through the sky, not an inch of gray for miles against the bright blue. Winter still sat in the air, but his wolf pranced and jumped in the sounds and sights of home. No curse, no clouds. Eldrick inhaled the vibrancy of the Vadon Mountains as he stood at the foot of Lār.

A few paces away, Kade and Bétar clasped forearms, saying their goodbyes.

"Send word, won't you?" Bétar said.

"It won't be too long," Eldrick said, joining them.

Kade smiled at his brother. "A month at most."

The day prior, they'd all gathered to discuss with Aramis and Claus about what they'd learned in Drystan and what came next. Kade and Evelyn would head east to the city of witches. If there was any research on how to get her magic *out* of the bloodstone, the Nūa library possessed it. Evelyn had also admitted it was time she returned home after being gone for so long. Kade hadn't objected, and in fact, stepped down as commander of the Gray Fenris and passed the title onto Bétar.

They'd decided to all reconvene at the end of the month with hopes Evelyn had gotten her magic back and they'd researched more of the prophecy thanks to her sister, Blair. In the meantime, Eldrick and his father planned to hold council, hosting the pack alphas to discuss the curse, the entirety of the prophecy, the missing werewolves, and the secured alliance with Princess Tovi Verena.

Their newest ally rounded the corner. Eldrick and Tovi hadn't spoken a word to one another since Sven's estate. They'd barely been in the same vicinity, aside from the planning session the day before, but Tovi had pretended as if he weren't there, never once making eye contact. He wasn't sure what hurt worse, the fact he'd caused the rift between them or her ability to move on so quickly. Between Evelyn and Yen, she smiled, nose scrunching as she laughed. The three had fallen into a natural friendship, and, according to Lucy, had racked up a tab at the Shield-maiden steep enough to compete with him and his brothers.

Eldrick sighed, shifting his attention to Kade. "I wrote to Lorkan and sent a missive this morning."

"Did you mention Mother?" Kade asked, amber eyes sad.

Eldrick sighed. "No. I thought it too great a risk to put it in writing, but I urged him to return home soon, that he was needed here. I'll tell him in person."

Other than the Gray Fenris, Kade and Eldrick had chosen to tell only their father that Nadia was still alive. As far as they knew, she was still a spy in Riven's court, and they intended to honor her wishes and duty until she returned home.

Behind Eldrick, Aramis ascended the stairs of Lār without a cane. Ever since learning his mate was alive, he had more pep to his step. Silver still lined his hair, but Eldrick wondered if the distance between mates had caused his ailments. How and when they saw his mother next, Eldrick wasn't sure, but his father's eyes shone with a new hope that had long been extinguished.

Kade and his father embraced, whispering their farewells and mumbling about leading with his heart. Kade's eyes glistened with understanding. They parted as Evelyn approached. The bloodstone resting on her chest had shifted to a shade of molten orange. Eldrick had only known Evelyn for a short while, but he admired her ability to keep going, despite whatever she faced. The last weeks had been difficult for all of them, but especially her.

She smiled at him. "I'm a little disappointed we can't tease Kade endlessly together."

"Same. I was looking forward to some little-sister bonding time."

Kade grumbled while Bleu beside him stomped his hoof like he agreed. Maxie weaved between his brother's legs, clearly picking a side.

"Traitor," Evelyn whispered.

The three laughed, and Eldrick brought Evelyn into a hug. It all felt too fast. A short time ago, he'd gotten his brother back, and duty, the prophecy, and the security of their homeland tugged them all in different directions.

"Take care of yourselves," he said to both of them.

Evelyn grasped his elbows. "I shouldn't meddle, but I think it's easy to forget Tovi's hurt is older than all our years combined. She won't make the first move, Eldrick, and if you don't want to lose her, talk to her."

Eldrick swallowed, but Evelyn had already swung atop Bleu and Kade had shifted into his wolf form before he could respond. The two headed out, and the rest of them waved their goodbyes and watched them leave until they passed under the village's gate.

Ahead, Yennifer dragged Tovi towards Drengr shops. The two mingled, laughing about something Yennifer had whispered into Tovi's ear. Eldrick drifted back to that day he first saw her, enchanted by her ethereal presence. She'd been standing between the same two vendors. Her hair had reminded him of the snow-capped mountains and those jade eyes had calmed his breath to a steady, even rhythm. He enjoyed her teasing tone, pushing his usually stern buttons. He grew excited at her secrets, because it meant there was more to learn about her, and he wanted to learn all he could. The good, the bad, the ugly, the wins, the losses, *all of it*.

He—

Eldrick shut his eyes.

One, two.

He wouldn't say a word. He wouldn't dare. He hadn't meant to hurt her or react so badly, and he hadn't meant to throw her cursed existence in her face. It didn't matter what she was or how the curse had changed her. Eldrick's heart knew she was no monster. It beat against the memory of her at Sven's farm, fighting fang and claw like a beast. She'd been fighting to save Eldrick, after all.

"She's a fighter," his father whispered. "There's no doubt about that."

Eldrick followed Aramis's line of sight. His throat closed. He feared if he agreed, he'd spill the secrets of his heart onto the ground.

His father clasped his shoulder. "Never fear the decisions we make from the heart. Those are usually the ones we're meant to make."

Before Eldrick met Tovi, he would've disagreed, but as he stared down at her, catching a glimpse of that breathtaking smile as she talked with a shopkeeper, he believed his father's words to be true. Not solely because of what he'd experienced with Tovi, but what he'd witnessed around him. The Gray Fenris's bond. Kade and Evelyn. Feelings, strong and deep, brought them together, made them stronger. They'd need it all with whatever came next.

"Thank you," he said, turning towards the stairs of Lār.

"Eldrick," his father said.

He stopped, not because of his name, but because of the tone his father used. Soft, endearing. Their eyes, the same green, met.

"I'm proud of you," his father said. "I don't tell you it enough. And if it is still something you want, I'd proudly allow you to ascend as alpha of the Drengr pack. We can announce it at the end of council."

The words Eldrick had wanted to hear for years brought nothing but joy to his entire being. His muscles zapped awake, yet he wished Tovi was hearing the news at his side. His father's approval, his words, finally made Eldrick realize he needed to speak with her.

"Thank you," he said, his words thick. "Let's discuss it this evening."

His father nodded, a small smile on his lips. "Your mother would be proud, too. I can feel it."

Eldrick swallowed, nodded, and headed off in the direction of the vampyr princess. His heart led him to her, the pull tugging him through the street to a leather maker's shop. Yennifer spied him over a shelf, her brow raising.

"Magu."

Beside her, Tovi stilled, hands halting over a set of fighting leathers. She blinked at the archer.

Yennifer winked. "I'll meet you at the Shield-maiden later. Be sure to drag Lou along!"

Tovi's eyes begged a direct *No!* but Yennifer scurried off regardless, leaving them alone. Tovi didn't pay him any mind, moving to the next vendor.

"Wait." He sidestepped her, blocking her path. "Can we talk?"

She opened her mouth and closed it. Her stare said enough. War raged in it, along with anger and hurt.

Stars above, maybe this had been a bad idea.

She made her way into the street. "There isn't anything to discuss."

Eldrick grabbed her wrist, halting her retreat. "Tovi, please."

He'd come here to say only a few words, and he didn't care how she responded. He simply needed to say them.

Tovi exhaled, her chest rising and falling. Tension, worse than it had ever been, buzzed between them like a thousand voices screaming whatever was unsaid.

"Eldrick—"

"I'm sorry."

Tovi's mouth fell open. She studied his face. As quickly as it had softened, her face hardened.

"Okay."

"Okay?"

That wasn't enough. He wanted more. *Needed* more. The thought of losing her drove him mad. He'd give up anything, he realized. Anything in this world. The sense it was too late crept over his inner wolf.

"There's nothing more between us, Eldrick," she said. "It's done."

Cold, agonizing fear shot through him. "I—"

"We'll go into the council as allies, yes?"

He stilled. That had been established during their meeting yesterday, along with his father and Claus present.

This had been the very thing she'd come here asking for. An alliance against her brother. What a fool he'd been to deny her, to see her only as a vampyr, his enemy. He'd been wrong. That she was a vampyr wasn't enough to determine anything. Because facts and logic weren't enough to make sound decisions. Getting to know her, learning about her, that had been enough and the beat of his heart, his instinct about her was enough, too.

"Yes, but you already know that."

Tovi gave a curt nod. "I'm a princess, you are an alpha, Eldrick. Nothing can get in the way of us being allies."

Eldrick's being deflated. A sharp pain lodged between his ribs, but he accepted her decision. She'd always be more to him than an ally against the darkness. Eldrick recognized his emotions, but he wasn't sure how to articulate them. He didn't have the stomach or courage to say it out loud, and it was clear this strong, proud, beautiful woman had given up on him.

"Alright."

Tovi retreated backward, leaving him stone and frozen to the muddy ground. "Thank you, Alpha Drengr."

Not Eldrick. Not wolf.

She fell into the throngs of the village, gone, and the reality he'd lost her forever carved itself across Eldrick's heart.

CHAPTER SIXTY-TWO

THE GREAT HALL OF Lār brimmed with wolfish energy. Arguments and whispers laced with frustration boomed against the stone walls. The council had begun early that morning, and yet as the noon sun reached through the tall window behind Eldrick and his father, so many questions and accusations continued.

Tovi stared, silent and observant.

Yennifer sat to her right, Bétar beside her. Todd still recovered from his injuries, and Linx had chosen to stay with him. Lou, without a bloodstone, remained at the Shield-maiden with Lucy, staying clear of the sun. Belle, on the other hand, had offered her accounts of Drystan to negate any naysayers. Tovi appreciated her efforts and had been impressed by the young witch's ability to face burly, indignant werewolves when they'd challenged her stories. Belle hadn't balked once.

With the ease and calm of a true leader, Eldrick had updated the alphas on the missing werewolves and the Lone Wolf. Sitting beside him, his father had supported his claims. Murmurs amongst the other alphas had worsened when he shed light on the vampyr curse. Once he spoke of the full prophecy, the energy shifted. Murmurs rippled across the room, rising higher and higher until an insult hit Eldrick like an arrow.

"Blasphemy!"

"Heretic!"

Tovi could not tell who flung the accusations. She gripped the arm of her chair, wood groaning. But Eldrick wasn't fazed. He wore finer clothes than he had during their travels—an all-black ensemble with black leather buckles lining the center of his quilted vest, fastening it tight across his lean frame. A sewn insignia over his heart was the only symbol of Drengr blue. A tight black tunic lined the curve of his arm's muscles as he clasped his hands behind his back, and his boots clanged against the stone as he entered the center of the hall. Tovi's heart skipped at the sight, and his gem eyes flicked over her.

"I understand the news you've learned today is difficult to accept, but place your doubts aside. We must prepare for the conflict to come."

"If this supposed Blood Moon has passed, what more do we have to fear from Prince Riven?" an alpha yelled.

"He will not stop," Tovi said. "The Blood Goddess is pulling his strings like a puppet. *She* is the true threat, and therefore we must be prepared for Riven to strike sooner or later."

"*We*? It's an absolute disgrace you sit in this hall, vampyr." He spat on the stone, and other alphas nodded their agreement.

Eldrick's jaw ticked. He stalked down the hall's center, stopping yards away from where the alpha sat.

"Alpha Johannes, you will regard Princess Tovi with respect."

The werewolf rose out of his seat. "I'll do no such—"

A younger werewolf, one Tovi recognized, stood up and grabbed the alpha's arm.

"Father, if it were not for her, I would not be home."

Sam Johannes.

He was one of the werewolves they'd set free and sent through the underground with Flynn. Relief washed through her to see him safe. She searched the rest of the werewolves gathered and found another standing. Beside her, a female alpha stared with pride in her eyes.

Siv Drabek.

"Sam is right. Tovi secured our passage home. We owe her our lives."

Those of the Drabek pack all nodded towards Tovi. Her shoulders straightened, and she nodded in return. For once, in a hall with so many others, respect vibrated through Tovi. More werewolves stood, others she didn't recognize, but those who must've been set free from the fighting rings. Murmurs of gratitude and hope filtered through the hall.

The air shifted. Eldrick's gaze found hers. The two stared at the other, like so many times before, finding a constant in the chaos.

The hall's doors groaned open, fracturing the peace the gathering had found.

Claus strode in, blood and sweat splattered across his face. He dragged a man behind him—someone else Tovi recognized. The human mercenary they'd let go in Drystan. The Gray Fenris erupted from their seats, and Tovi stepped from hers. *This* man had tried to kill Eldrick, and her hackles rose.

"How in the stars did Claus find him?" Yennifer whispered, joining her side.

Tovi shared a similar question. Unease swam in her gut.

Eldrick met his uncle halfway, rushing to meet him. Claus threw the bound mercenary at his feet while the rest of his uncle's team funneled from the door, stationing themselves throughout the hall. For the second time, the air shifted, and Tovi's animal side detected a threat, her spine itched, like a predator stalked from behind, and yet, her focus only settled on the mercenary heaving in the center of the hall.

"Claus, what is the meaning of this?" Eldrick asked.

His uncle paced, locking eyes with each of the alphas. "My nephew has at this point told you about the Lone Wolf, yes?"

Agreement hummed amongst the werewolves.

"It may seem an enemy is in our mist, but after Eldrick told me all he learned, I refused to believe a werewolf would do such a thing. We've been at peace for centuries, have we not?"

Werewolves howled and thumped their hands against the chairs.

Claus held up his hand, silencing them all. He looked to Eldrick.

"My team and I found this man gambling the money he received, bragging he hadn't even needed to kill you to keep the coin."

Eldrick remained calm, but Tovi caught the twitch in his jaw. She peered at Yennifer and Bétar, the two shared a worrisome glance with her.

"I don't like this," Belle whispered beside her, and Tovi agreed.

"But I found something far better," Claus said. "An actual name. Not a code, but the one who has been taking our werewolves and who wanted the next Drengr Alpha dead."

The werewolves began to whisper, and Tovi's heart raced with anticipation.

"Who?" Aramis had stood out of his chair.

Tovi snapped her attention back to Claus.

Who stared directly at her. He gripped the hair of the mercenary and yanked him back. "Tell them! Who hired you?"

With a shaky hand, the man pointed straight at Tovi. "It was her! She hired us!"

The hall exploded into growls. The sound of dozens of werewolves rumbled through it.

"What?" Tovi hissed, stepping back as if the accusation hit her physically. "That is a lie!"

"He's wrong!" Yennifer shouted, shielding Tovi.

Tovi tried to make her way towards Eldrick, but hands grabbed her arms from behind. She struggled, but it was too late. Claus's men had surrounded her. Belle fought to get to her, rushing water at her assailants, but two werewolves tackled the witch to the ground.

"Stop!" Tovi cried.

Those holding her had an unrelenting grip, and they dragged her to the head of the hall, steps away from Aramis and the Drengr Alpha's seats. His expression was stone, eyes wide as he watched her with distrust.

"Unhand me!" she shouted.

"Claus," Eldrick said. Evenly, stoic. It was impossible to read his tone, and as she pushed against those that held her firm, she couldn't make him out in the frenzy of werewolves.

"Stop!" Bétar roared, hand going to the hilt of his sword.

Other werewolves reached for theirs, growling at the Gray Fenris's new commander. Yennifer joined his side, approaching Tovi. But Yen and Bétar were intercepted by werewolves who'd chosen Claus's side. They pushed them back near their seats. Yennifer's eyes met Tovi's, wide and blue and frightened.

Tovi cried out as someone kicked the back of her knees and they hit the stone floor. Anger rippled through her, and she didn't stop pulling and tugging against those who held her firmly to the ground. She hissed, baring her fangs.

Werewolves growled again, swords ringing as they were unsheathed.

"Don't you see. There isn't an enemy amongst us. It is a plot, a ploy to deter us from the real enemy. *Her.*" Claus jabbed a finger in her direction.

"You're a liar!" Tovi cried. "It is not true! Eldrick, you know this!"

For the first time since the chaos happened, their gazes connected.

And Tovi's heart sank.

Wrath encompassed him. Every last muscle of his lean frame twitched with it. Hatred, loathing, malice. All of it warred in his beautiful gaze.

All for her.

"Are you certain?" he said, calm and deadly.

"Eldrick." Tovi's eyes stung. A tear fell down her cheek. Did he really believe his uncle? After everything?

Claus grunted at the mercenary.

"Tell him."

"During the night of the attack, she met me and my team at an establishment with dancers. She told us where you and your team were staying and to follow once you all left Drystan."

The words were a lie, but they were damning all the same—Tovi had never shared with Eldrick exactly where she'd gone that night or what came of finding her brother. For all he knew, it had all been a ruse, a ploy to get away from him.

"It's not true." The words slipped from Tovi like her last breath. "It's not true!"

She tried with all her might to escape the hold of those who held her down, but she couldn't. They'd added a fourth werewolf, two seizing her on each side. Eldrick wouldn't look at her, his gem eyes darkened, staring at the stone floor.

She peered over to Yennifer and Bétar. "It's not true."

Yennifer gave her a curt not, and Bétar mouthed, "We know." They believed her. She felt it in their stares, but her heart broke as the one man she needed to trust her wouldn't even *look* at her.

"I see," Eldrick finally said.

His words were absolute, a deafening gavel resounding of her fate.

Something in Tovi snapped. Her tears ceased. Her heartbeat evened out. Her shoulders snapped back.

A hundred eyes stared at her, and she didn't feel a goddamn one. For the first time in Tovi's life, she didn't give a fuck what they saw, thought, or *judged.* These were lies. She *wasn't* the Lone Wolf. Yet, she was so, so, so tired of trying to make the rest of the world see who she'd become. She'd changed. She knew she had. All these years. The secrets. The allies. The plots. The betrayals. *Bloody hel,* she'd cared so deeply for her people. She cared for this continent and its well-being. She cared so fiercely it thrummed like war drums in her veins.

Perhaps it didn't matter if the world or Eldrick saw it.

"She must pay for her crimes!" an alpha shouted.

Eldrick retrieved his axe and started prowling towards her. The resolve to make him see vanished. It didn't matter anymore.

All that mattered was that Tovi knew. She believed she'd changed, and as she took her last shaky breath, she appreciated the mistakes of her past. She didn't loathe them. She loved who she'd become through it all and without them, she wouldn't be who she was.

Who gave a *bloody hel* what anyone saw or judged her for?

Eldrick stopped, a few yards between them left, the edge of his axe glinting in the sunlight escaping into the hall.

With her head held high, Tovi accepted her fate. She met Eldrick's stare head-on.

Kill me, I dare you.

Tovi didn't stand proud for anyone else. It wasn't armor, it wasn't a defense. It was her, purely, infinitely, wildly her.

Strong, fierce, and loyal.

Chapter Sixty-Three

Eldrick

Hate marred Tovi's beautiful eyes, and Eldrick's heart broke.

"Keep her steady," he said, words like shards of glass in his throat. He swallowed the pain. Kept up his ruse. Schooled himself to appear passive and stoic.

As if he didn't care. As if the vampyr his heart beat for didn't face a hall full of those ready to end her life.

He stepped closer to the front of the hall, closer to *her*, placing himself between Tovi and Claus. Purposeful, tactful. A small movement no one else batted an eye against. But his muscles shook. His wolf raged at the sight of the vampyr princess on her knees, she too shook with rage and ire, all directed at him.

It's all right, dove, he wanted to say, but couldn't. His insides churned so violently he threatened to empty them onto the stone floor.

One, two.

Eldrick couldn't look away, didn't dare break his stare with her for a second, wishing, *begging*, hoping she saw his true intent shining in his gaze back to her.

"Uncle," Eldrick said, evenly, cool, though his heart raced, and body flushed cold. "For so many years, I've looked to you for guidance. How do you suggest we proceed? She's the princess, after all."

Bait. Eldrick dangled the question, knowing full well what his uncle would suggest. Lies. All of it had been lies—his uncle's teachings, the push to leave and prove he could be alpha. Eldrick's wrath was ice. His wolf was chaos and fury. Pushing and howling to be set free. Eldrick had *felt* the deceit the moment his uncle had thrown the mercenary at his feet. Weeks ago, hesitation would've cost Tovi her life, but today, Eldrick trusted his intuition.

Other alphas screamed for retribution. For the dungeons. For death. Eldrick's wolf growled. He wasn't sure what was more difficult—reining in his beast or witnessing Tovi hate him, believing he'd hurt her. Did he play the part well? Or worse, was her perception of him not that far from this truth?

Behind him, Claus stomped against the stone floor as he approached. "Her death may start a war, but war is inevitable, isn't it? Remove the princess, the true heir to the throne, and we weaken our opponent."

Tovi pushed against those who held her steady. *Moons*, he needed her still, calm.

"Hold her!" Eldrick growled, his composure moments from fracturing. He stepped closer again, minding his distance between her and Claus.

"Eldrick, you can't do this!" Bétar shouted.

His stomach roiled at his friends words. He didn't look to him, didn't have time to make him see. Sweat prickled on his palms, and the leather wrapped around the shaft of his axe strained against his hold.

"I'll kill her," Claus said, unsheathing his sword. "If it is too difficult for you to do, given your history with her."

"No." Eldrick's Alpha baritone rang through the hall—too harsh, too angry. He rallied it in as he said, "I'll do it."

Eldrick finished the distance between him and Tovi. He fought the shake in his hand as he steadied his axe against her bare flesh. It may as well have been piercing him, wedged between his ribs.

She didn't falter. She didn't even blink. The fracture in his heart tore wider as tears welled in her beautiful eyes. Fate had an interesting way of writing beginnings and endings—they'd stood like this before.

Time slowed as voices rang out behind him. Bétar shouted for him to stop. Claus's team held him and the rest of the Gray Fenris back. Yennifer cried. Even his father begged him to reconsider.

He paid them no mind, focusing on the vampyr under his blade. He gripped her chin. *Please, dove. Look at me.* Silent tears started streaming down her face, and Tovi's anguish grasped Eldrick's heart and strangled it. He caressed her throat with the pad of his thumb. Softly, sweetly. The thrum of her pulse calmed him, rooted him.

Never fear the decisions we make from the heart.

"If I am to be alpha, I must be willing to do what it takes to protect my pack." He bent down to the shell of her ear. "And the woman I love."

Tovi sucked in a breath, and Eldrick moved. His axe slit the throat of the werewolf on the right first. He embedded his next blow in the left's shoulder. The two remaining let Tovi go, grasping hold of their weapons. Eldrick threw his axe. It landed in one's chest, and before the last fled, he drew the weapon from one of the fallen and sliced the male down.

Blood slicked the floors, and four dead bodies lay around them.

In two long strides, Eldrick tugged his axe out of the werewolf's chest. He whirled, pointing it at Claus. "How dare you lie in the hall of my home?"

Everyone had risen from their seats. Confusion filled Lār with static. The Gray Fenris stared, mouths agape. Alphas jumped their attention between him and his uncle.

"You killed your own kind for her? What kind of alpha are you?" Claus shouted.

"A kind that trusts his instincts!" Eldrick growled.

"You are weak! Like your father!" Claus said.

Werewolves gasped around them. Eldrick paid them no mind, helping Tovi rise. She placed her hand in his, peering up at him under long lashes. Eldrick swallowed, his heart skipping a beat. With her looking at him like that and the feel of her skin against his, he knew right then, he'd do more than kill his kind for her. The steely, wild emotion didn't frighten him.

It fueled him and his wolf.

Eldrick addressed the packs. "Tovi Verena has saved my life on more than one occasion these past few weeks. I've witnessed her kindness, loyalty, and devotion to not only her people, but to this continent. What is more important, though, is I have *felt* all of these things from her. It has not only been her actions I have witnessed, but her heart."

Eldrick's own heart ballooned at the words.

Claus's shoulders vibrated, his wolf edging at the surface. "She has poisoned your mind!"

"The only poison here is you, Claus," a smooth, stern woman's voice said.

Everyone's attention spun towards the end of the hall. Tovi gasped, and behind them, Eldrick's father sobbed.

Nadia Drengr, his mother, stood in the doorway. Shock soaked the air. Alphas rushed from their seats, crowding around each other at a chance to get a better glimpse of her as she strode towards Claus. With all the news they'd revealed today, the fact the female Drengr Alpha had lived, had not been one.

"Stars above."

One werewolf in particular, Eldrick's father, stood on shaky legs. Disbelief and wonder fell over his face, and Aramis Drengr appeared more alive than he had in over a decade. Nadia's attention fell on him for a moment. A small tug of her lips. Sheen coating her eyes.

Eldrick's chest swelled, snapping his shoulders straighter and taller. His mother was back in the halls of the Drengr Village. Their home. She stood like a fierce warrior, as if that part of her had never been gone. Black fighting leathers, dark hair braided to the side. Golden eyes as sharp as the axe fastened to her belt. He knew she was alive, had found relief with that fact, but seeing her back at Lār far sooner than he ever imagined had him rejuvenated with adrenaline. It was more real than ever, and Eldrick sent a small pray of thanks to the Moon God.

His mother focused back on Claus.

Eldrick pulled Tovi with him, unable to let the vampyr princess out of his hold or sights. His uncle's chest rose and fell, and he spun wildly as he realized Eldrick and his mother had him locked between them.

Nadia thrust a wooden chest at Claus's his feet. Coin burst from its chambers—*Drystan* coin. Next she thrust letters atop the gleaming gold. A symbol snagged Eldrick's memory.

A growl rumbled through his chest. "You're the Lone Wolf."

Claus gritted his teeth, eyes downcast on the upside down pawprint. "That is an appalling accusation. I have been nothing but loyal to my kind!"

"I found all of this in your quarters, Claus. Try and deny it," Nadia said. "Once you learned Eldrick hadn't been killed, you went looking for an explanation as to why the job hadn't been done. Lucky for you, this mercenary was a sleaze, already spending his unearned coin at the very establishment you had him lie about. Again, try and deny it, but I witnessed your little conversation. I've been trailing you ever since you left Drystan."

Eldrick's heart hammered in his chest. Beside him, Tovi bent down, grasping hold of a letter. Claus moved to swipe it from her hand, but Eldrick blocked him, baring his teeth.

"The Lone Wolf—I'm delighted to hear your next shipment of werewolves will consist of alpha blood. It's a shame you can't join us and enjoy the fights and splendor your business brings to court. Nothing thrills me more to hear your continued—" Tovi glanced at Eldrick. He nodded for her to go on. "Your continued efforts in ailing your brother are still going as planned. Once your nephew ascends, name the price and I'll happily pay it to have the Drengr pack eliminated entirely. Sincerely, Princess Visha."

Tovi's hand trembled as she lowered the letter. No gasps. No murmurs. No growls. The hall was silent, eerie as the beasts all focused on the same prey. Cold dripped over Eldrick's skin, and his wolf snarled.

Nadia reached inside her pocket and retrieved a vile. Eldrick sniffed and a sweet, earthy aroma filled his nose. It sickened him.

"Wolfsbane."

Eldrick released Tovi's hand and lunged at Claus. His uncle was faster, pivoting out of reach. Tovi moved after him next, but Claus backhanded her across the face. Blood splattered over the stone, and Eldrick saw red. His hands shifted to claws, and his teeth sharpened.

He advanced. Claus stumbled, whirling with his sword in circles as others advanced, too.

"Why?" Eldrick demanded, half wolf, half man.

His uncle's dark stare flicked over to his mother.

Eldrick blinked, swallowing bile. "You knew she was alive?"

His uncle sneered. "I hoped she wasn't herself. That turning into a vampyr changed her, breaking the mating bond with your father."

"You sold werewolves to gain favor into court, didn't you?" Tovi said.

"I wanted to get close to her. She should've been mine!" Claus roared.

He moved to run but halted. Yennifer emerged from the crowd, bow knocked and arrowhead glinting from the afternoon sun. Pointed straight at Claus's nose. His uncle backed away and then spun. Yennifer pulled the string but stopped.

Eldrick's uncle had made it up to the steps to the hall's front. He held Aramis in his arms, claws out and against his father's neck.

"No!" Eldrick ran, but a black mass raced passed him.

The slim silhouette, all black fur, grabbed hold of Claus by the arm and thrust him across the hall. His body flew through the air, and Eldrick's mother, shifted in her werewolf form but *different*, bared her sharper, slimmer teeth.

Fangs.

Her fur was glossier, darker. Red warped against the gold in her eyes, and her claws, now black talons, clanked against the stone as she approached Claus. She was still a werewolf as well as part vampyr.

Claus crawled straight into Eldrick's shins. He grabbed his uncle's beefy neck, forcing him still. Tovi joined his side and passed him the vile. His uncle struggled, but Eldrick only tightened his hold.

He didn't peer at this father for permission. He didn't glance at Tovi, either. Eldrick's instinct screamed vengeance, and as a leader, he couldn't let this go. Not when his life, his father's, and so many others had been threatened. *Lost.* In this instance, he ignored the facts completely, because this may have been his uncle, but he didn't know this man at all.

Eldrick yanked his uncle's head and shoved the entire contents of the wolfsbane's vile down his throat. Satisfied enough had traveled down his gullet, he released Claus. His uncle groaned against the pain, and his body writhed as his face grew bulbous and red. He clawed at his throat, back arching against the stone until he stilled completely, dead and gone.

There was a beat of deafening silence in the presence of fresh death, and Eldrick's instinct snapped his attention to the woman he loved. She was already staring at him, and the horridness of the last few moments fell away. Death didn't linger. Neither did pain etch his heart. There was only her, keeping him grounded, steady and strong.

They reached each other in two long strides as the hall erupted around them. Yet, Eldrick didn't hear the shouts of alphas or the commotion near his uncle's dead body. He lay his brow onto Tovi's, shutting his eyes so he could fill his lungs with plum and lilac scent, listen to the beat of her heart.

She was his constant in the chaos.

CHAPTER SIXTY-FOUR

DUSK IN THE VADON Mountains had turned into Tovi's favorite hour.

The sun dropped between the wedge of two mountains, orange and white stretching across the army of pines, redwoods, and evergreens. Songbirds fleeted across a sky that bled indigo on one end, daylight blue the other. When Tovi inhaled, the air was crisp and fresh, not the nibbling bites of a cold curse.

After Claus's death, the council had shifted their attention to Nadia. She'd not only returned home to protect her son and save her mate, but she'd returned for good. Happiness chimed through Tovi like the bluebird's song. Relieved for her friend, a decade chapter of her past seemed to snap shut, so Tovi soaked in the dusk, relishing in the promise of tomorrow's dawn, a new start for the Drengr pack.

Steps approached behind her, and Tovi didn't need to turn to catch Eldrick making his way across the training grounds. It was the emptiest part of Lār, and seeing as the female Drengr Alpha had returned, the village was brimming with celebration. Tovi craved peace and stillness, both of which came in the presence of Eldrick.

Lemon and basil overtook the dirt and sap, and the rivets of dark green in his eyes brightened under the sun's perusal. He joined her atop the picnic table she sat on. The higher ground gave a better view of the forest and mountains. Despite the beauty of the hour, she found herself lost to another beauty, a beastly kind that sang to her soul.

When Eldrick finally looked at Tovi, a breath rushed out of her.

"I trust your mother is settling in nicely," she said, averting her gaze.

"Yes. Well, she and my father disappeared, and I'd rather not think about what that entails."

Tovi smiled. "I imagine we might not see them for days."

Eldrick grimaced. "Again, I'd rather not think about it."

Tovi laughed so hard, her cheeks ached like a bruise, but she stilled her excitement for her friend for a moment and assessed Eldrick.

"How are you doing?" she asked. She'd not witnessed hesitation when he'd killed Claus, but the loss of family, no matter the complicated circumstances, left a mark.

He blinked and stared at the ground. "I'm grieving a man who never existed while also relieved we have at least one more problem behind us."

She nodded, understanding. He'd killed the Lone Wolf, an ally of her brother. She wasn't sure how much that weakened Riven's plans with some witch in Nūa and the Blood Goddess, but it ended the capture of innocent werewolves. His people were better for it. Conflict still sat on the horizon. The Blood Moon may have passed by, but Tovi didn't forget the words of the prophecy. *A new dawn will rise.* The land felt different, she felt different. Though she didn't dare consider that one line. She sighed.

"Eldrick—"

"Tovi—"

The both stopped, uneasy laughs bubbling from them.

He grabbed her hand, tracing his fingers across the lines of her palm. "I never once believed him. The moment he dared to say your name, I knew it was a lie. I only pretended because I needed to get close to you."

She nodded—it hadn't made sense at the time, but after he'd killed those werewolves and their warm blood had stained her dress, she knew his wrath hadn't been aimed at her. Because she, too, had been overcome with the same feeling a week ago outside Sven's estate with the need to protect him. But Tovi didn't dare speak of that as the sun sank deeper past the mountains.

"I also meant what I said," he whispered.

The woman I love.

His words in the hall had driven her to get fresh air. She'd needed space and time to think. So much lay ahead of them, and his heartfelt revelation was like gravity, pulling and receding tides over her heart. Her soul sang to return the sentiment, but for some reason, she couldn't bring herself to say them back.

She swallowed, glass lodged in her throat. "I know."

"Even if you never say it back, I don't care. Even if I've lost you—"

"You haven't lost me, Eldrick," she said.

No. She was lost to him. Tovi floated, suspended and off kilter as she tried to regain her sense of poise, but it was too late. Since the moment they'd met at the Shield-maiden, her future had been written.

The wolf and dove.

The prophecy whispered—nothing and something at the same time—into her ear. She ignored it, meeting Eldrick's stare.

"Stay," he breathed.

"What?" she asked.

"Stay in my village."

"Eldrick, I need to secure more allies—"

"Exactly. Stay with me. I think you and I can bring the werewolves and vampyrs together."

You and I.

More words that unraveled Tovi's insides. Again, she didn't have it in her to say the right words or the words she wanted to say. Sweet and tangy, that sat on her tongue. She let them dissolve, not meeting Eldrick's expectant stare. He'd given her an option, an out if she wished it.

But he'd also given her an opportunity, one her body, soul, and mind wanted to seize.

"Alright," she said. "I'll stay."

Tovi moved closer to him, resting her head on his shoulder. Eldrick relaxed at her nearness. They sat together, anchor for the other as they watched the peace of the evening settle across the Vadon Mountains, promise thrumming between them.

Chapter Sixty-Five

Autumn's sticky humidity still fought against the crisp, evening air of Nūa, the city of witches. Winter hadn't made its way east yet, its toe still at the coast's doorstep. The sun beat down in a cloudless sky and gulls glided on the briny wind.

Evelyn and Kade passed under the east entrance's arch, straight into the bustle of the largest city square. After dropping Bleu off at a stable to rest, Evelyn and Kade kept their hoods up and Maxie hidden as they made for their next destination. Neither had a desire to attract attention in a city where their union had always gained such fascination.

The flower boxes, bakeries, and restaurants washed a wave of nostalgia through her. There, the coffee shop she'd met her sister at every morning—the chive and cheddar biscuits were sinful. There, as they rounded the corner adjacent to where her apartment sat, the brick townhomes and copper lampposts lined the arts district. Evelyn veered them farther north, passing a wine bar situated in a garden courtyard and decorated with string lights—she'd frequented the spot with Tovi too many times to count. With each beat of her boots against the sidewalk, her courage built to an unbending tempo.

As she guided Kade, the roads and streets came back to her like she'd never left. Yet, it didn't have a sense of home. It had nothing to do with the time away or her magic locked inside the bloodstone, her essence of a witch absent. Evelyn's home walked beside her, and she grabbed his hand, holding it as they turned down the last street.

Kade paused, peering down at her. "Everything will be alright."

"I know," she said, believing it.

Rather than seeking forgiveness from her sisters, she looked forward to seeing them. Simply *seeing* them, being with them again. She expected Blair's laugh, and Mirella's older-sister tone. It added a pep to her strides and a faster pace as she and Kade continued down the block of townhomes, hand in hand. Of course, she'd apologize for lying, leaving, and running for so long, but Evelyn's chest pulsed with the grace she'd granted herself.

The metal number plates went up... *35, 36, 37...* until they stood outside Blair's home. Evelyn swallowed, releasing her breath.

"Do you want me to stay here?" Kade asked.

"No," Evelyn said. "I'd like you to be with me."

Kade kissed her temple. "Always."

Evelyn's walk turned hesitant, her limbs brimming with anticipation. She was mindful of her boots against the steps and hovered her hand over the door. Her sister's front window was cracked open, and the sound and smell of fatty bacon sizzling on the kitchen stove wafted through. A hum trickled outside, and Evelyn fought the tickle of tears at the corner of her eyes.

She knocked.

The humming stopped on the other side and steps approached the door. Evelyn's heart hammered in her chest. All words and thoughts emptied from her mind. What would she say? What would she do? The door swung open and—

Blair froze. Her dark eyes drank Evelyn in, and she couldn't take it any longer.

Evelyn launched at her sister and dragged her into the fiercest hug. Words weren't right. Touch was. *Feeling* her sister in her arms. Holding her close for the first time in so long, the thud of her middle sister's heart beating against hers.

And thank the goddesses, her sister held her back. Tightly. Fiercely. A sob broke from one of them, and the tears welling in Evelyn's eyes spilled. A tingling surged through her chest and warmth radiated through her body. Her tears didn't stop as she pulled away.

Blair blinked, looking over her shoulder. "You found one another."

"Yes, we did." Evelyn didn't let go of her sister who ushered them both into her townhome.

Uncooked bacon waited on a plate, and eggs had been whipped in a bowl beside the stove. A bottle of sparkling wine sat on the table—for the Carson sisters, that only meant one thing.

"Breakfast for dinner?" Evelyn asked. "Is it someone's birthday?"

She hadn't checked dates. She knew the seasons, but not the months or days. A lot of it had gotten lost since leaving Callum.

"Yours."

Evelyn stilled as Blair wiped away tears. "Mine?"

Kade chuckled beside her, kissing her cheek. "You didn't tell me it was your birthday, love."

"I didn't know," Evelyn whispered.

Blair gripped the back of a chair. "Hold on a second, the two of you are *together* together?"

"We're mated," Kade said, setting his shoulders back.

"*Kade.*"

Though fateds and mates were similar in regard to feelings and bindings, werewolves were rather prideful and forthcoming, and more detail oriented compared to witches. They were not shy about staking their claim.

She turned to her sister. "I'm sorry. Also, I'm sorry for running and leaving you without an explanation."

Blair fought more tears and ran a hand through her messy hair. "All that matters is you're home now and—wait, I can't feel your magic." She studied Evelyn head to foot, skeptical eyes landing on the bloodstone. "What happened?"

"I think we should all sit," Kade said.

Evelyn told her sister everything, starting the night she left after her dress fitting up until she placed the magic in the bloodstone at Sven's estate. An account of the years away tumbled from her, but not in a rush, not a desperation for her sister to see what she'd been through. She simply told her, like two sisters who'd not seen one another, catching up. The months and years didn't hold the wretched weight they once did, and in fact, certain moments and instances made Evelyn smile, excited to tell her sister. Blair listened, intently, and only said one thing after.

"I'm sorry, too."

Evelyn leaned back in her chair. "You're sorry? For what?"

"You didn't think you could come to me about your lost flame."

Evelyn smiled, softly, grabbing her sister's hand. "I didn't think I could go to anyone, Blair."

She shook her head, brows pinched. "But I'm your older sister. The fact you didn't trust me enough means I did something wrong along the way, and I'm sorry for that."

"We'd just lost Mom and Dad." Pain lanced through Evelyn at the memory.

"True," Blair said. "Let's promise ourselves to be honest with one another from here on out. No matter what."

"No matter what," Evelyn said.

Kade sent her a smile, and she couldn't help but smile back. A sense of rightness settled over her, like a new dawn was rising.

The front door opened.

"You will not believe the day I had!" Mirella called. "Seven patients. I barely had time to grab the cinnamon rolls—"

Evelyn's oldest sister stopped dead in her tracks and dropped the parchment bag she'd been clutching. Her blue-eyed gaze, similar to Evelyn's, scurried over all three of them.

"Evelyn." Her sister hurried over and grasped her face in her hands. "You came back."

Tears welled again in Evelyn's eyes, like they'd never really stopped. "Yes."

"I'm so sorry," Mirella whispered. Tears streamed down her face. Their mother's eyes stared back at Evelyn. "I was terrible, awful. If you ran because of me, it's completely and utterly justifiable."

"Mirella, it's alright," Evelyn said, grasping her sister's hands that still held her face and giving them a reassuring squeeze. "I never ran from you but know I'm never running again."

Her eldest sister chuckled. "You better not, I swear to the Goddess, Evelyn."

A laugh burst out of her—there was that stern tone she'd missed.

Her sister blinked, gaze landing on Kade for the first time. Her attention jumped between the two of them.

"Wait." She backed away from Evelyn. "Did anyone see you in the city?"

Kade leaned across the table. "No, we were sure to not attract attention to ourselves."

Mirella rushed from her position on the floor and closed the curtains of Blair's home.

"What are you doing?" Evelyn asked.

Mirella ignored her, rummaging through her satchel. She grabbed Evelyn's hand while pulling a daily pamphlet from the bag. "It's slander and lies. I didn't believe a word it when I saw it, but you have to read this."

She handed Evelyn the paper, and her heart dropped like a stone to her gut.

Evelyn peered up at Kade and said, "Everyone knows."

Thank You!

Dear Reader...

T HANK YOU FOR READING! It means the world to me as a writer that you picked up my book and gave it a chance. If you enjoyed this enemies to lovers, adventure-filled romantic fantasy, I'd greatly appreciate if you could **leave a review on Goodreads and/or Amazon.**

Again, thank you so much and happy reading!

Acknowledgements

Drew—It's no secret you're the inspiration behind Kade. You're loyal, encouraging, kind, and thoughtful. You fight for my dreams and believe in me every single day. This book challenged me in so many new ways compared to book one, and yet you kept pushing and supporting me each step of the process. When I had moments of doubt about the story's direction, you kept telling me, "You got this!" or "Go for it!". You attend all my author events and have the best supportive husband energy an author can ask for. I wouldn't be able to do this without you and our incredible partnership. Thank you, and I love you (Sincerely, Chicken).

The Family—I'm so grateful to have a family who supports my dreams. It's tremendously encouraging each time we talk on the phone or see one another and discuss my books and writing life so casually yet with so much enthusiasm. Thank you for celebrating my wins, listening to my losses, and ultimately always being there when I need. Love you, Mom, Dad, and Ian.

My Friends—Thank you, thank you, thank you for the continuous support. To showing up at events, recommending my book to other readers, and entertaining me with your character theories. You make writing this series and the world more fun!

The best CP on the planet—Neerali, I don't know where this story would be without you. Thank you for rereading the same act three times. Thank you for putting up with the unhinged, ranting text ideas I sent. Thank you for the

FaceTime chats where we talk about story, problem characters, author goals, and everything in between. Thank you!

My Beta Reader—Emily, thank you (yet again) for reading my book and revisiting these characters. Your feedback and comments are always helpful, constructive, and positive. You push me to be a better writer, and I appreciate that. Thank you!

My Editors—I can't thank my editors enough. This book, again, challenged me in so many ways. I had a vision. My characters demanded it be told a certain way. Megan, Mallori, Whitney, and Krista: thank you for supporting the vision, making it better, and expressing genuine belief in what I was aiming to do with this story. It would not be where it is today without your ideas, one one-on-one calls, and feedback. Thank you!

My Writing Groups—To Tenacious Writing and Drafting Club. Thank you for the sprint channels, live writing sessions, and overall great community.

My Street Team—If someone told me a year ago I'd have a hype team full of lovely, kind readers, I'd never believe them! I'm still in shock I have a street team who are interested in my cozy with plenty of stakes romantasy books. Thank you so much for getting this book in front of other readers.

To Tovi & Eldrick—Thank you Tovi for helping me heal from the invisible audience and leading me to authenticity over approval. Thank you Eldrick for teaching me that some of us have big, loud feelings, and that's okay.

About the Author

A lover of fantasy since childhood, C.C. discovered her passion for storytelling during high school. With a bachelor's in creative writing and psychology plus a master's in mental health counseling, she likes to blend romantic fantasy elements with an understanding of the human psyche. Beyond writing, she's obsessed with a good latte, and can often be found enjoying one with her husband as they set out on adventures of their own, traveling to various places fit for a fantasy-novel backdrop.

If you want to stay up to date on C.C.'s book news, updates, and bonus content, sign up for her newsletter at authorcctyler.com or follow her on Instagram.

instagram.com/authorcctyler